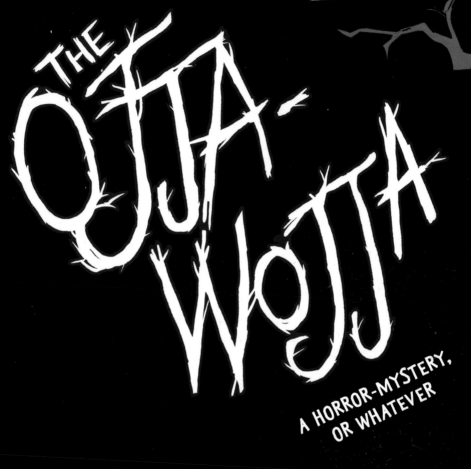

THE OJJA-WOJJA

A HORROR-MYSTERY, OR WHATEVER

WRITTEN BY
MAGDALENE ViSAGGIO

ILLUSTRATED BY
JENN St-ONGE

BALZER+BRAY

Imprints of HarperCollinsPublishers

HARPER
alley

Balzer + Bray is an imprint of HarperCollins Publishers.
HarperAlley is an imprint of HarperCollins Publishers.

The Ojja-Wojja

Library of Congress Control Number: 2022940777
ISBN 978-0-06-285239-7 — ISBN 978-0-06-285242-7 (pbk)

The artist used Clip Studio Paint Pro and a Wacom Intuos Pro M
to create the digital illustrations for this book.
Colors by Avery Bacon
Flatting assists by Arif Kudus
Lettering by Micah Myers
Design by Andrea Vandergrift
22 23 24 25 26   GPS   10 9 8 7 6 5 4 3 2 1
❖
First Edition

For that goofball who has my heart.
—M. V.

To my own Val—
the most wonderful tiny gremlin cat daughter
this meat suit could have ever wished for.
And, of course—for Theo. Always for Theo.
—J. S.

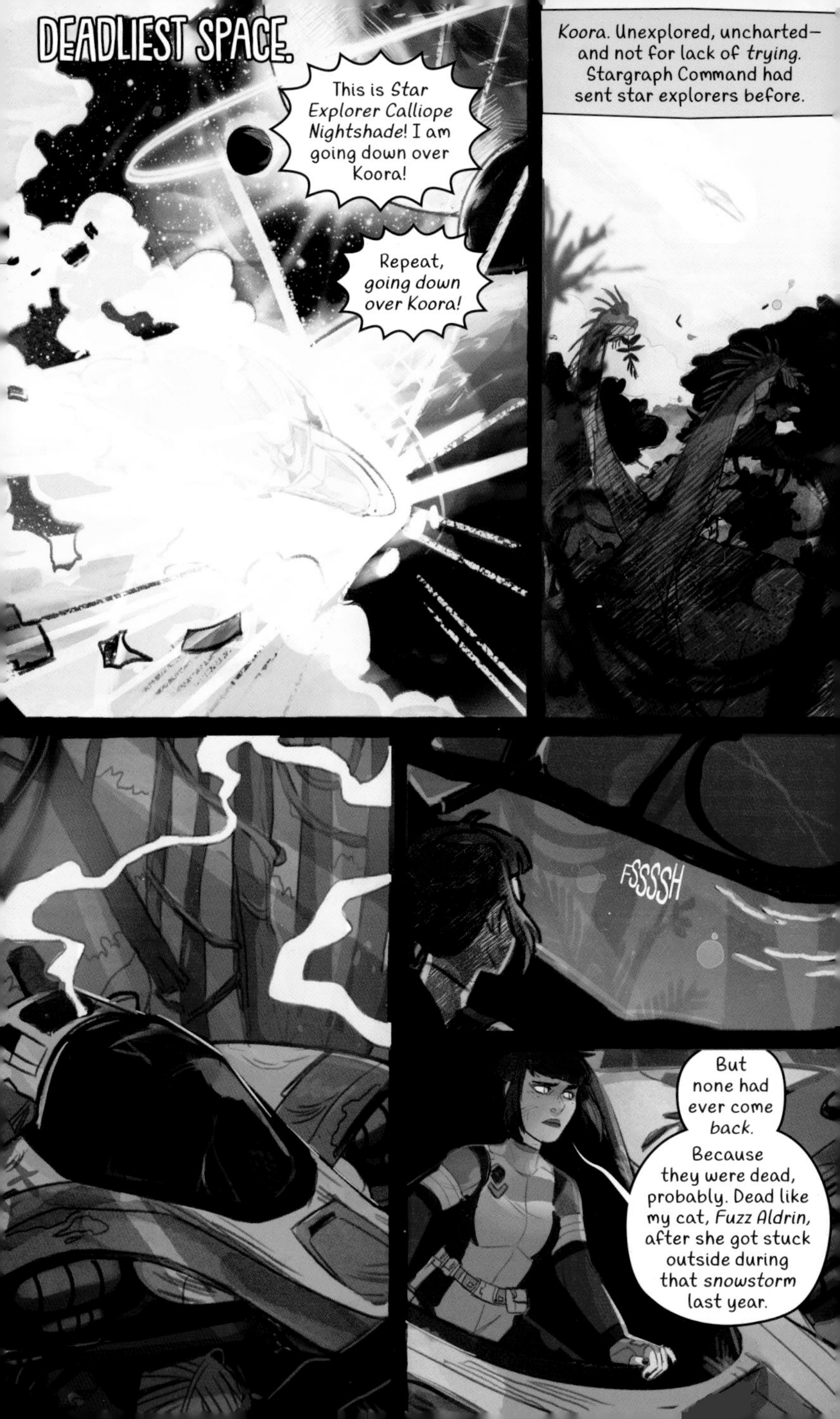
DEADLIEST SPACE.
This is *Star Explorer Calliope Nightshade*! I am going down over Koora!
Repeat, *going down* over Koora!
Koora. Unexplored, uncharted—and not for lack of *trying*. Stargraph Command had sent star explorers before.
FSSSSH
But none had ever come *back*.
Because they were dead, probably. Dead like my cat, *Fuzz Aldrin*, after she got stuck outside during that *snowstorm* last year.

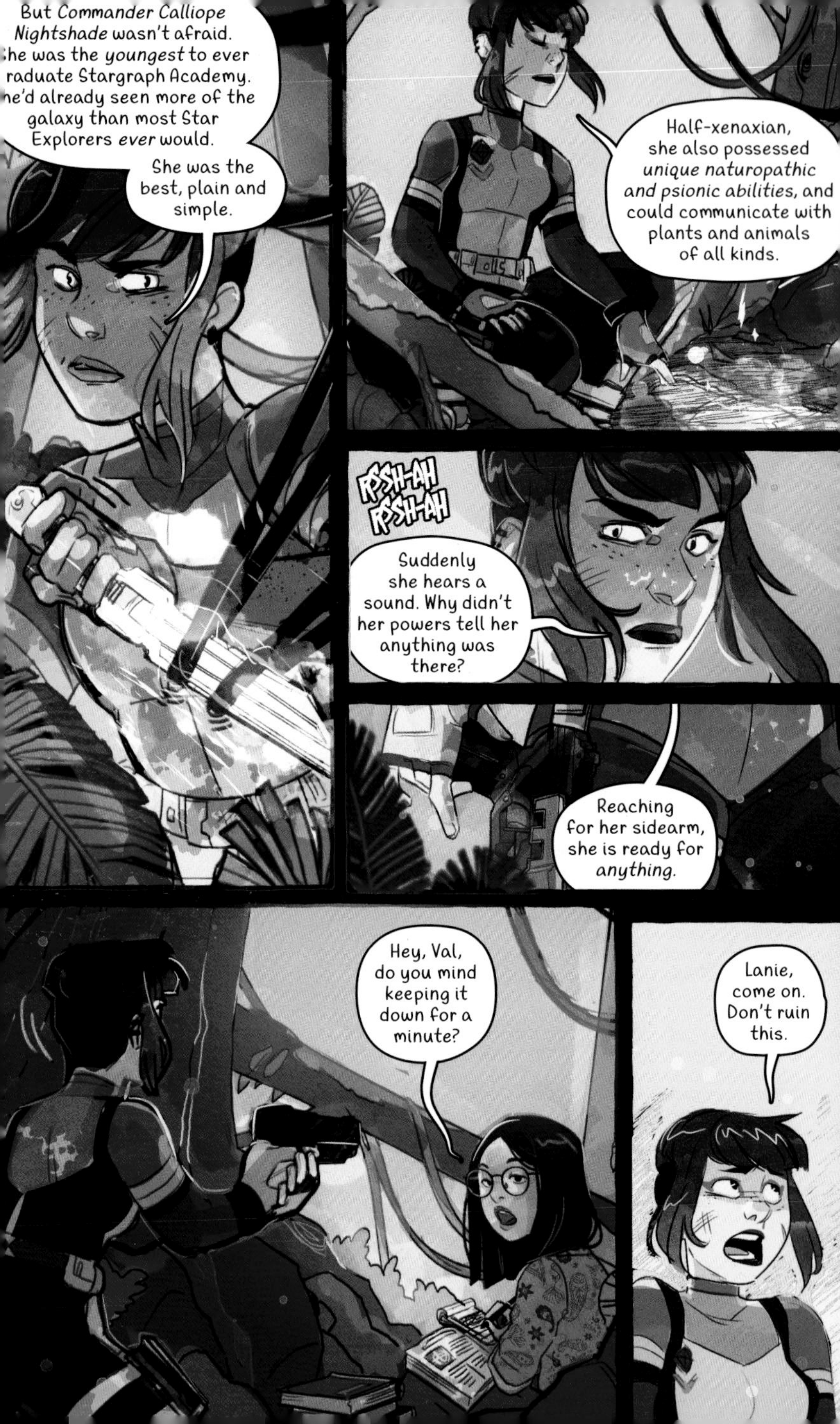

But Commander Calliope Nightshade wasn't afraid. he was the youngest to ever raduate Stargraph Academy. he'd already seen more of the galaxy than most Star Explorers ever would.
She was the best, plain and simple.
Half-xenaxian, she also possessed unique naturopathic and psionic abilities, and could communicate with plants and animals of all kinds.
RSSH-AH RSSH-AH
Suddenly she hears a sound. Why didn't her powers tell her anything was there?
Reaching for her sidearm, she is ready for anything.
Hey, Val, do you mind keeping it down for a minute?
Lanie, come on. Don't ruin this.

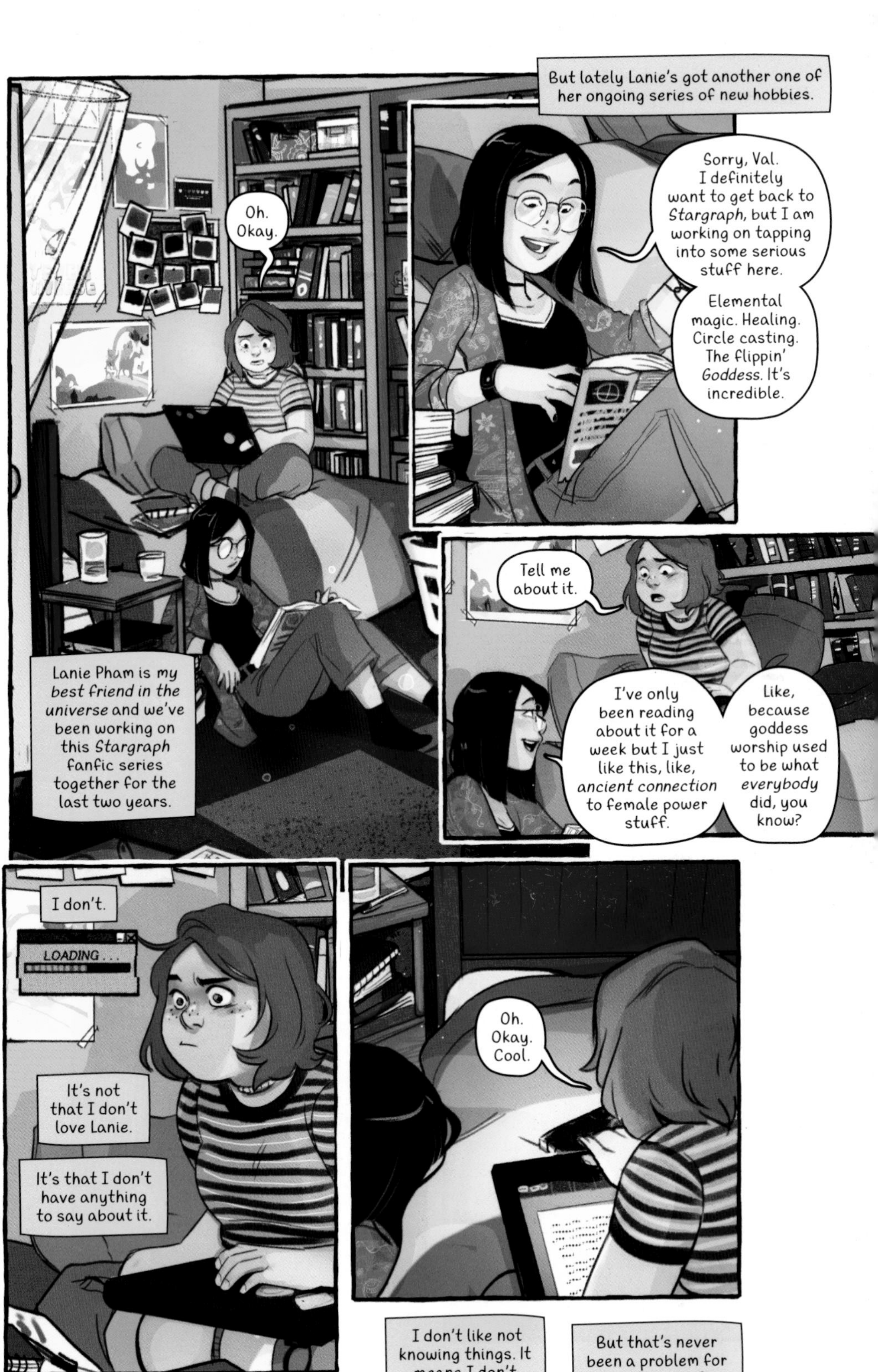
But lately Lanie's got another one of her ongoing series of new hobbies.
Oh. Okay.
Sorry, Val. I definitely want to get back to *Stargraph*, but I am working on tapping into some serious stuff here.
Elemental magic. Healing. Circle casting. The flippin' *Goddess*. It's incredible.
Lanie Pham is my *best friend in the universe* and we've been working on this *Stargraph* fanfic series together for the last two years.
Tell me about it.
I've only been reading about it for a week but I just like this, like, *ancient connection* to female power stuff.
Like, because goddess worship used to be what *everybody* did, you know?
I don't.
LOADING . . .
It's not that I don't love Lanie.
It's that I don't have anything to say about it.
Oh. Okay. Cool.
I don't like not knowing things. It means I don't know how to talk.
But that's never been a problem for me and Lanie before.

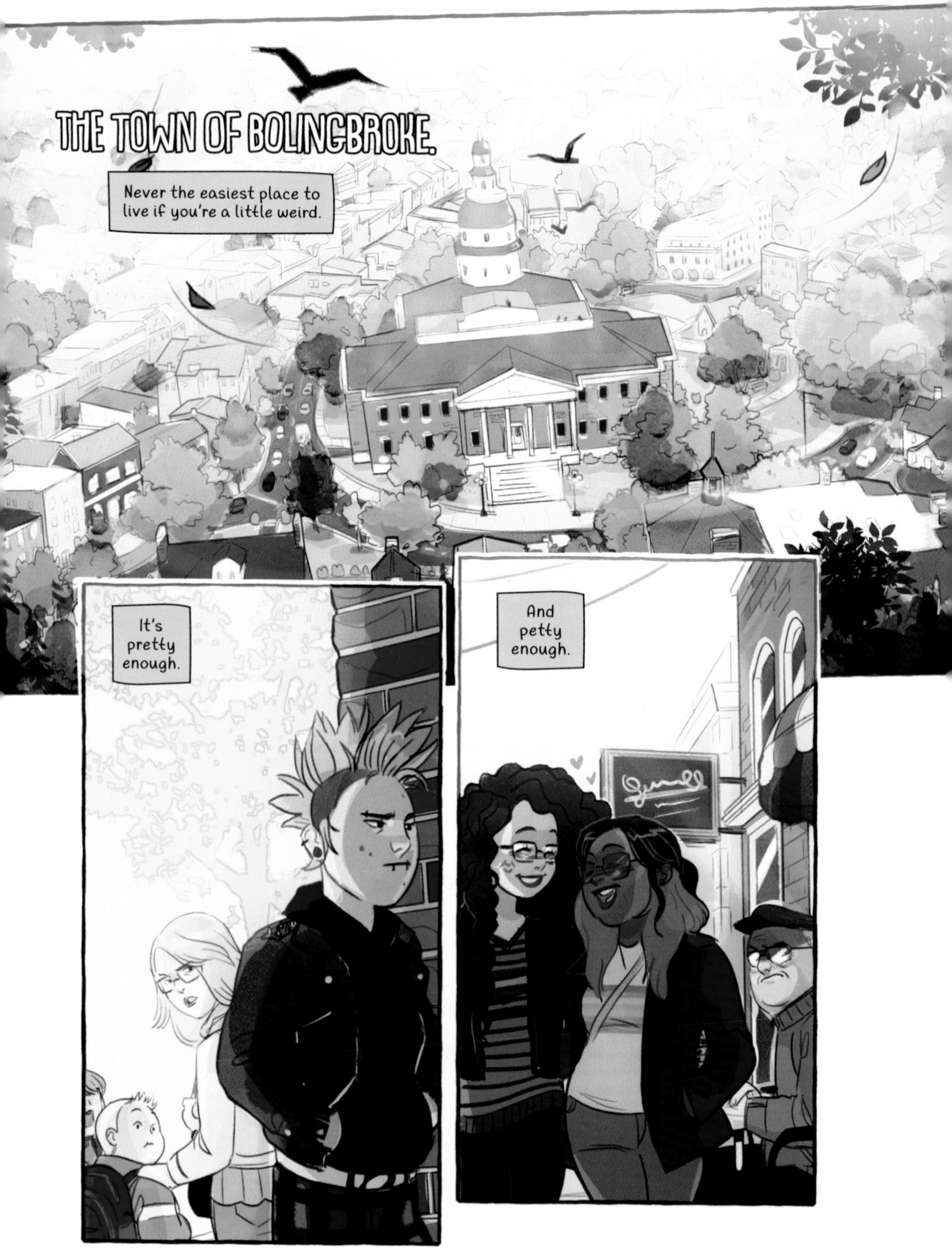
THE TOWN OF BOLINGBROKE.
Never the easiest place to live if you're a little weird.
It's pretty enough.
And petty enough.

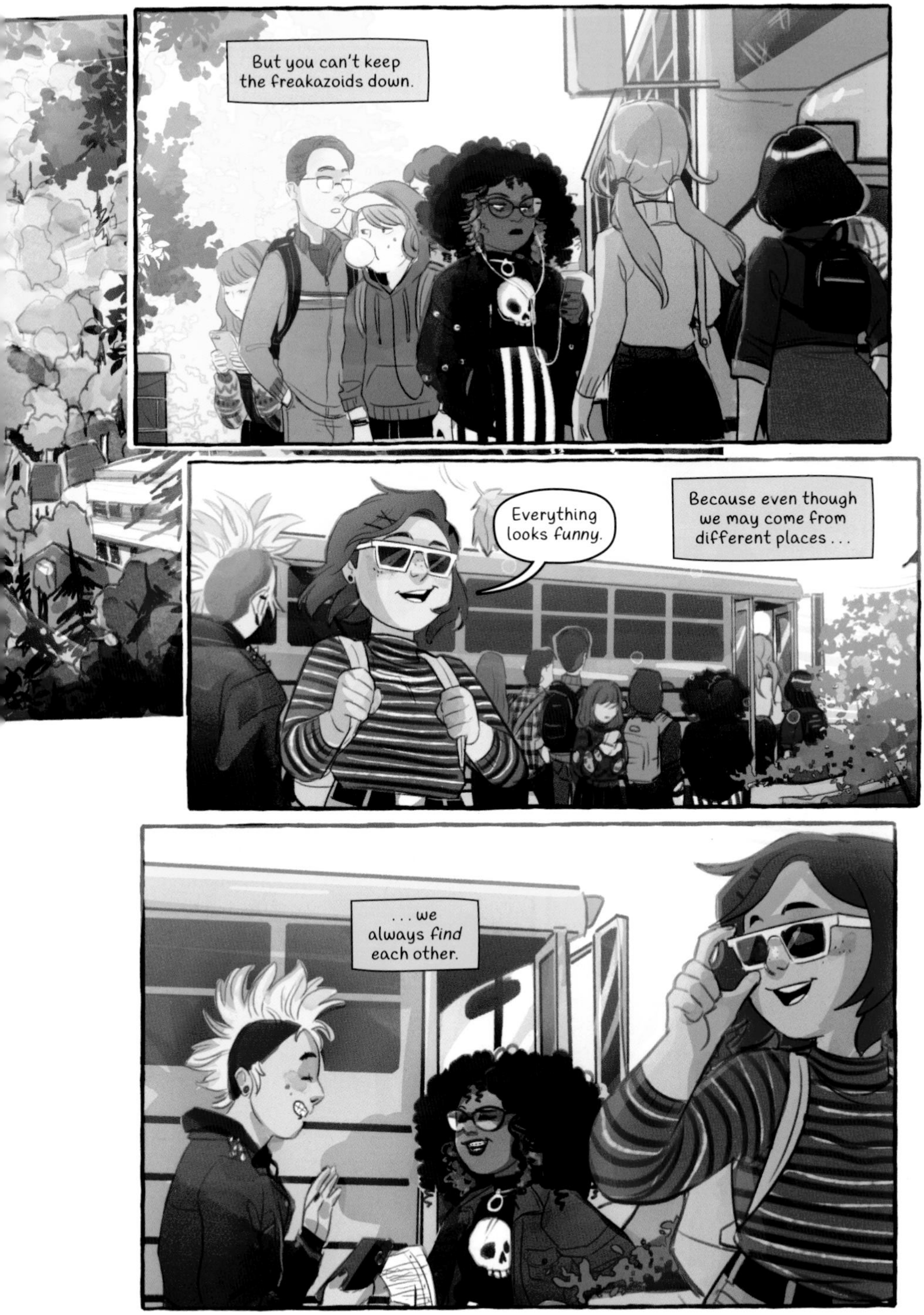
But you can't keep the freakazoids down.
Everything looks funny.
Because even though we may come from different places . . .
. . . we always find each other.

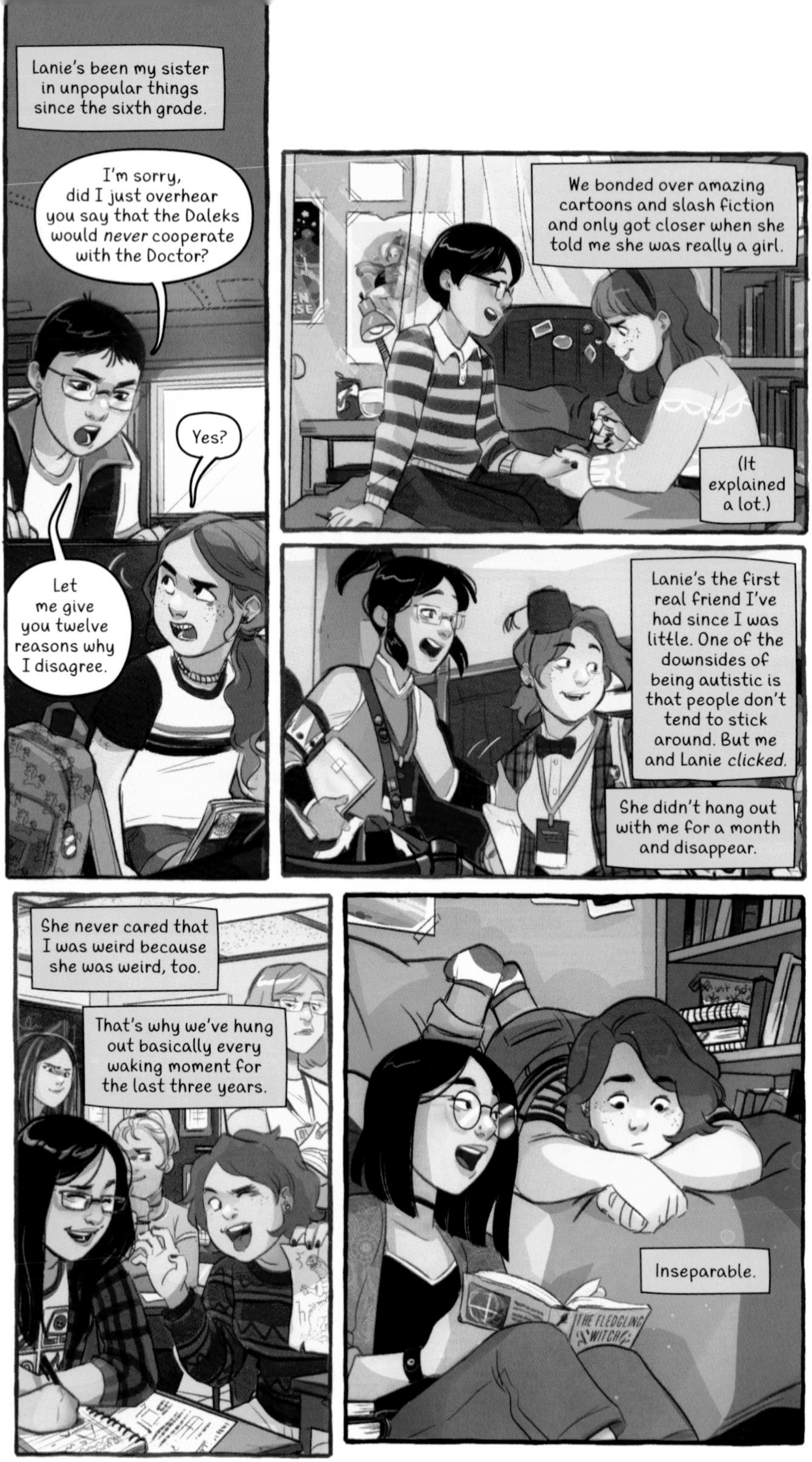
Lanie's been my sister in unpopular things since the sixth grade.
I'm sorry, did I just overhear you say that the Daleks would *never* cooperate with the Doctor?
Yes?
Let me give you twelve reasons why I disagree.
We bonded over amazing cartoons and slash fiction and only got closer when she told me she was really a girl.
(It explained a lot.)
Lanie's the first real friend I've had since I was little. One of the downsides of being autistic is that people don't tend to stick around. But me and Lanie *clicked*.
She didn't hang out with me for a month and disappear.
She never cared that I was weird because she was weird, too.
That's why we've hung out basically every waking moment for the last three years.
Inseparable.
THE FLEDGLING WITCH

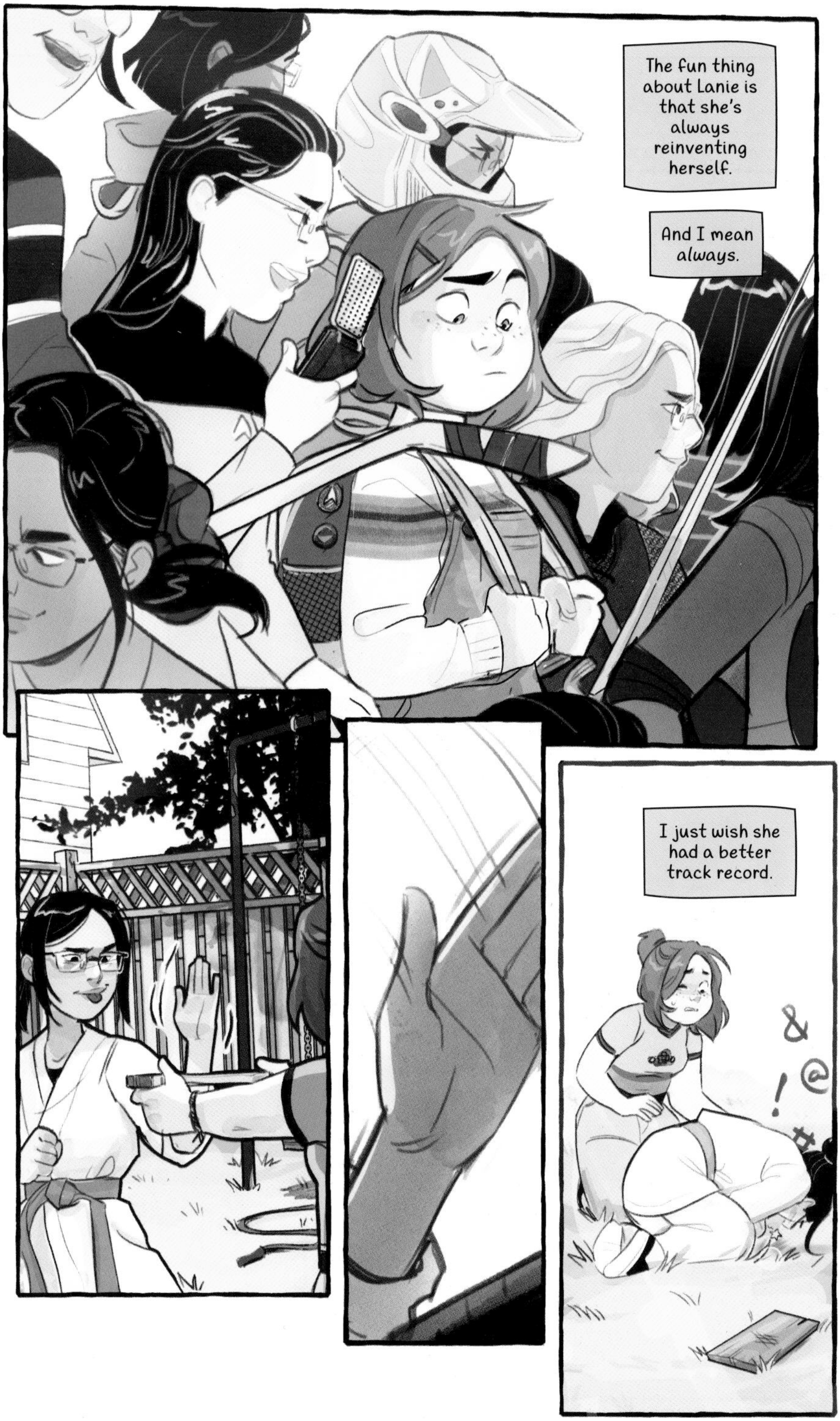
The fun thing about Lanie is that she's always reinventing herself.
And I mean always.
I just wish she had a better track record.
& @ ! #

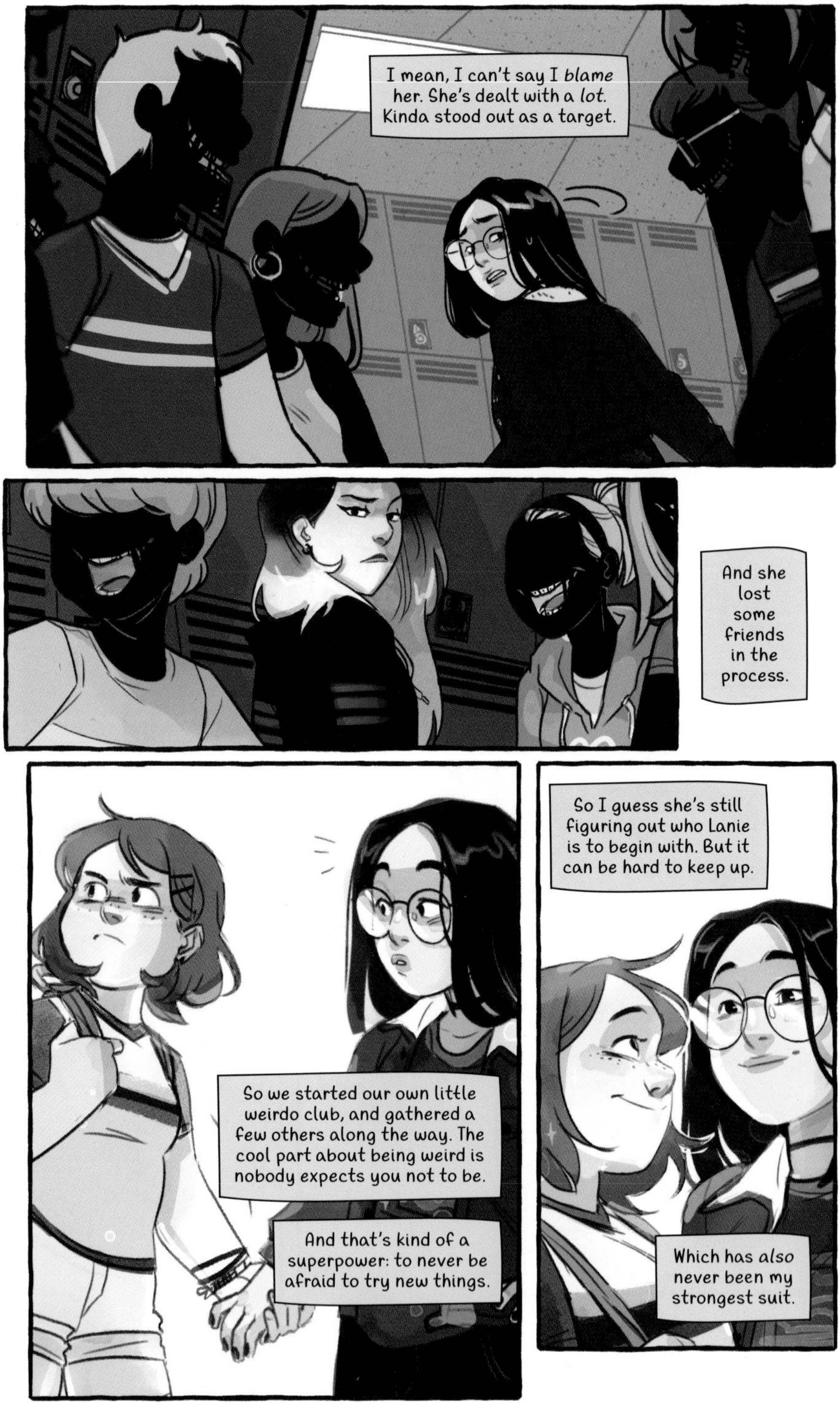

I mean, I can't say I *blame* her. She's dealt with a *lot*. Kinda stood out as a target.
And she lost some friends in the process.
So we started our own little weirdo club, and gathered a few others along the way. The cool part about being weird is nobody expects you not to be.
And that's kind of a superpower: to never be afraid to try new things.
So I guess she's still figuring out who Lanie is to begin with. But it can be hard to keep up.
Which has *also* never been my strongest suit.

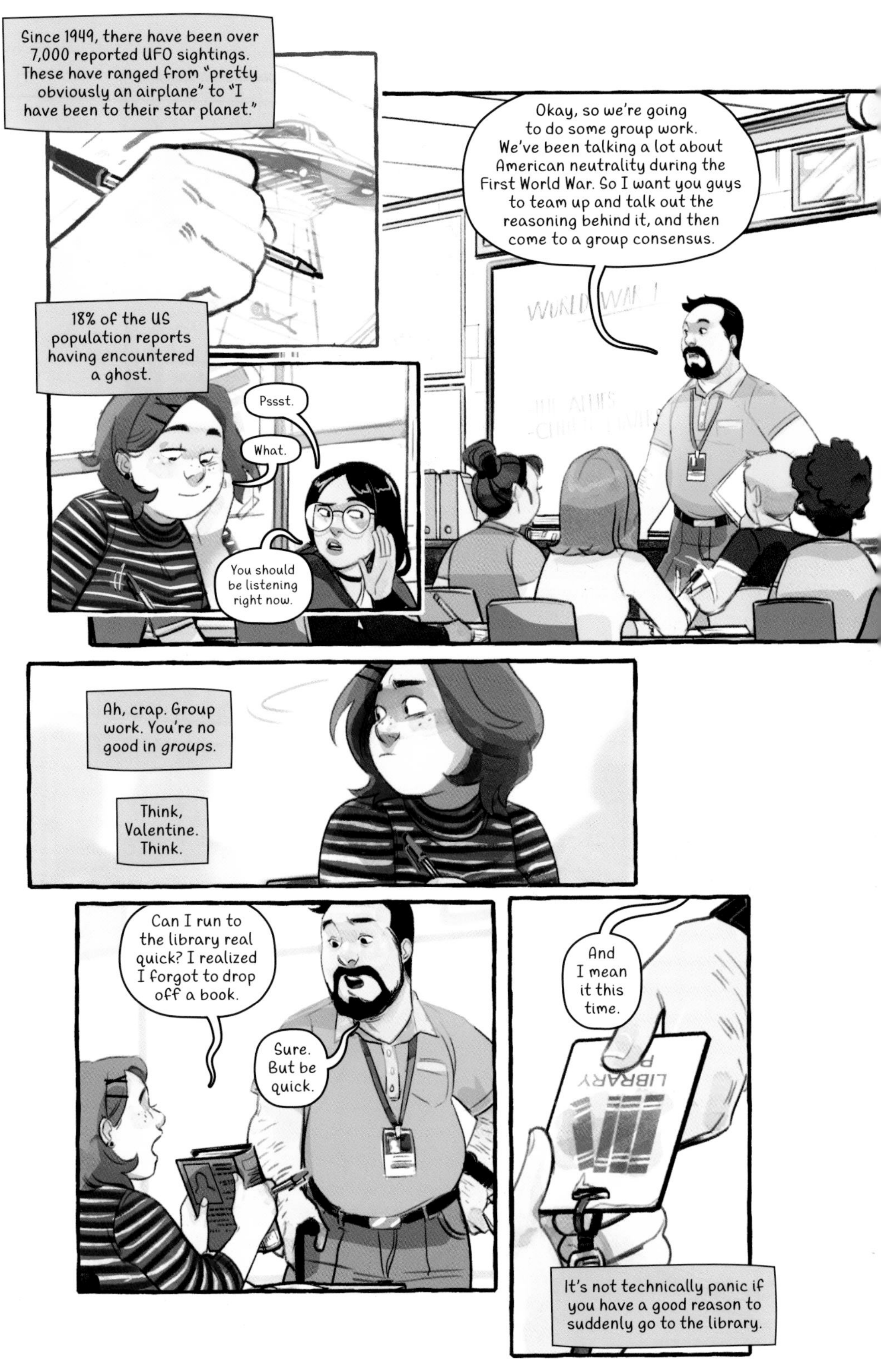

Since 1949, there have been over 7,000 reported UFO sightings. These have ranged from "pretty obviously an airplane" to "I have been to their star planet."
Okay, so we're going to do some group work. We've been talking a lot about American neutrality during the First World War. So I want you guys to team up and talk out the reasoning behind it, and then come to a group consensus.
18% of the US population reports having encountered a ghost.
Pssst.
What.
You should be listening right now.
Ah, crap. Group work. You're no good in *groups*.
Think, Valentine. Think.
Can I run to the library real quick? I realized I forgot to drop off a book.
Sure. But be quick.
And I mean it this time.
It's not technically panic if you have a good reason to suddenly go to the library.

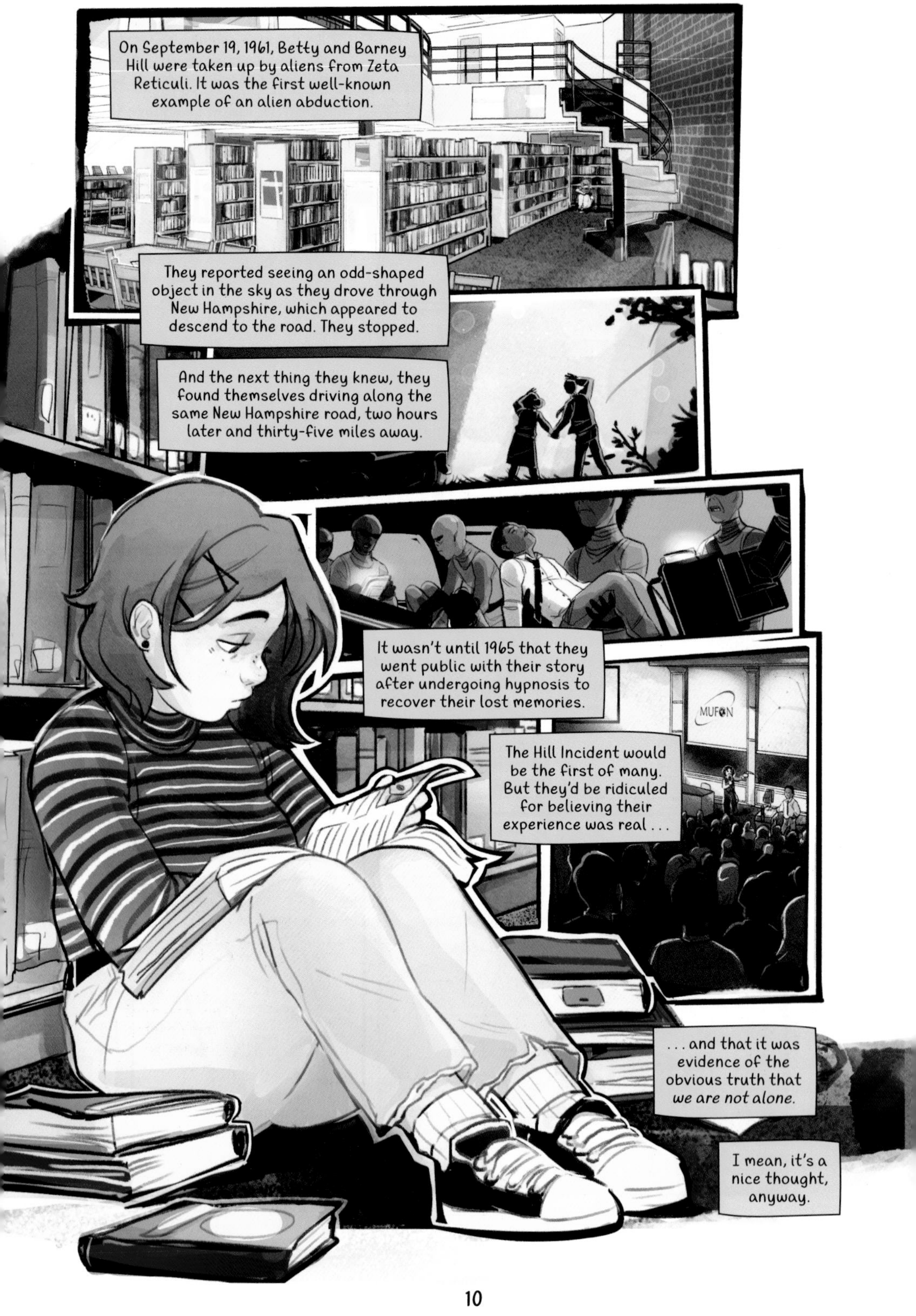
On September 19, 1961, Betty and Barney Hill were taken up by aliens from Zeta Reticuli. It was the first well-known example of an alien abduction.
They reported seeing an odd-shaped object in the sky as they drove through New Hampshire, which appeared to descend to the road. They stopped.
And the next thing they knew, they found themselves driving along the same New Hampshire road, two hours later and thirty-five miles away.
It wasn't until 1965 that they went public with their story after undergoing hypnosis to recover their lost memories.
MUFON
The Hill Incident would be the first of many. But they'd be ridiculed for believing their experience was real . . .
. . . and that it was evidence of the obvious truth that *we are not alone.*
I mean, it's a nice thought, anyway.

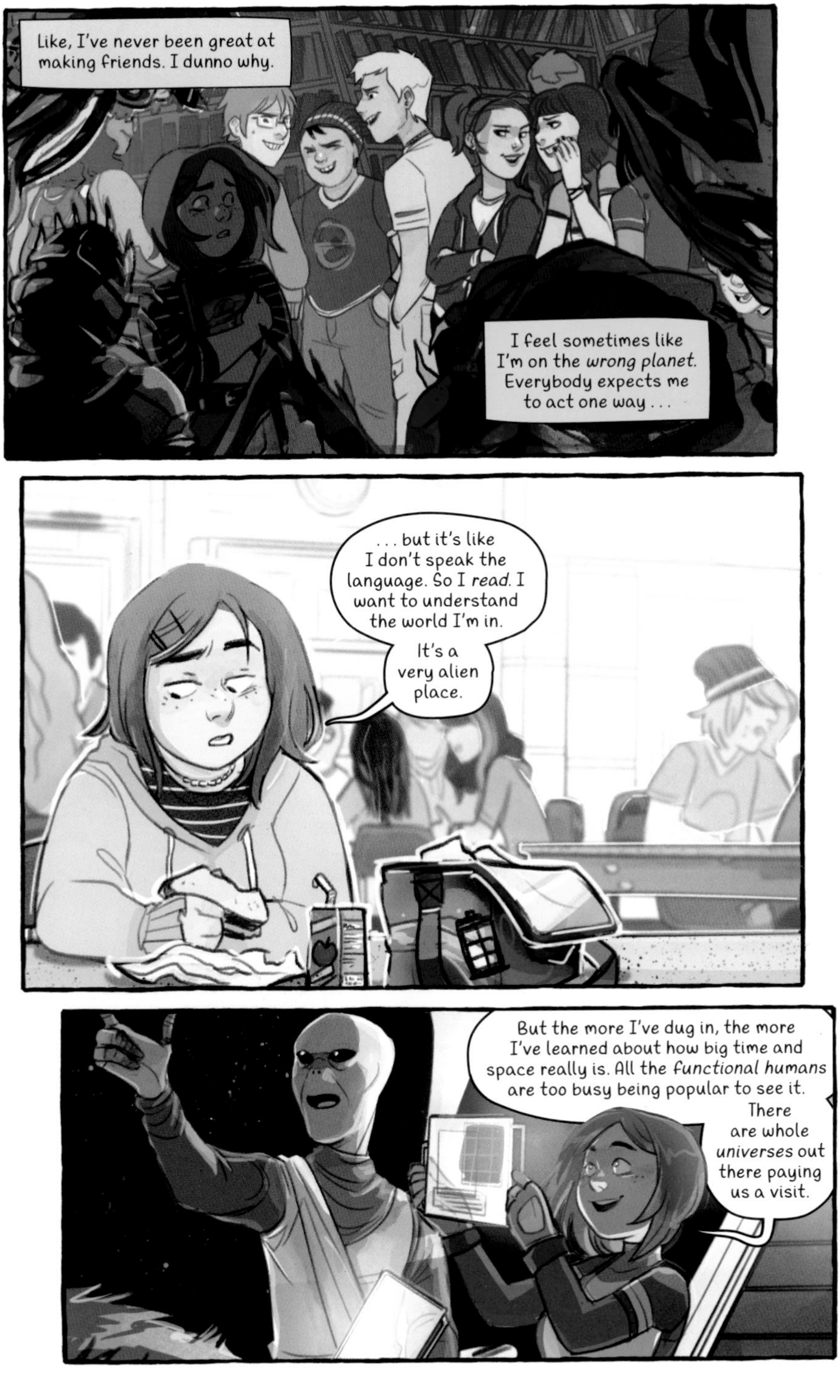

Like, I've never been great at making friends. I dunno why.
I feel sometimes like I'm on the *wrong planet.* Everybody expects me to act one way . . .
. . . but it's like I don't speak the language. So I *read.* I want to understand the world I'm in.
It's a very alien place.
But the more I've dug in, the more I've learned about how big time and space really is. All the *functional humans* are too busy being popular to see it.
There are whole *universes* out there paying us a visit.

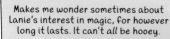

Makes me wonder sometimes about Lanie's interest in magic, for however long it lasts. It can't all be hooey.

Hey, Val.

A PHILOSOPHY OF MAGICKAL THINGS

You didn't come back to class, you know.

Oh my *God*, I am so sorry, Mr. Betancourt. I lost track of time. I can come back right now—

It's a little late for that. Class ended five minutes ago.

So what stole your attention?

Uh . . .

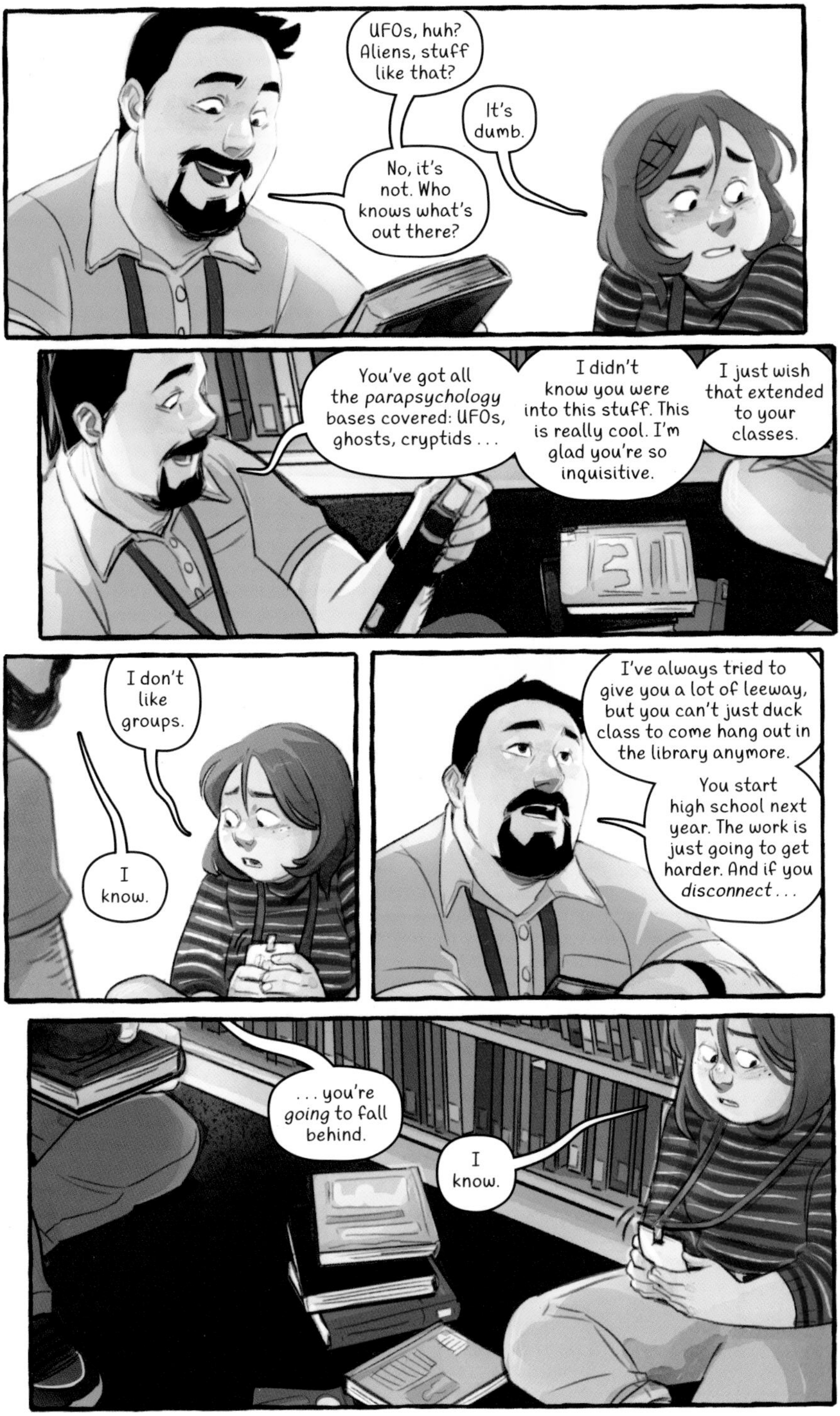
UFOs, huh? Aliens, stuff like that?
It's dumb.
No, it's not. Who knows what's out there?
You've got all the *parapsychology* bases covered: UFOs, ghosts, cryptids . . .
I didn't know you were into this stuff. This is really cool. I'm glad you're so inquisitive.
I just wish that extended to your classes.
I don't like groups.
I know.
I've always tried to give you a lot of leeway, but you can't just duck class to come hang out in the library anymore.
You start high school next year. The work is just going to get harder. And if you *disconnect* . . .
. . . you're *going* to fall behind.
I know.

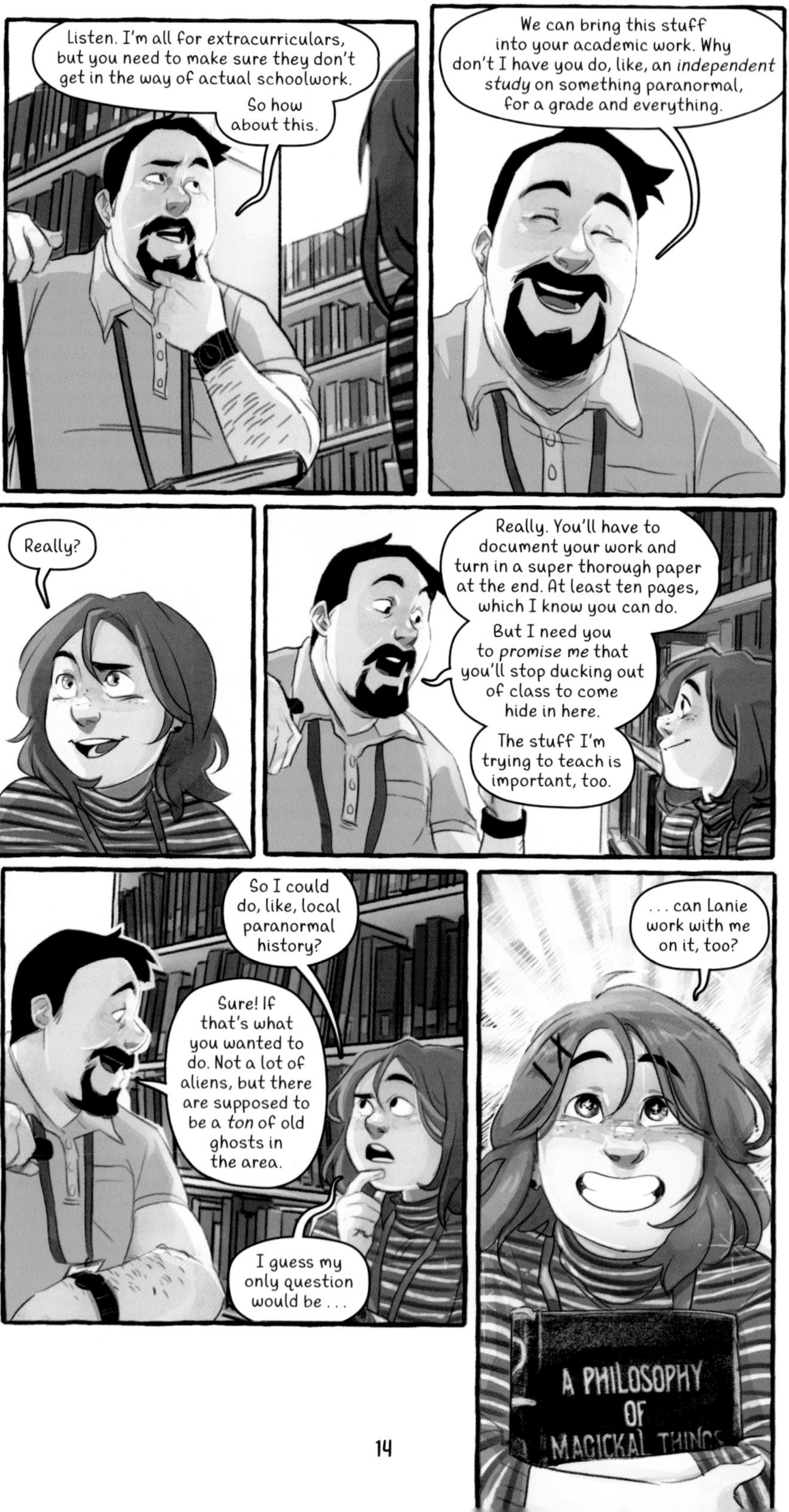
Listen. I'm all for extracurriculars, but you need to make sure they don't get in the way of actual schoolwork.
So how about this.
We can bring this stuff into your academic work. Why don't I have you do, like, an *independent study* on something paranormal, for a grade and everything.
Really?
Really. You'll have to document your work and turn in a super thorough paper at the end. At least ten pages, which I know you can do.
But I need you to *promise me* that you'll stop ducking out of class to come hide in here.
The stuff I'm trying to teach is important, too.
So I could do, like, local paranormal history?
Sure! If that's what you wanted to do. Not a lot of aliens, but there are supposed to be a *ton* of old ghosts in the area.
I guess my only question would be . . .
. . . can Lanie work with me on it, too?
A PHILOSOPHY OF MAGICKAL THINGS

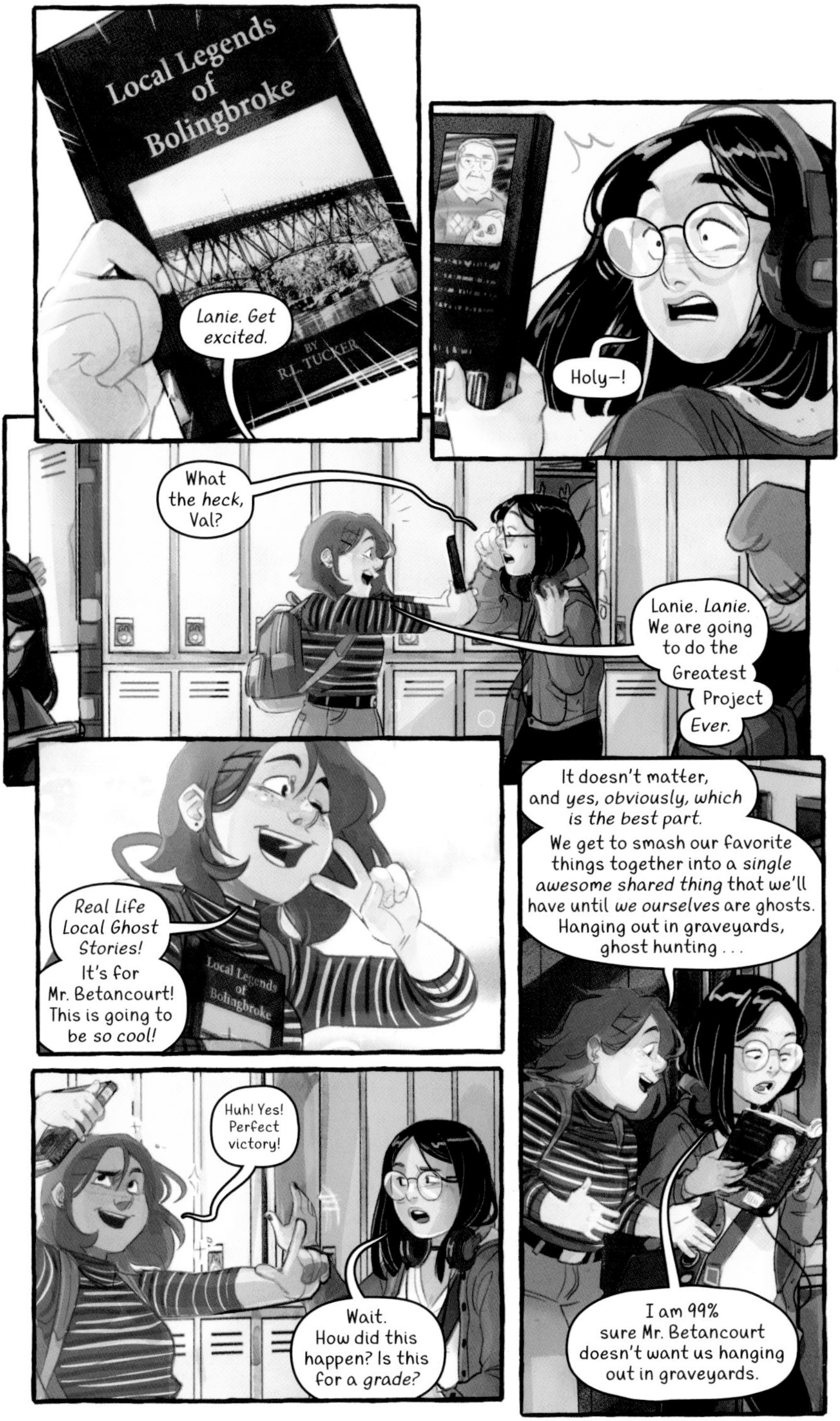
Local Legends of Bolingbroke
BY R.L. TUCKER
Lanie. Get excited.
Holy—!
What the heck, Val?
Lanie. Lanie. We are going to do the Greatest Project Ever.
Real Life Local Ghost Stories!
It's for Mr. Betancourt! This is going to be so cool!
Local Legends of Bolingbroke
It doesn't matter, and yes, obviously, which is the best part.
We get to smash our favorite things together into a single awesome shared thing that we'll have until we ourselves are ghosts. Hanging out in graveyards, ghost hunting . . .
I am 99% sure Mr. Betancourt doesn't want us hanging out in graveyards.
Huh! Yes! Perfect victory!
Wait. How did this happen? Is this for a grade?

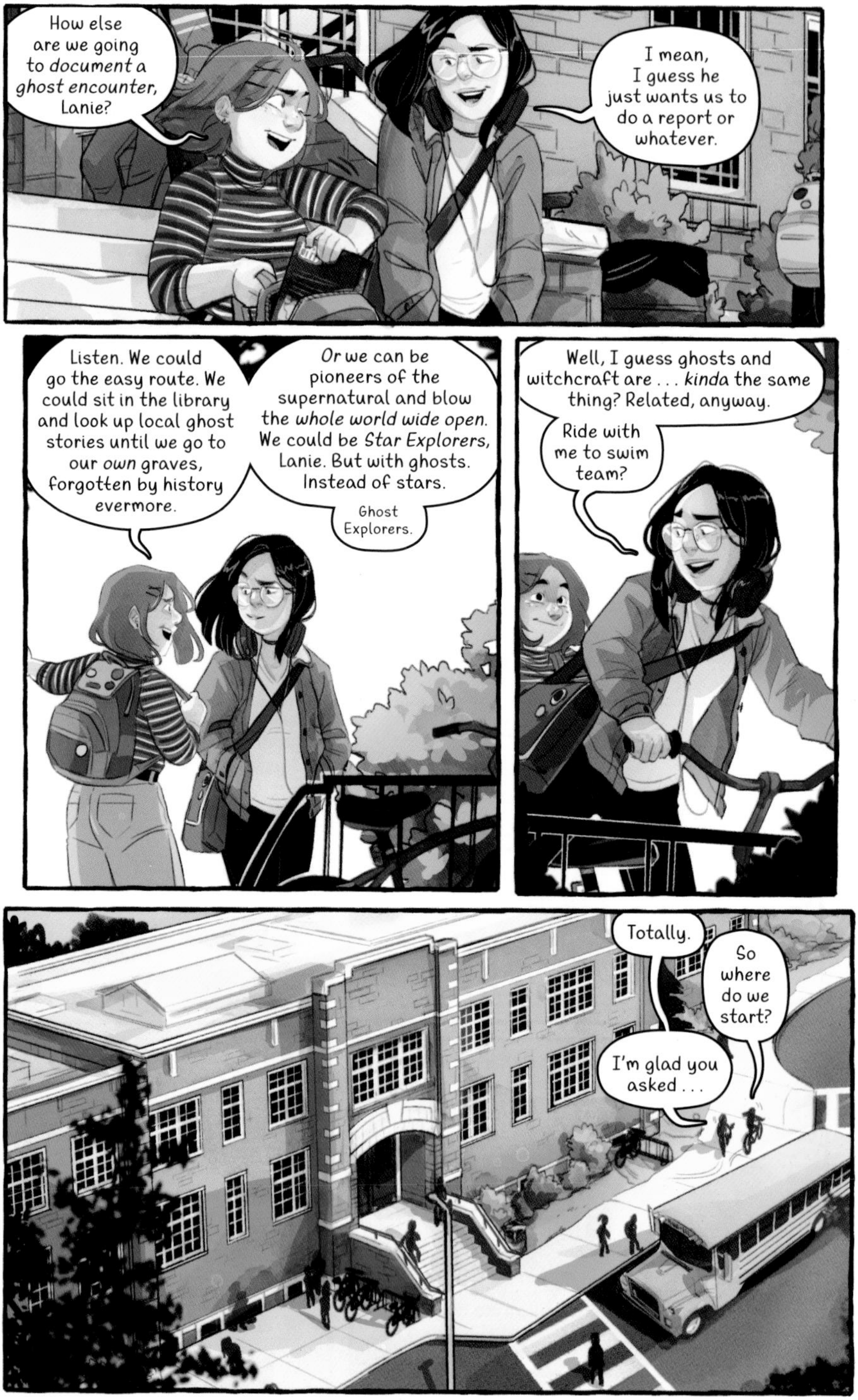
How else are we going to *document* a *ghost encounter*, Lanie?
I mean, I guess he just wants us to do a report or whatever.
Listen. We could go the easy route. We could sit in the library and look up local ghost stories until we go to our *own* graves, forgotten by history evermore.
Or we can be pioneers of the supernatural and blow the *whole world wide open*. We could be *Star Explorers*, Lanie. But with ghosts. Instead of stars.
Ghost Explorers.
Well, I guess ghosts and witchcraft are . . . *kinda* the same thing? Related, anyway.
Ride with me to swim team?
Totally.
So where do we start?
I'm glad you asked . . .

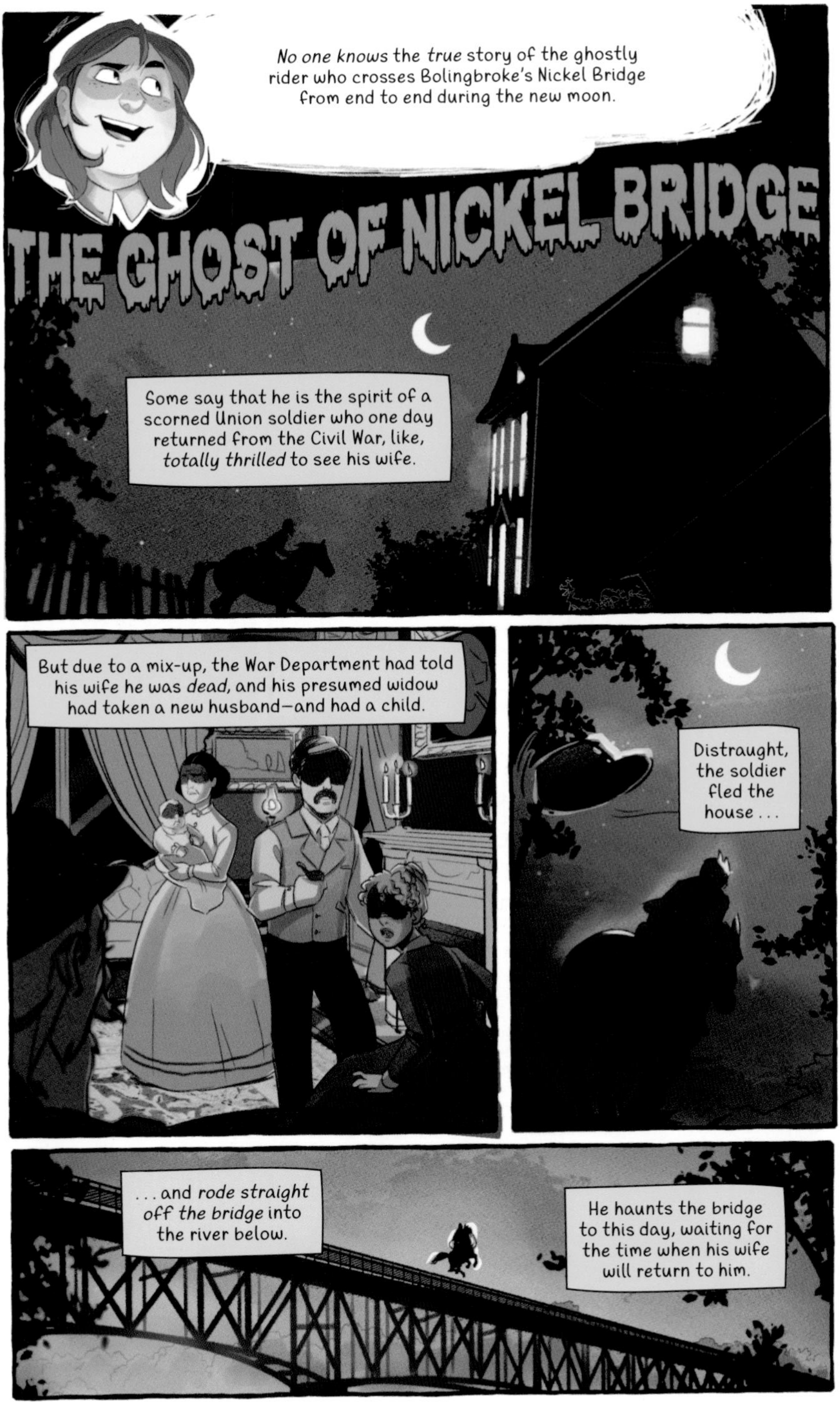
No one knows the true story of the ghostly rider who crosses Bolingbroke's Nickel Bridge from end to end during the new moon.
THE GHOST OF NICKEL BRIDGE
Some say that he is the spirit of a scorned Union soldier who one day returned from the Civil War, like, totally thrilled to see his wife.
But due to a mix-up, the War Department had told his wife he was dead, and his presumed widow had taken a new husband—and had a child.
Distraught, the soldier fled the house . . .
. . . and rode straight off the bridge into the river below.
He haunts the bridge to this day, waiting for the time when his wife will return to him.

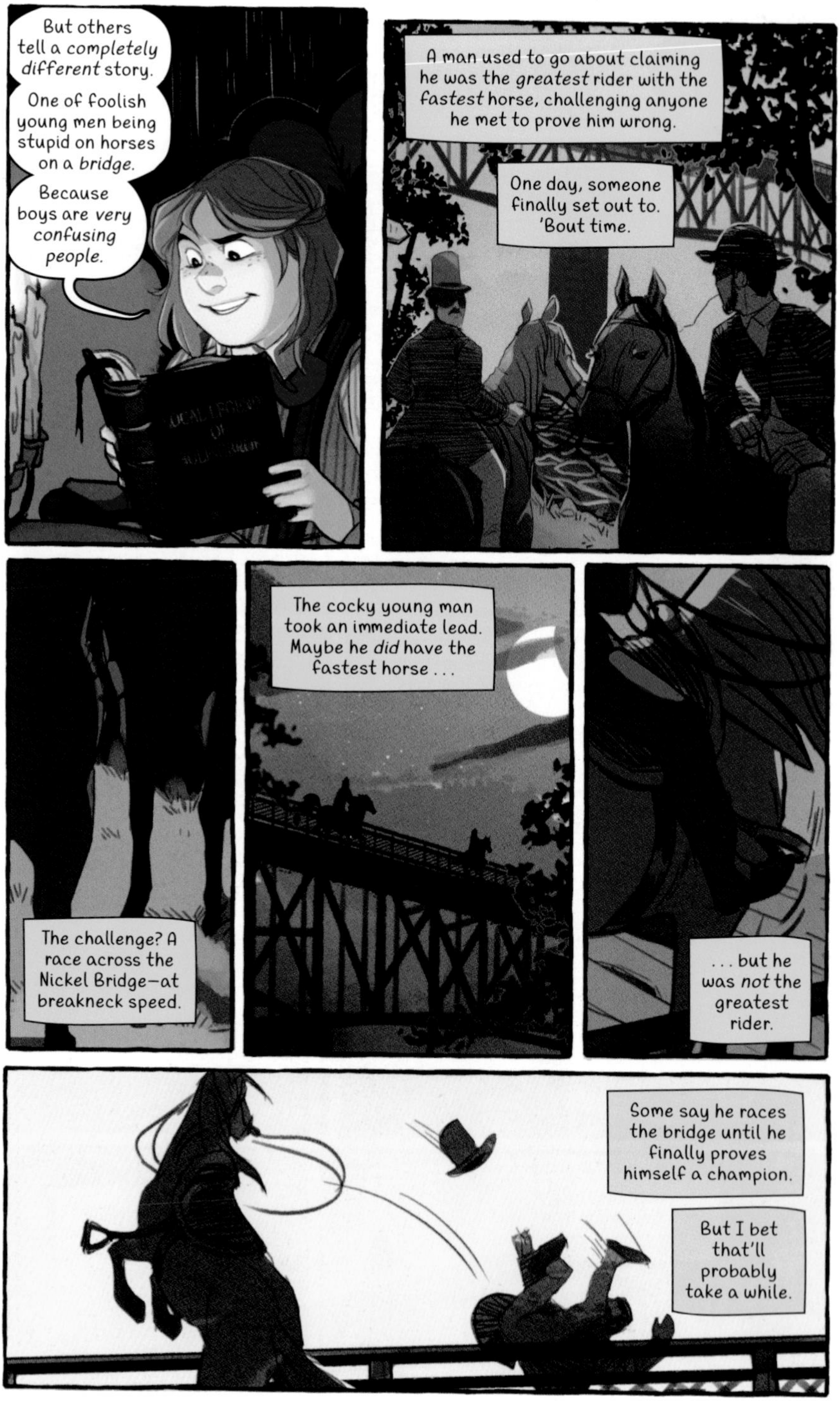
But others tell a *completely different* story.
One of foolish young men being stupid on horses on a *bridge*.
Because boys are *very* confusing people.
A man used to go about claiming he was the *greatest* rider with the *fastest* horse, challenging anyone he met to prove him wrong.
One day, someone finally set out to. 'Bout time.
The challenge? A race across the Nickel Bridge—at breakneck speed.
The cocky young man took an immediate lead. Maybe he *did* have the fastest horse . . .
. . . but he was *not* the greatest rider.
Some say he races the bridge until he finally proves himself a champion.
But I bet that'll probably take a while.

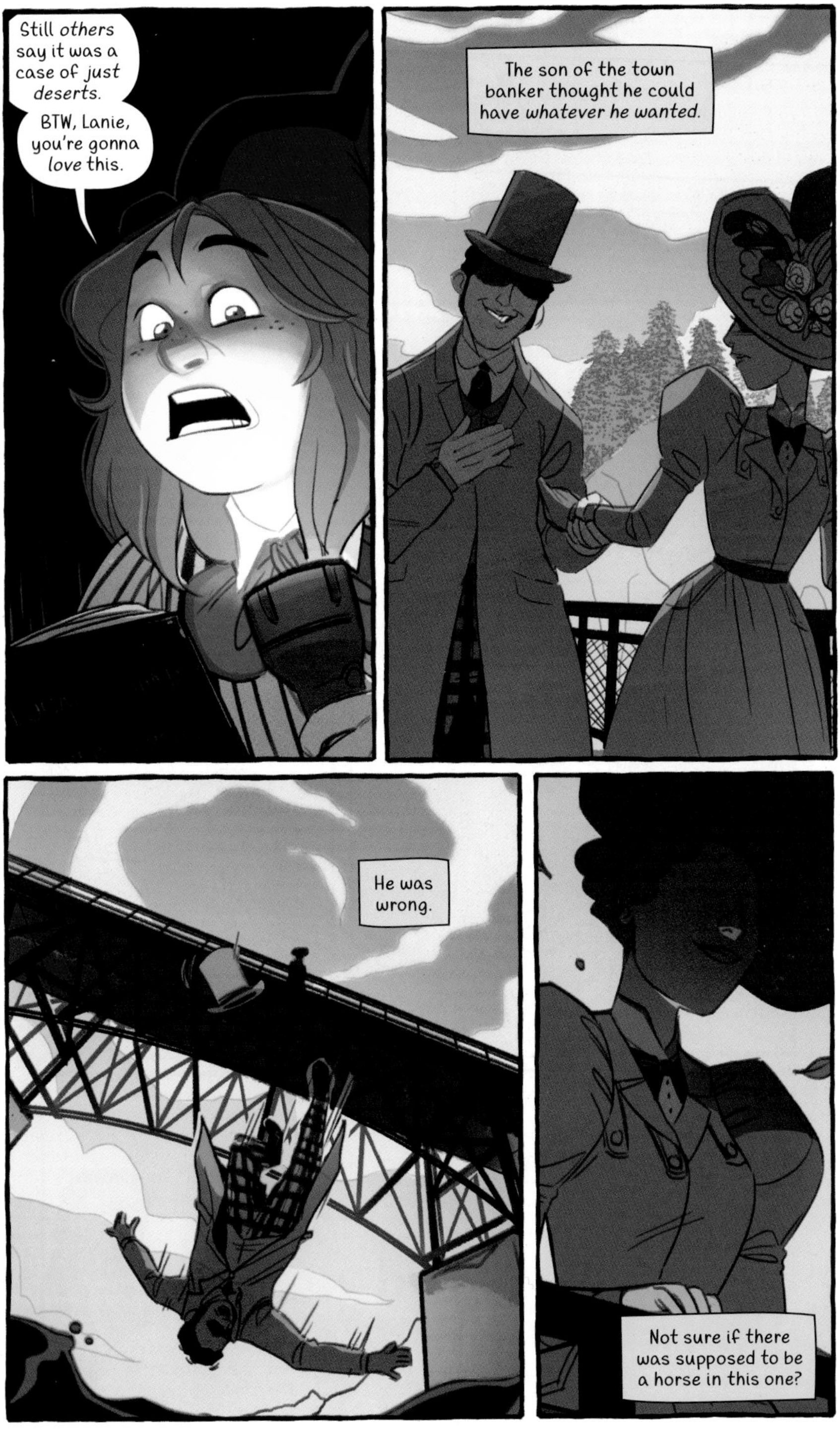
Still *others* say it was a case of *just deserts.*
BTW, Lanie, you're gonna *love* this.
The son of the town banker thought he could have *whatever he wanted.*
He was wrong.
Not sure if there was supposed to be a horse in this one?

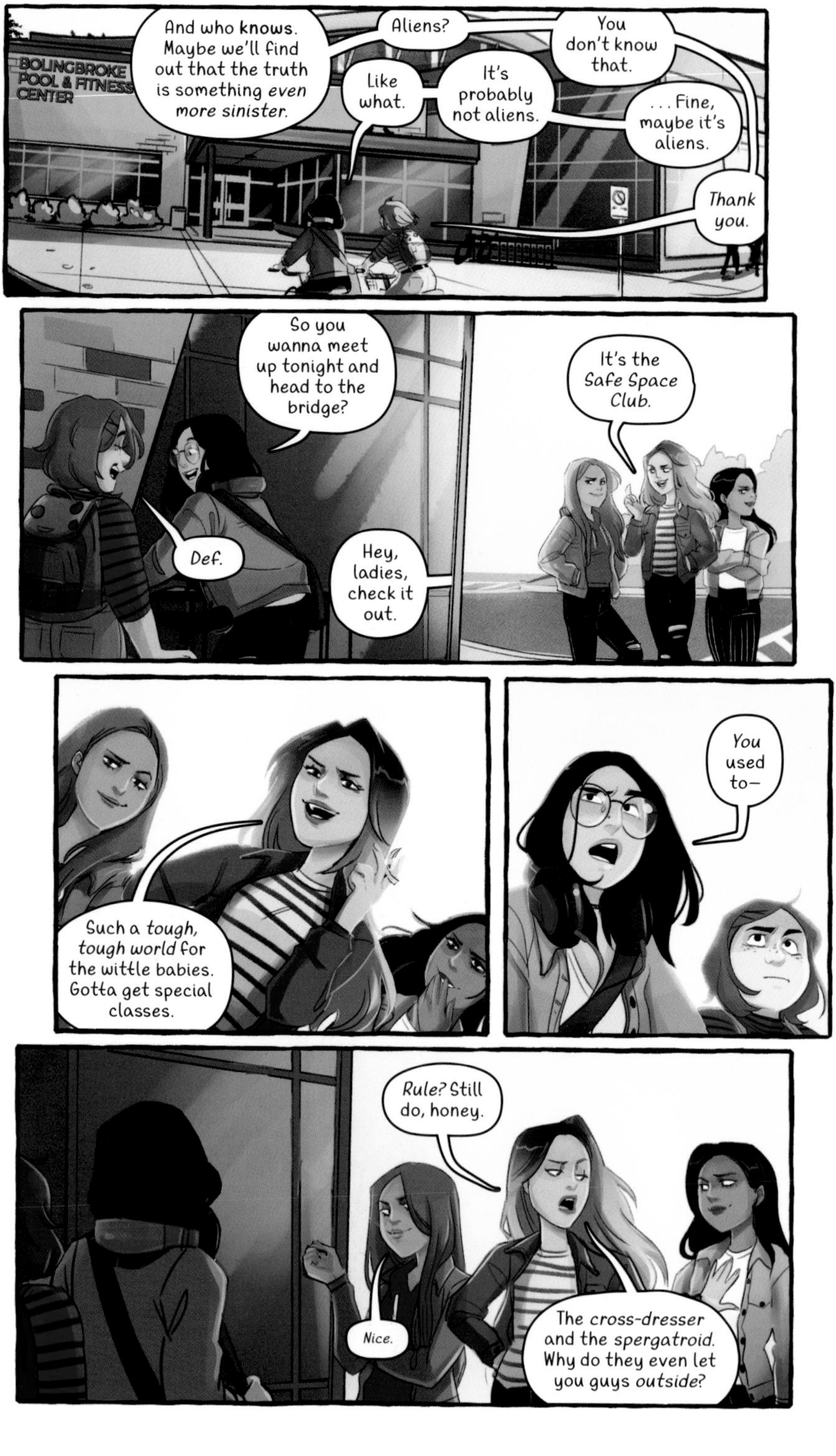
BOLINGBROKE POOL & FITNESS CENTER
And who **knows**. Maybe we'll find out that the truth is something *even more sinister*.
Aliens?
Like what.
It's probably not aliens.
You don't know that.
. . . Fine, maybe it's aliens.
Thank you.
So you wanna meet up tonight and head to the bridge?
Def.
Hey, ladies, check it out.
It's the *Safe Space Club*.
Such a *tough*, *tough world* for the wittle babies. Gotta get special classes.
You used to—
Rule? Still do, honey.
Nice.
The *cross-dresser* and the *spergatroid*. Why do they even let you guys *outside*?

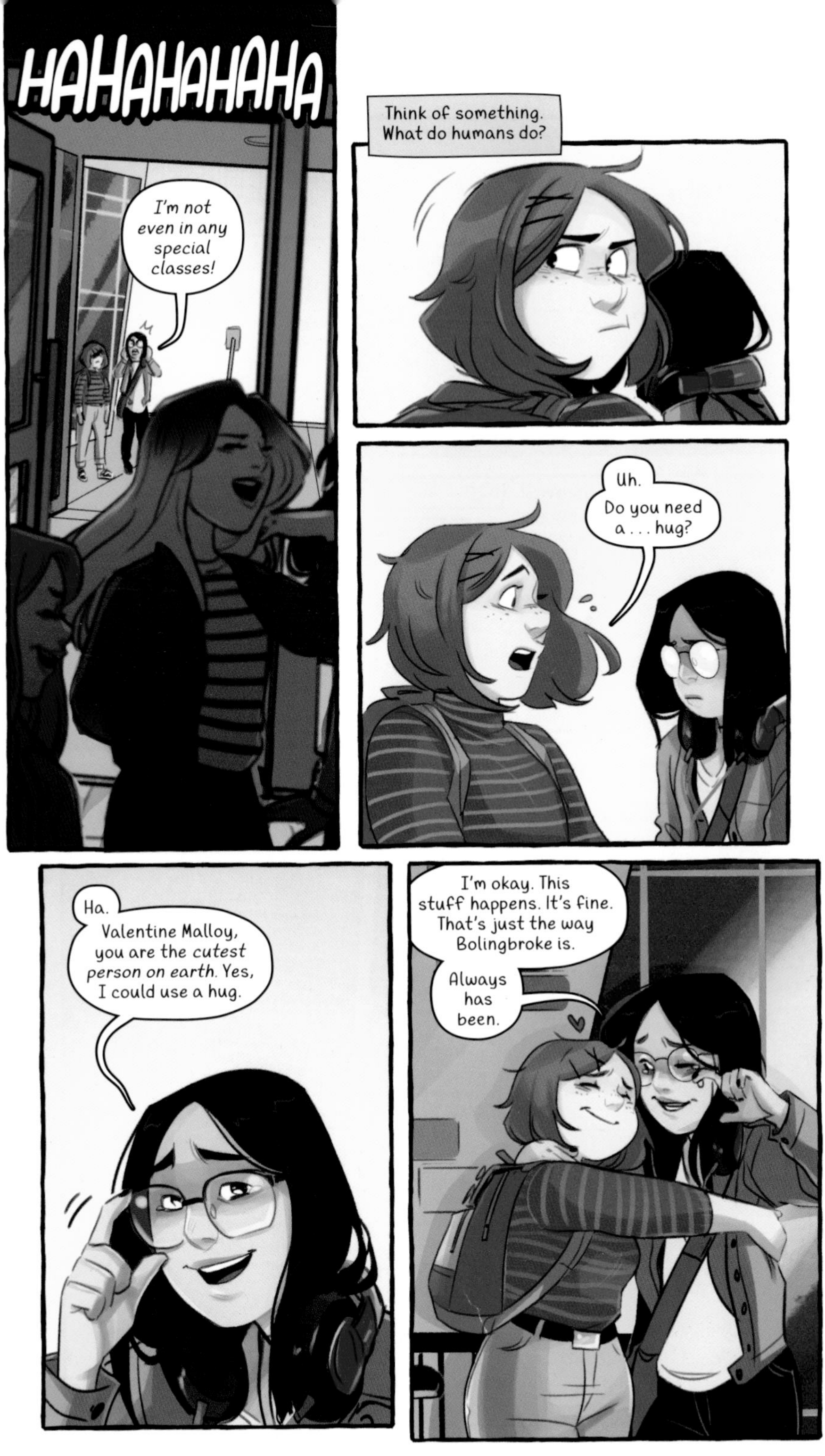
HAHAHAHAHA
I'm not even in any special classes!
Think of something. What do humans do?
Uh.
Do you need a . . . hug?
Ha.
Valentine Malloy, you are the *cutest* person on earth. Yes, I could use a hug.
I'm okay. This stuff happens. It's fine. That's just the way Bolingbroke is.
Always has been.

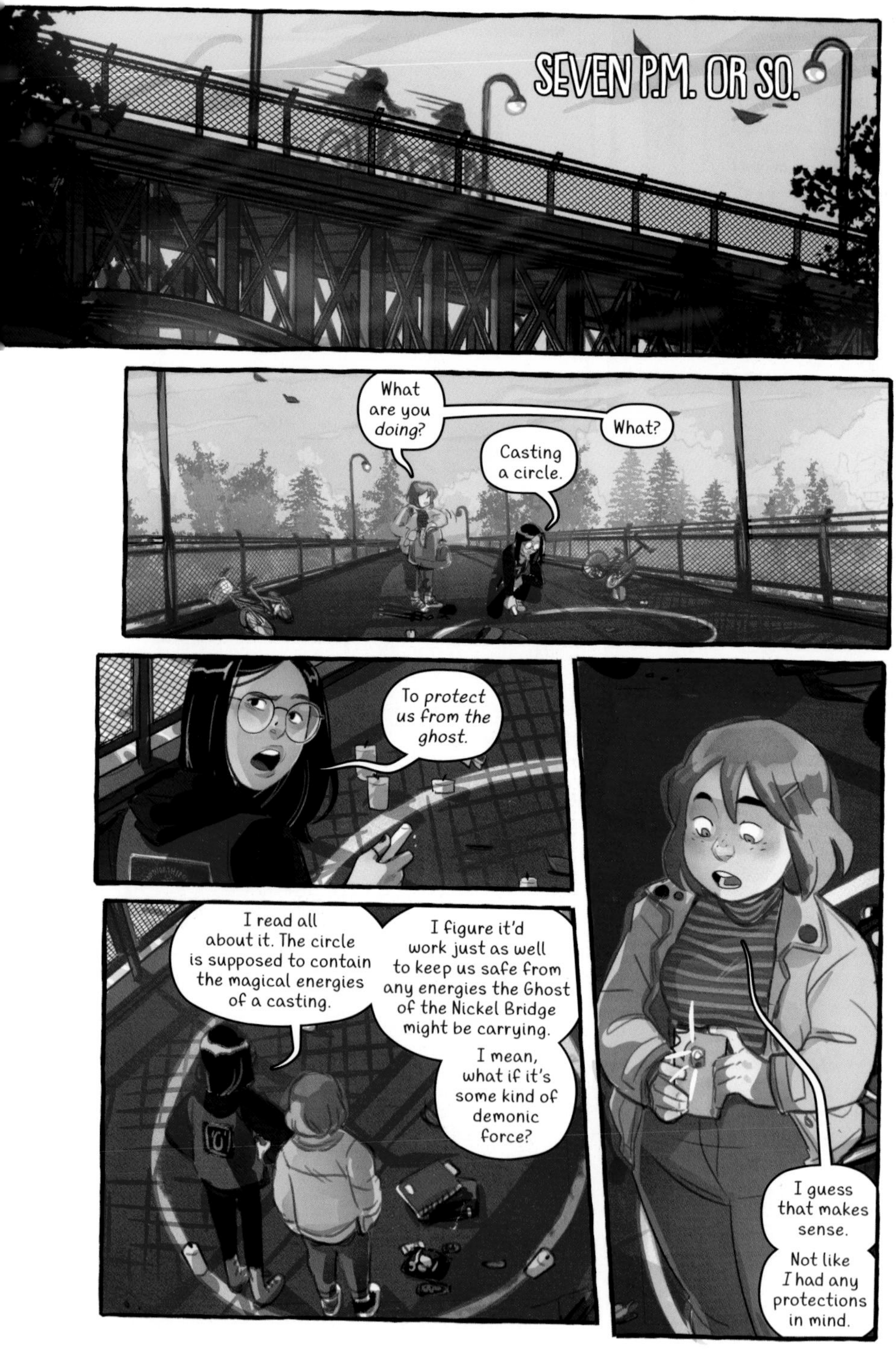
SEVEN P.M. OR SO.
What are you doing?
Casting a circle.
What?
To protect us from the ghost.
I read all about it. The circle is supposed to contain the magical energies of a casting.
I figure it'd work just as well to keep us safe from any energies the Ghost of the Nickel Bridge might be carrying.
I mean, what if it's some kind of demonic force?
I guess that makes sense.
Not like *I* had any protections in mind.

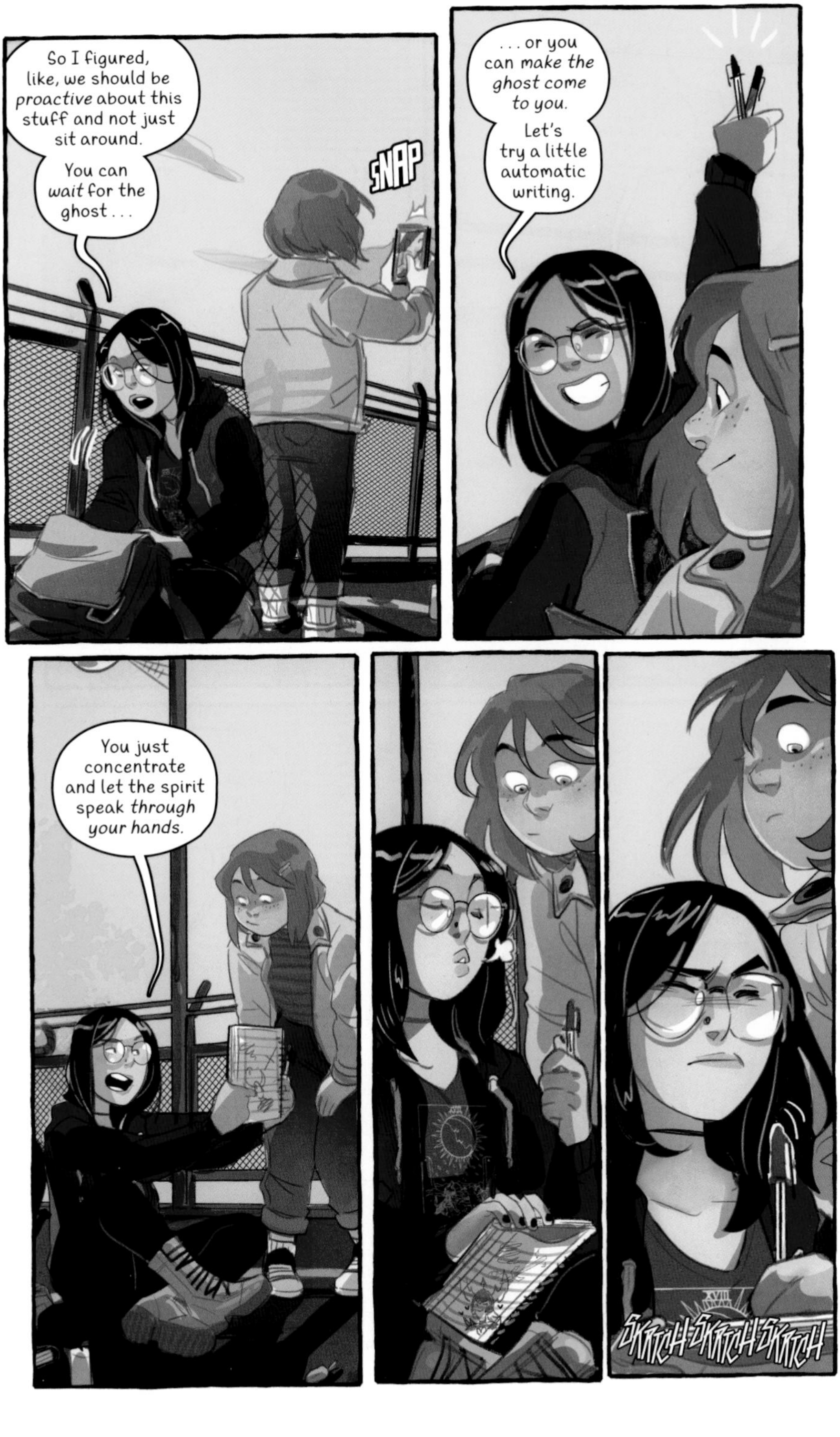
So I figured, like, we should be *proactive* about this stuff and not just sit around.
You can *wait* for the ghost . . .
SNAP
. . . or you can make the *ghost come to you*.
Let's try a little automatic writing.
You just concentrate and let the spirit speak *through your hands*.
SKRTCH SKRTCH SKRTCH

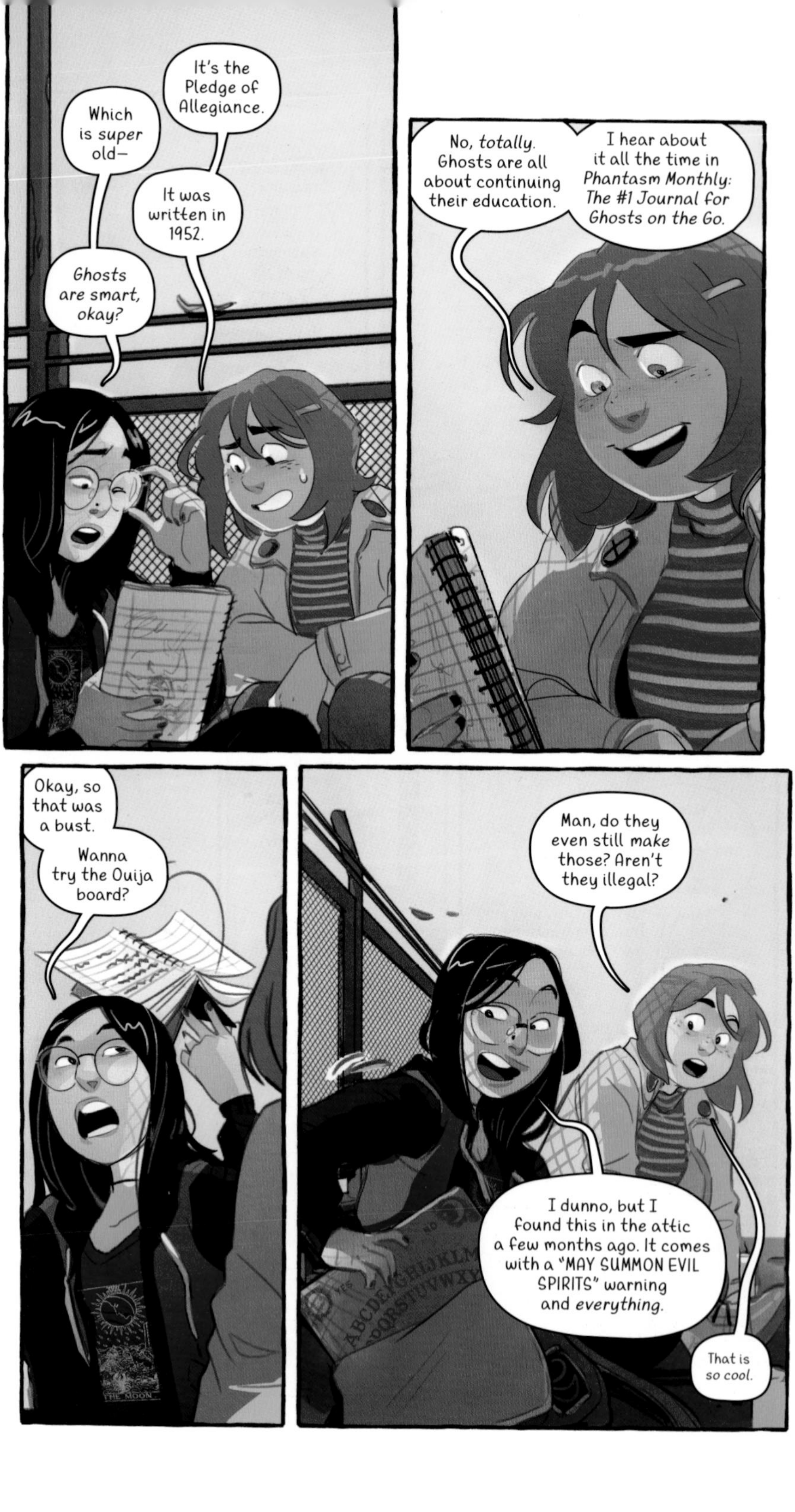
Which is super old—
It's the Pledge of Allegiance.
It was written in 1952.
Ghosts are smart, okay?
No, totally. Ghosts are all about continuing their education.
I hear about it all the time in Phantasm Monthly: The #1 Journal for Ghosts on the Go.
Okay, so that was a bust.
Wanna try the Ouija board?
Man, do they even still make those? Aren't they illegal?
I dunno, but I found this in the attic a few months ago. It comes with a "MAY SUMMON EVIL SPIRITS" warning and everything.
That is so cool.

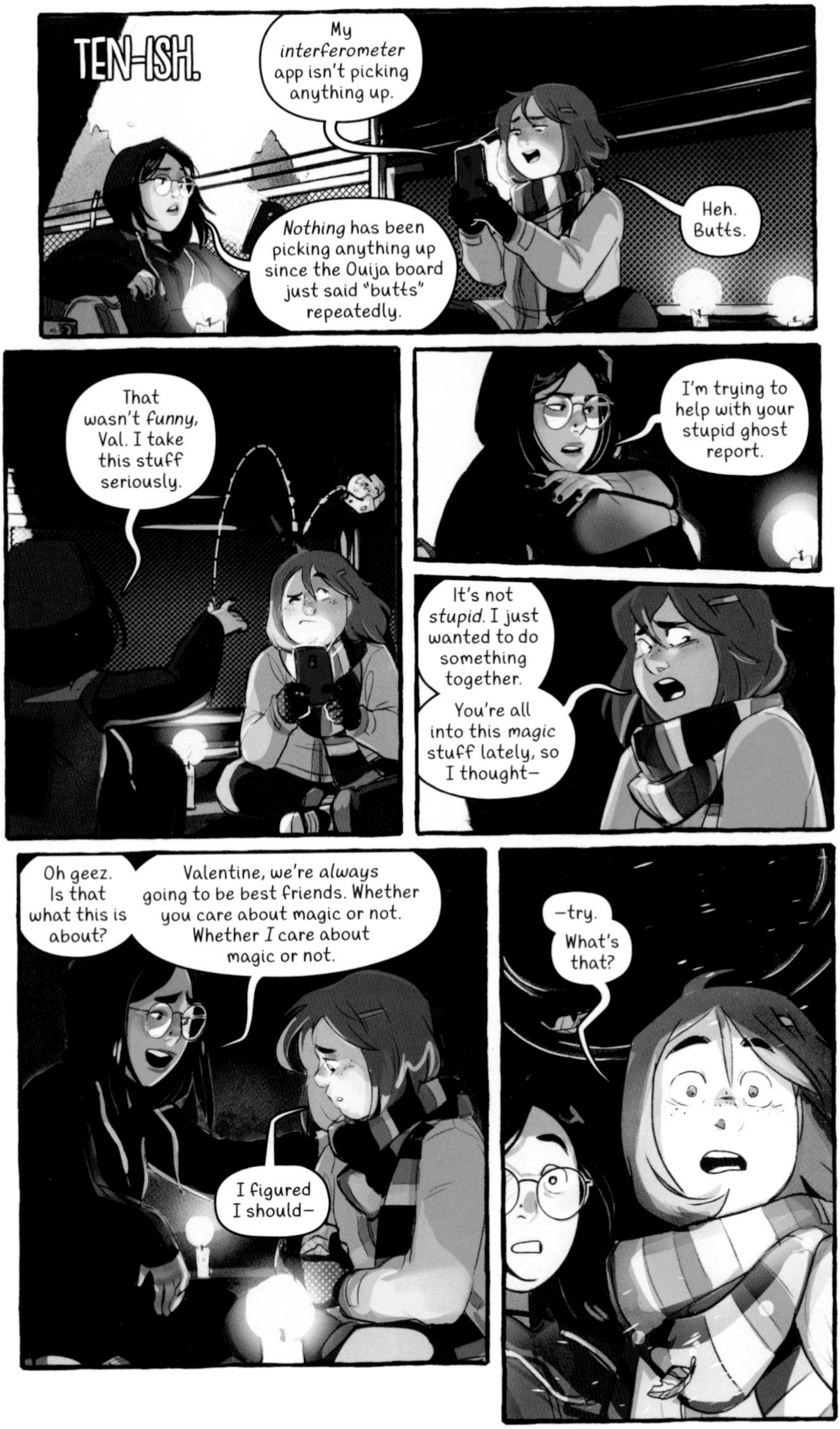
TEN-ISH.
My *interferometer* app isn't picking anything up.
Nothing has been picking anything up since the Ouija board just said "butts" repeatedly.
Heh. Butts.
That wasn't *funny*, Val. I take this stuff seriously.
I'm trying to help with your stupid ghost report.
It's not *stupid*. I just wanted to do something together.
You're all into this *magic* stuff lately, so I thought—
Oh geez. Is that what this is about?
Valentine, we're *always* going to be best friends. Whether you care about magic or not. Whether *I* care about magic or not.
I figured I should—
—try. What's that?

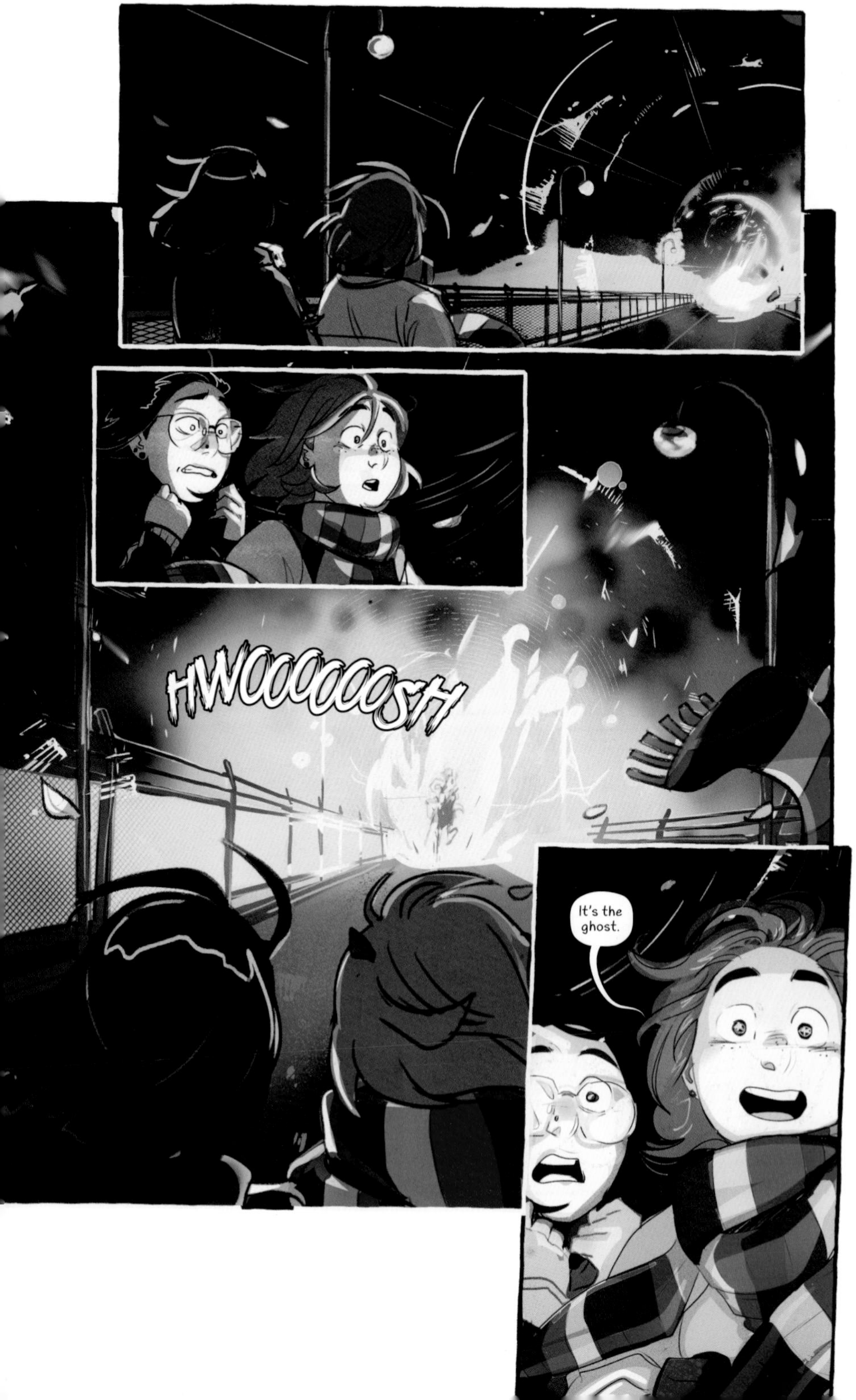
HWOOOOOOSH
It's the ghost.

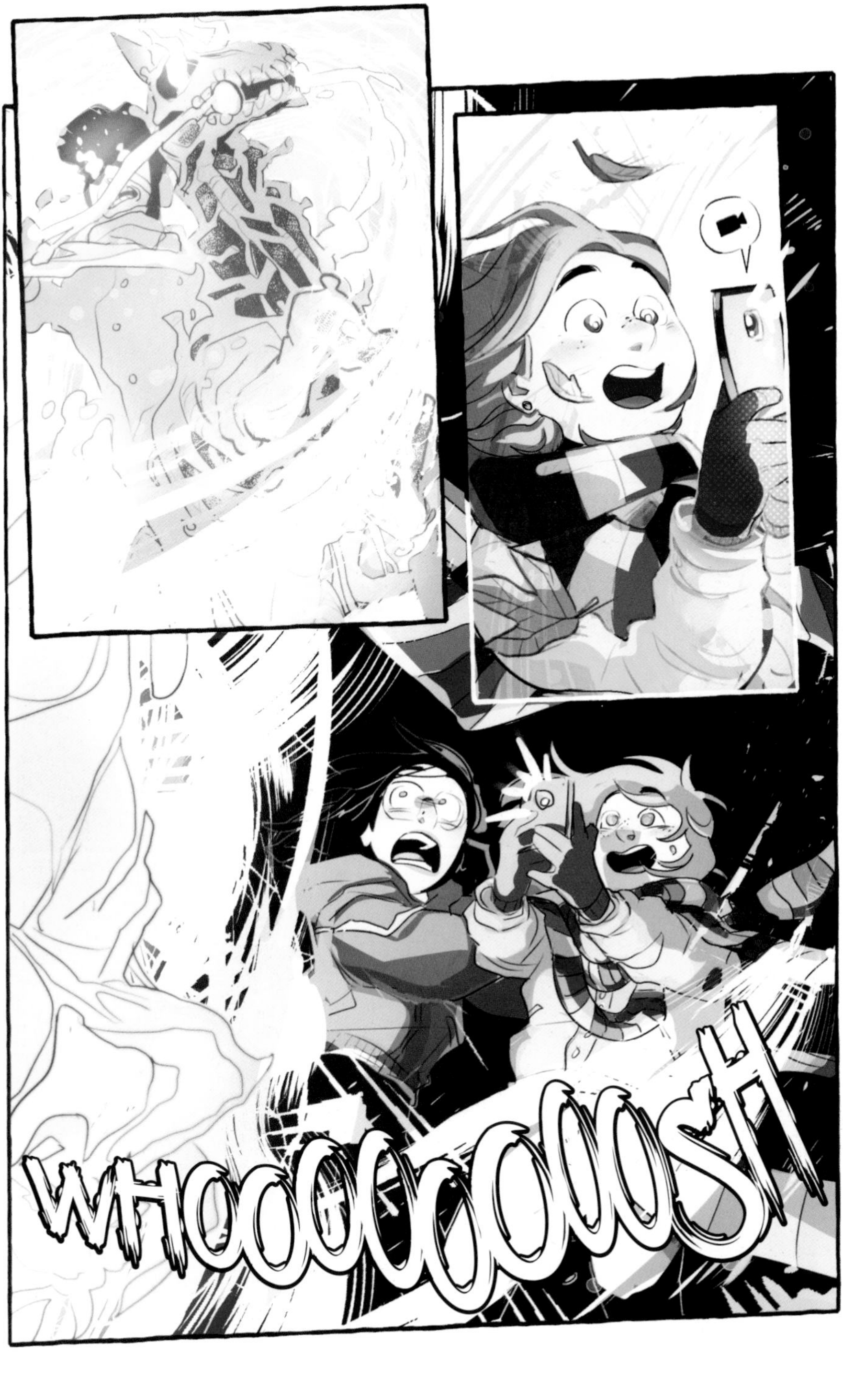
WHOOOOOOOOOSH

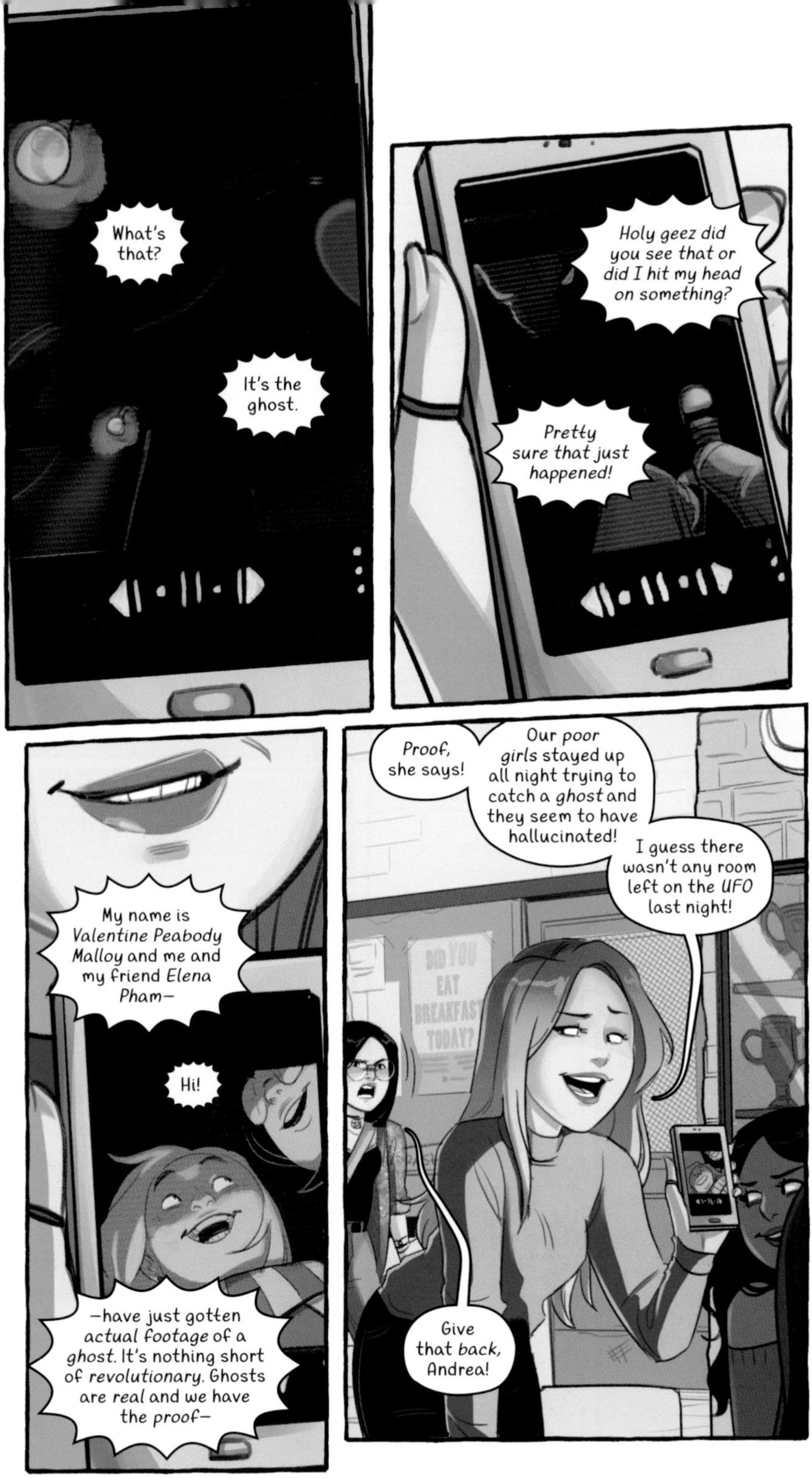
What's that?
It's the ghost.
Holy geez did you see that or did I hit my head on something?
Pretty sure that just happened!
My name is Valentine Peabody Malloy and me and my friend Elena Pham—
Hi!
—have just gotten actual footage of a ghost. It's nothing short of revolutionary. Ghosts are real and we have the proof—
Proof, she says!
Our poor girls stayed up all night trying to catch a ghost and they seem to have hallucinated!
I guess there wasn't any room left on the UFO last night!
DID YOU EAT BREAKFAST TODAY?
Give that back, Andrea!

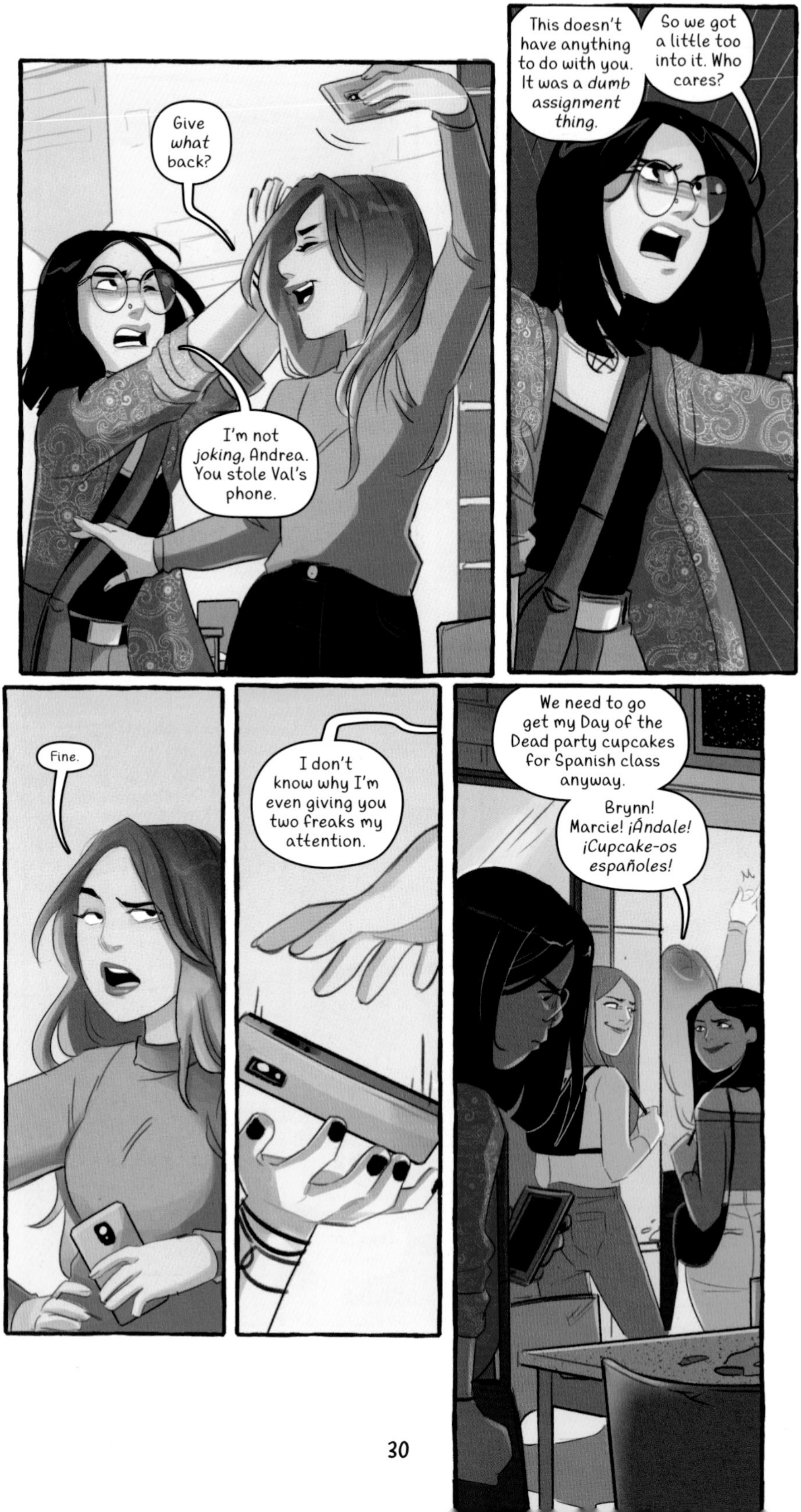
Give *what* back?
I'm not *joking*, Andrea. You stole Val's phone.
This doesn't have anything to do with you. It was a *dumb* assignment thing.
So we got a little too into it. Who cares?
Fine.
I don't know why I'm even giving you two freaks my attention.
We need to go get my Day of the Dead party cupcakes for Spanish class anyway.
Brynn! Marcie! ¡Ándale! ¡Cupcake-os españoles!

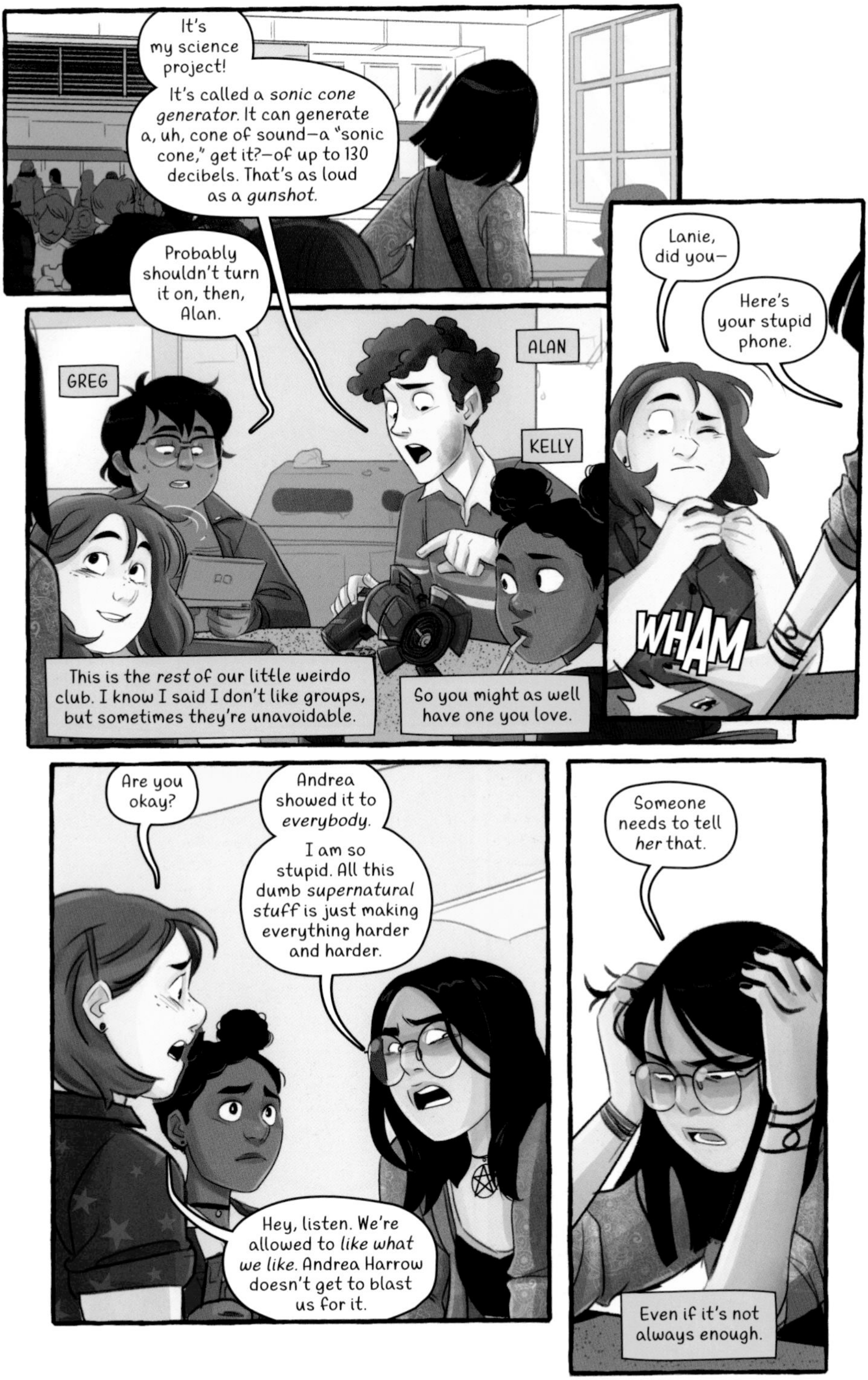
It's my science project!
It's called a *sonic cone generator*. It can generate a, uh, cone of sound—a "sonic cone," get it?—of up to 130 decibels. That's as loud as a *gunshot*.
Probably shouldn't turn it on, then, Alan.
GREG
ALAN
KELLY
This is the *rest* of our little weirdo club. I know I said I don't like groups, but sometimes they're unavoidable.
So you might as well have one you love.
Lanie, did you—
Here's your stupid phone.
WHAM
Are you okay?
Andrea showed it to *everybody*.
I am so stupid. All this dumb *supernatural stuff* is just making everything harder and harder.
Hey, listen. We're allowed to *like what we like*. Andrea Harrow doesn't get to blast us for it.
Someone needs to tell *her* that.
Even if it's not always enough.

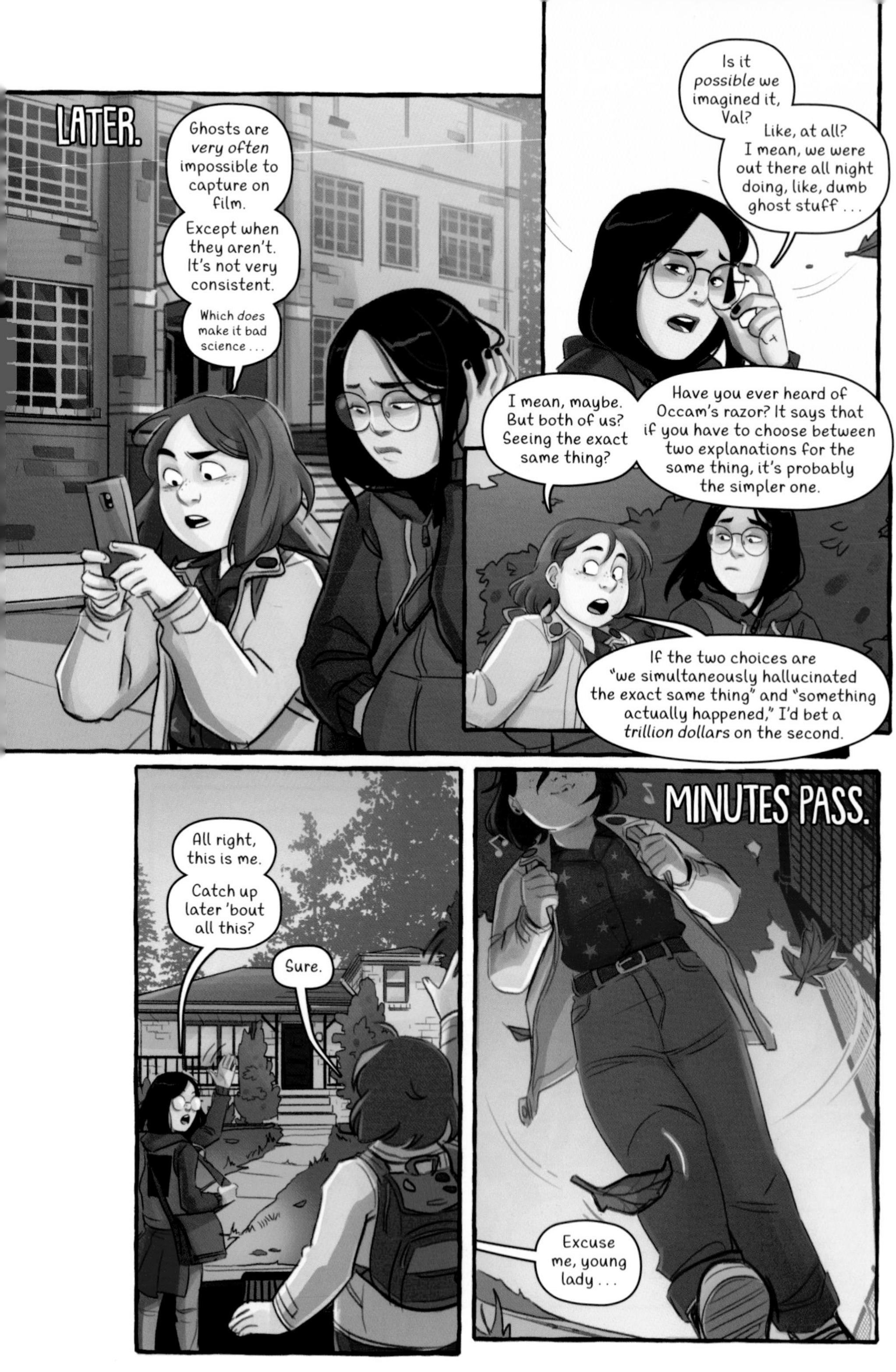
LATER.
Ghosts are *very often* impossible to capture on film.
Except when they aren't. It's not very consistent.
Which *does* make it bad science . . .
Is it *possible* we imagined it, Val?
Like, at all? I mean, we were out there all night doing, like, dumb ghost stuff . . .
I mean, maybe. But both of us? Seeing the exact same thing?
Have you ever heard of Occam's razor? It says that if you have to choose between two explanations for the same thing, it's probably the simpler one.
If the two choices are "we simultaneously hallucinated the exact same thing" and "something actually happened," I'd bet a *trillion dollars* on the second.
All right, this is me.
Catch up later 'bout all this?
Sure.
MINUTES PASS.
Excuse me, young lady . . .

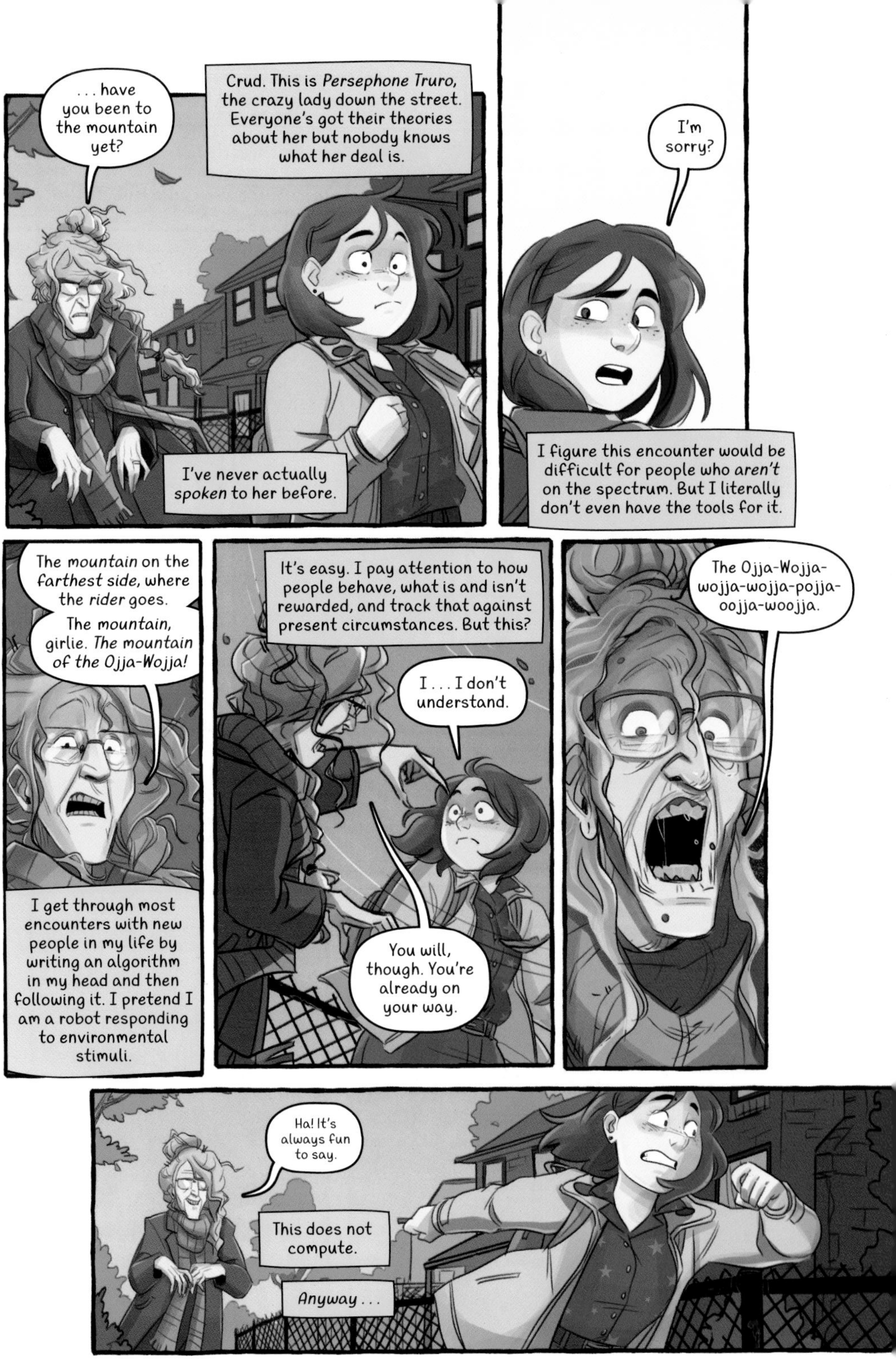
. . . have you been to the mountain yet?
Crud. This is *Persephone Truro,* the crazy lady down the street. Everyone's got their theories about her but nobody knows what her deal is.
I've never actually *spoken* to her before.
I'm sorry?
I figure this encounter would be difficult for people who *aren't* on the spectrum. But I literally don't even have the tools for it.
The *mountain* on the *farthest side,* where the *rider* goes.
The *mountain,* girlie. *The mountain of the Ojja-Wojja!*
I get through most encounters with new people in my life by writing an algorithm in my head and then following it. I pretend I am a robot responding to environmental stimuli.
It's easy. I pay attention to how people behave, what is and isn't rewarded, and track that against present circumstances. But this?
I . . . I don't understand.
You will, though. You're already on your way.
The Ojja-Wojja-wojja-wojja-pojja-oojja-woojja.
Ha! It's always fun to say.
This does not compute.
Anyway . . .

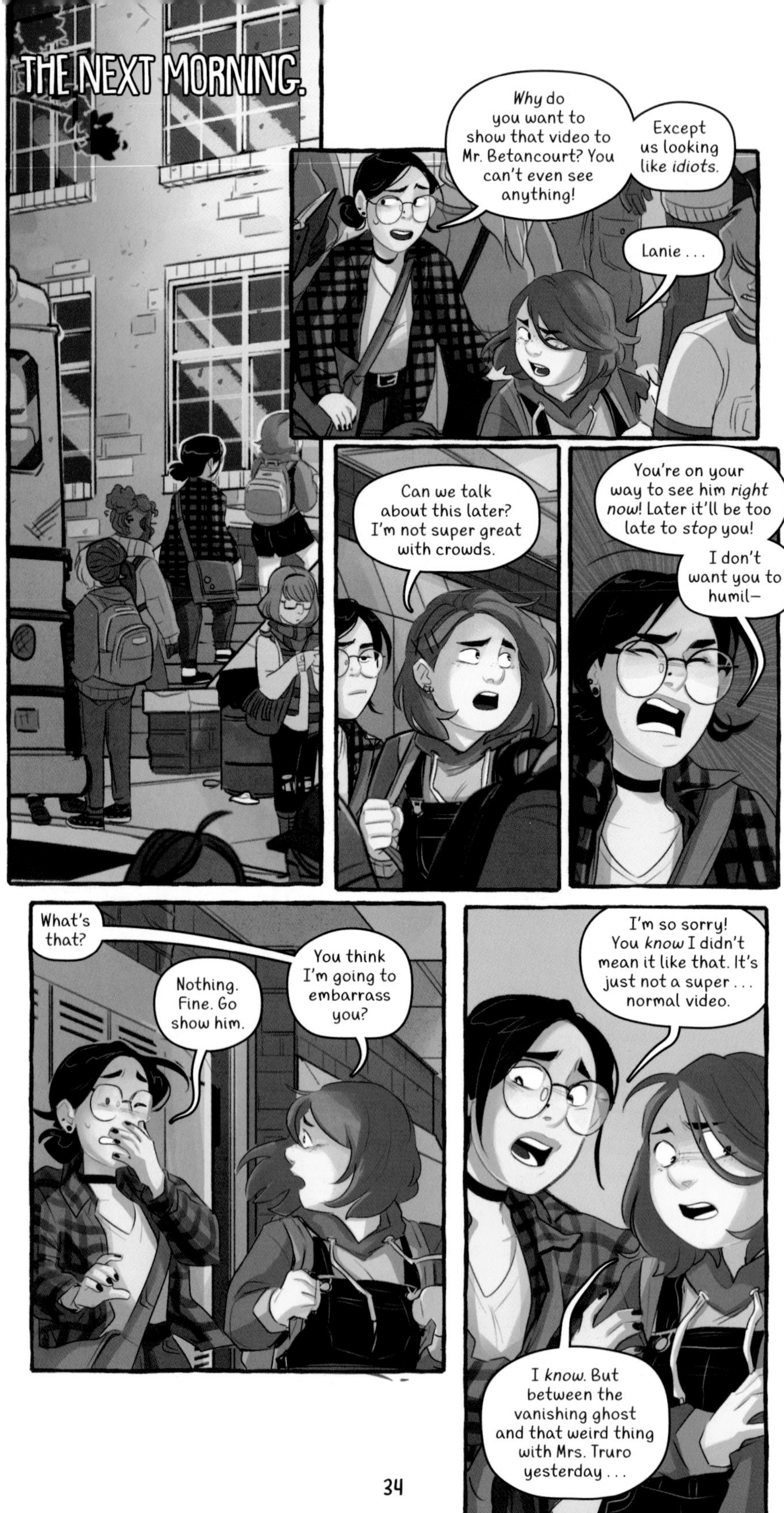
THE NEXT MORNING.
Why do you want to show that video to Mr. Betancourt? You can't even see anything!
Except us looking like *idiots*.
Lanie . . .
Can we talk about this later? I'm not super great with crowds.
You're on your way to see him *right now*! Later it'll be too late to *stop* you!
I don't want you to humil—
What's that?
You think I'm going to embarrass you?
Nothing. Fine. Go show him.
I'm so sorry! You *know* I didn't mean it like that. It's just not a super . . . normal video.
I *know*. But between the vanishing ghost and that weird thing with Mrs. Truro yesterday . . .

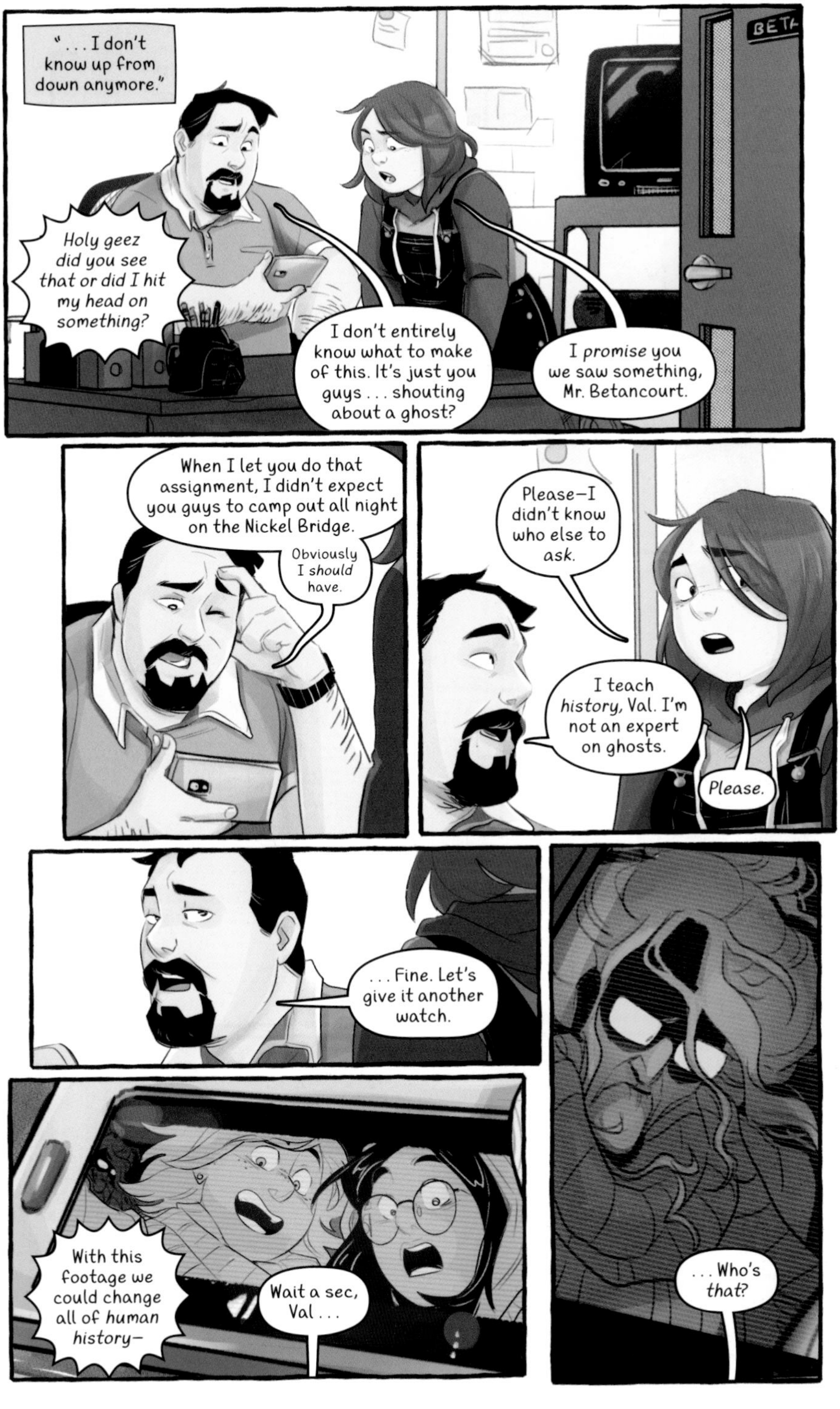
". . . I don't know up from down anymore."
Holy geez did you see that or did I hit my head on something?
I don't entirely know what to make of this. It's just you guys . . . shouting about a ghost?
I *promise* you we saw something, Mr. Betancourt.
When I let you do that assignment, I didn't expect you guys to camp out all night on the Nickel Bridge.
Obviously I *should* have.
Please—I didn't know who else to ask.
I teach *history*, Val. I'm not an expert on ghosts.
Please.
. . . Fine. Let's give it another watch.
With this footage we could change all of *human history*—
Wait a sec, Val . . .
. . . Who's *that*?

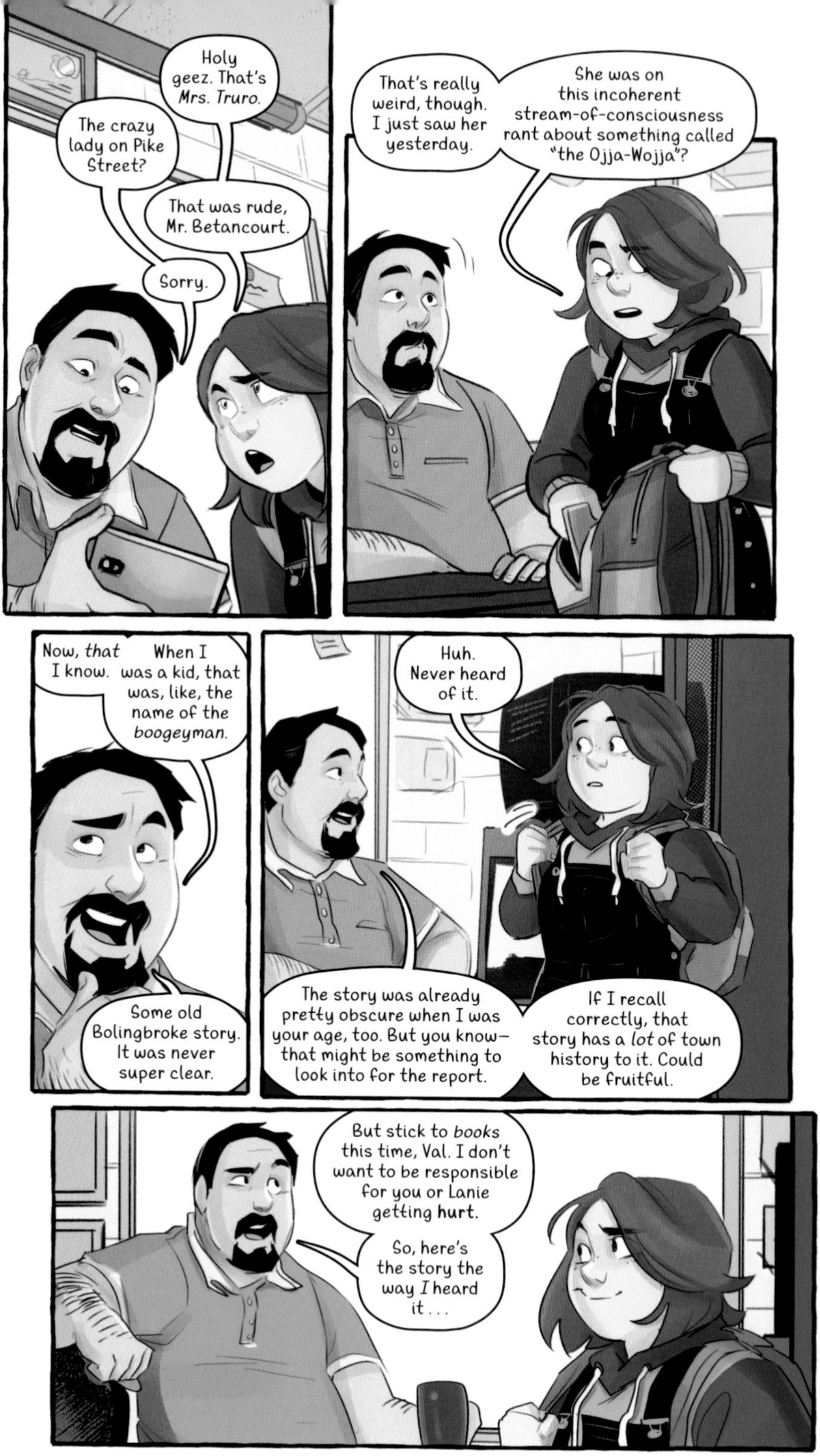
The crazy lady on Pike Street?
Holy geez. That's *Mrs. Truro.*
That was rude, Mr. Betancourt.
Sorry.
That's really weird, though. I just saw her yesterday.
She was on this incoherent stream-of-consciousness rant about something called "the Ojja-Wojja"?
Now, *that* I know.
When I was a kid, that was, like, the name of the *boogeyman.*
Some old Bolingbroke story. It was never super clear.
Huh. Never heard of it.
The story was already pretty obscure when I was your age, too. But you know— that might be something to look into for the report.
If I recall correctly, that story has a *lot* of town history to it. Could be fruitful.
But stick to *books* this time, Val. I don't want to be responsible for you or Lanie getting **hurt**.
So, here's the story the way *I* heard it . . .

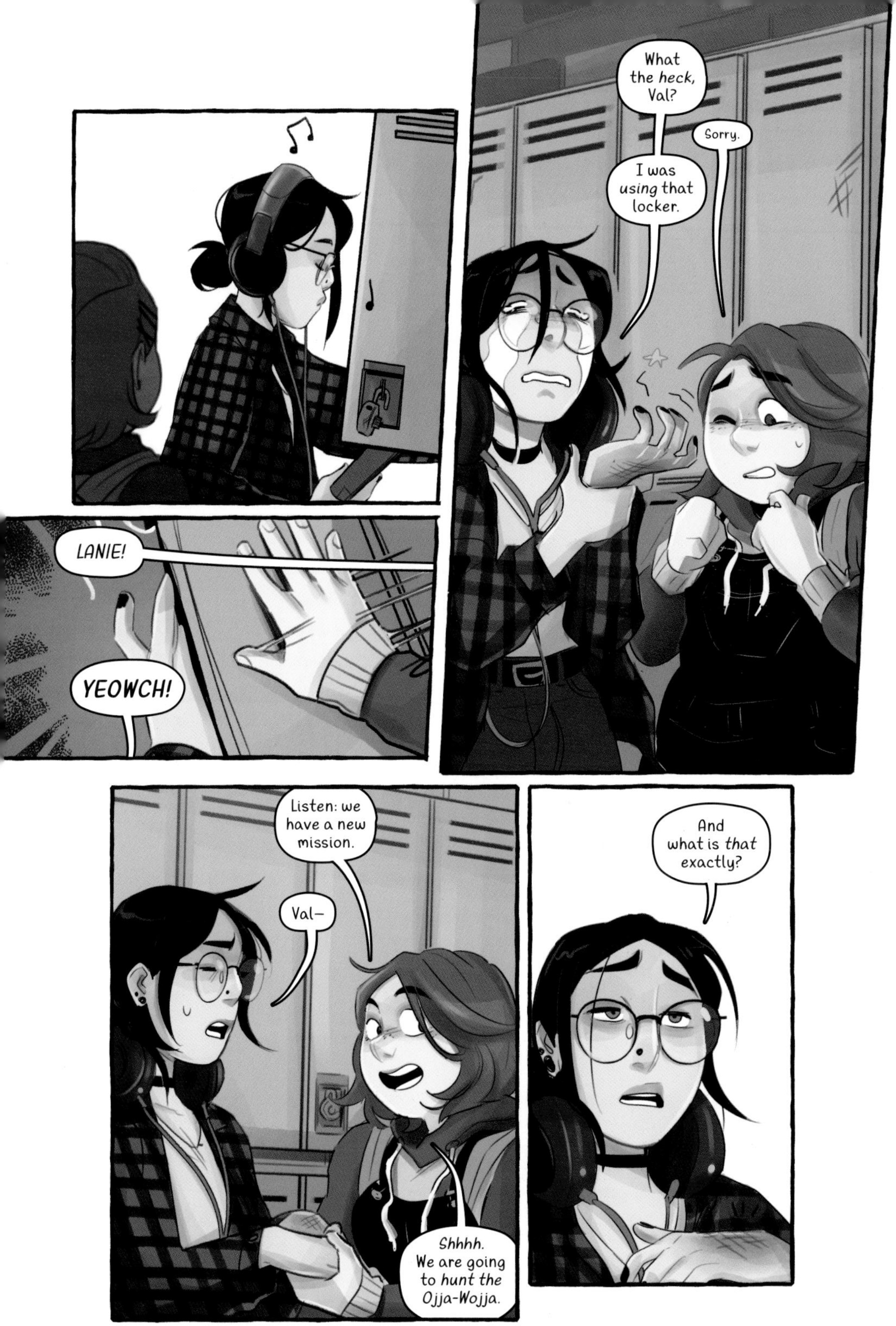
LANIE!
YEOWCH!
What the *heck*, Val?
I was *using* that locker.
Sorry.
Listen: we have a new mission.
Val–
Shhhh. We are going to *hunt* the Ojja-Wojja.
And what is *that* exactly?

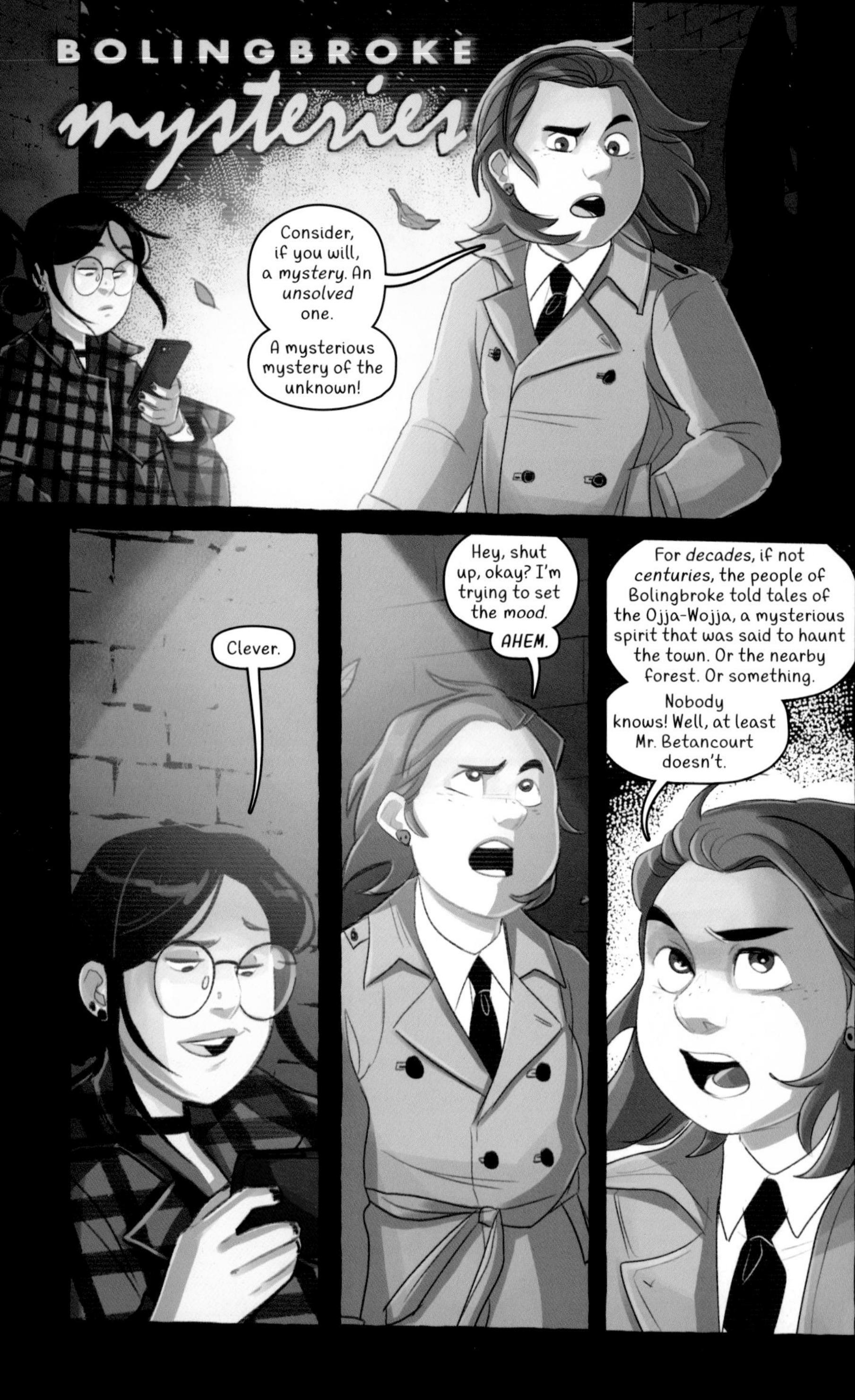
BOLINGBROKE mysteries
Consider, if you will, a *mystery*. An *unsolved* one.
A mysterious mystery of the unknown!
Clever.
Hey, shut up, okay? I'm trying to set the *mood*.
AHEM.
For *decades*, if not *centuries*, the people of Bolingbroke told tales of the Ojja-Wojja, a mysterious spirit that was said to haunt the town. Or the nearby forest. Or something.
Nobody knows! Well, at least Mr. Betancourt doesn't.

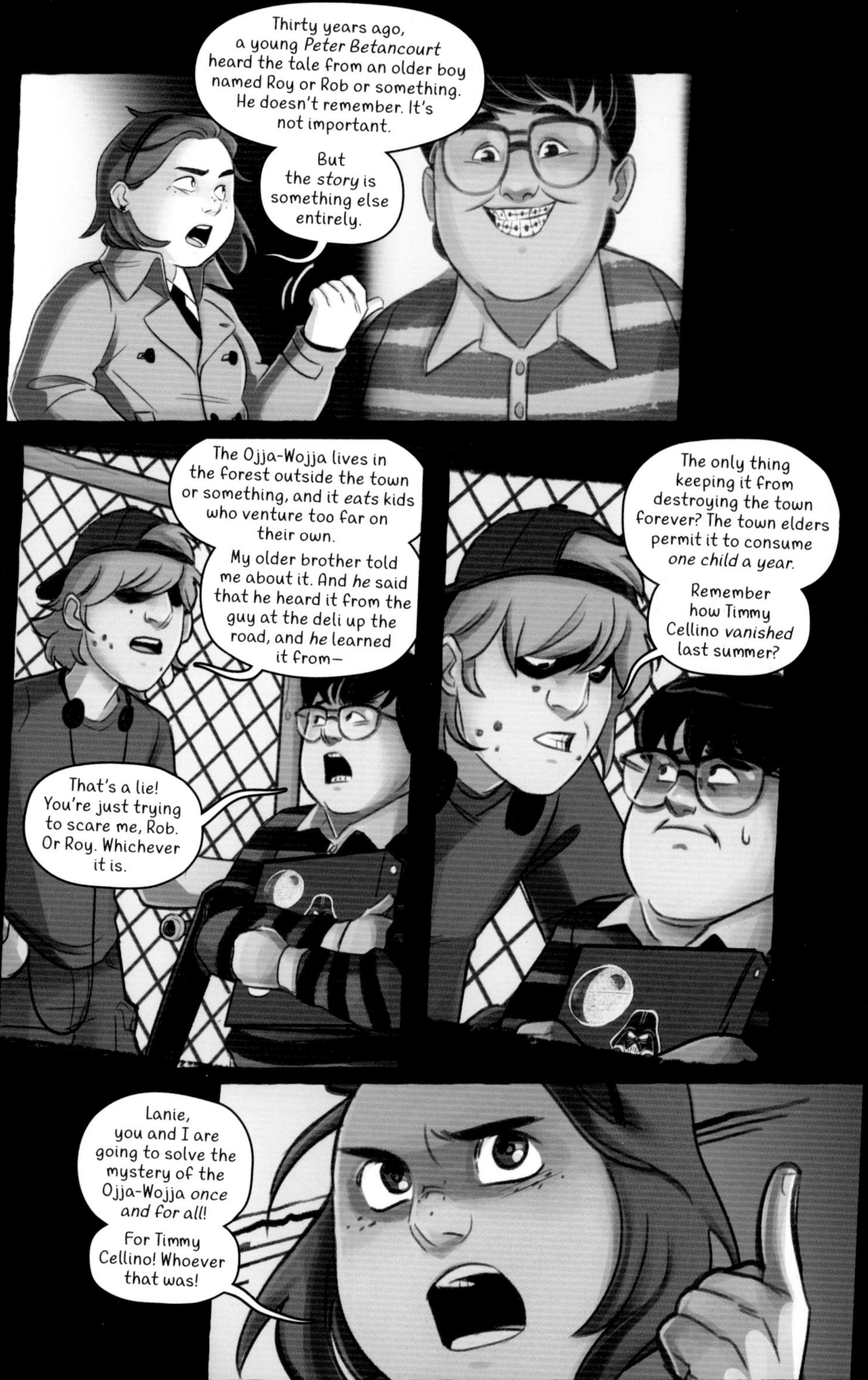
Thirty years ago, a young *Peter Betancourt* heard the tale from an older boy named Roy or Rob or something. He doesn't remember. It's not important.
But the *story* is something else entirely.
The Ojja-Wojja lives in the forest outside the town or something, and it *eats* kids who venture too far on their own.
My older brother told me about it. And *he* said that he heard it from the guy at the deli up the road, and *he* learned it from—
That's a lie! You're just trying to scare me, Rob. Or Roy. Whichever it is.
The only thing keeping it from destroying the town forever? The town elders permit it to consume *one child a year.*
Remember how Timmy Cellino *vanished* last summer?
Lanie, you and I are going to solve the mystery of the Ojja-Wojja *once and for all!*
For Timmy Cellino! Whoever that was!

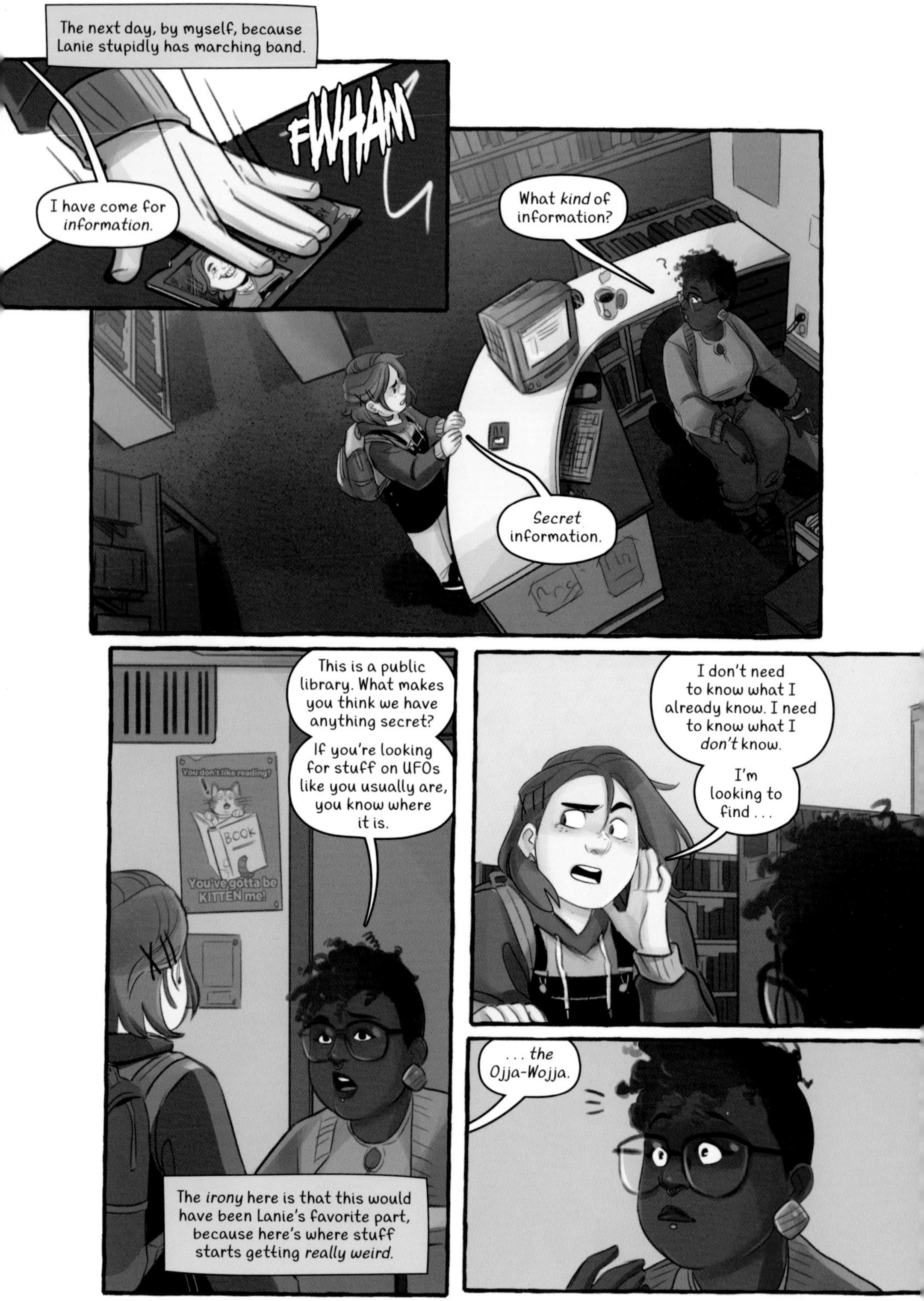
The next day, by myself, because Lanie stupidly has marching band.
FWHAM
I have come for *information*.
What *kind* of information?
?
Secret information.
This is a public library. What makes you think we have anything secret?
If you're looking for stuff on UFOs like you usually are, you know where it is.
You don't like reading?
BOOK
You've gotta be KITTEN me!
The *irony* here is that this would have been Lanie's favorite part, because here's where stuff starts getting *really weird*.
I don't need to know what I already know. I need to know what I *don't* know.
I'm looking to find . . .
. . . the Ojja-Wojja.

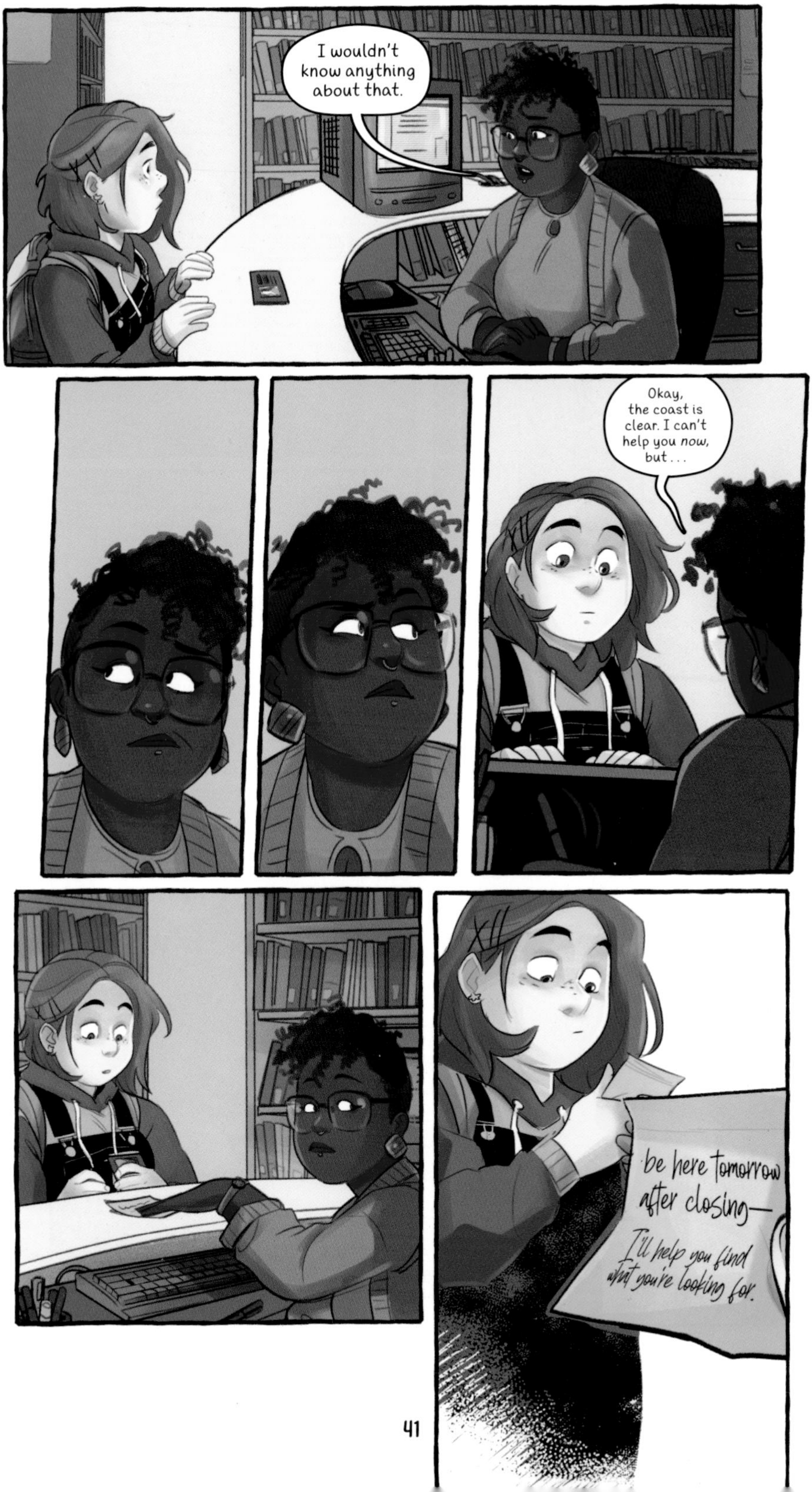
I wouldn't know anything about that.
Okay, the coast is clear. I can't help you *now*, but . . .
be here tomorrow after closing—
I'll help you find what you're looking for.

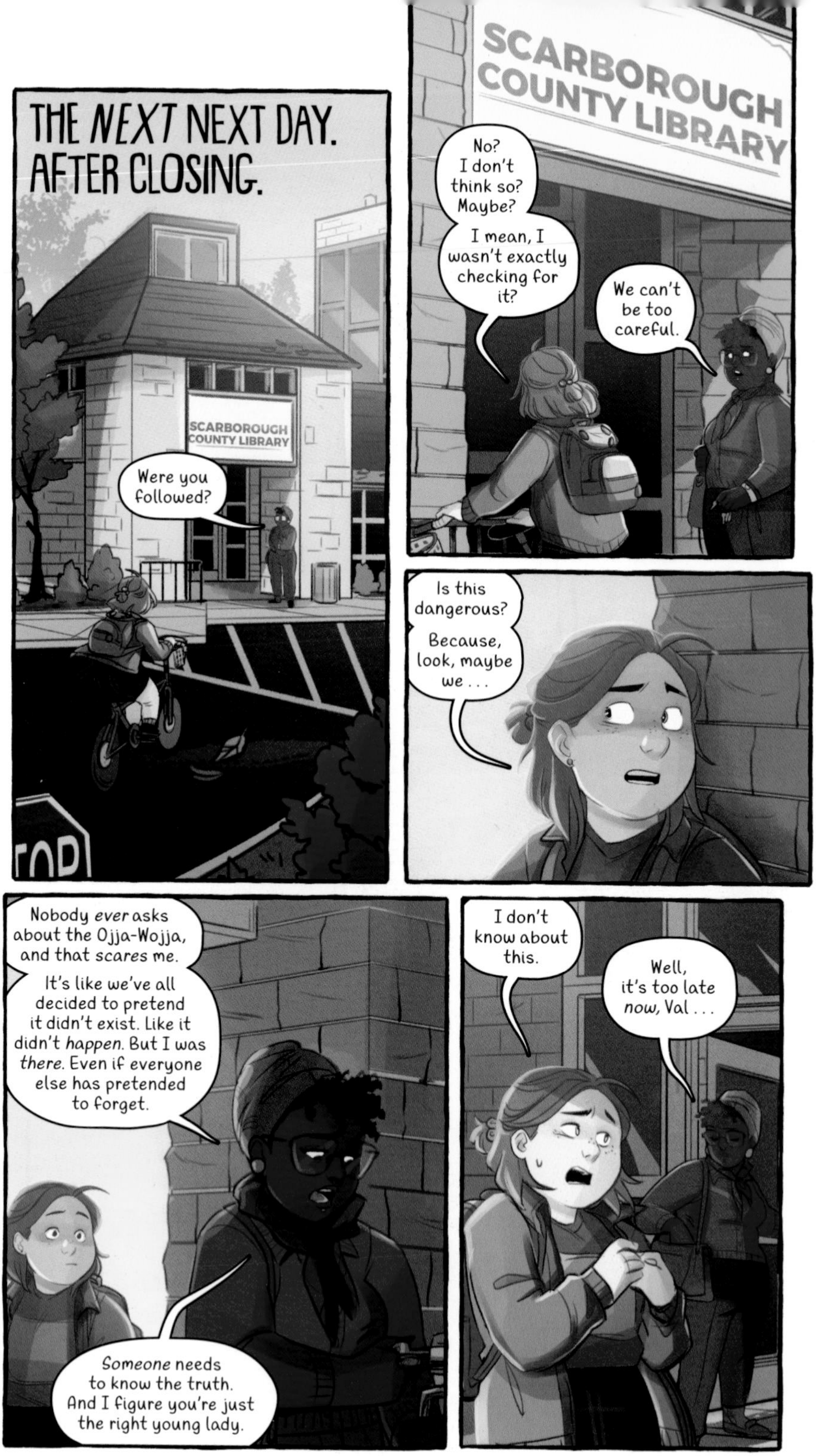
THE *NEXT* NEXT DAY. AFTER CLOSING.
SCARBOROUGH COUNTY LIBRARY
Were you followed?
SCARBOROUGH COUNTY LIBRARY
No? I don't think so? Maybe?
I mean, I wasn't exactly checking for it?
We can't be too careful.
Is this dangerous?
Because, look, maybe we . . .
Nobody *ever* asks about the Ojja-Wojja, and that *scares* me.
It's like we've all decided to pretend it didn't exist. Like it didn't *happen*. But I was *there*. Even if everyone else has pretended to forget.
Someone needs to know the truth. And I figure you're just the right young lady.
I don't know about this.
Well, it's too late *now*, Val . . .

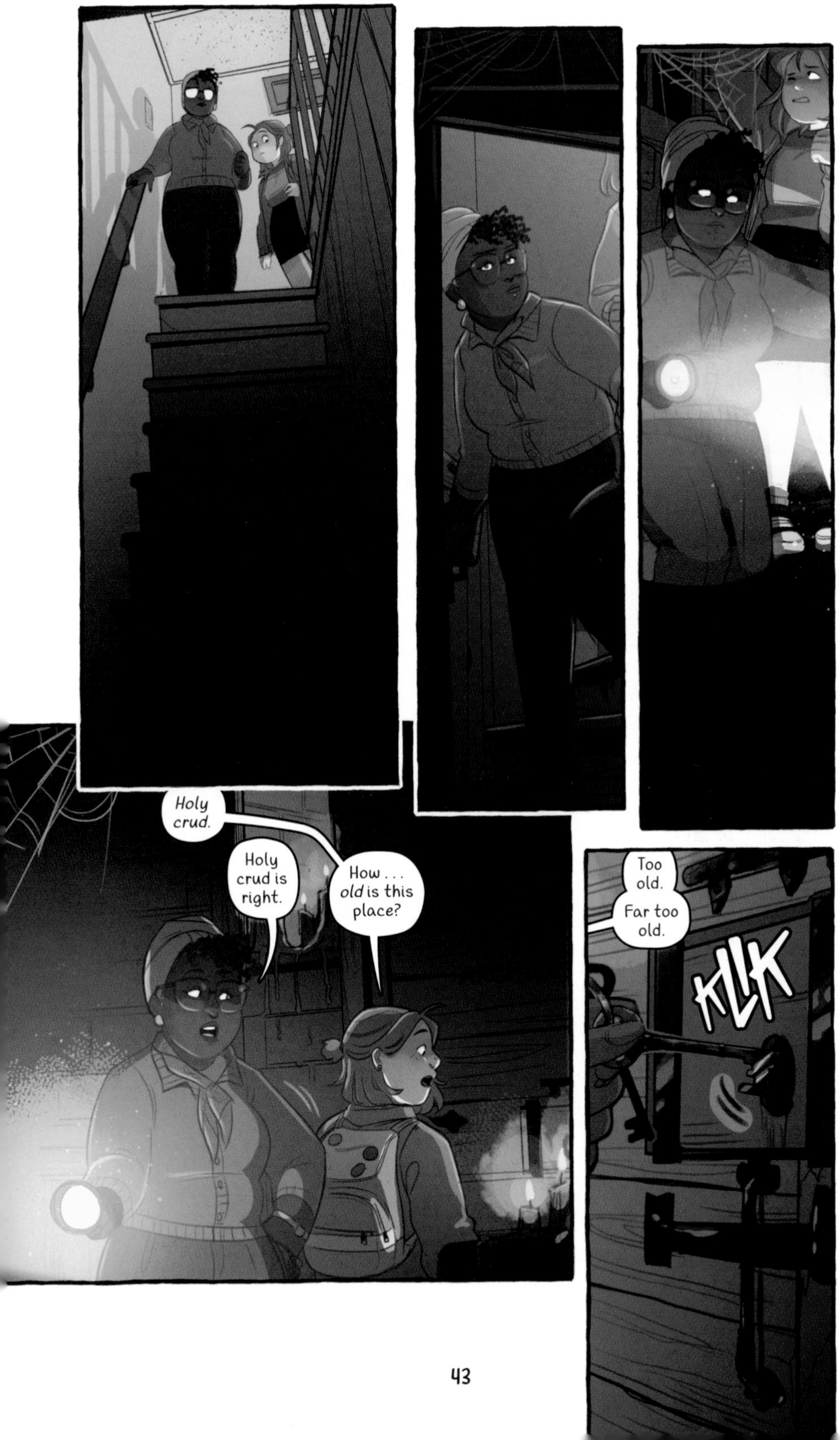
Holy crud.
Holy crud is right.
How . . . *old* is this place?
Too old.
Far too old.
KLIK

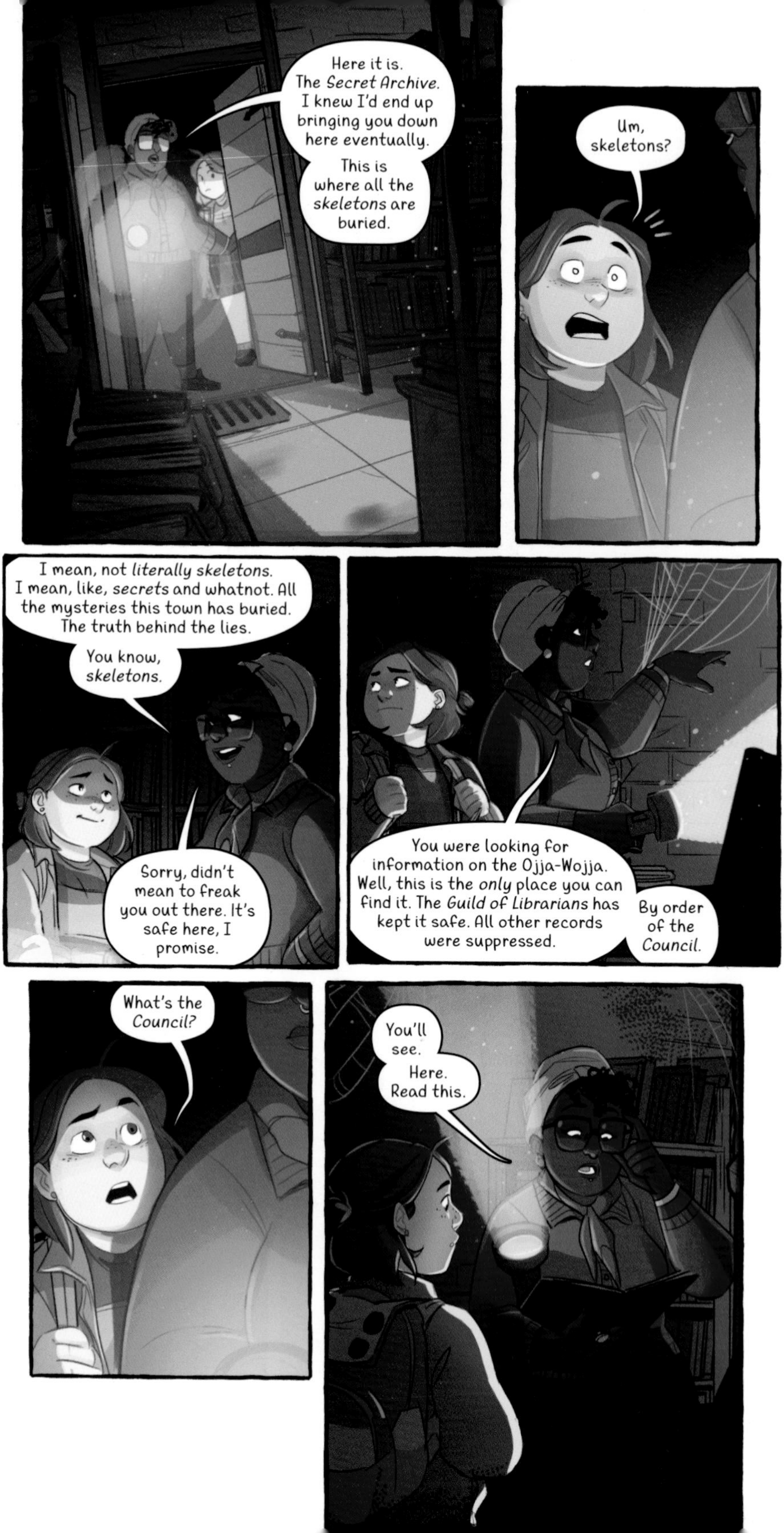
Here it is. The *Secret Archive.* I knew I'd end up bringing you down here eventually.
This is where all the *skeletons* are buried.
Um, skeletons?
I mean, not *literally skeletons.* I mean, like, *secrets* and whatnot. All the mysteries this town has buried. The truth behind the lies.
You know, *skeletons.*
Sorry, didn't mean to freak you out there. It's safe here, I promise.
You were looking for information on the Ojja-Wojja. Well, this is the *only* place you can find it. The *Guild of Librarians* has kept it safe. All other records were suppressed.
By order of the *Council.*
What's the *Council?*
You'll see.
Here. Read this.

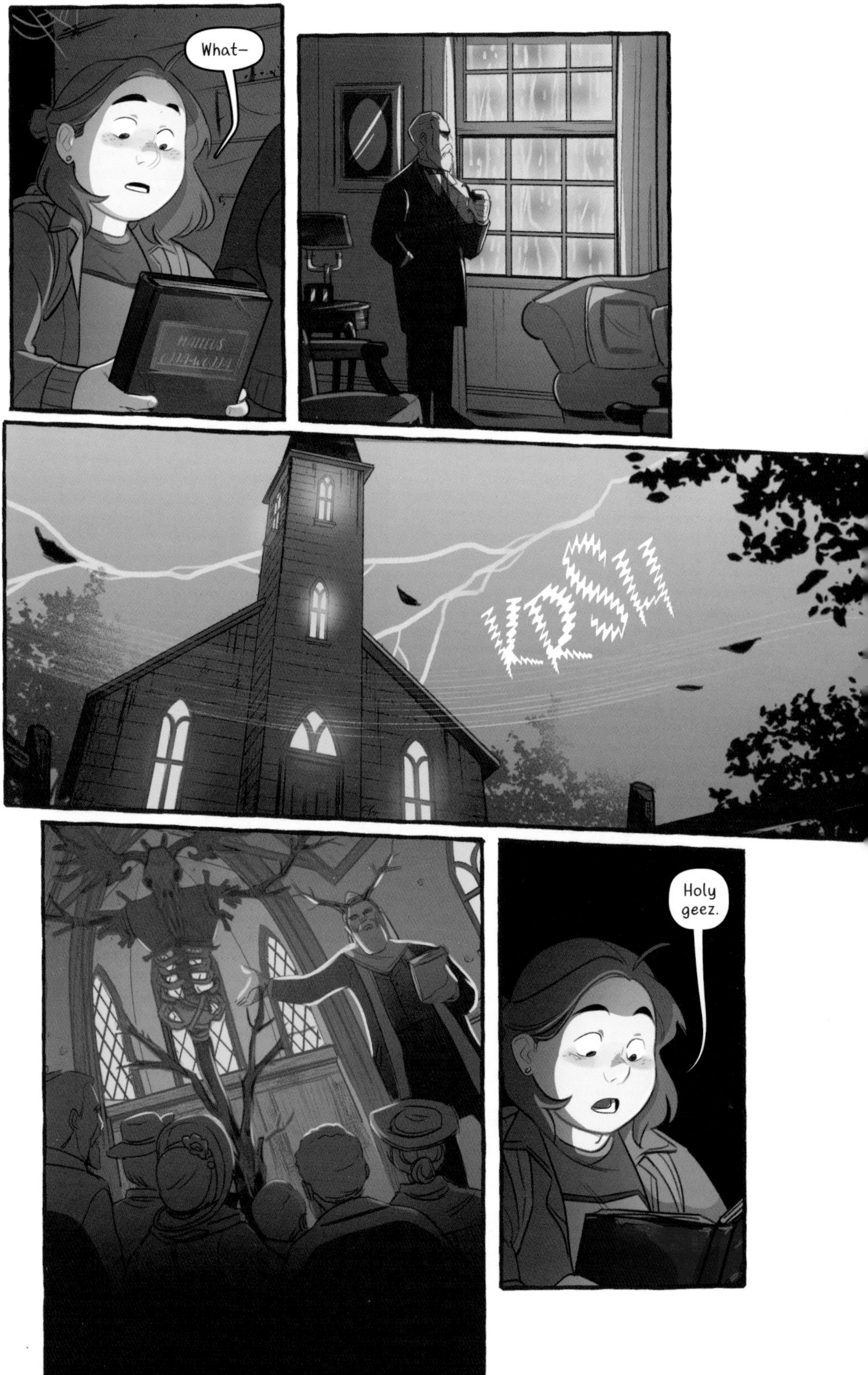
What–
KRSH
Holy geez.

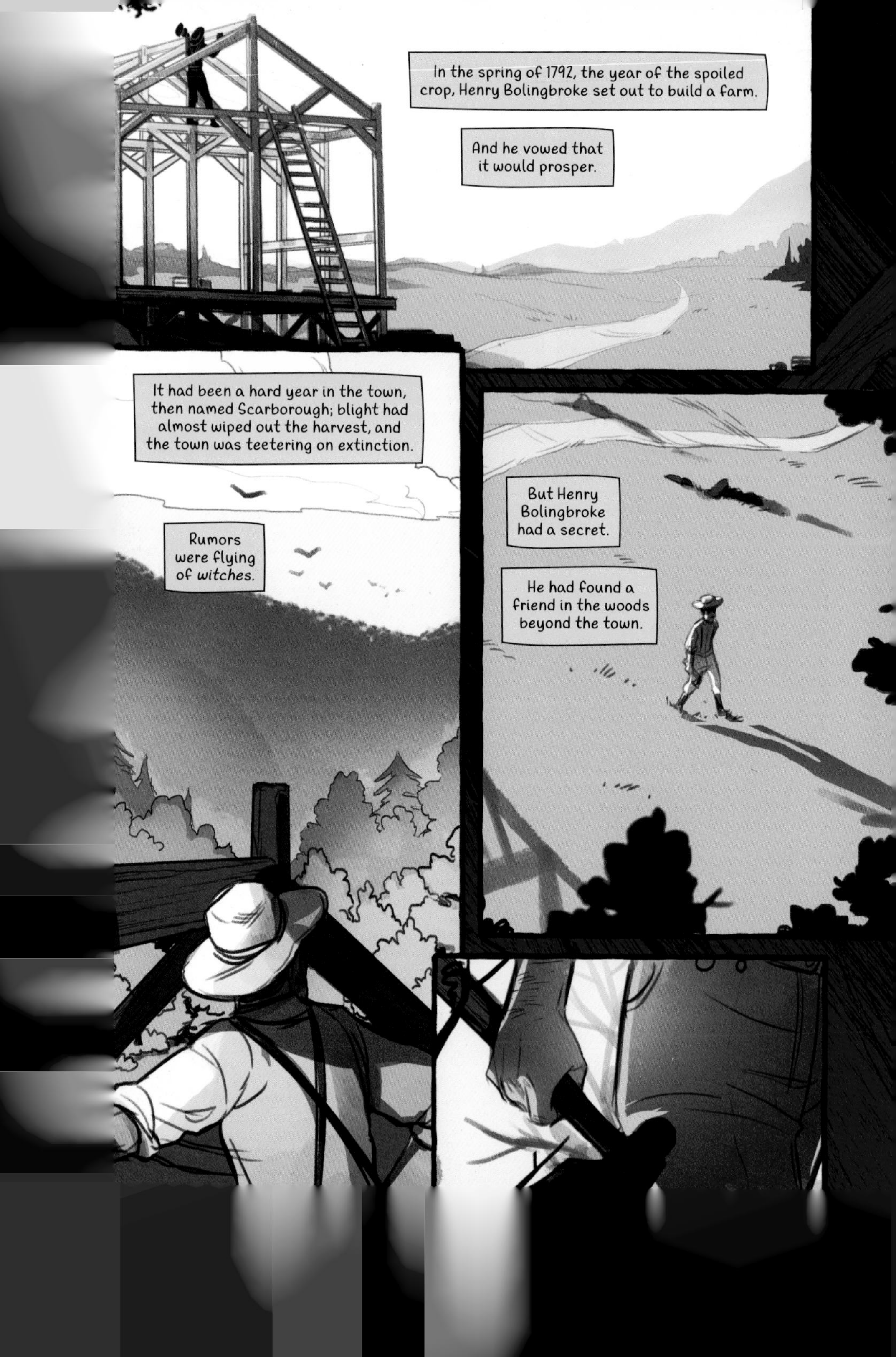
In the spring of 1792, the year of the spoiled crop, Henry Bolingbroke set out to build a farm.
And he vowed that it would prosper.
It had been a hard year in the town, then named Scarborough; blight had almost wiped out the harvest, and the town was teetering on extinction.
Rumors were flying of *witches.*
But Henry Bolingbroke had a secret.
He had found a friend in the woods beyond the town.

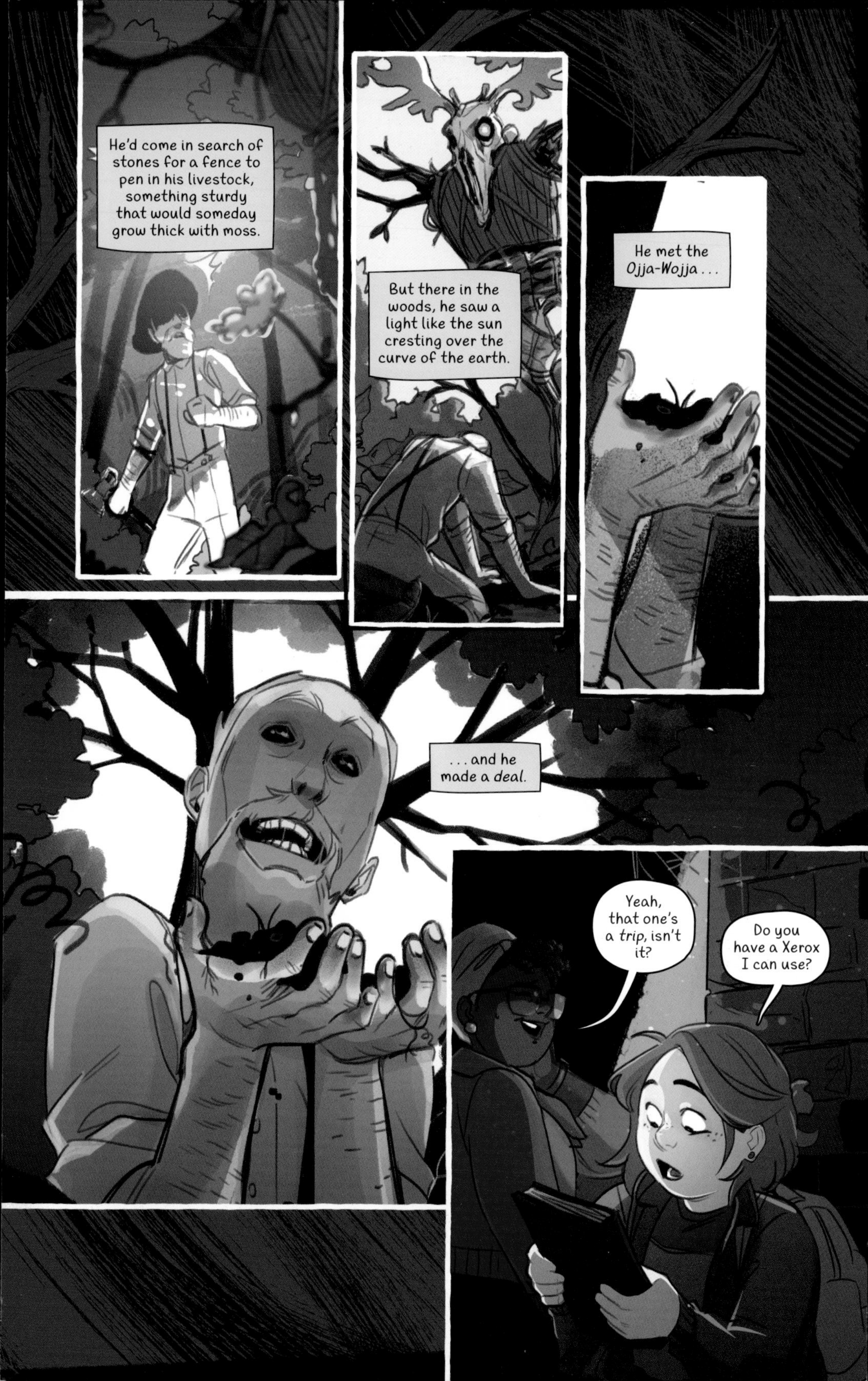
He'd come in search of stones for a fence to pen in his livestock, something sturdy that would someday grow thick with moss.
But there in the woods, he saw a light like the sun cresting over the curve of the earth.
He met the Ojja-Wojja . . .
. . . and he made a deal.
Yeah, that one's a trip, isn't it?
Do you have a Xerox I can use?

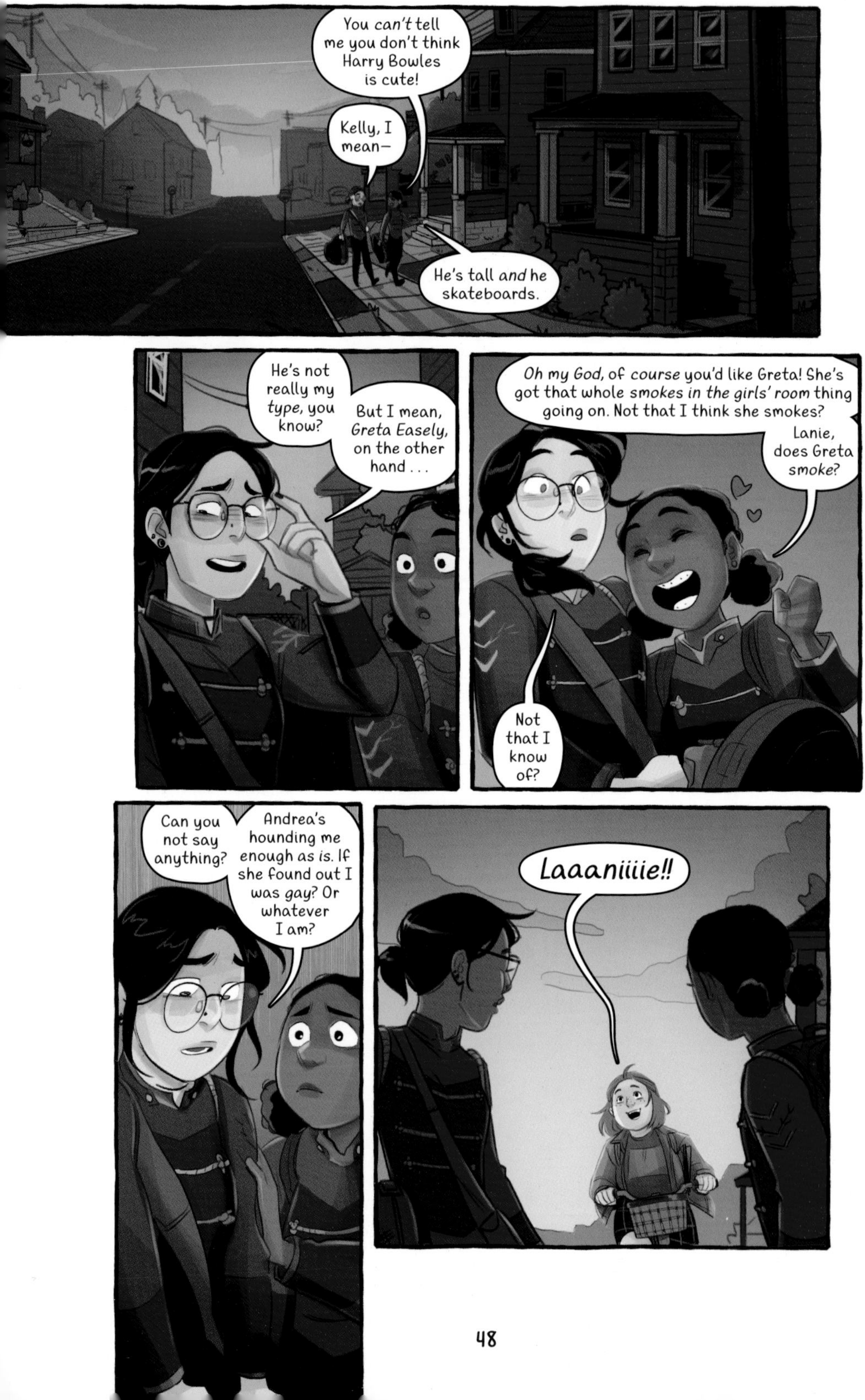

You *can't* tell me you don't think Harry Bowles is cute!
Kelly, I mean—
He's tall *and* he skateboards.
He's not really my *type*, you know?
But I mean, *Greta Easely*, on the other hand . . .
Oh my God, of *course* you'd like Greta! She's got that whole *smokes in the girls' room* thing going on. Not that I think she smokes?
Lanie, does Greta *smoke?*
Not that I know of?
Can you not say anything?
Andrea's hounding me enough as *is*. If she found out I was *gay?* Or whatever I am?
Laaaniiiie!!

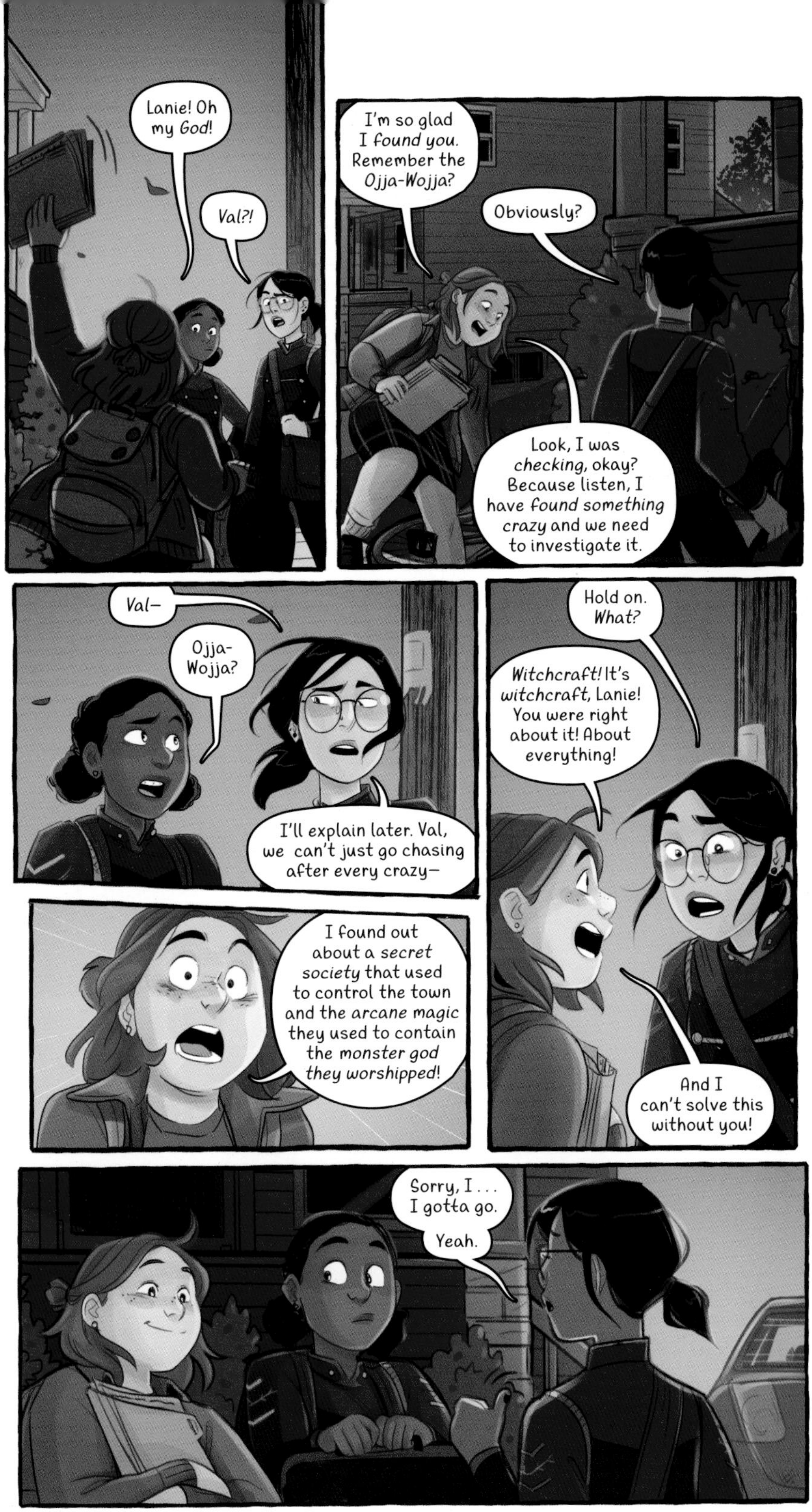

Lanie! Oh my God!
Val?!
I'm so glad I found you. Remember the Ojja-Wojja?
Obviously?
Look, I was checking, okay? Because listen, I have found something crazy and we need to investigate it.
Val—
Ojja-Wojja?
I'll explain later. Val, we can't just go chasing after every crazy—
Hold on. What?
Witchcraft! It's witchcraft, Lanie! You were right about it! About everything!
I found out about a secret society that used to control the town and the arcane magic they used to contain the monster god they worshipped!
And I can't solve this without you!
Sorry, I . . . I gotta go.
Yeah.

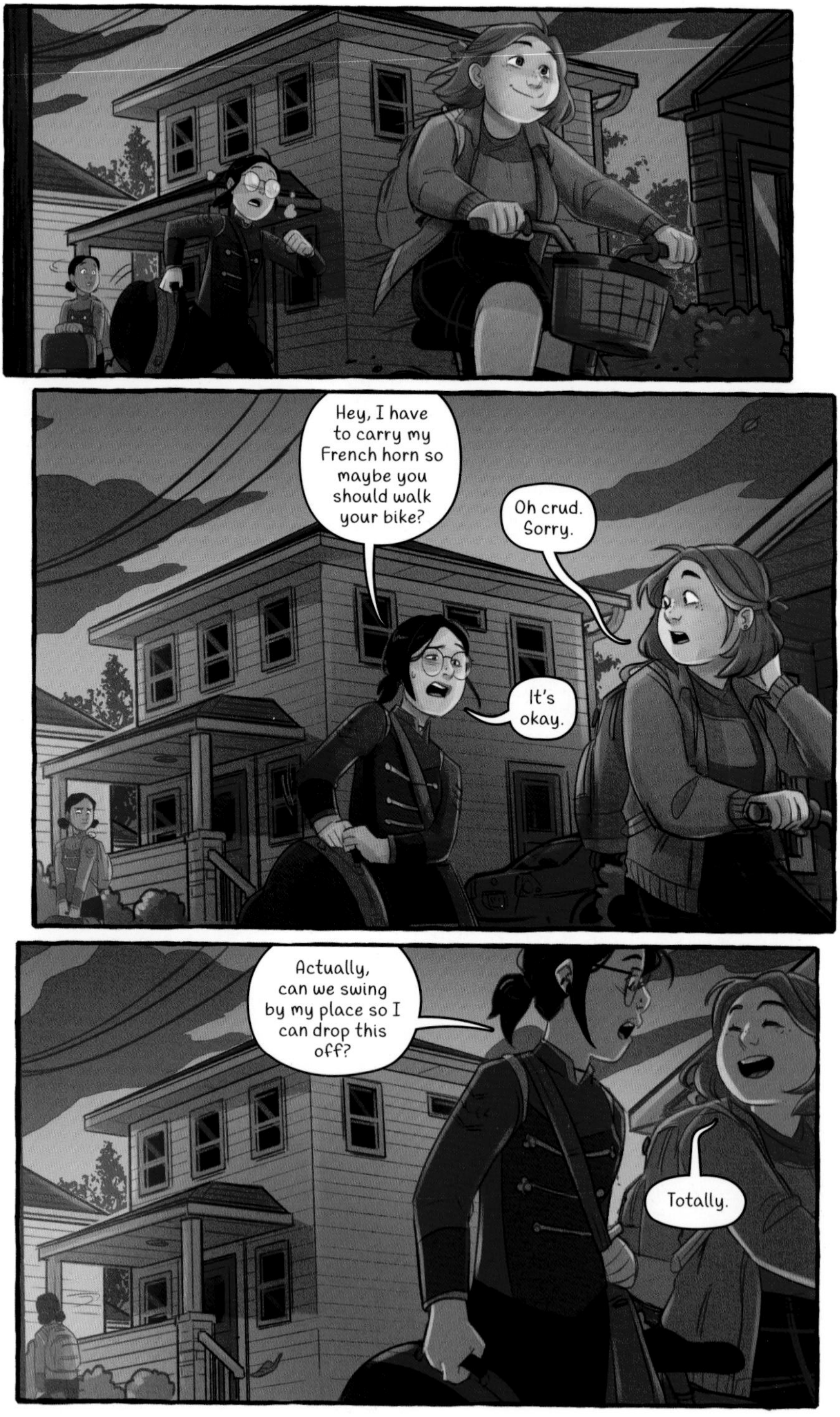
Hey, I have to carry my French horn so maybe you should walk your bike?
Oh crud. Sorry.
It's okay.
Actually, can we swing by my place so I can drop this off?
Totally.

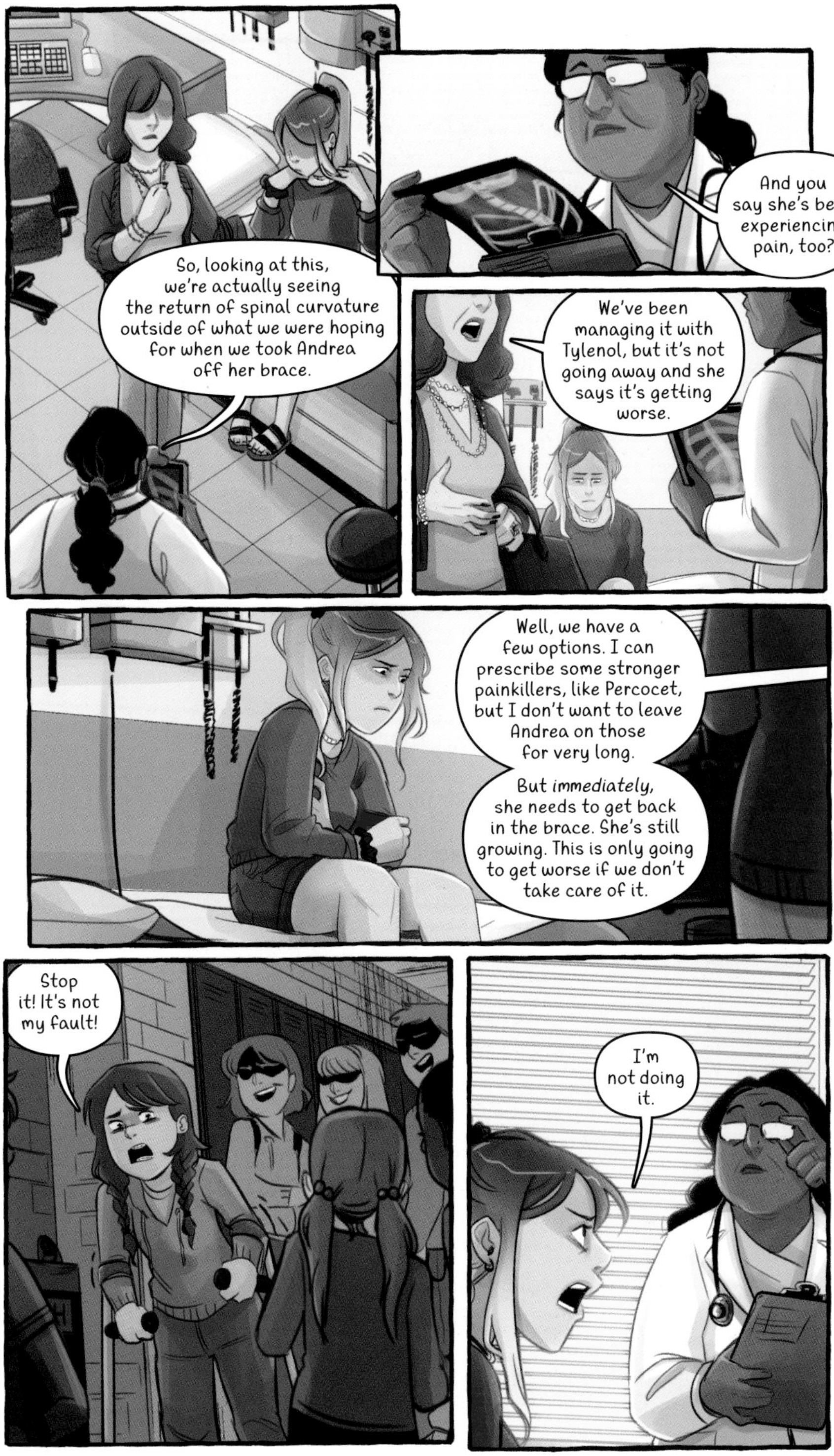
And you say she's been experiencing pain, too?
So, looking at this, we're actually seeing the return of spinal curvature outside of what we were hoping for when we took Andrea off her brace.
We've been managing it with Tylenol, but it's not going away and she says it's getting worse.
Well, we have a few options. I can prescribe some stronger painkillers, like Percocet, but I don't want to leave Andrea on those for very long.
But *immediately*, she needs to get back in the brace. She's still growing. This is only going to get worse if we don't take care of it.
Stop it! It's not my fault!
I'm not doing it.

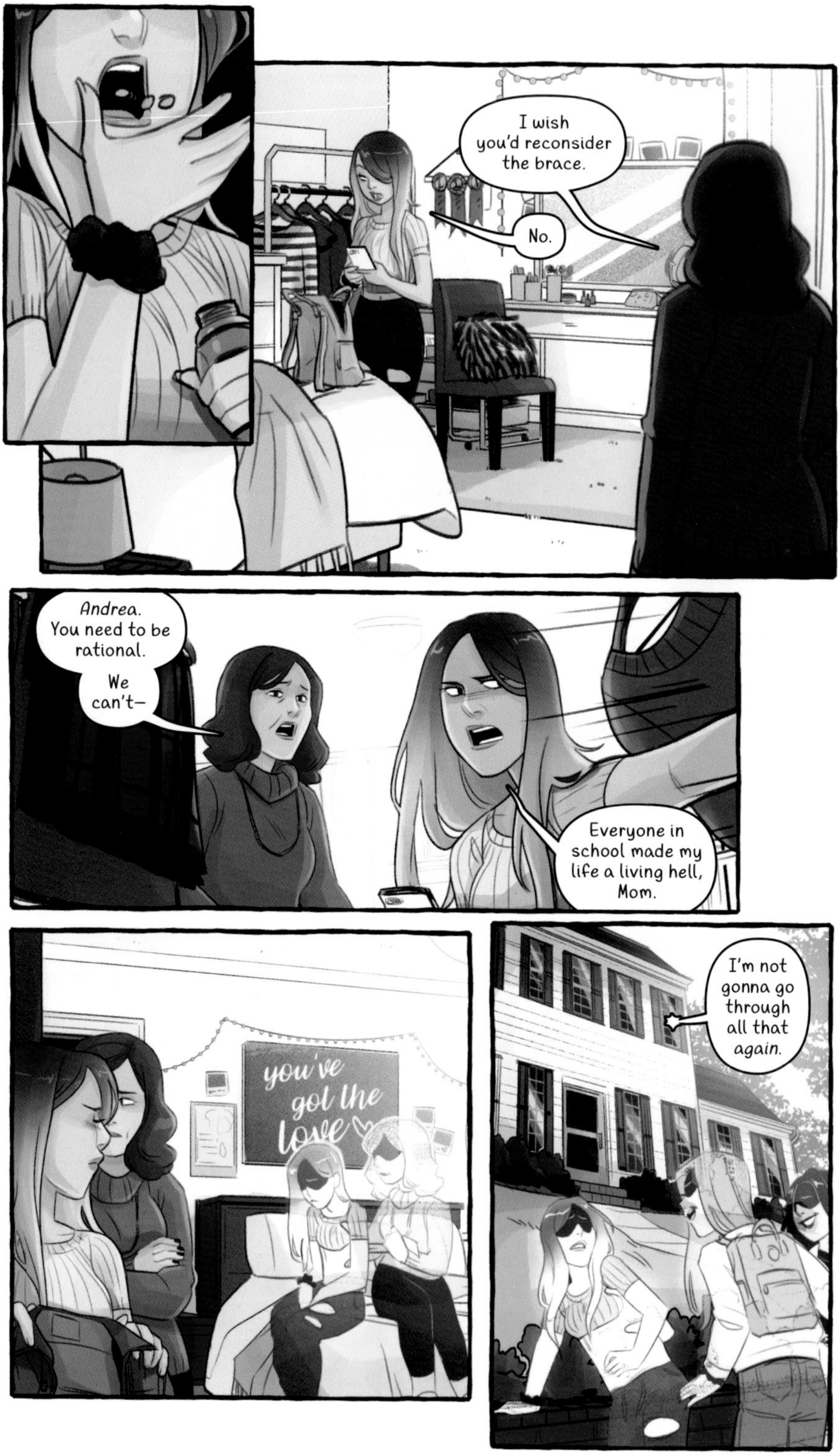
I wish you'd reconsider the brace.
No.
Andrea. You need to be rational.
We can't–
Everyone in school made my life a living hell, Mom.
you've got the love
I'm not gonna go through all that again.

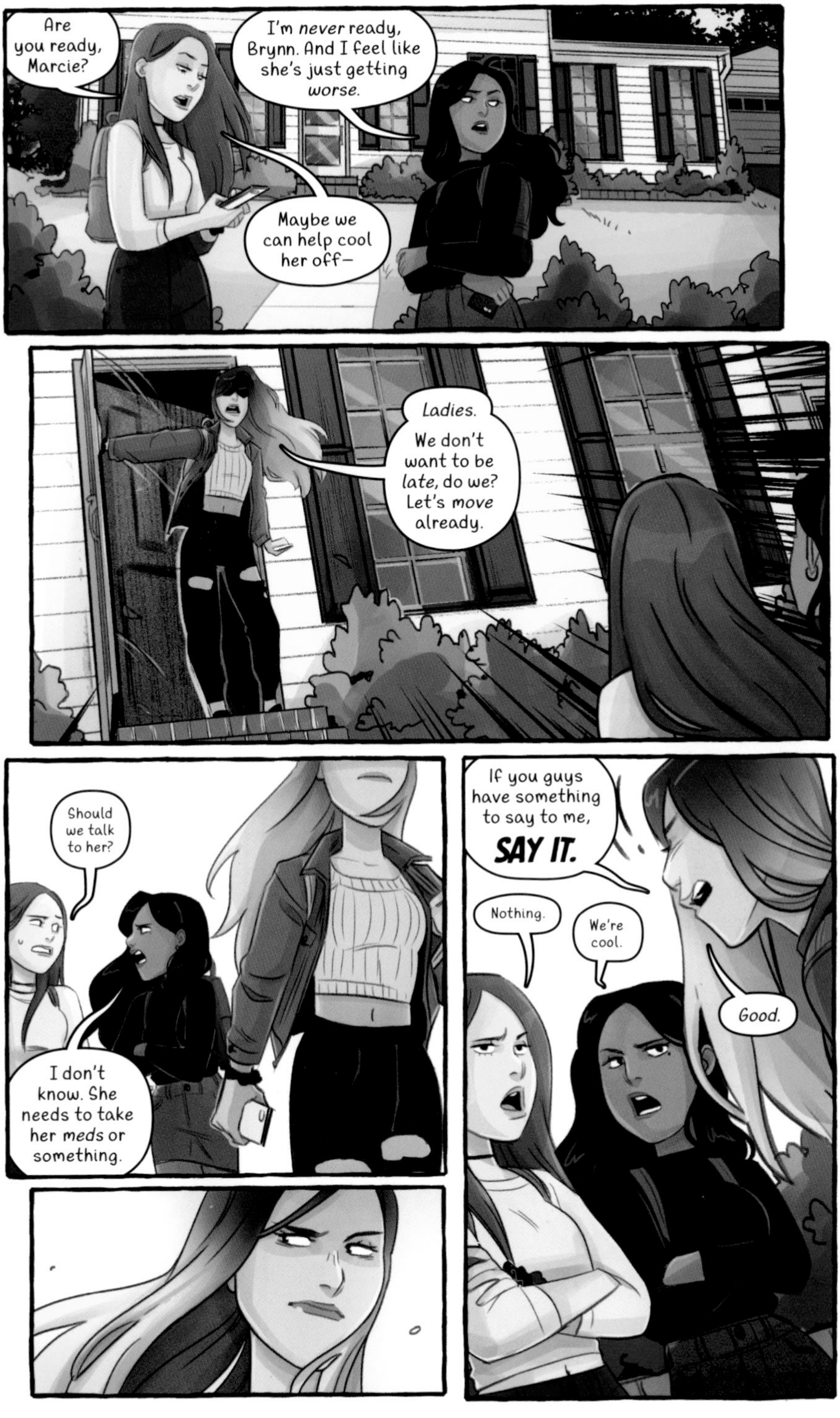
Are you ready, Marcie?
I'm *never* ready, Brynn. And I feel like she's just getting *worse*.
Maybe we can help cool her off—
Ladies.
We don't want to be *late*, do we? Let's *move* already.
Should we talk to her?
I don't know. She needs to take her *meds* or something.
If you guys have something to say to me, **SAY IT.**
Nothing.
We're cool.
Good.

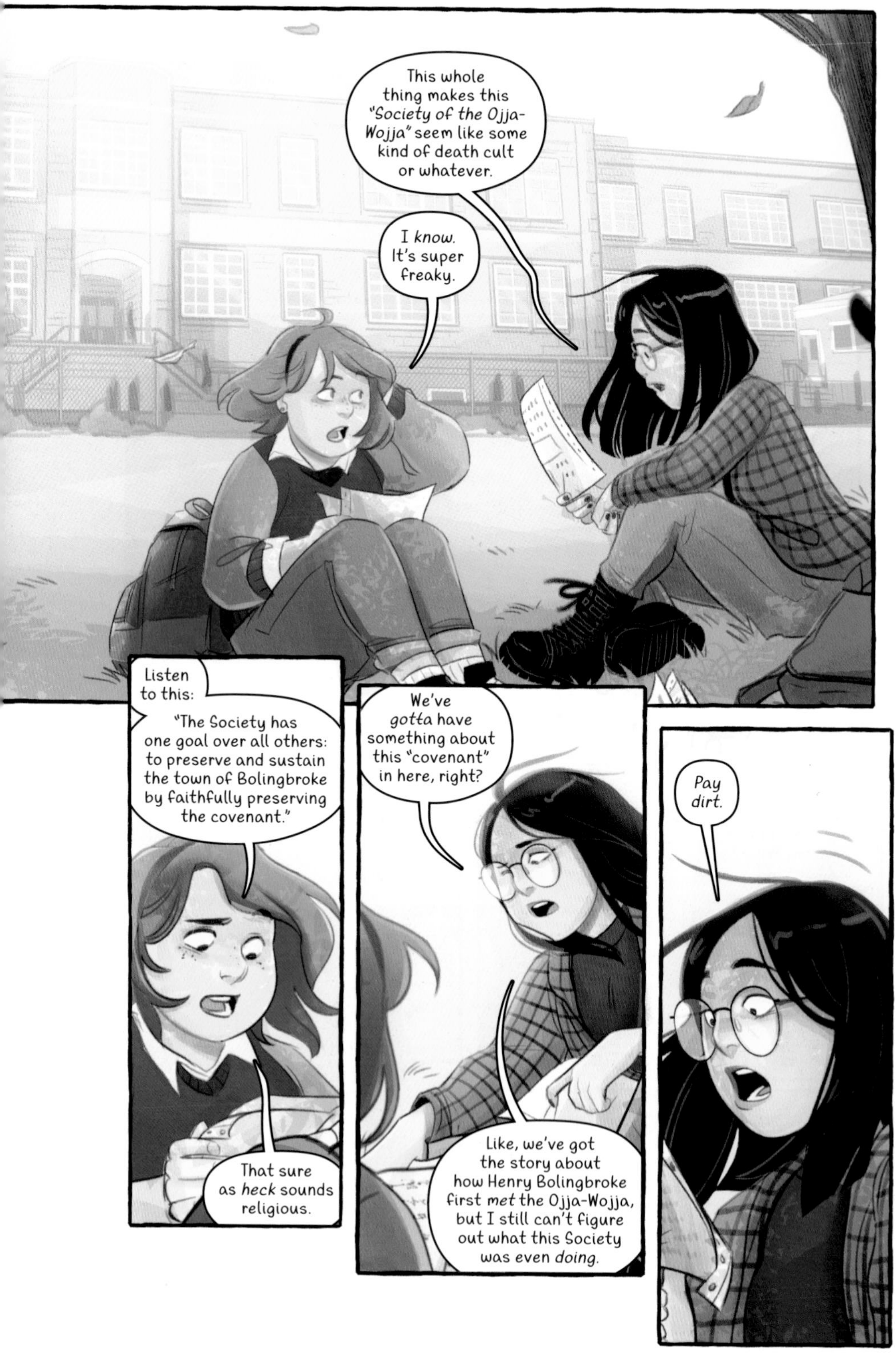
This whole thing makes this "Society of the Ojja-Wojja" seem like some kind of death cult or whatever.
I know. It's super freaky.
Listen to this:
"The Society has one goal over all others: to preserve and sustain the town of Bolingbroke by faithfully preserving the covenant."
That sure as heck sounds religious.
We've gotta have something about this "covenant" in here, right?
Like, we've got the story about how Henry Bolingbroke first met the Ojja-Wojja, but I still can't figure out what this Society was even doing.
Pay dirt.

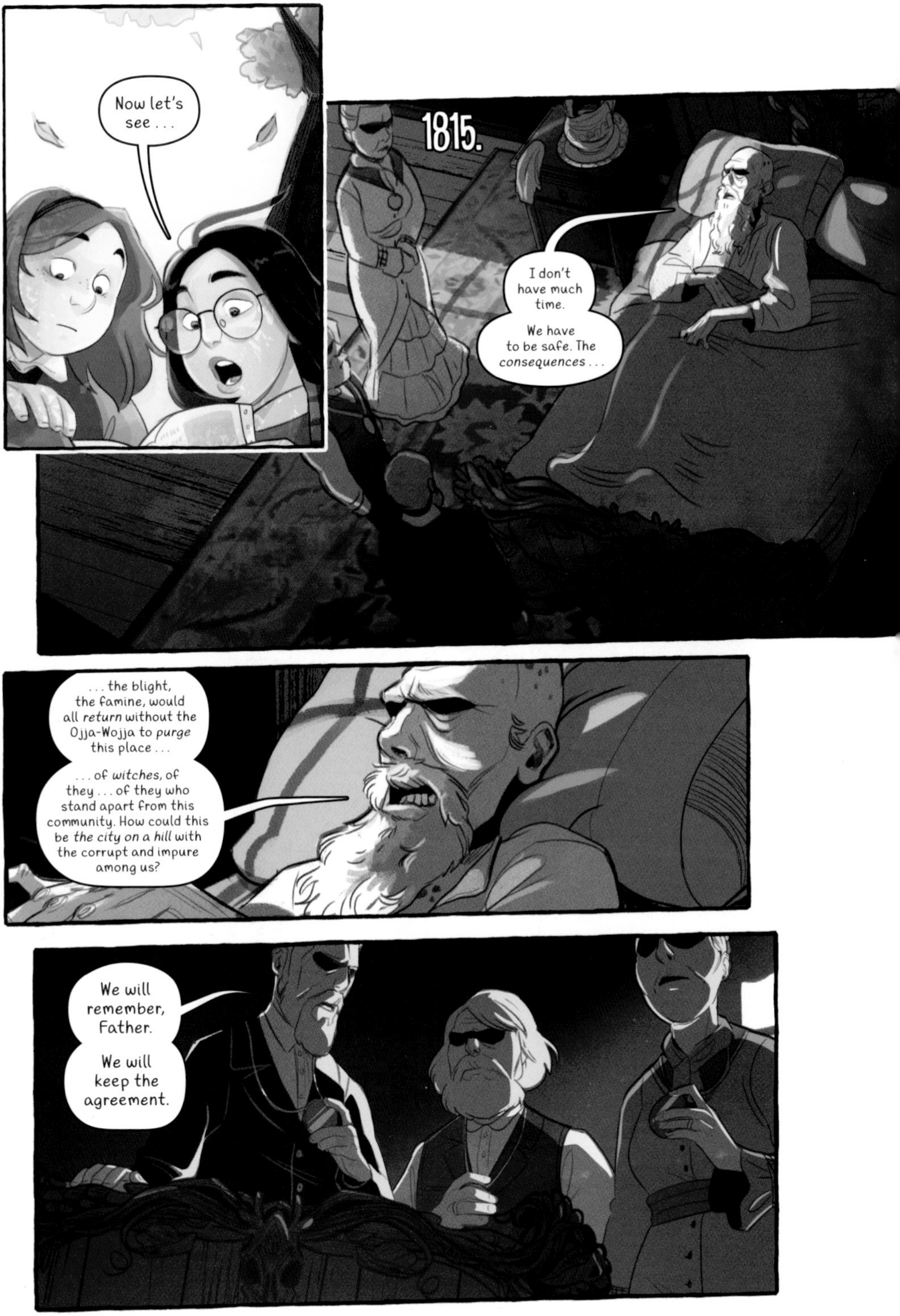
Now let's see . . .
1815.
I don't have much time.
We have to be safe. The *consequences* . . .
. . . the blight, the famine, would all *return* without the Ojja-Wojja to *purge* this place . . .
. . . of *witches*, of they . . . of they who stand apart from this community. How could this be *the city on a hill* with the corrupt and impure among us?
We will remember, Father.
We will keep the agreement.

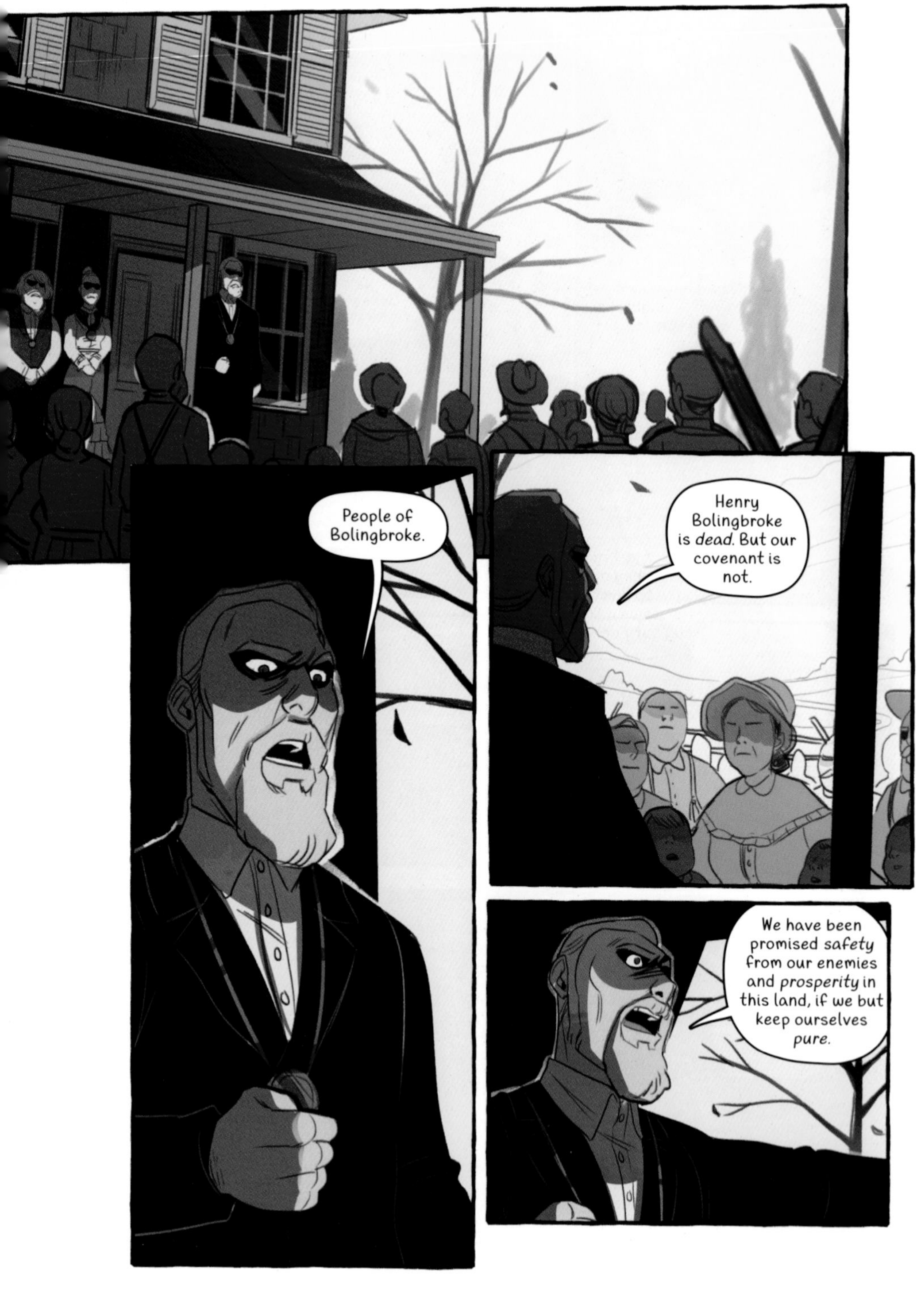
People of Bolingbroke.
Henry Bolingbroke is *dead*. But our covenant is not.
We have been promised *safety* from our enemies and *prosperity* in this land, if we but keep ourselves *pure*.

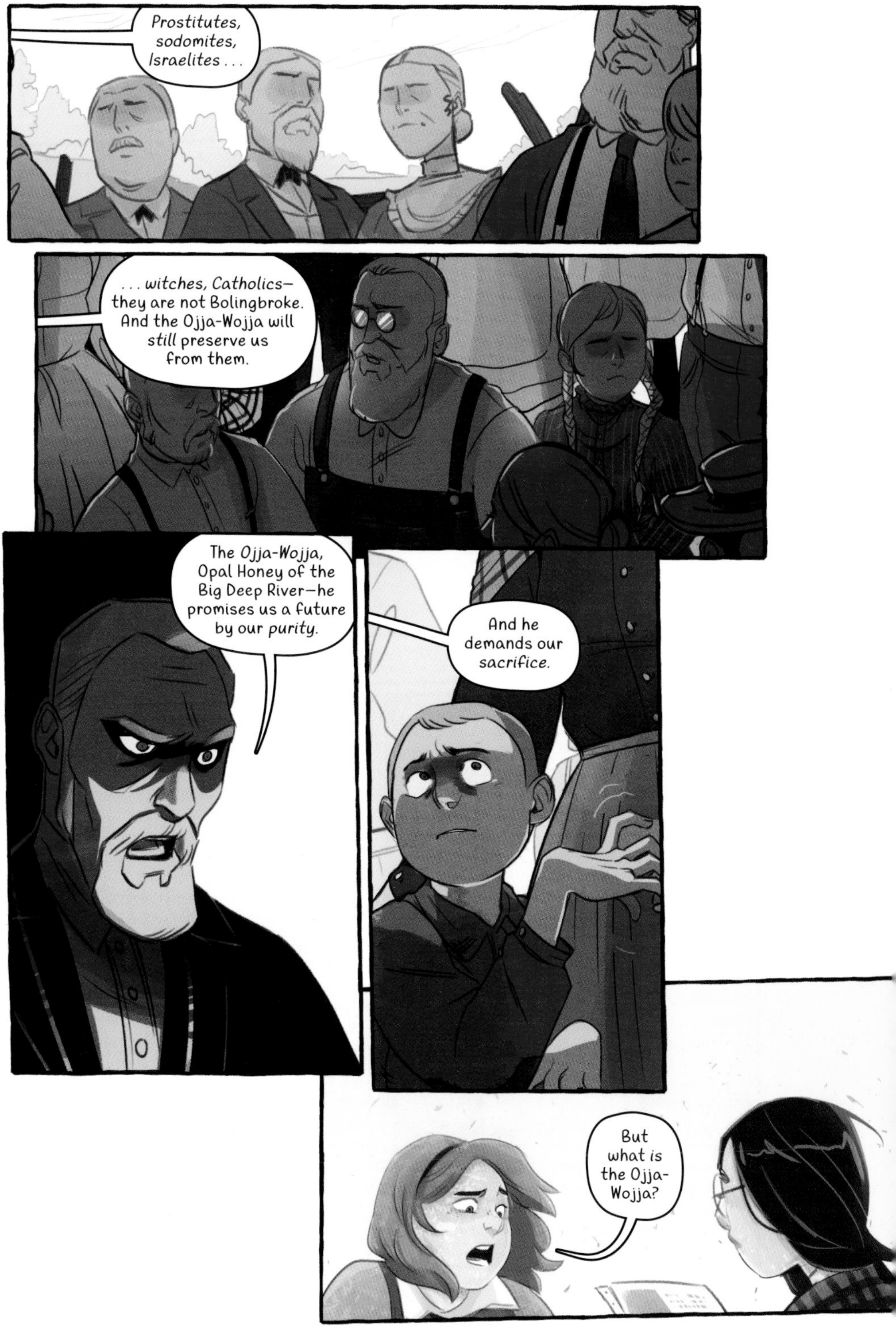

Prostitutes, sodomites, Israelites . . .
. . . witches, Catholics—they are not Bolingbroke. And the Ojja-Wojja will *still* preserve us from them.
The *Ojja-Wojja*, Opal Honey of the Big Deep River—he promises us a future by our *purity*.
And he demands our *sacrifice*.
But what *is* the Ojja-Wojja?

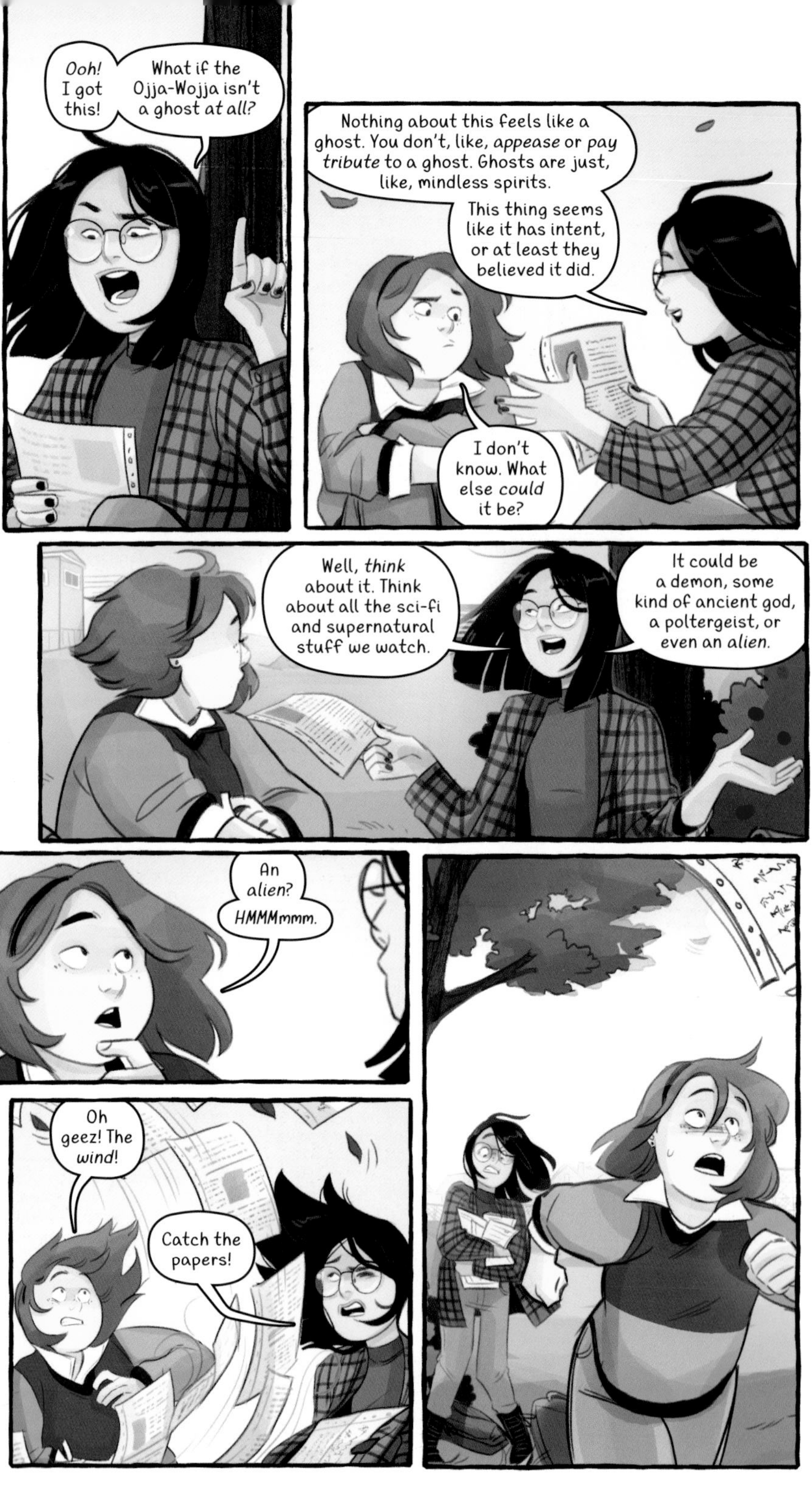
Ooh! I got this!
What if the Ojja-Wojja isn't a ghost *at all?*
Nothing about this feels like a ghost. You don't, like, *appease* or *pay tribute* to a ghost. Ghosts are just, like, mindless spirits.
This thing seems like it has intent, or at least they believed it did.
I don't know. What else *could* it be?
Well, *think* about it. Think about all the sci-fi and supernatural stuff we watch.
It could be a demon, some kind of ancient god, a poltergeist, or even an *alien.*
An *alien?*
HMMMmmm.
Oh geez! The *wind*!
Catch the papers!

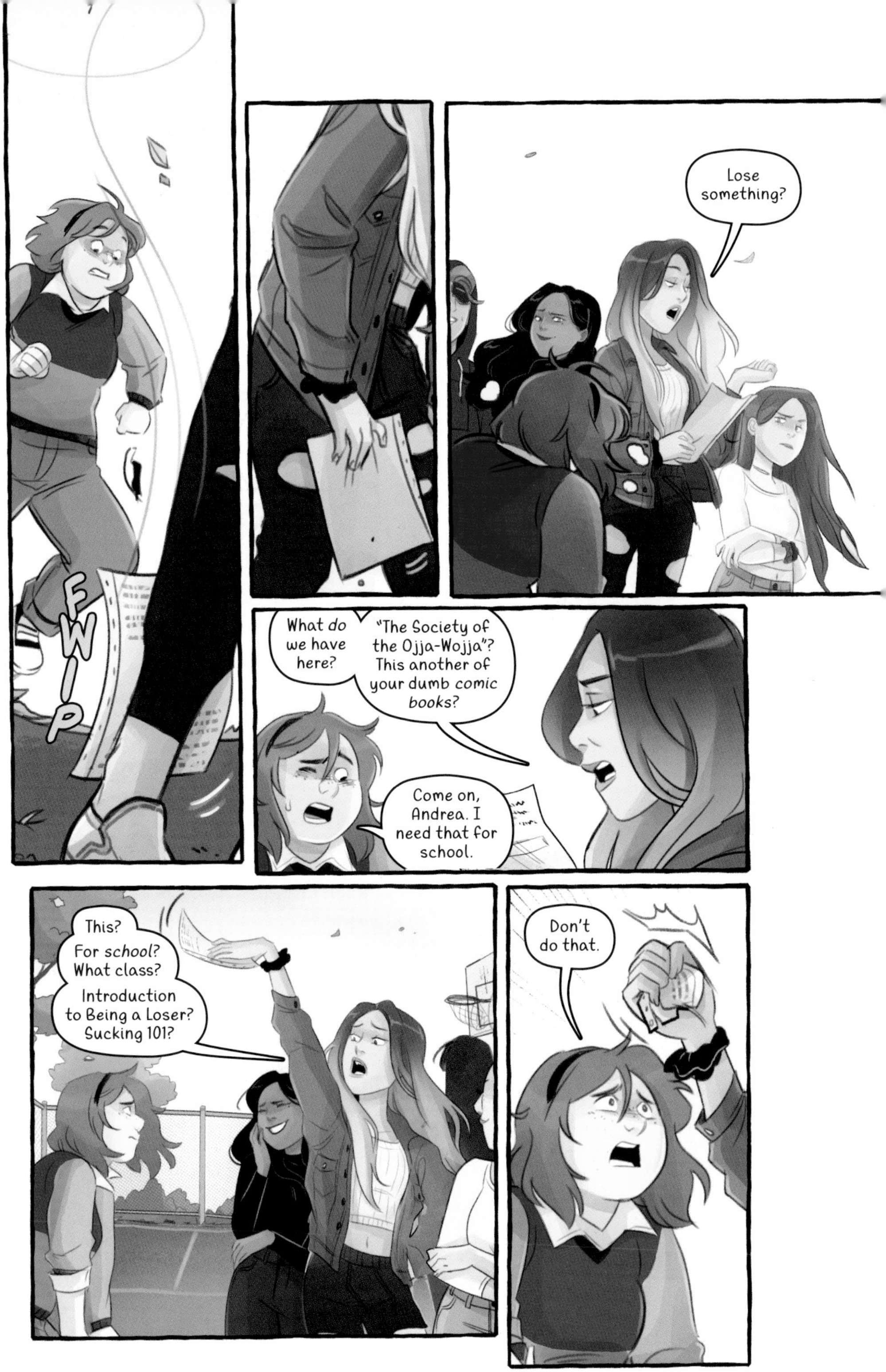
FWIP
Lose something?
What *do* we have here?
"The Society of the Ojja-Wojja"? This another of your dumb *comic* *books*?
Come on, Andrea. I need that for school.
This?
For *school*? What class?
Introduction to Being a Loser? Sucking 101?
Don't do that.

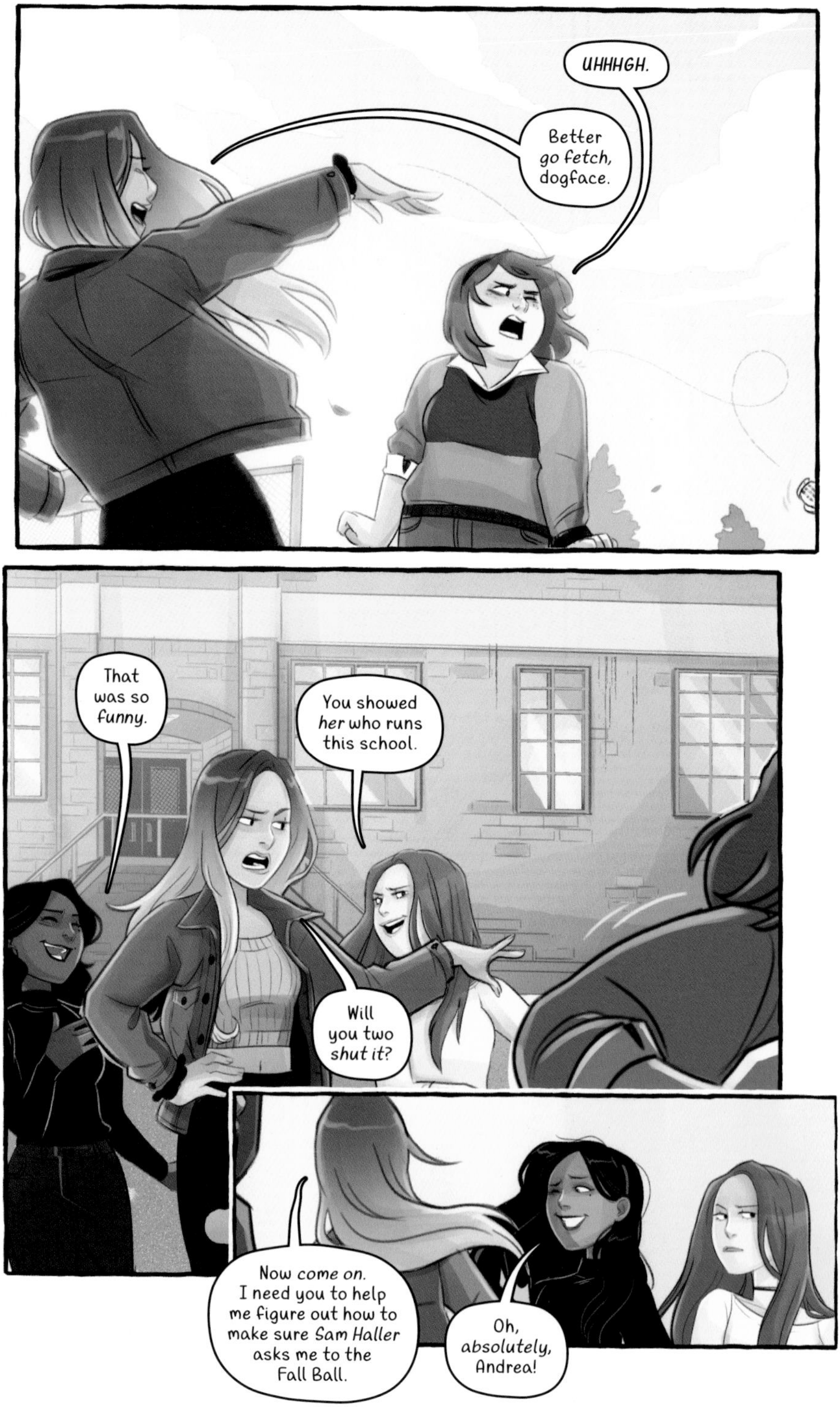
UHHHGH.
Better go fetch, dogface.
That was so funny.
You showed her who runs this school.
Will you two shut it?
Now come on. I need you to help me figure out how to make sure Sam Haller asks me to the Fall Ball.
Oh, absolutely, Andrea!

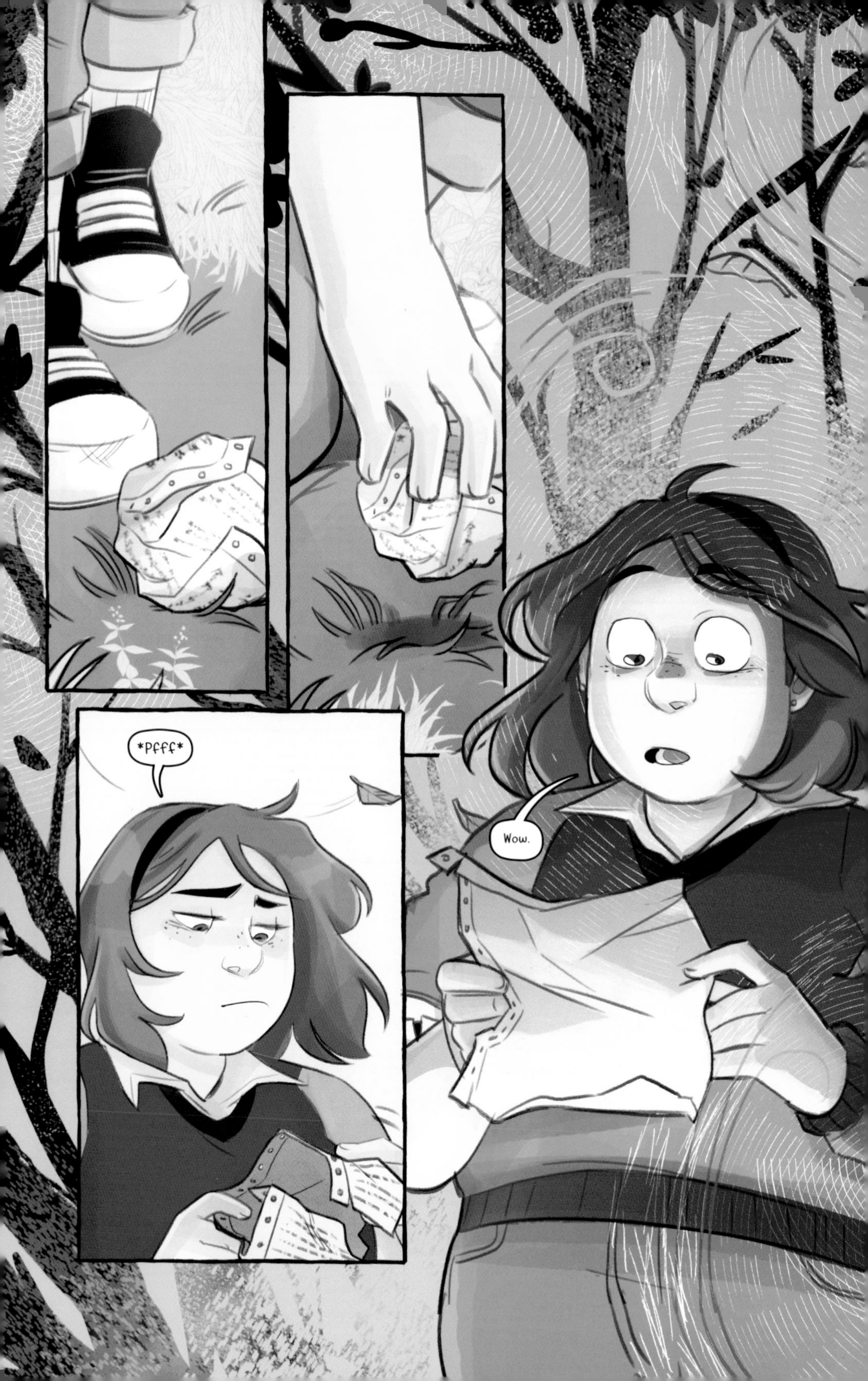
Pfff
Wow.

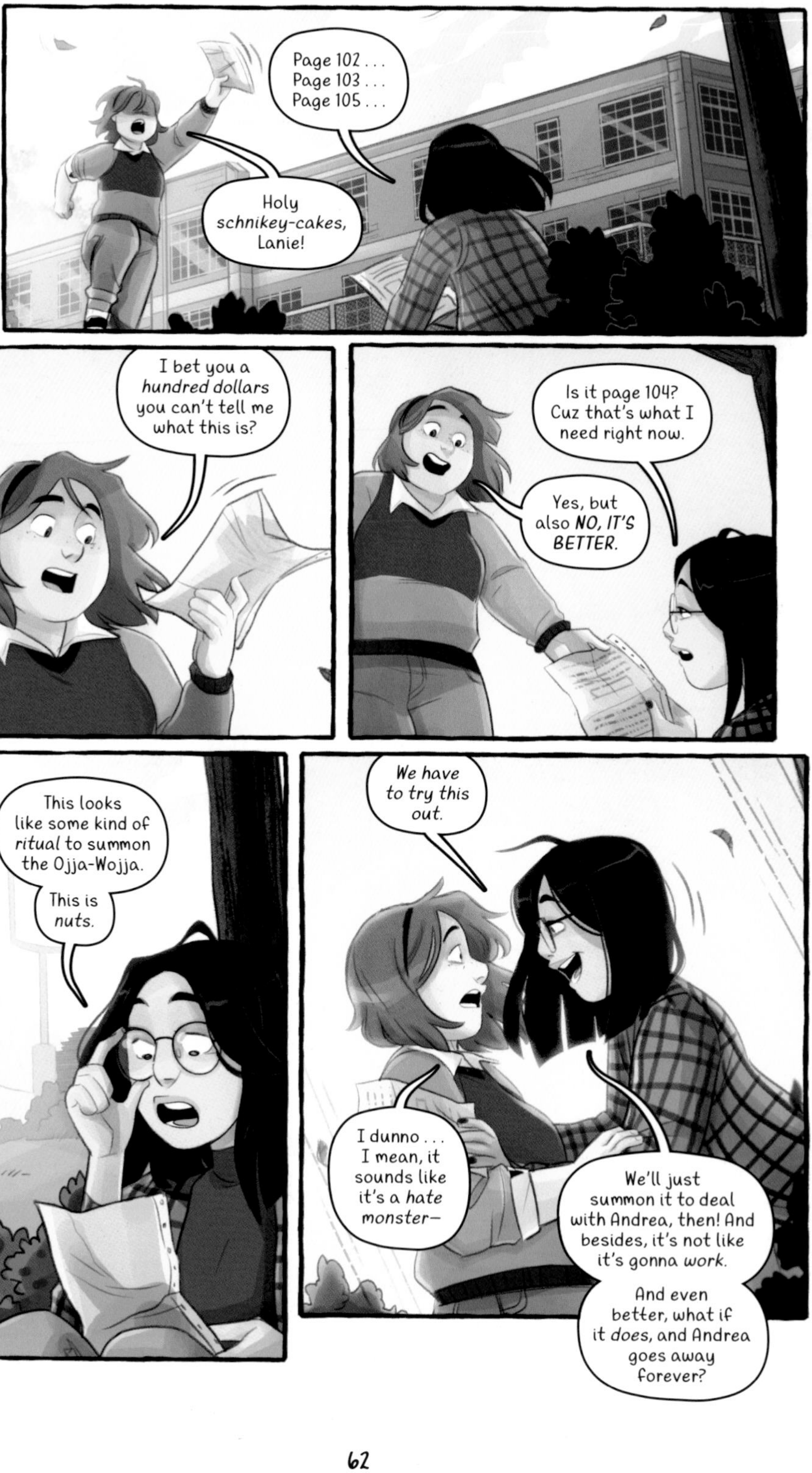
Page 102 . . .
Page 103 . . .
Page 105 . . .
Holy *schnikey-cakes*, Lanie!
I bet you a *hundred dollars* you can't tell me what this is?
Is it page 104? Cuz that's what I need right now.
Yes, but also *NO, IT'S BETTER.*
This looks like some kind of *ritual* to summon the Ojja-Wojja.
This is *nuts.*
We have to try this out.
I dunno . . . I mean, it sounds like it's a *hate* monster—
We'll just summon it to deal with Andrea, then! And besides, it's not like it's gonna *work*.
And even better, what if it *does*, and Andrea goes away forever?

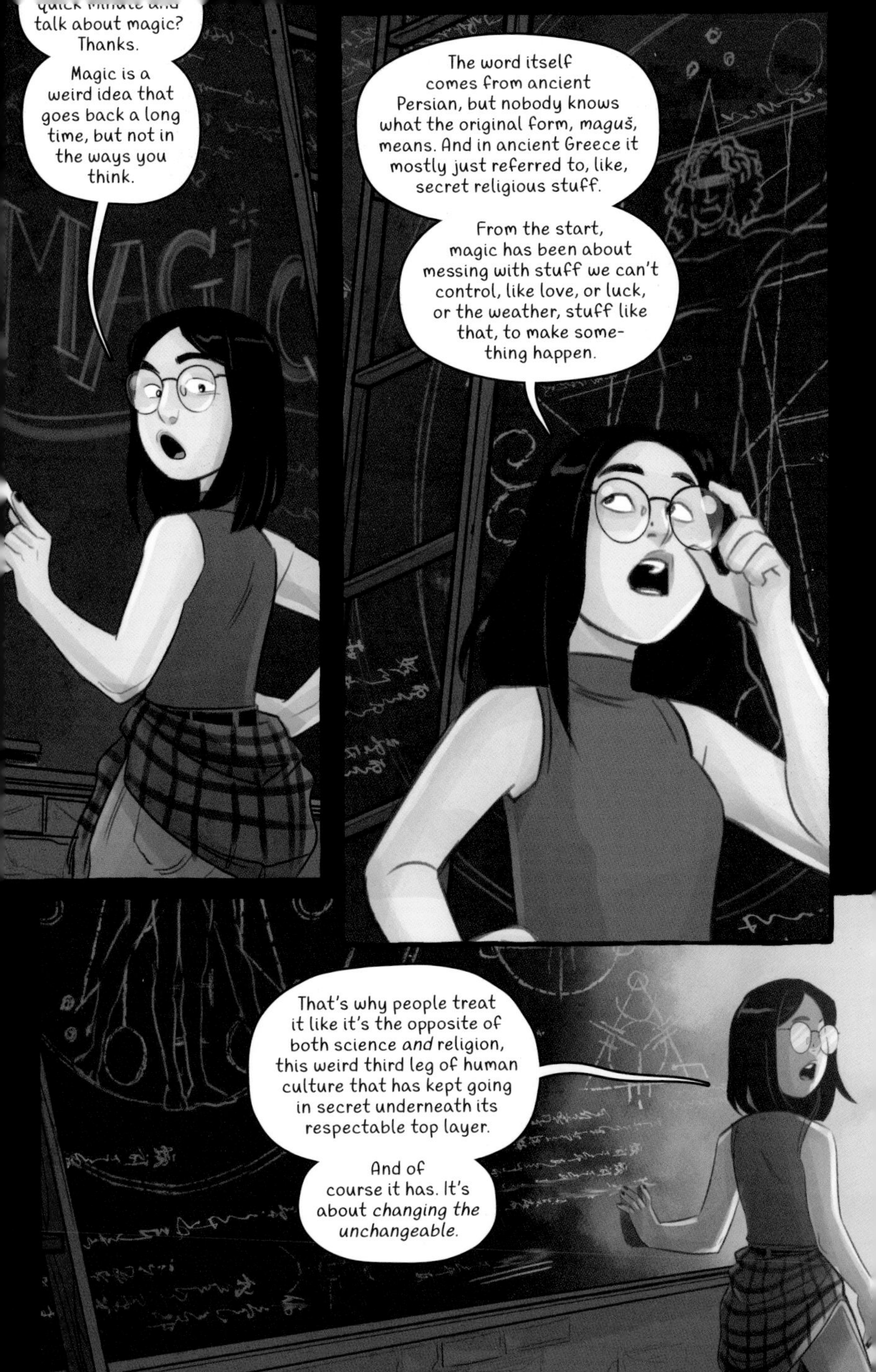
talk about magic? Thanks.
Magic is a weird idea that goes back a long time, but not in the ways you think.
The word itself comes from ancient Persian, but nobody knows what the original form, *maguš*, means. And in ancient Greece it mostly just referred to, like, secret religious stuff.
From the start, magic has been about messing with stuff we can't control, like love, or luck, or the weather, stuff like that, to make some-thing happen.
That's why people treat it like it's the opposite of both science *and* religion, this weird third leg of human culture that has kept going in secret underneath its respectable top layer.
And of course it has. It's about *changing the unchangeable.*

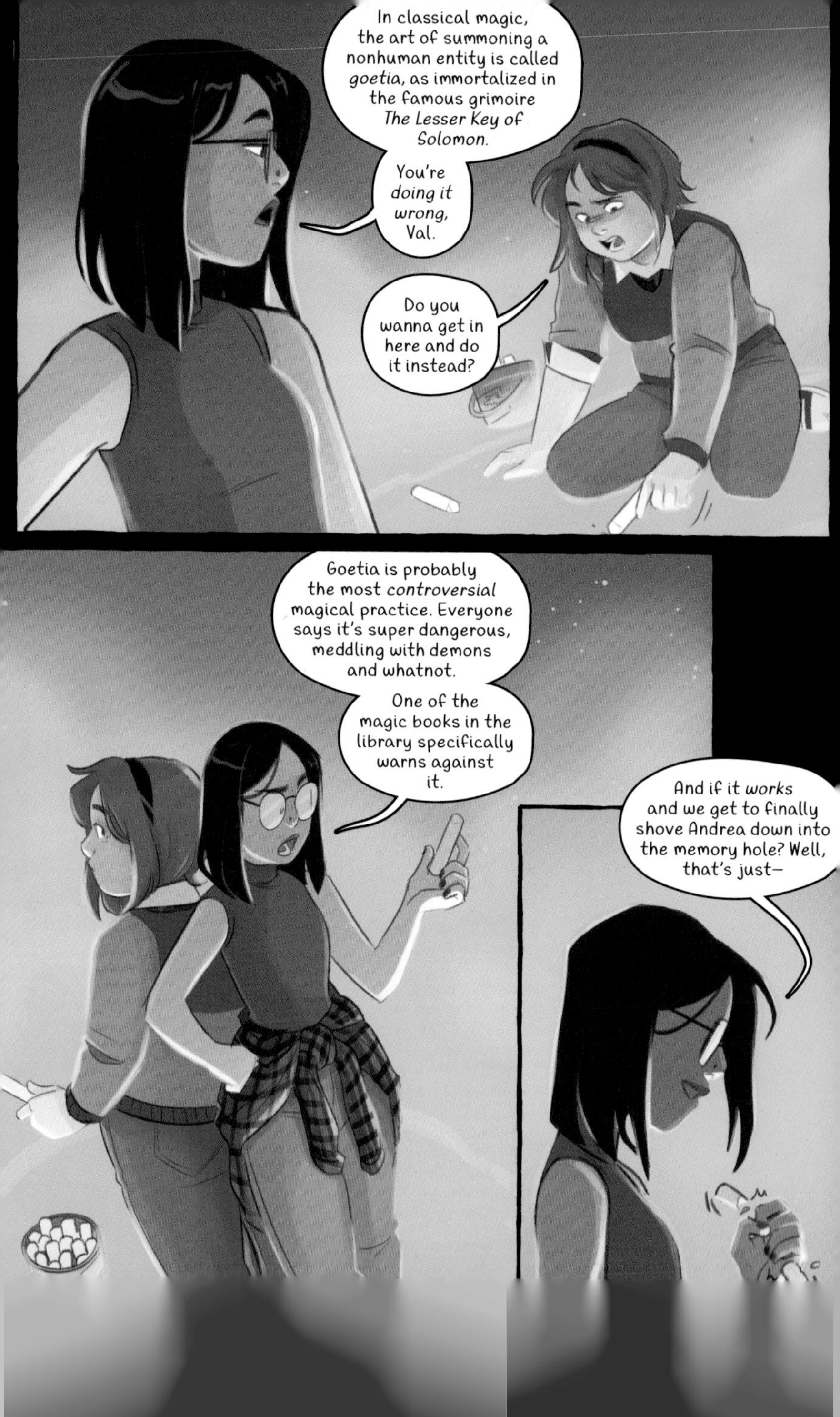
In classical magic, the art of summoning a nonhuman entity is called goetia, as immortalized in the famous grimoire The Lesser Key of Solomon.
You're doing it wrong, Val.
Do you wanna get in here and do it instead?
Goetia is probably the most controversial magical practice. Everyone says it's super dangerous, meddling with demons and whatnot.
One of the magic books in the library specifically warns against it.
And if it works and we get to finally shove Andrea down into the memory hole? Well, that's just—

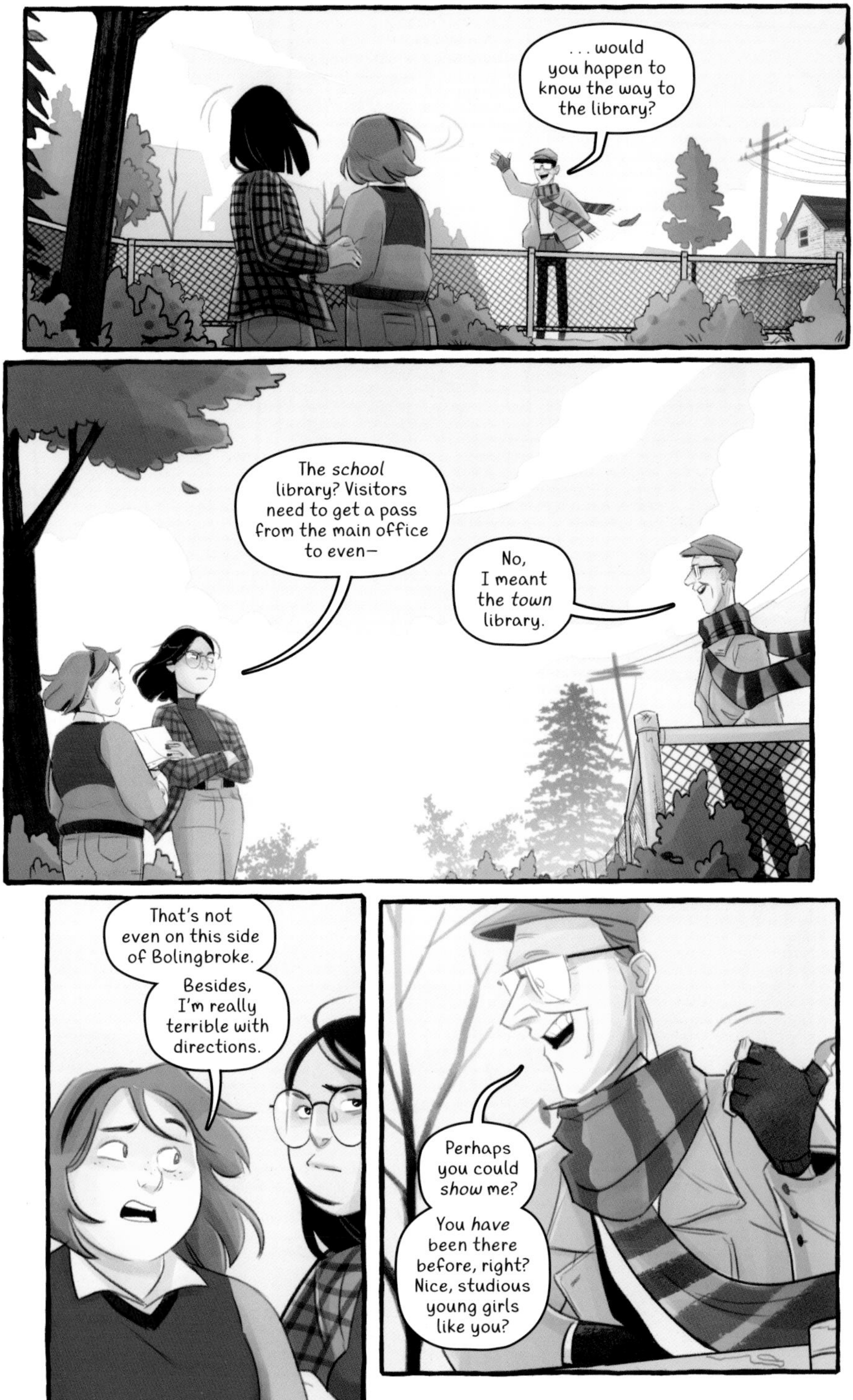
. . . would you happen to know the way to the library?
The *school* library? Visitors need to get a pass from the main office to even—
No, I meant the *town* library.
That's not even on this side of Bolingbroke.
Besides, I'm really terrible with directions.
Perhaps you could *show me?*
You *have* been there before, right? Nice, studious young girls like you?

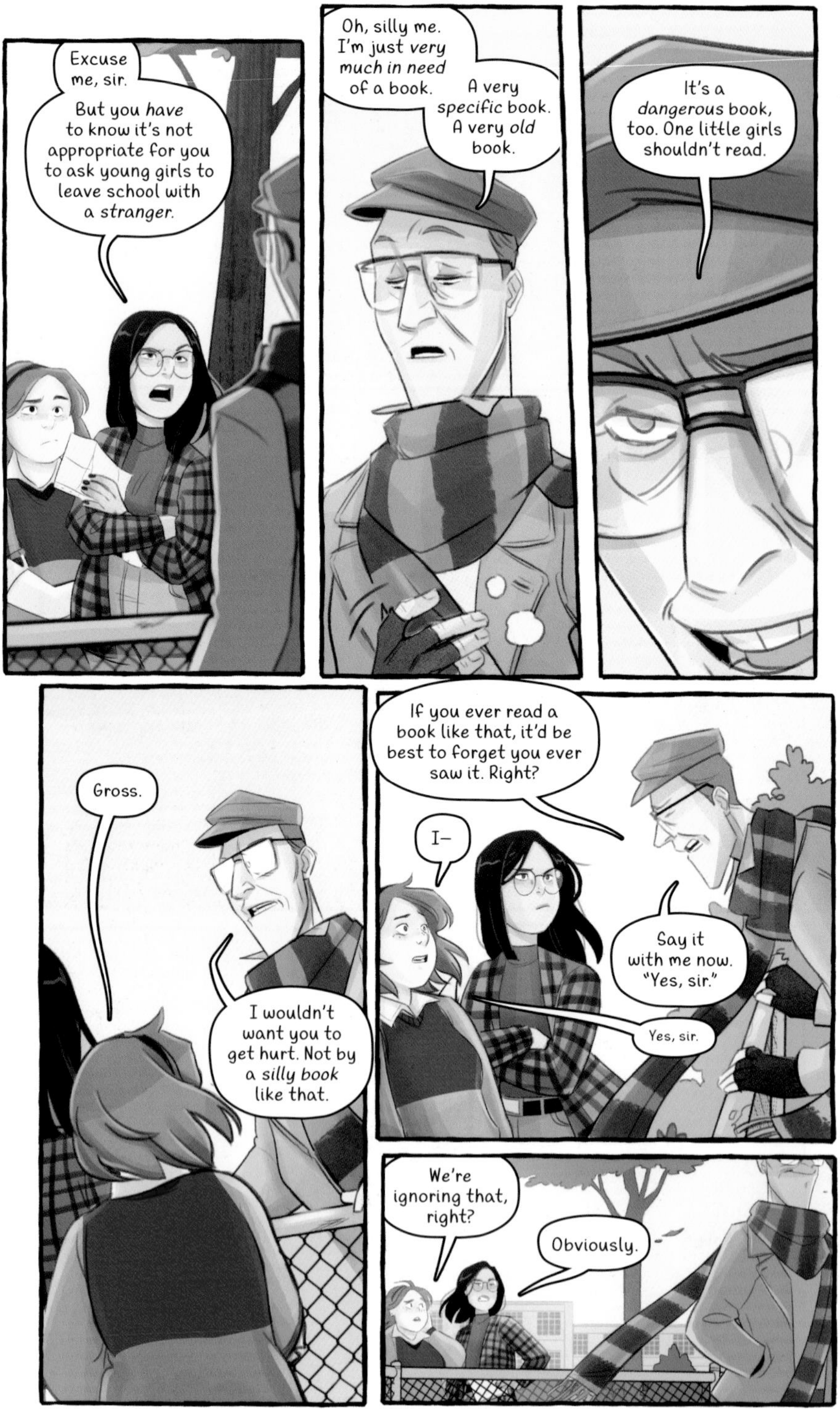
Excuse me, sir.
But you *have* to know it's not appropriate for you to ask young girls to leave school with a *stranger*.
Oh, silly me. I'm just *very much in need* of a book.
A very *specific* book. A very *old* book.
It's a *dangerous* book, too. One little girls shouldn't read.
Gross.
I wouldn't want you to get hurt. Not by a *silly book* like that.
If you ever read a book like that, it'd be best to forget you ever saw it. Right?
I–
Say it with me now. "Yes, sir."
Yes, sir.
We're ignoring that, right?
Obviously.

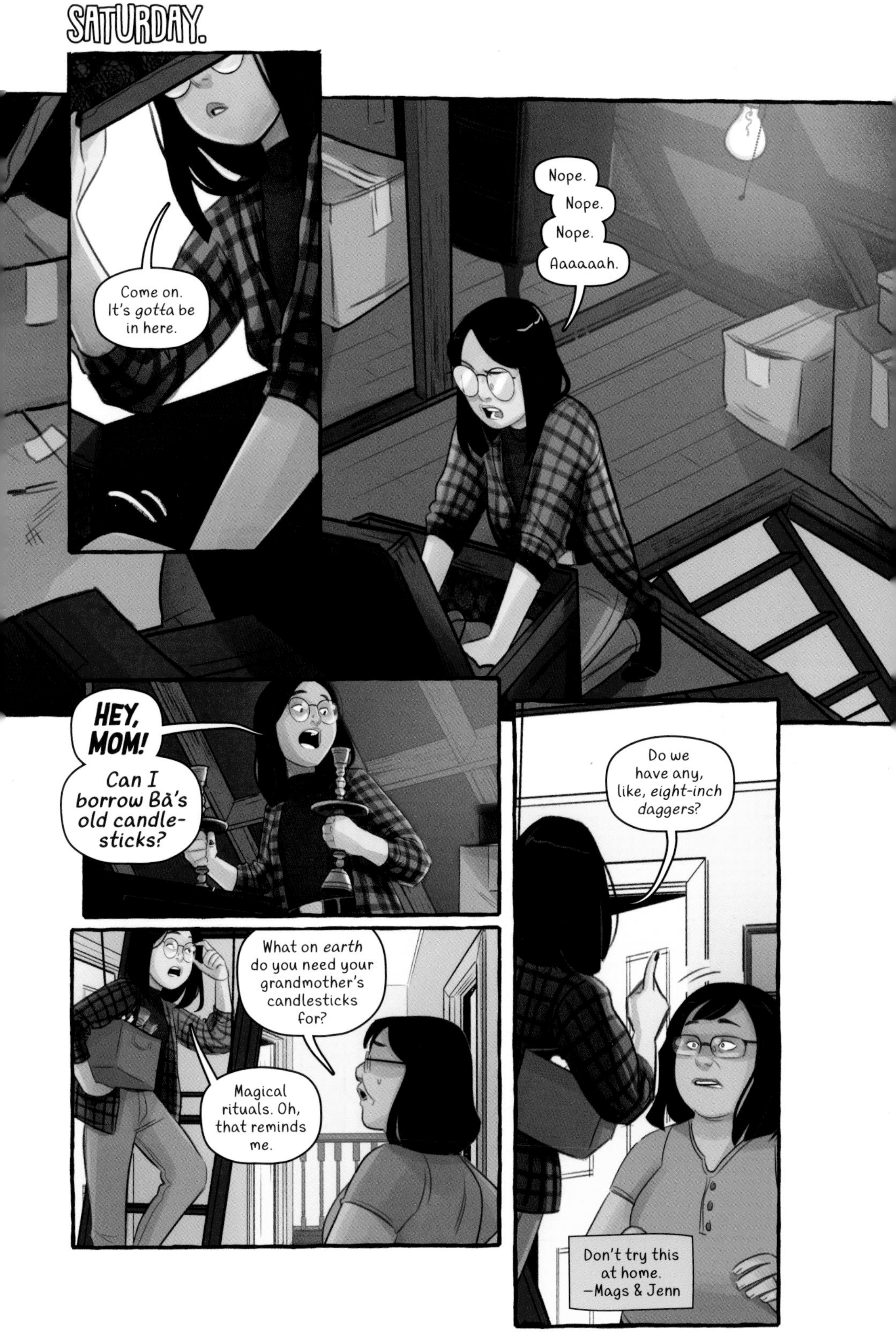
SATURDAY.
Come on. It's *gotta* be in here.
Nope.
Nope.
Nope.
Aaaaaah.
HEY, MOM!
Can I borrow Bà's old candlesticks?
Do we have any, like, *eight-inch* daggers?
What on *earth* do you need your grandmother's candlesticks for?
Magical rituals. Oh, that reminds me.
Don't try this at home. —Mags & Jenn

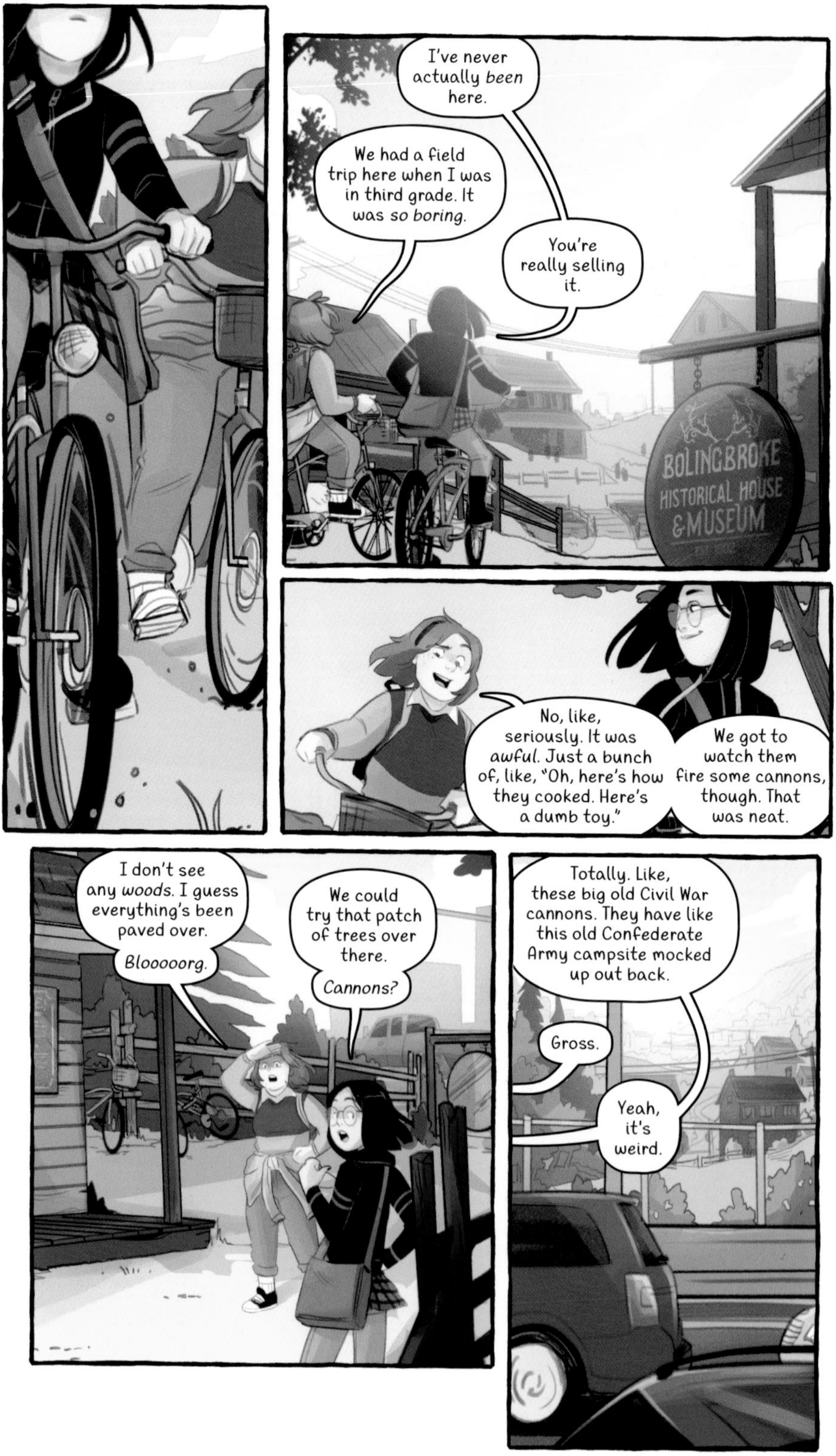
I've never actually *been* here.
We had a field trip here when I was in third grade. It was *so boring*.
You're really selling it.
BOLINGBROKE HISTORICAL HOUSE & MUSEUM
No, like, seriously. It was *awful*. Just a bunch of, like, "Oh, here's how they cooked. Here's a dumb toy."
We got to watch them fire some cannons, though. That was neat.
I don't see any *woods*. I guess everything's been paved over.
Blooooorg.
We could try that patch of trees over there.
Cannons?
Totally. Like, these big old Civil War cannons. They have like this old Confederate Army campsite mocked up out back.
Gross.
Yeah, it's weird.

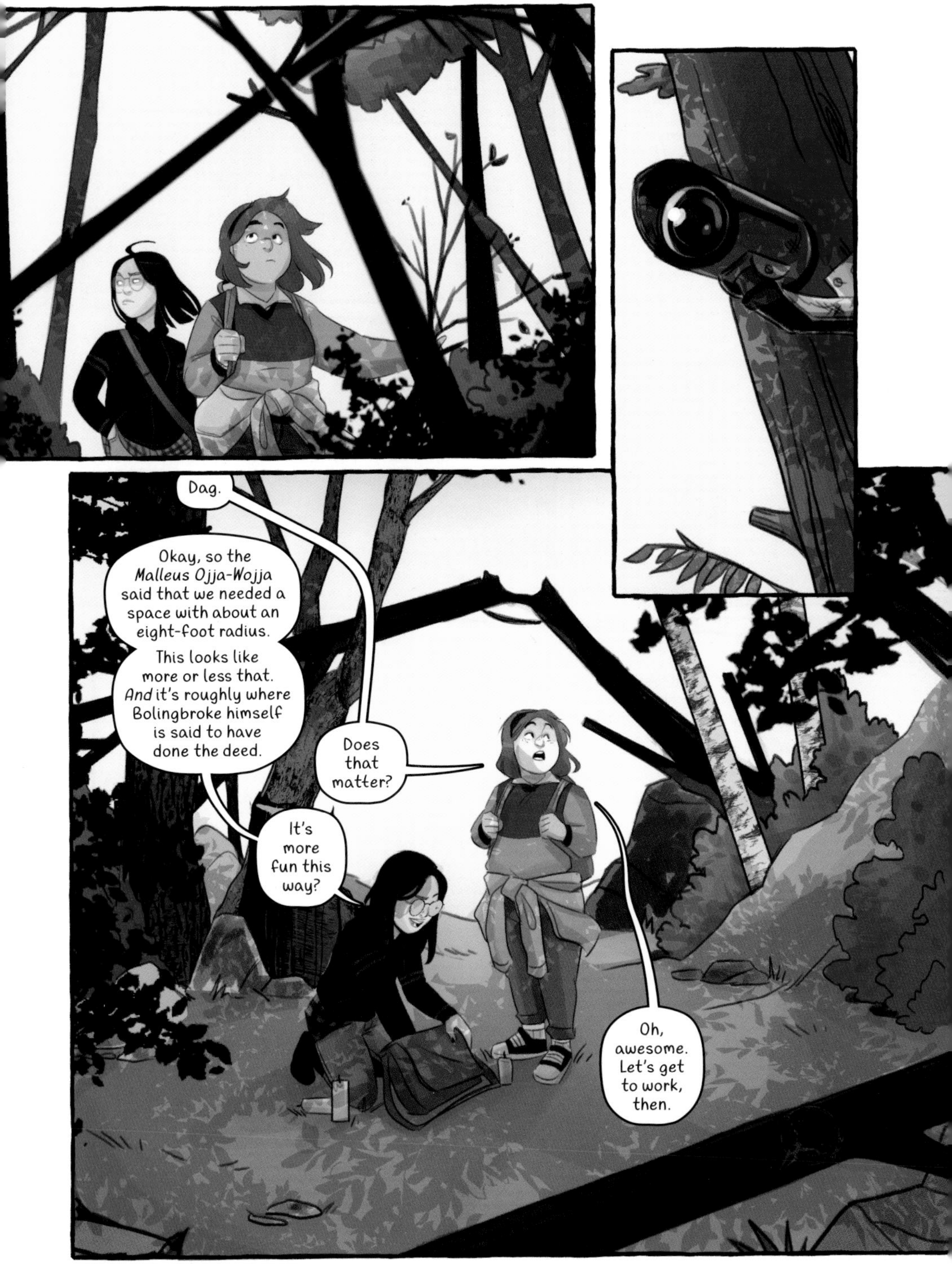
Dag.
Okay, so the *Malleus Ojja-Wojja* said that we needed a space with about an eight-foot radius.
This looks like more or less that. *And* it's roughly where Bolingbroke himself is said to have done the deed.
Does that matter?
It's more fun this way?
Oh, awesome. Let's get to work, then.

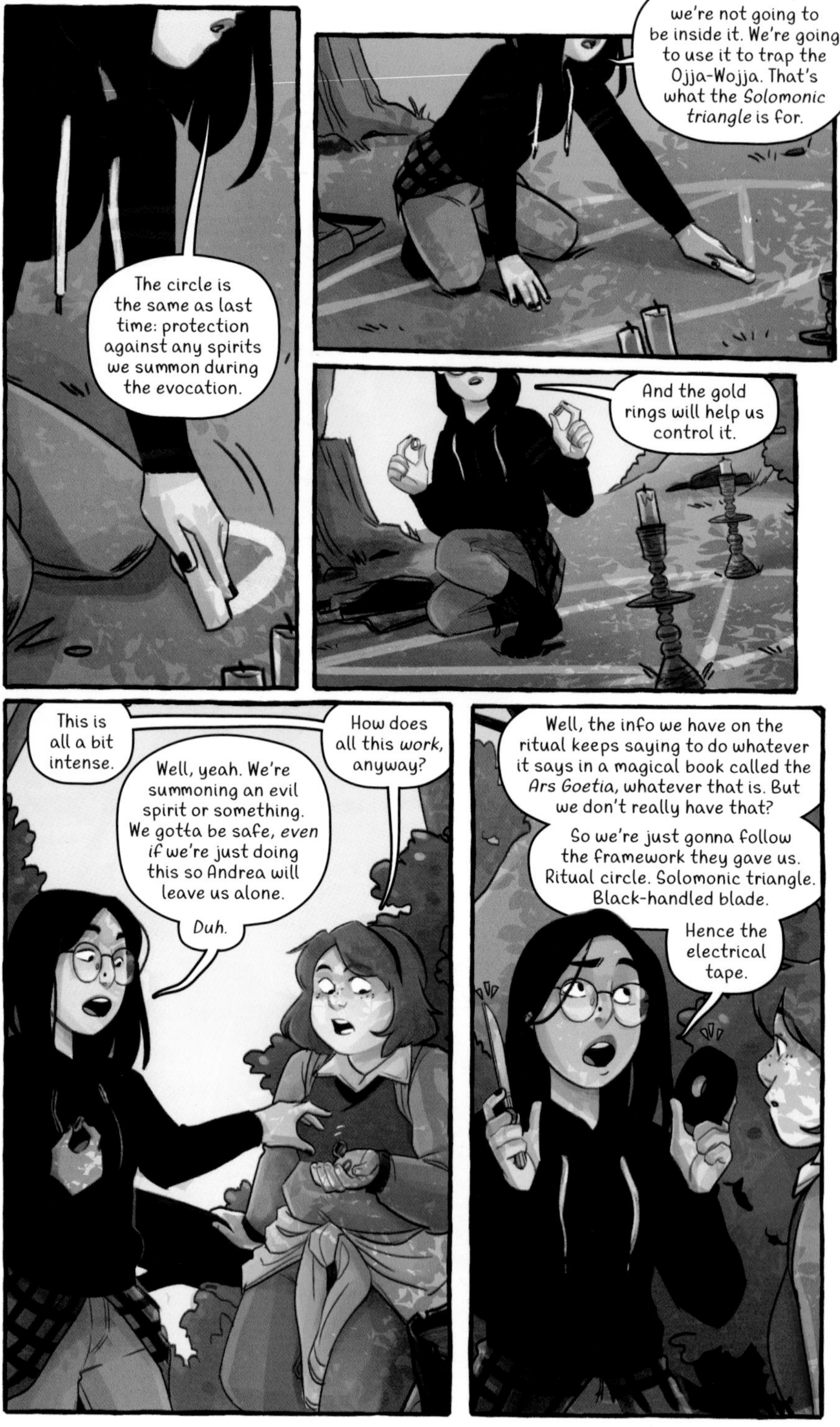

But this time we're not going to be inside it. We're going to use it to trap the Ojja-Wojja. That's what the *Solomonic triangle* is for.
The circle is the same as last time: protection against any spirits we summon during the evocation.
And the gold rings will help us control it.
This is all a bit intense.
How does all this *work*, anyway?
Well, yeah. We're summoning an evil spirit or something. We gotta be safe, *even if* we're just doing this so Andrea will leave us alone.
Duh.
Well, the info we have on the ritual keeps saying to do whatever it says in a magical book called the *Ars Goetia*, whatever that is. But we don't really have that?
So we're just gonna follow the framework they gave us. Ritual circle. Solomonic triangle. Black-handled blade.
Hence the electrical tape.

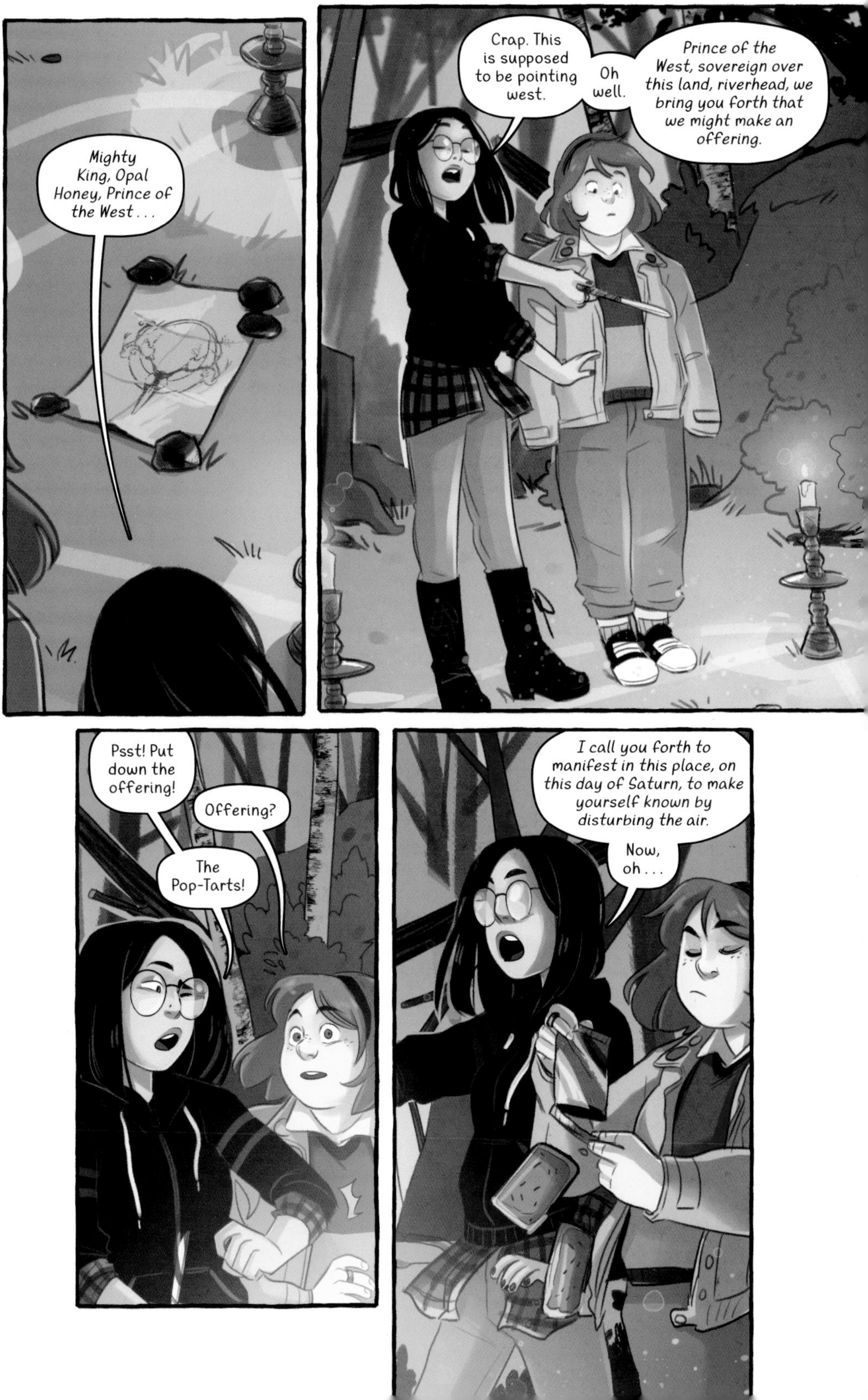

Mighty King, Opal Honey, Prince of the West . . .
Crap. This is supposed to be pointing west.
Oh well.
Prince of the West, sovereign over this land, riverhead, we bring you forth that we might make an offering.
Psst! Put down the offering!
Offering?
The Pop-Tarts!
I call you forth to manifest in this place, on this day of Saturn, to make yourself known by disturbing the air.
Now, oh . . .

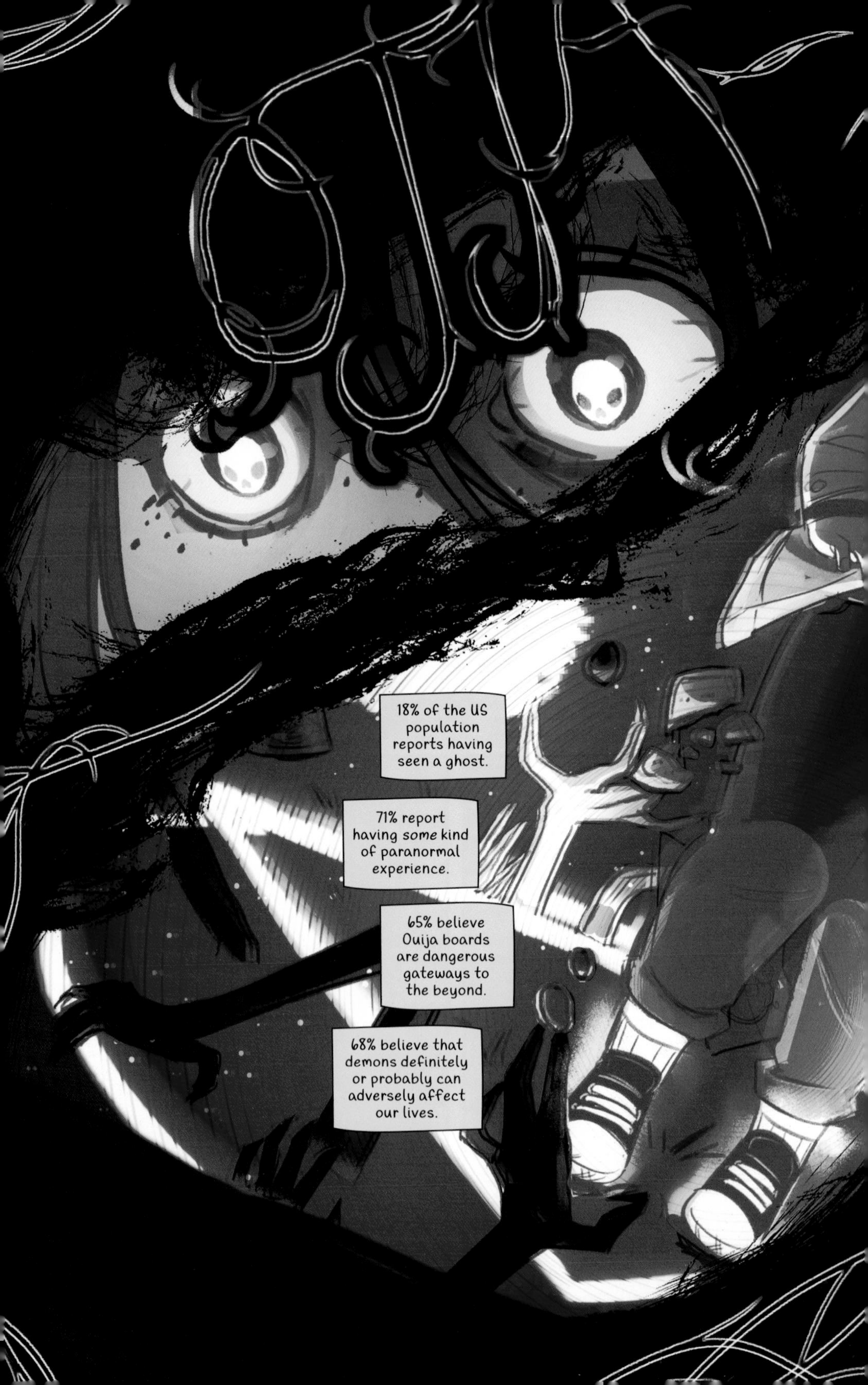
18% of the US population reports having seen a ghost.
71% report having *some* kind of paranormal experience.
65% believe Ouija boards are dangerous gateways to the beyond.
68% believe that demons definitely or probably can adversely affect our lives.

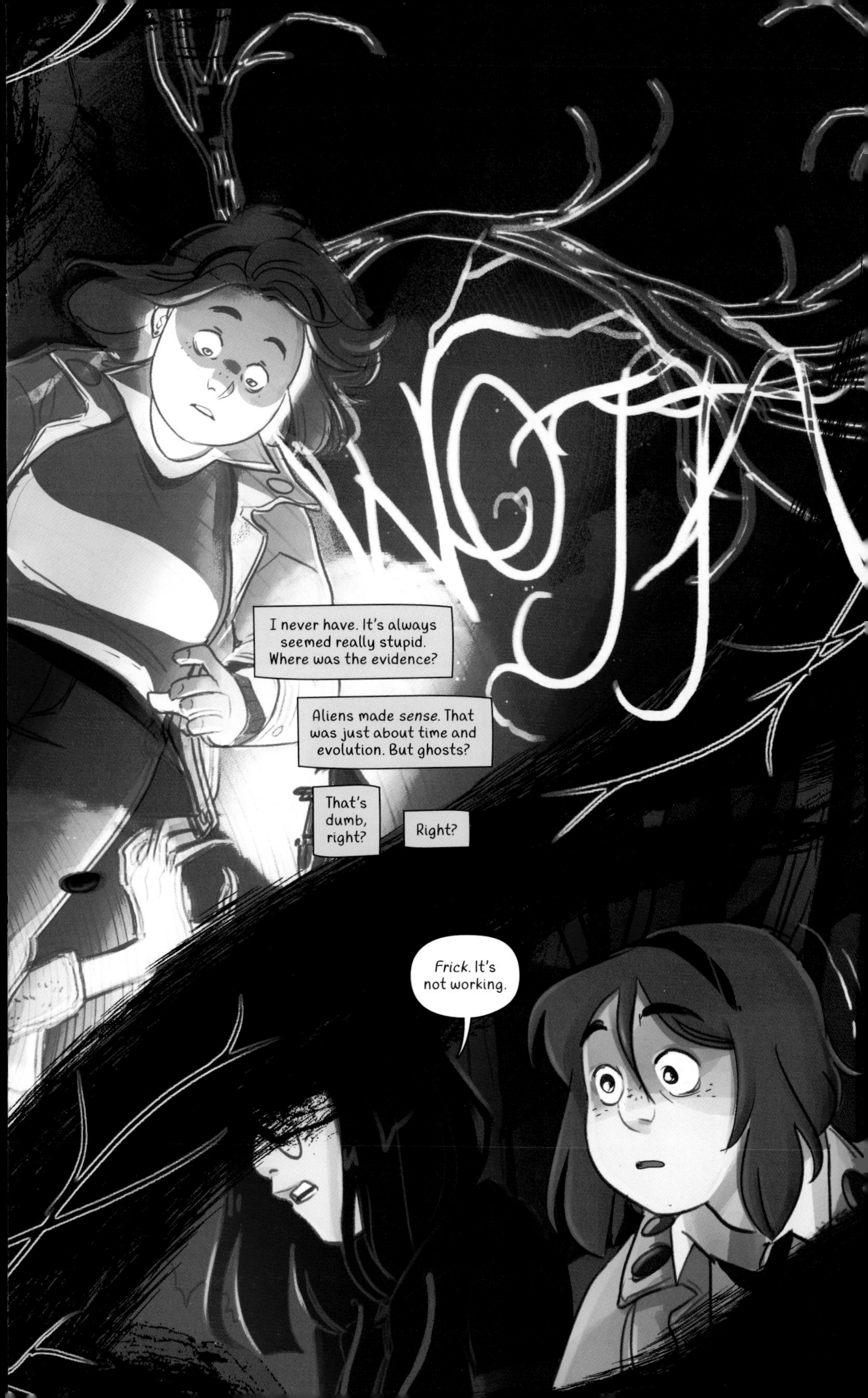

I never have. It's always seemed really stupid. Where was the evidence?
Aliens made *sense*. That was just about time and evolution. But ghosts?
That's dumb, right?
Right?
Frick. It's not working.

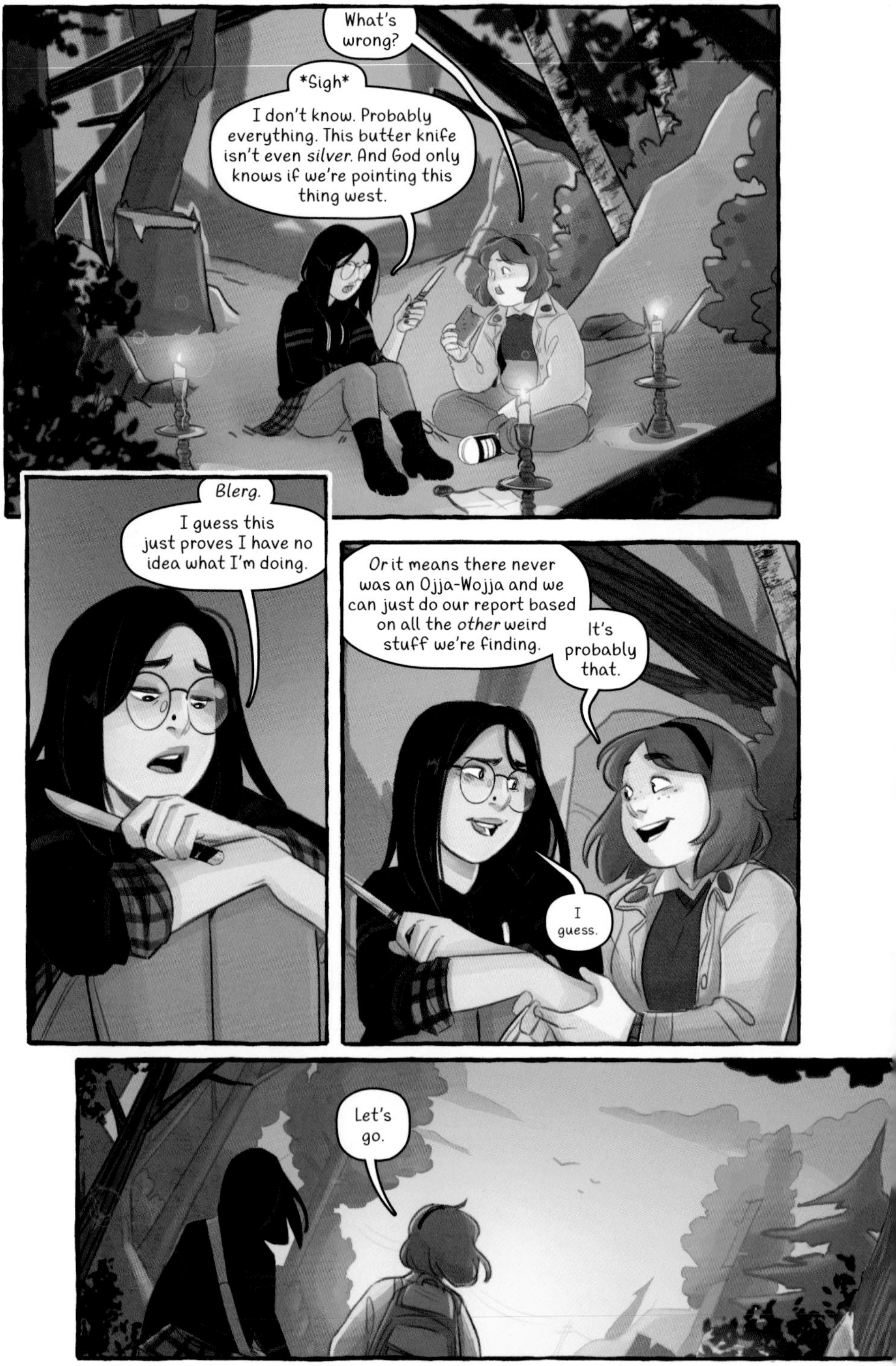
What's wrong?
Sigh
I don't know. Probably everything. This butter knife isn't even *silver*. And God only knows if we're pointing this thing west.
Blerg.
I guess this just proves I have no idea what I'm doing.
Or it means there never was an Ojja-Wojja and we can just do our report based on all the *other* weird stuff we're finding.
It's probably that.
I guess.
Let's go.

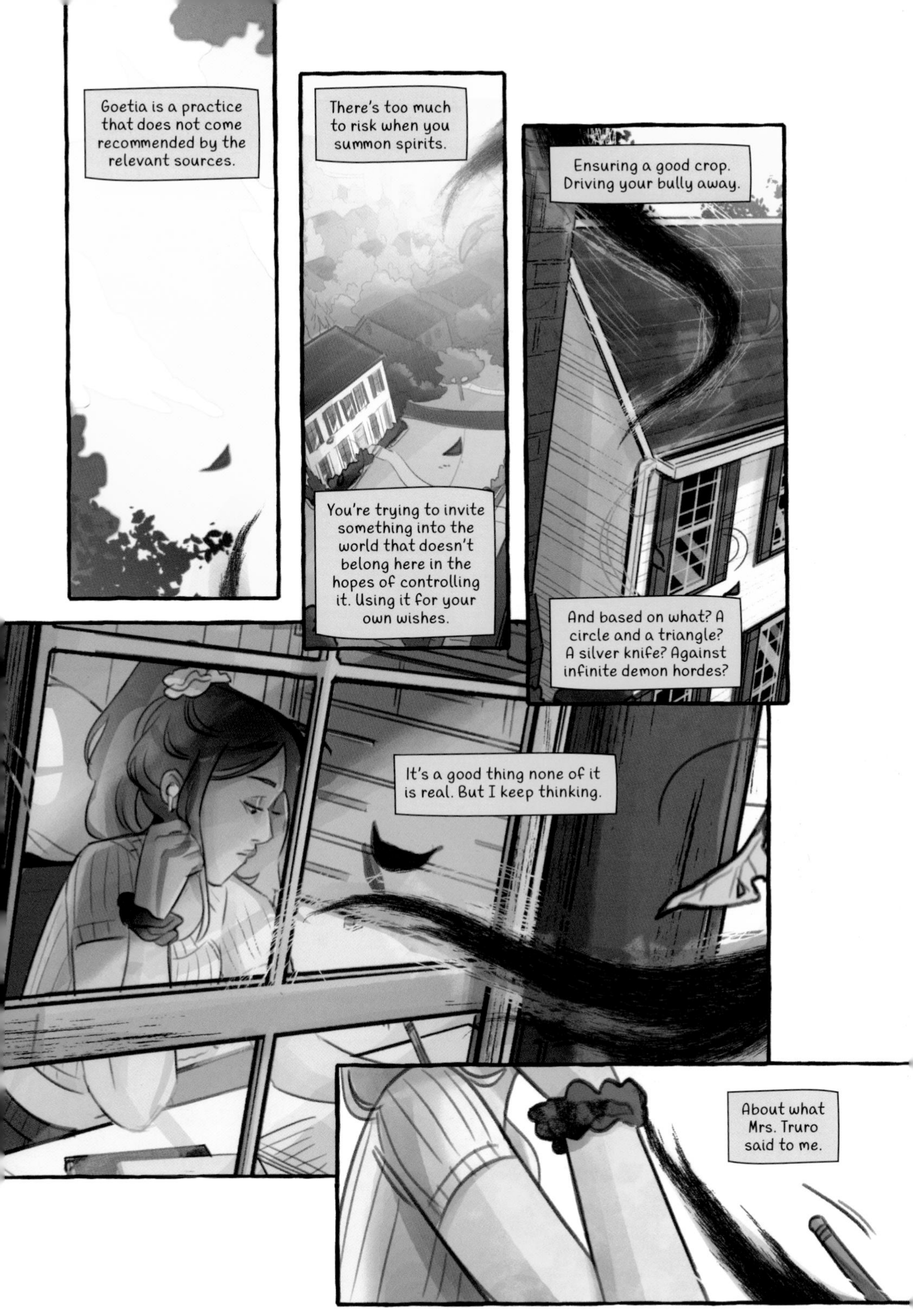
Goetia is a practice that does not come recommended by the relevant sources.
There's too much to risk when you summon spirits.
You're trying to invite something into the world that doesn't belong here in the hopes of controlling it. Using it for your own wishes.
Ensuring a good crop. Driving your bully away.
And based on what? A circle and a triangle? A silver knife? Against infinite demon hordes?
It's a good thing none of it is real. But I keep thinking.
About what Mrs. Truro said to me.

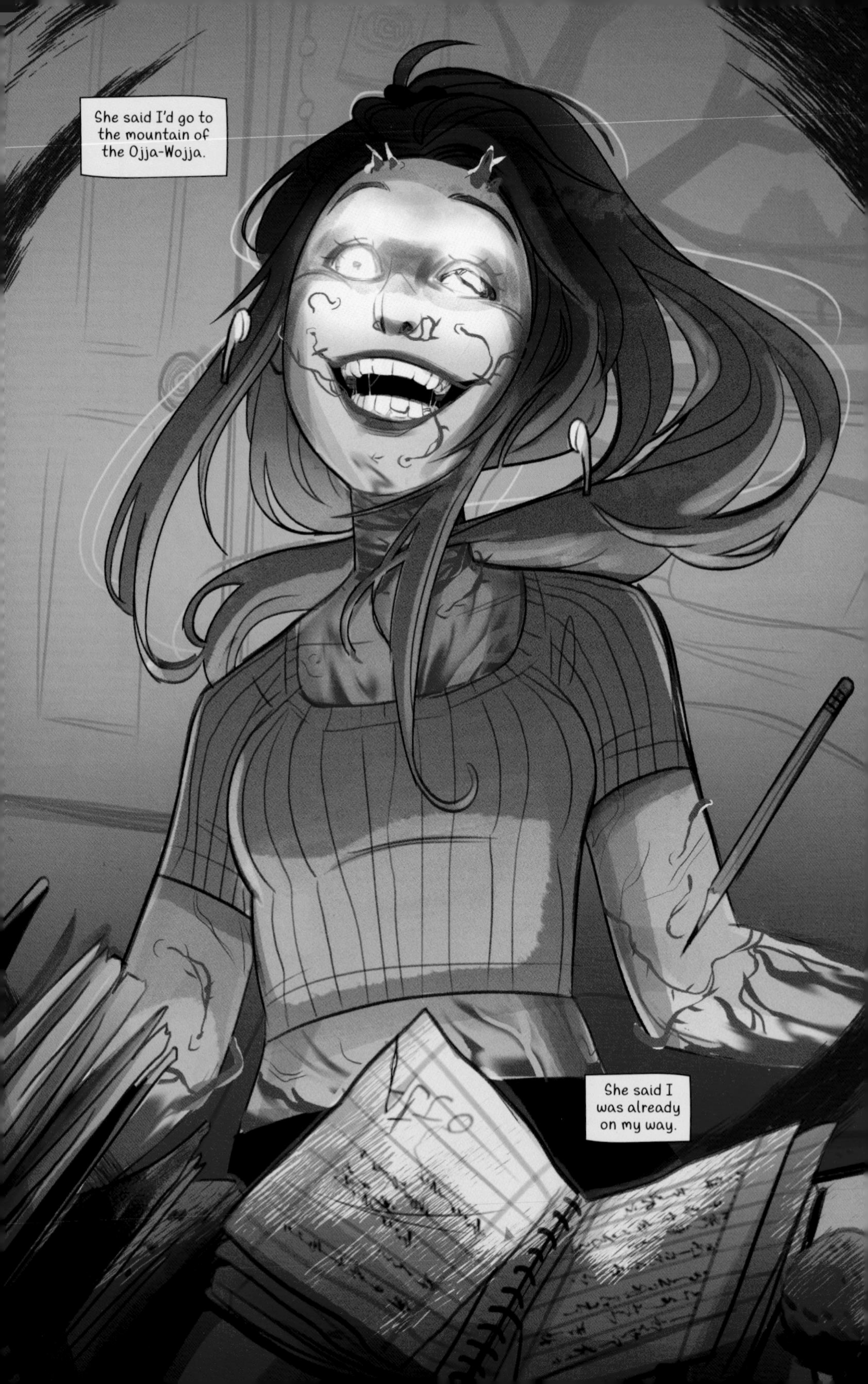
She said I'd go to the mountain of the Ojja-Wojja.
She said I was already on my way.

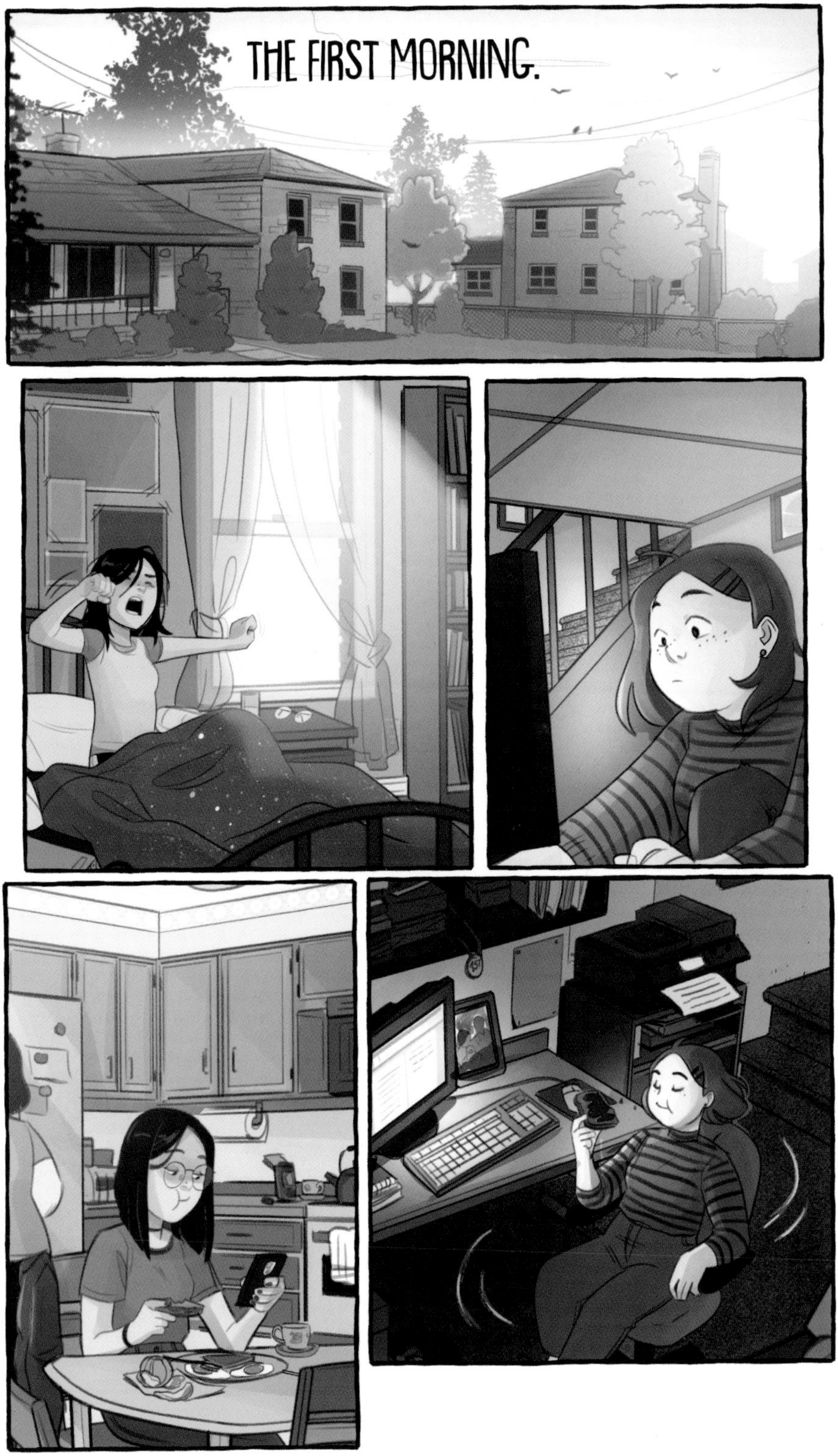
THE FIRST MORNING.

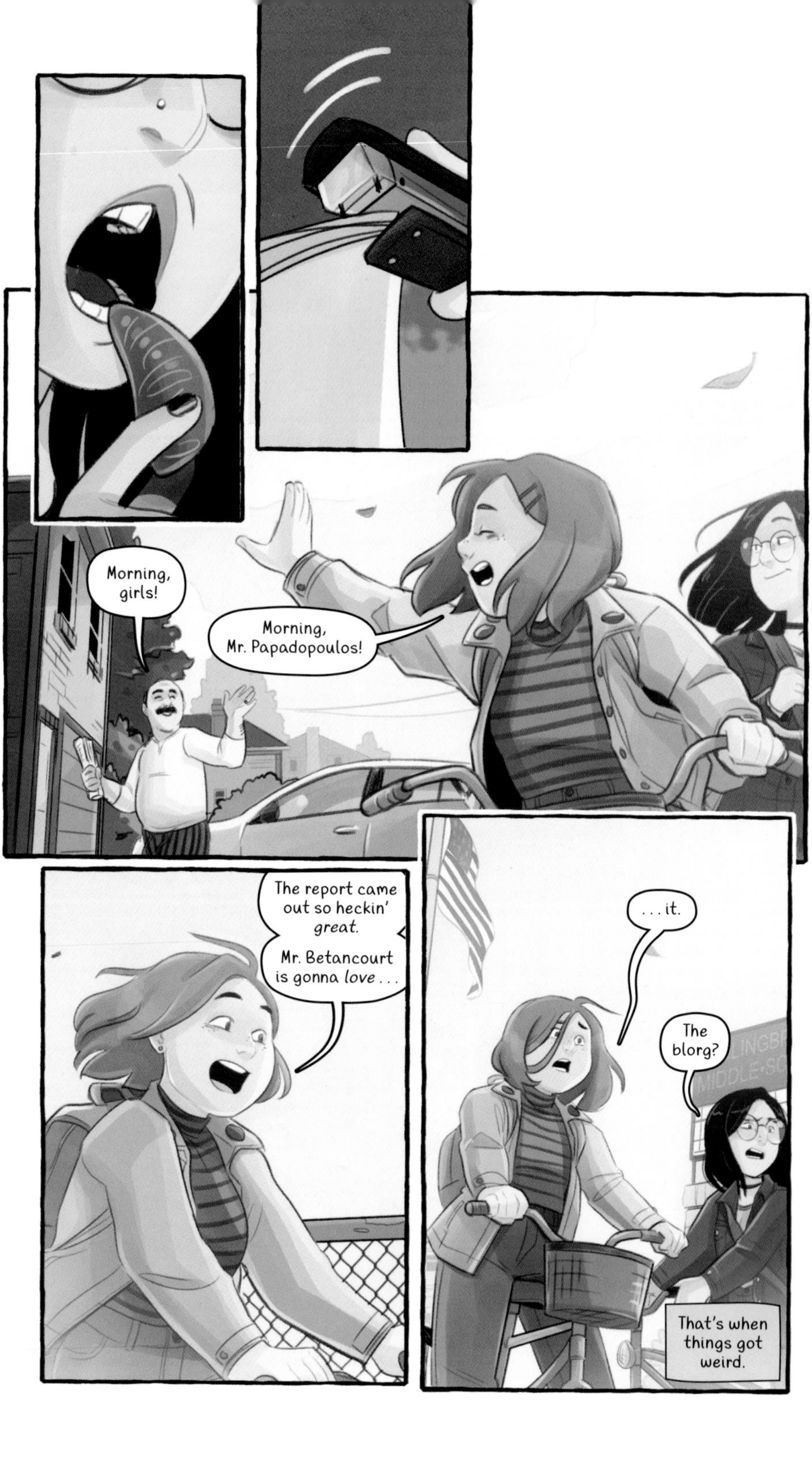
Morning, girls!
Morning, Mr. Papadopoulos!
The report came out so heckin' *great.*
Mr. Betancourt is gonna *love* . . .
. . . it.
The blorg?
That's when things got weird.

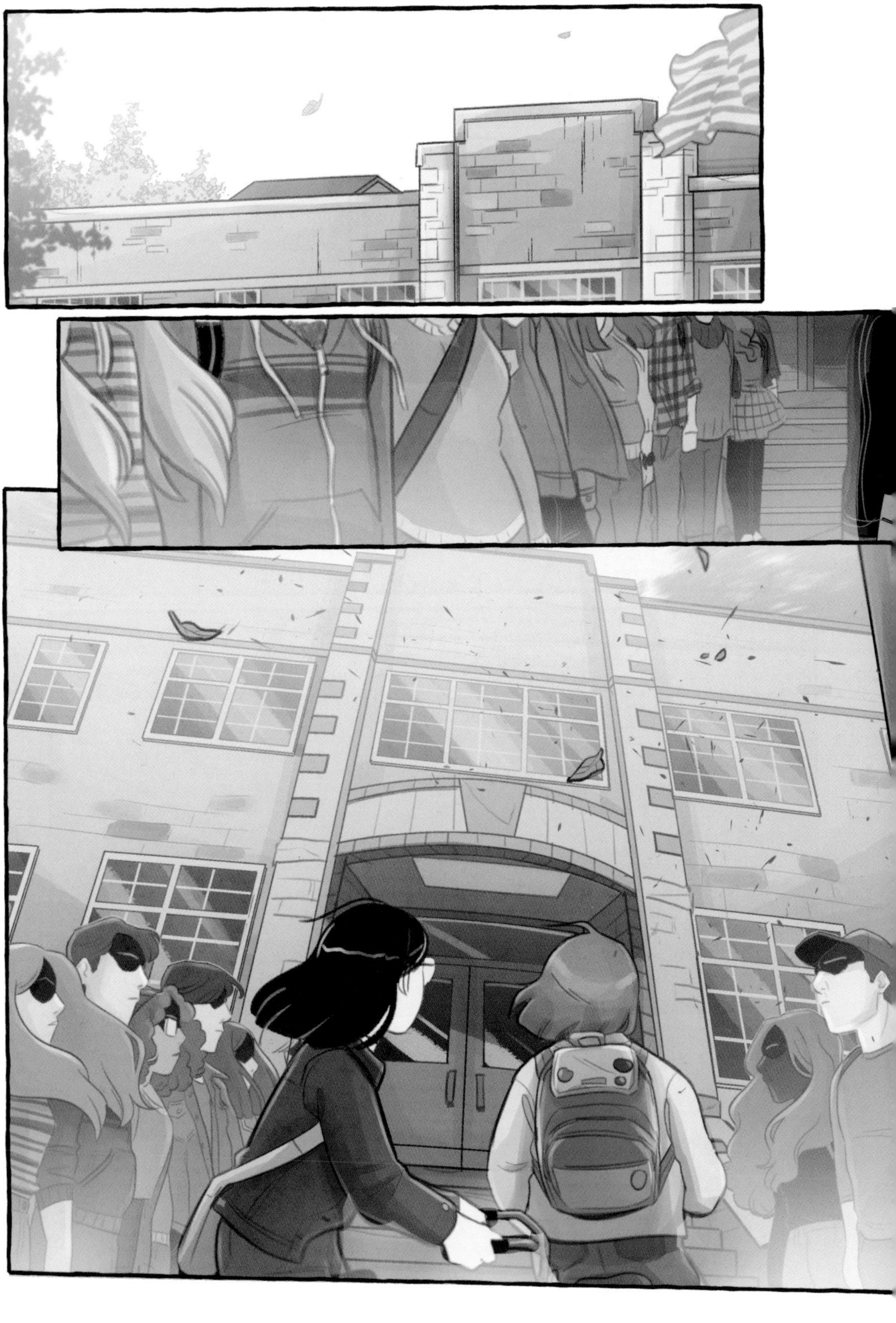

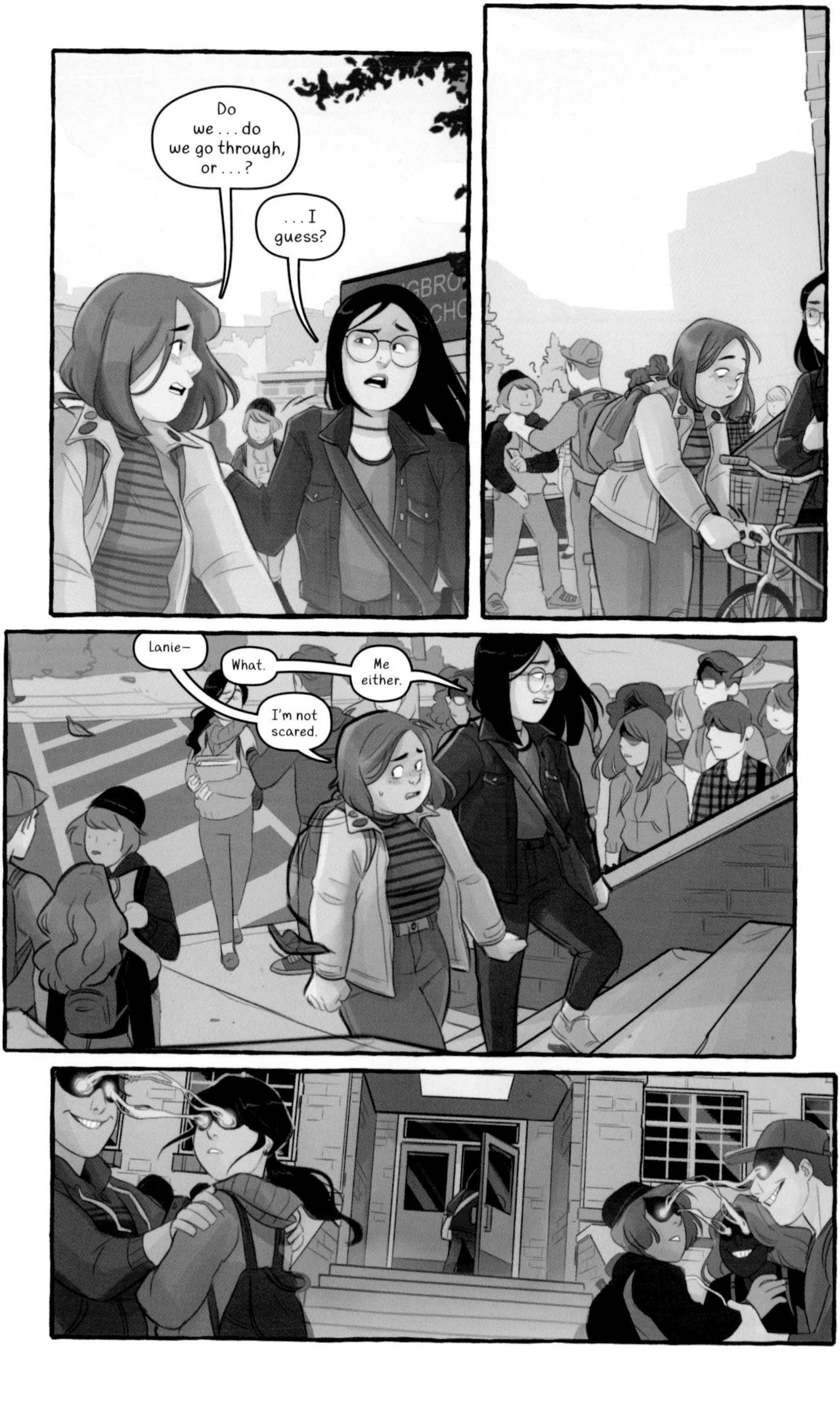
Do we . . . do we go through, or . . . ?
. . . I guess?
Lanie—
What.
I'm not scared.
Me either.

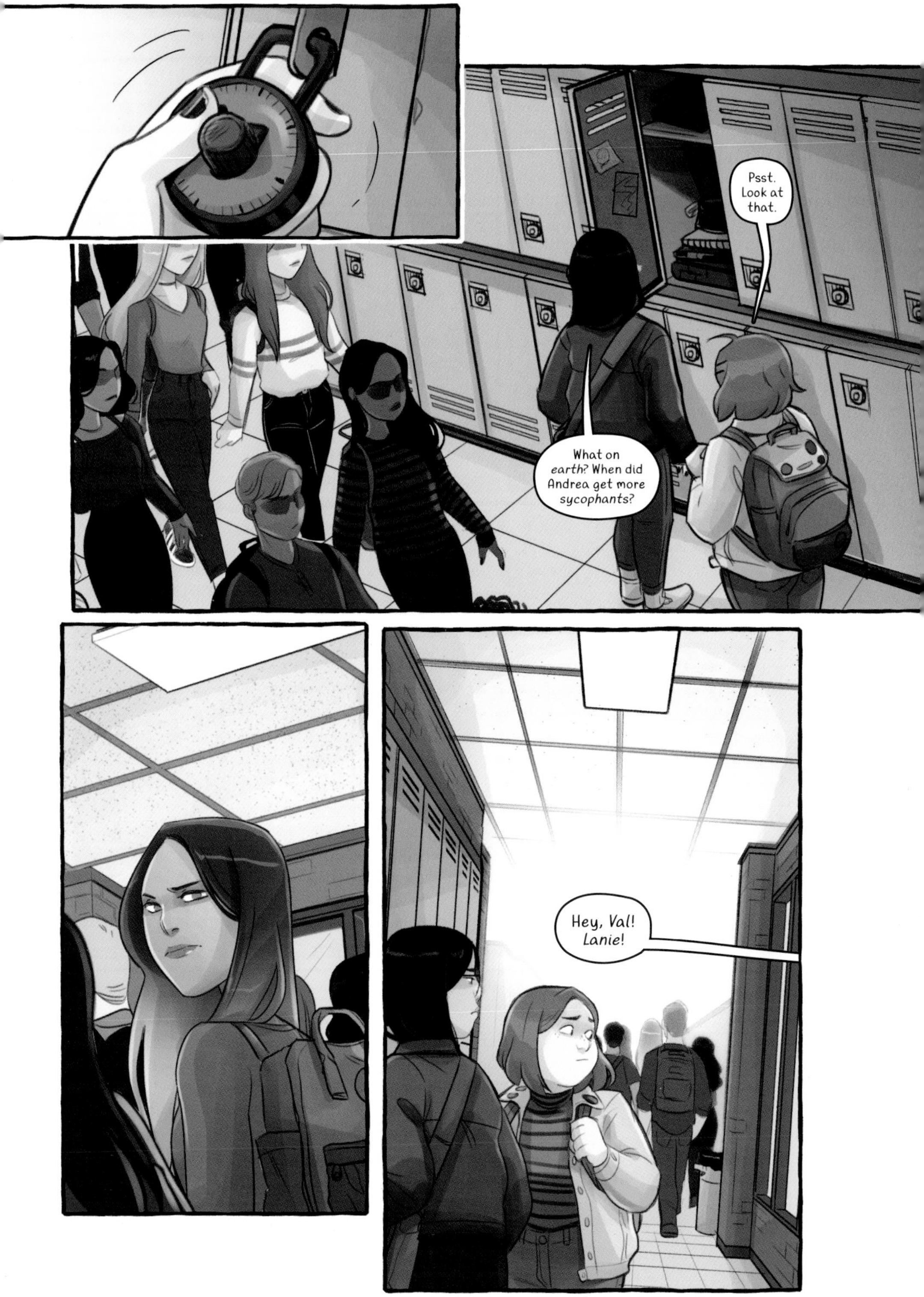
Psst. Look at that.
What on *earth*? When did Andrea get more sycophants?
Hey, Val! Lanie!

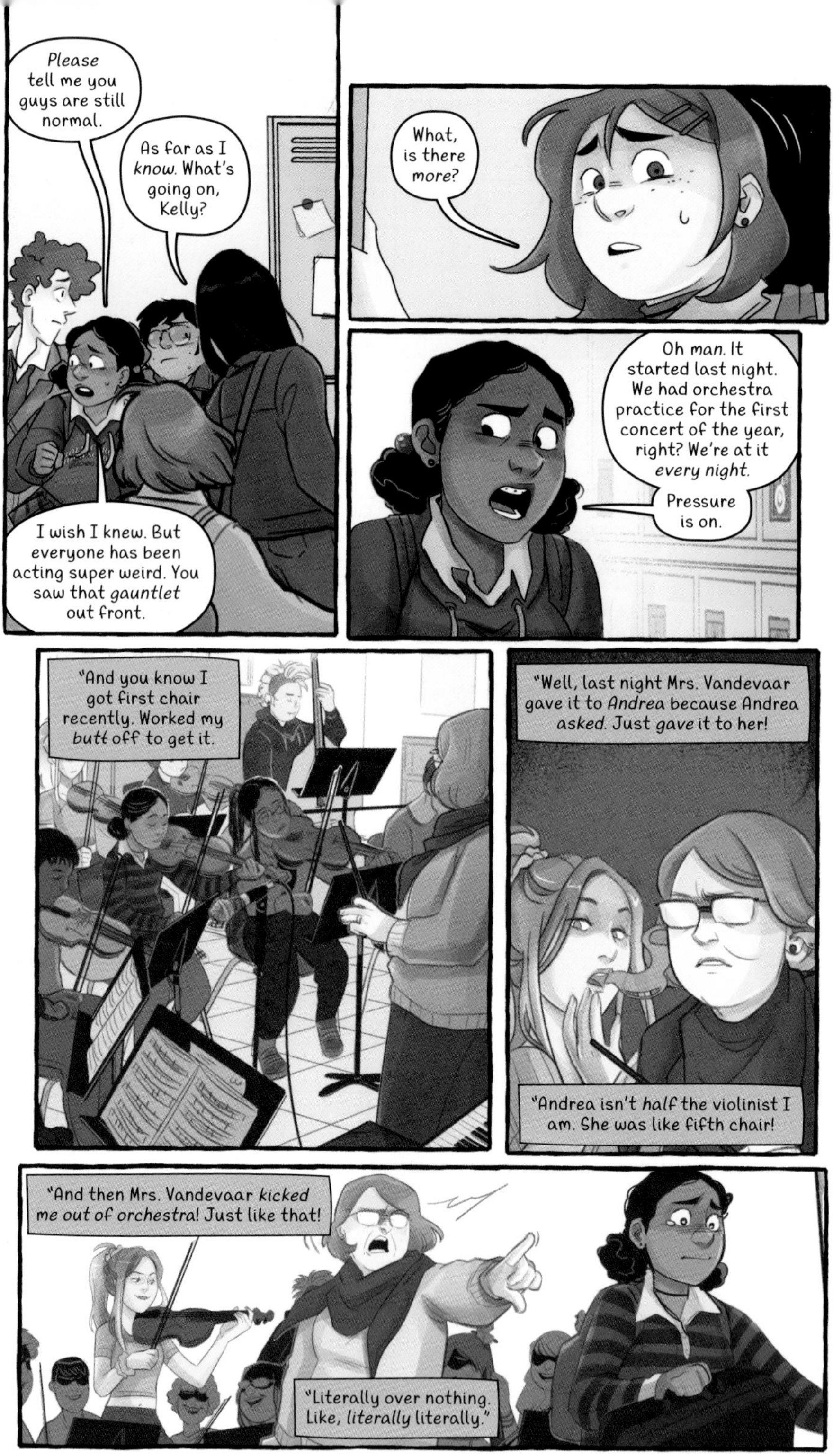
Please tell me you guys are still normal.
As far as I *know*. What's going on, Kelly?
I wish I knew. But everyone has been acting super weird. You saw that *gauntlet* out front.
What, is there *more*?
Oh *man*. It started last night. We had orchestra practice for the first concert of the year, right? We're at it *every night*.
Pressure is on.
"And you know I got first chair recently. Worked my *butt* off to get it.
"Well, last night Mrs. Vandevaar gave it to *Andrea* because Andrea *asked*. Just *gave* it to her!
"Andrea isn't *half* the violinist I am. She was like fifth chair!
"And then Mrs. Vandevaar *kicked me out of orchestra*! Just like that!
"Literally over nothing. Like, *literally* literally."

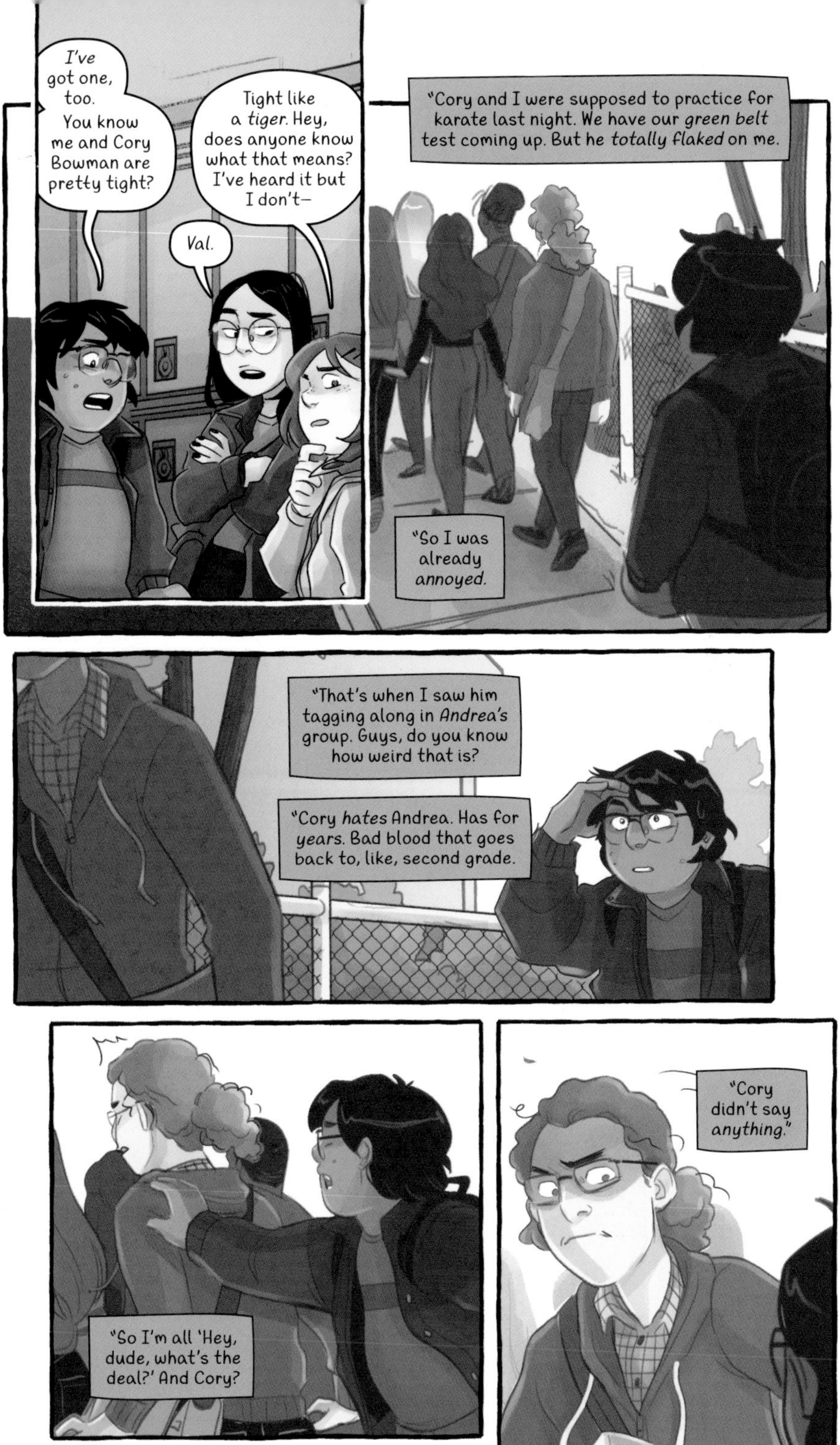
I've got one, too. You know me and Cory Bowman are pretty tight?
Val.
Tight like a *tiger*. Hey, does anyone know what that means? I've heard it but I don't–
"Cory and I were supposed to practice for karate last night. We have our *green belt* test coming up. But he *totally flaked* on me.
"So I was already *annoyed*.
"That's when I saw him tagging along in *Andrea's* group. Guys, do you know how weird that is?
"Cory *hates* Andrea. Has for *years*. Bad blood that goes back to, like, second grade.
"So I'm all 'Hey, dude, what's the deal?' And Cory?
"Cory didn't say *anything*."

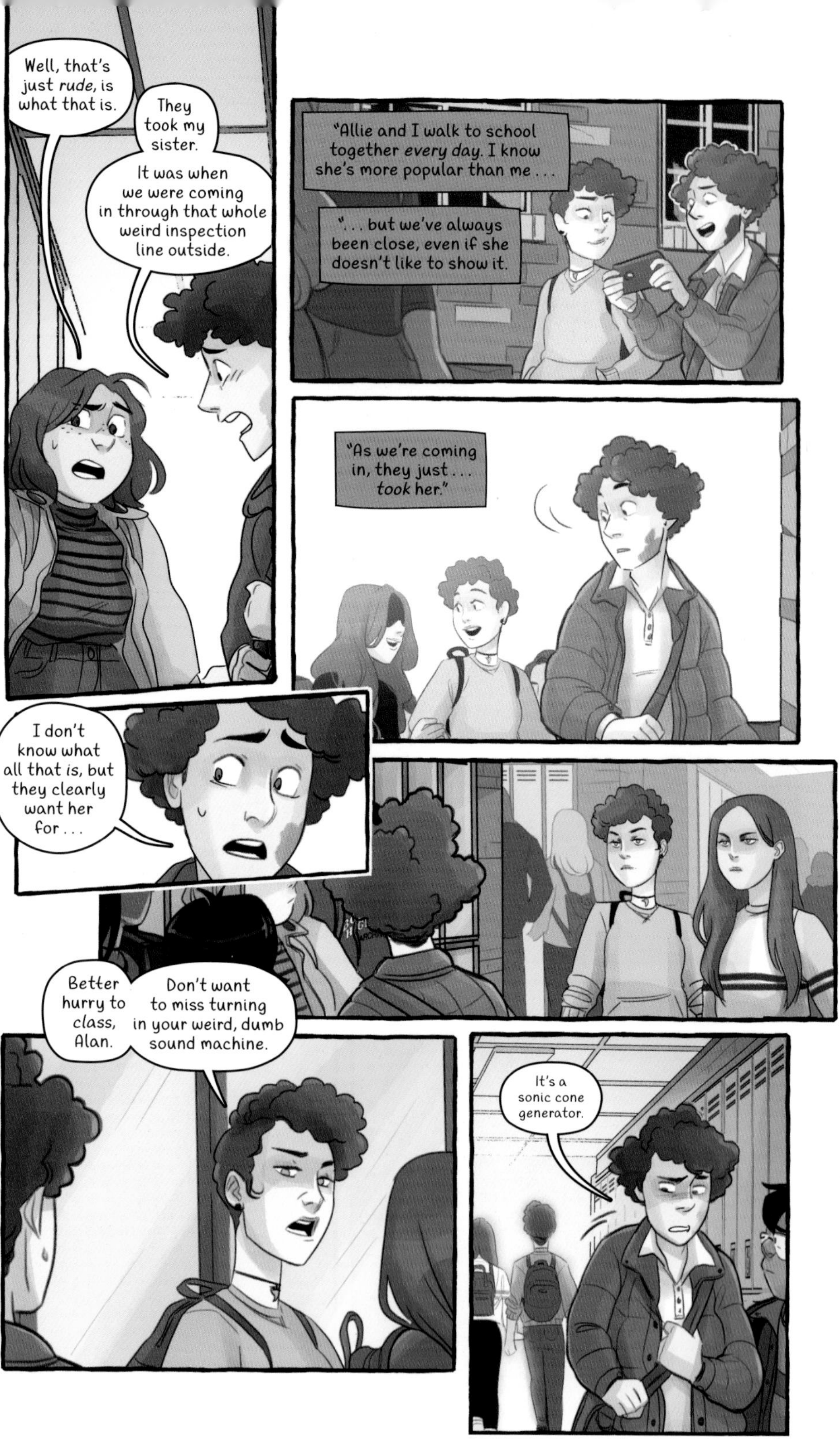

Well, that's just *rude*, is what that is.
They took my sister.
It was when we were coming in through that whole weird inspection line outside.
"Allie and I walk to school together *every day*. I know she's more popular than me . . .
". . . but we've always been close, even if she doesn't like to show it.
"As we're coming in, they just . . . *took* her."
I don't know what all that *is*, but they clearly want her for . . .
Better hurry to *class*, Alan.
Don't want to miss turning in your weird, dumb sound machine.
It's a sonic cone generator.

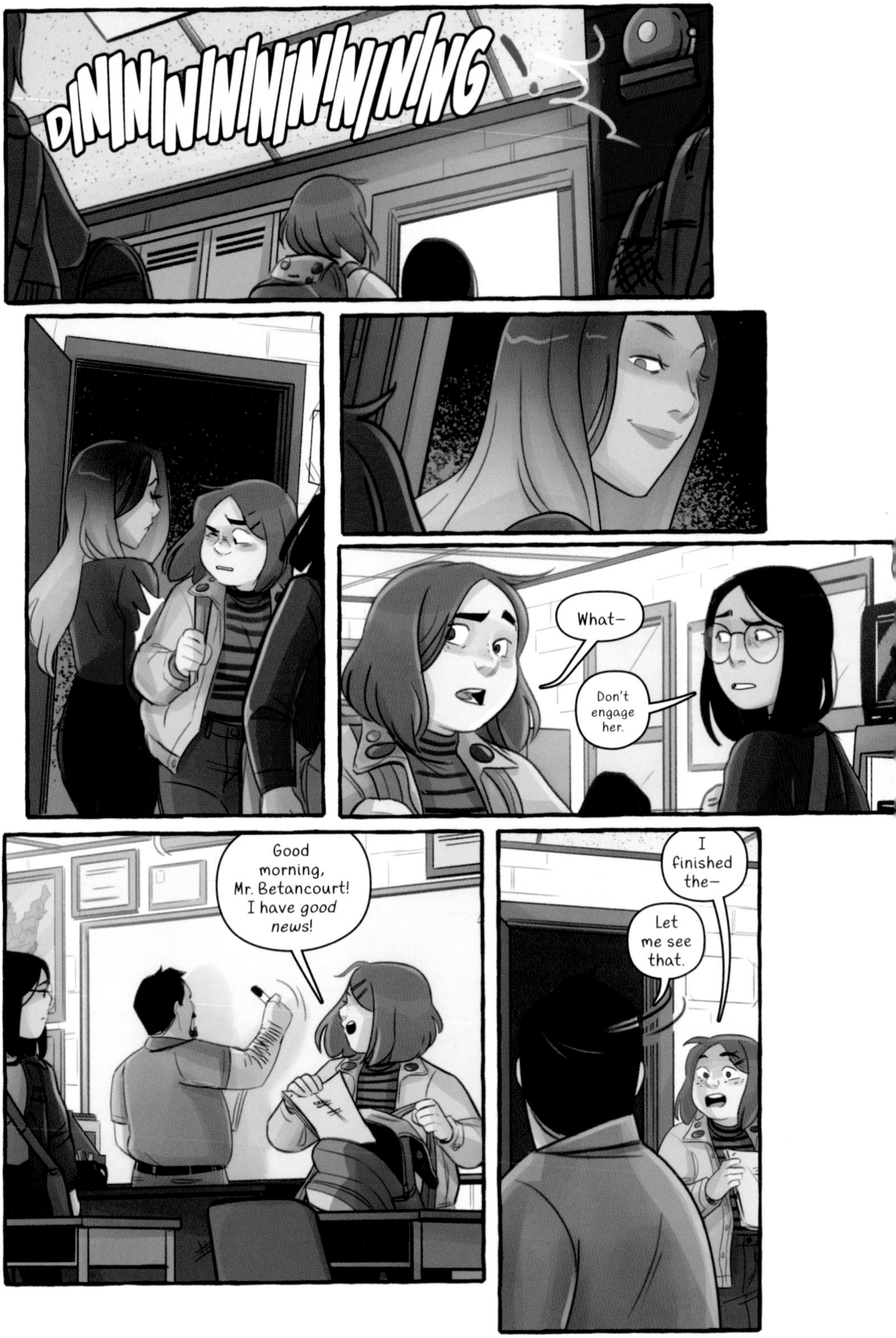
DINININININININING
What–
Don't engage her.
Good morning, Mr. Betancourt! I have *good* news!
I finished the–
Let me see that.

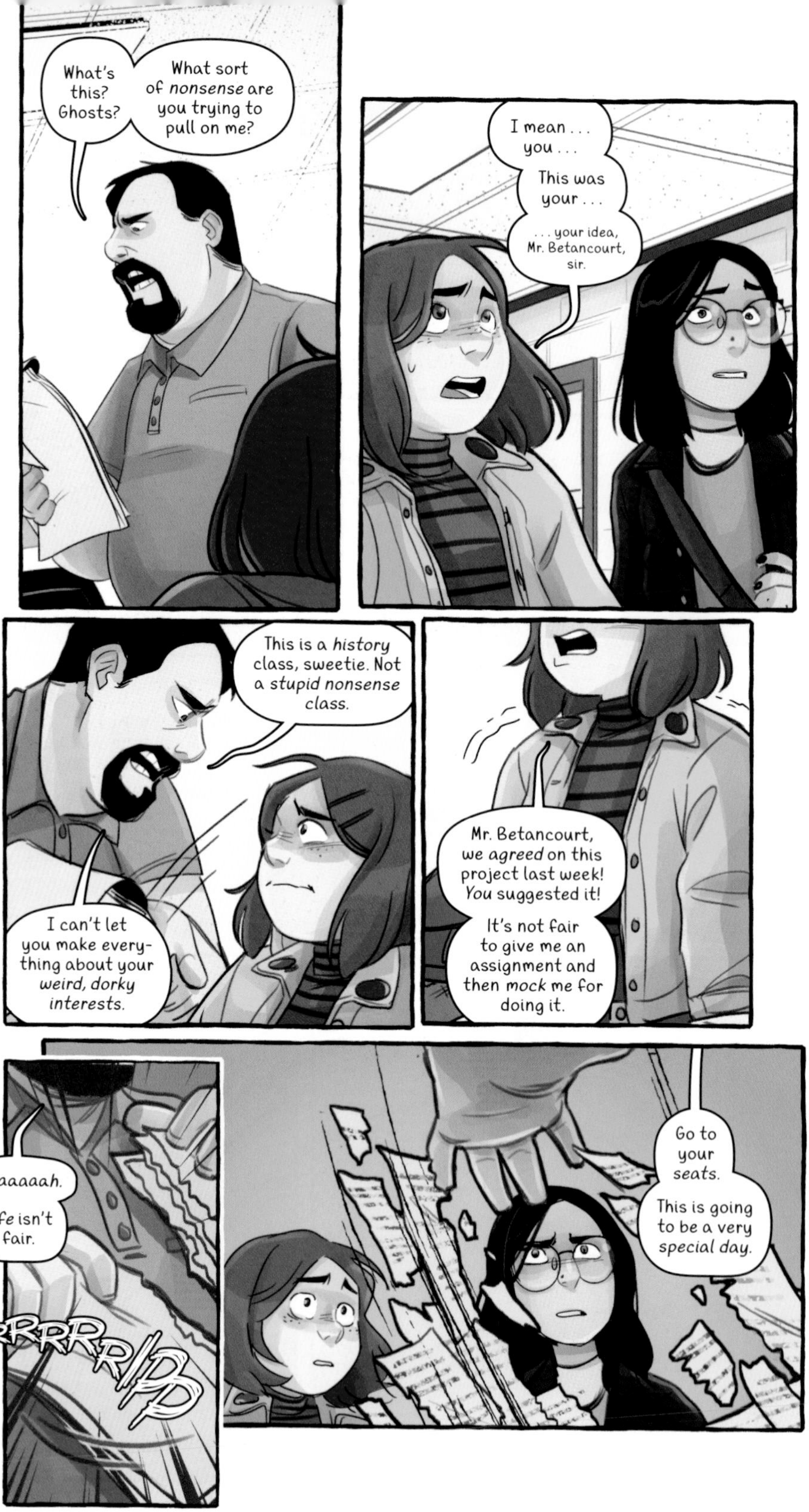
What's this? Ghosts?
What sort of *nonsense* are you trying to pull on me?
I mean . . . you . . .
This was your . . .
. . . your idea, Mr. Betancourt, sir.
This is a *history* class, sweetie. Not a *stupid nonsense* class.
I can't let you make every-thing about your *weird, dorky interests.*
Mr. Betancourt, we *agreed* on this project last week! *You* suggested it!
It's not fair to give me an assignment and then *mock* me for doing it.
Waaaaaah.
Life isn't fair.
RRRRRIP
Go to your seats.
This is going to be a very *special day.*

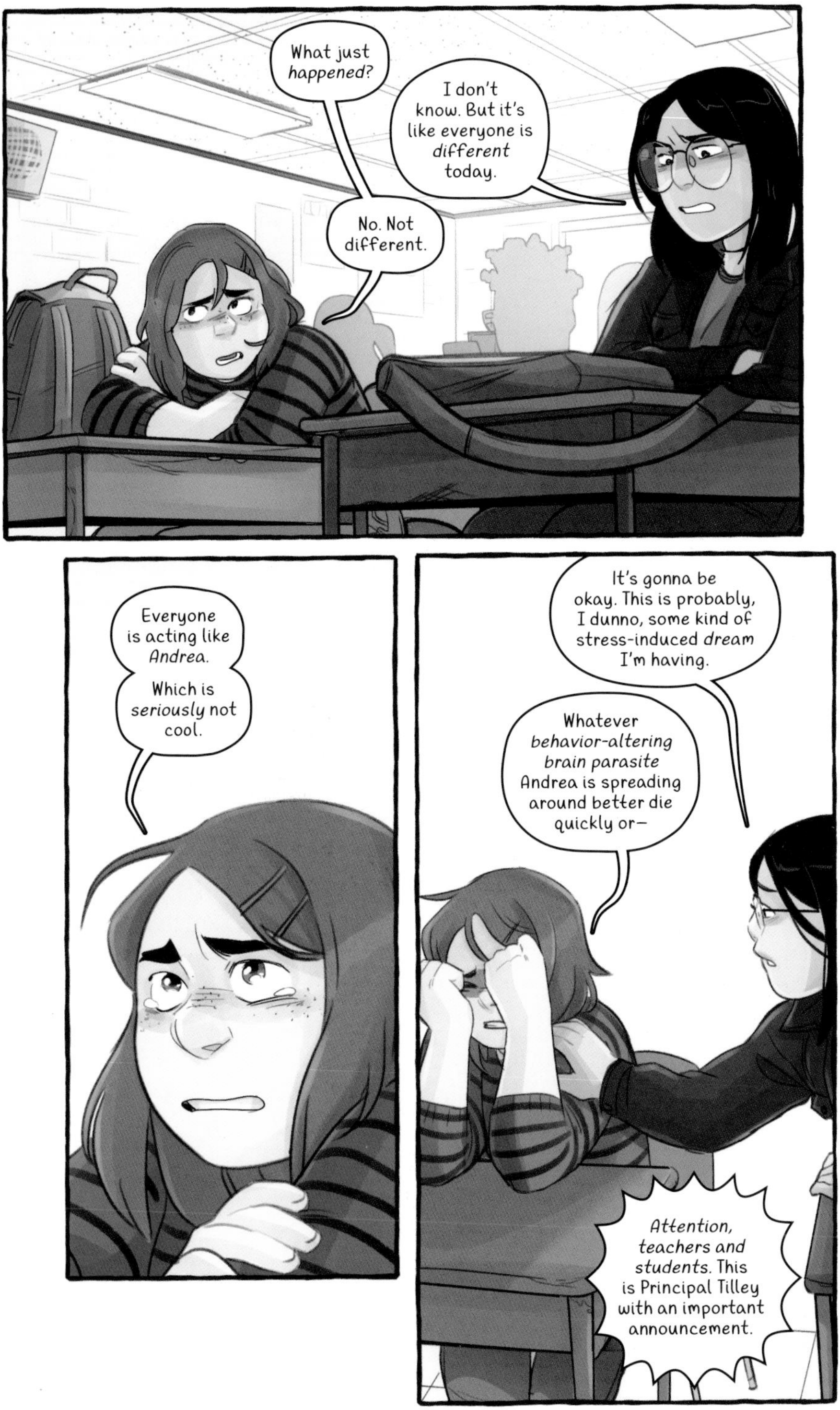
What just happened?
I don't know. But it's like everyone is different today.
No. Not different.
Everyone is acting like Andrea.
Which is seriously not cool.
It's gonna be okay. This is probably, I dunno, some kind of stress-induced dream I'm having.
Whatever behavior-altering brain parasite Andrea is spreading around better die quickly or—
Attention, teachers and students. This is Principal Tilley with an important announcement.

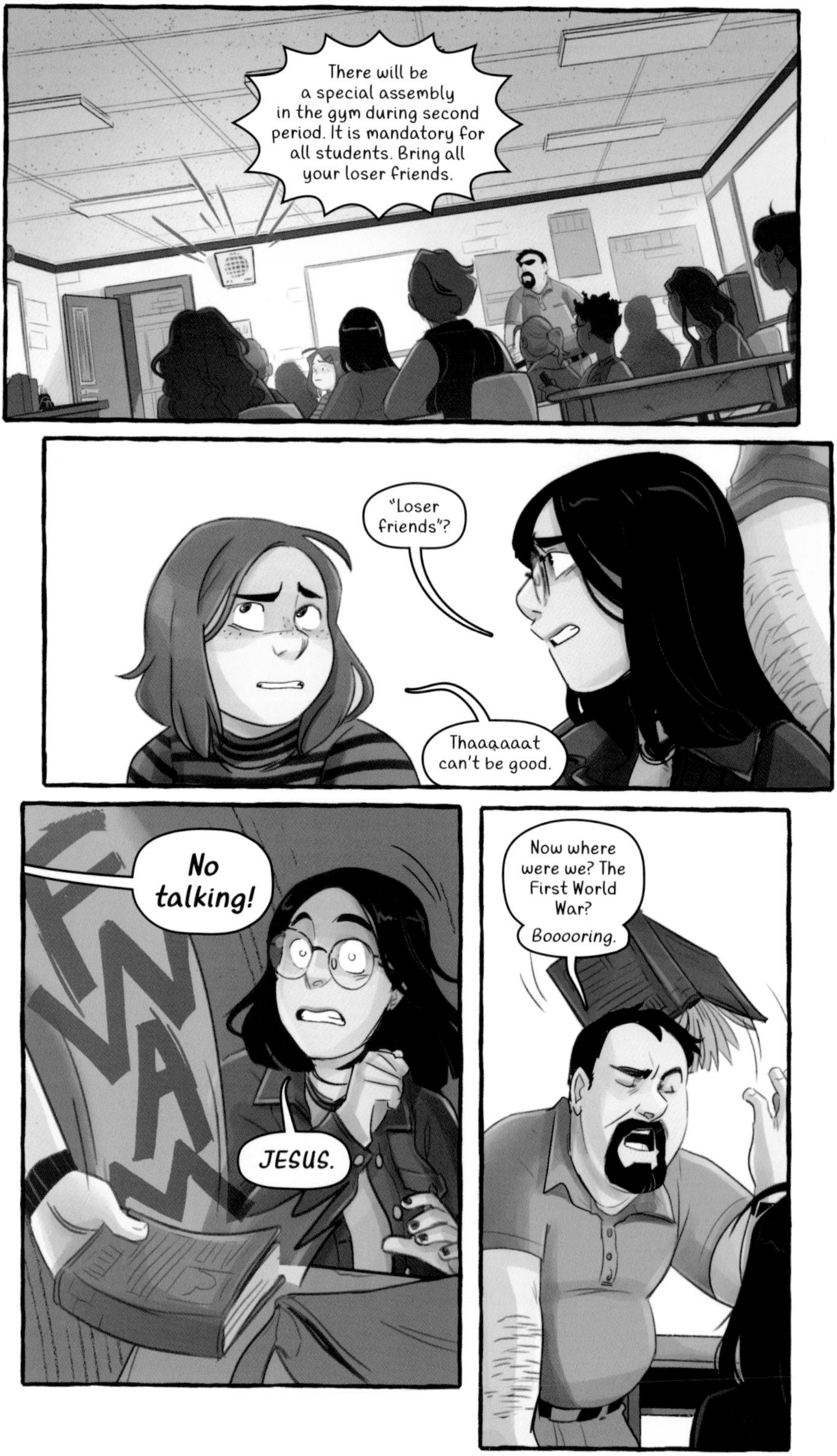
There will be a special assembly in the gym during second period. It is mandatory for all students. Bring all your loser friends.
"Loser friends"?
Thaaqaaat can't be good.
No talking!
FWAM
JESUS.
Now where were we? The First World War?
Booooring.

SO. SECOND PERIOD.

School assemblies are the *worst* even under the best circumstances.

The entire school together in *one room?* That's such an incredibly bad idea unless you *want* to put unstable elements side by side.

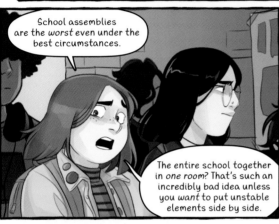

The weird cliques get shunted to the side, and the cheerleaders take center stage.

Half the crowd doesn't wanna be there at all, and the ones that do? They're the ones *kicking social butt.*

But all this?

I feel like this is going to get *dangerous.*

We have to get out of here.

Hmmm...

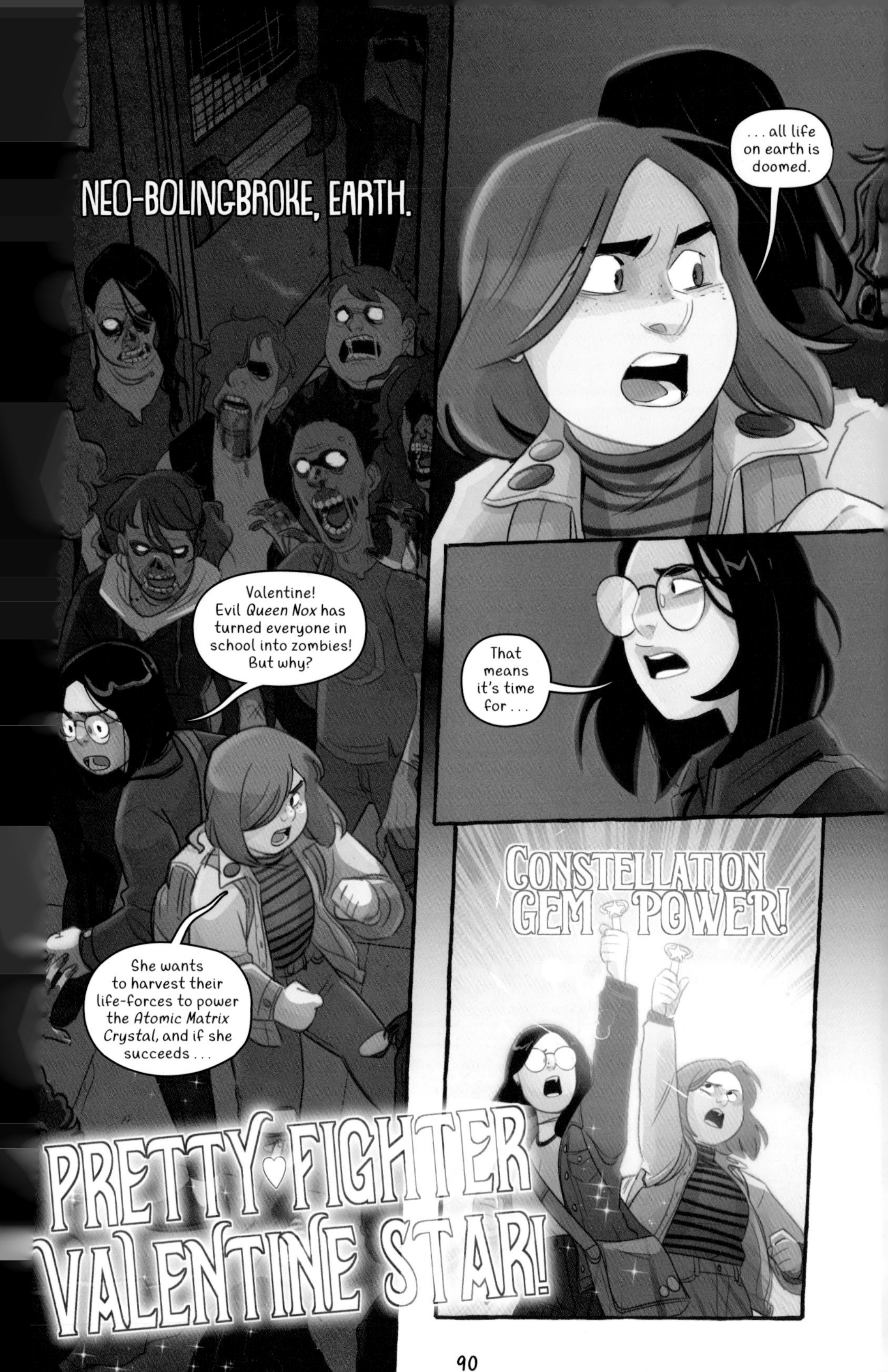
NEO-BOLINGBROKE, EARTH.
Valentine! Evil *Queen Nox* has turned everyone in school into zombies! But why?
She wants to harvest their life-forces to power the *Atomic Matrix Crystal*, and if she succeeds . . .
. . . all life on earth is doomed.
That means it's time for . . .
CONSTELLATION GEM POWER!
PRETTY♥FIGHTER VALENTINE STAR!

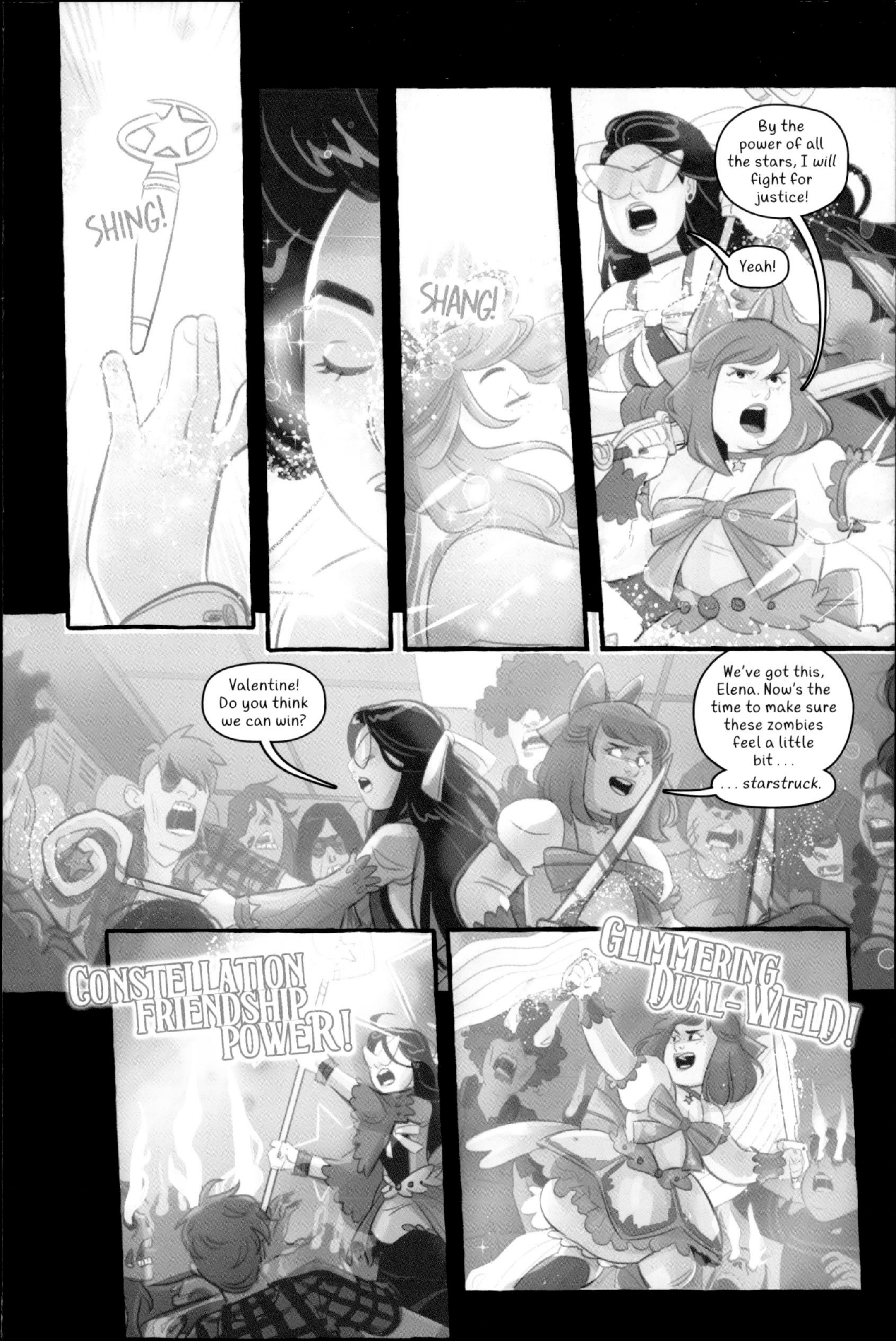
SHING!
SHANG!
By the power of all the stars, I will fight for justice!
Yeah!
Valentine! Do you think we can win?
We've got this, Elena. Now's the time to make sure these zombies feel a little bit . . .
. . . starstruck.
CONSTELLATION FRIENDSHIP POWER!
GLIMMERING DUAL-WIELD!

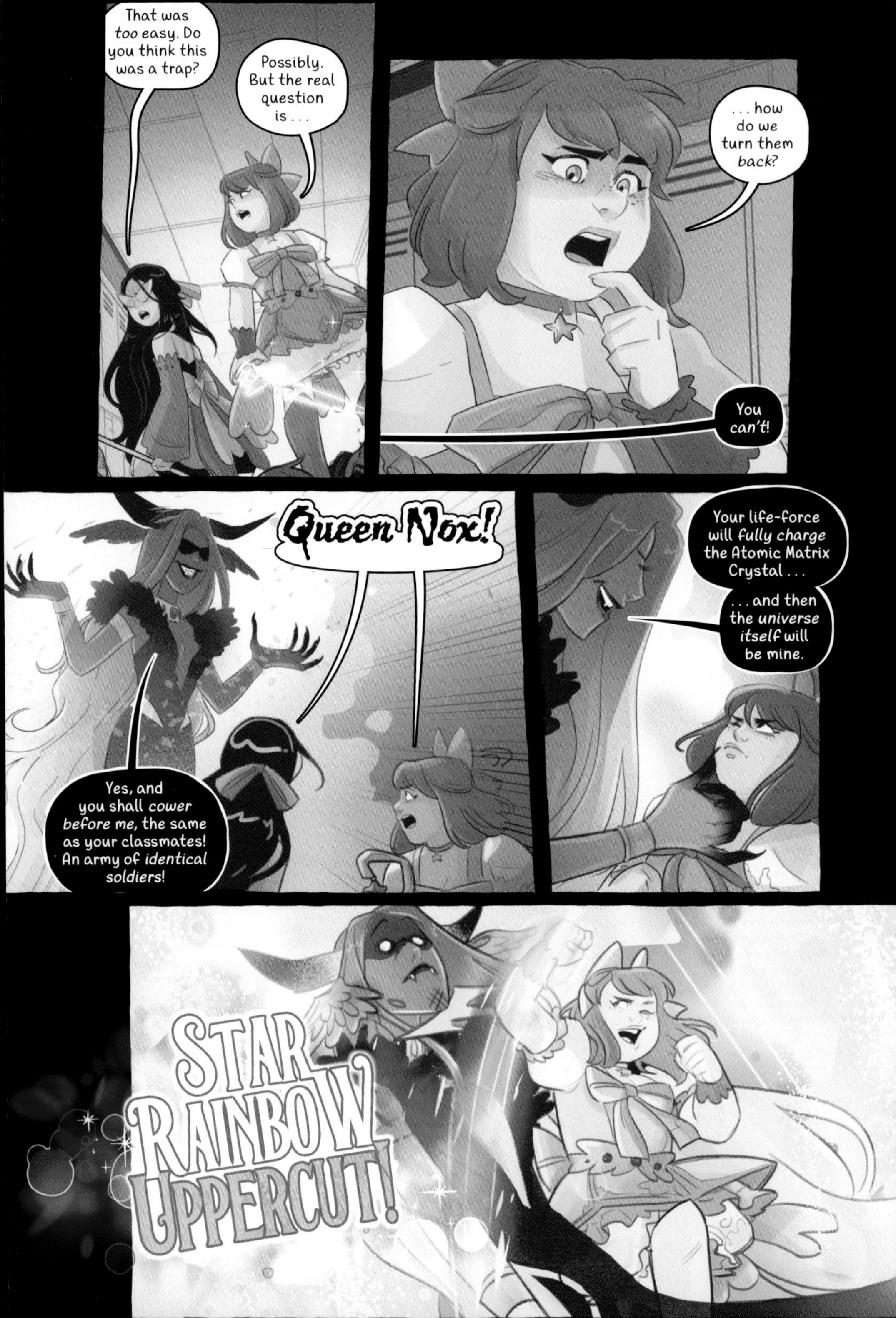
That was *too* easy. Do you think this was a trap?
Possibly. But the real question is . . .
. . . how do we turn them *back*?
You can't!
Queen Nox!
Yes, and you shall *cower before me*, the same as your classmates! An army of *identical* soldiers!
Your life-force will *fully charge* the Atomic Matrix Crystal . . .
. . . and then the *universe itself* will be mine.
STAR RAINBOW UPPERCUT!

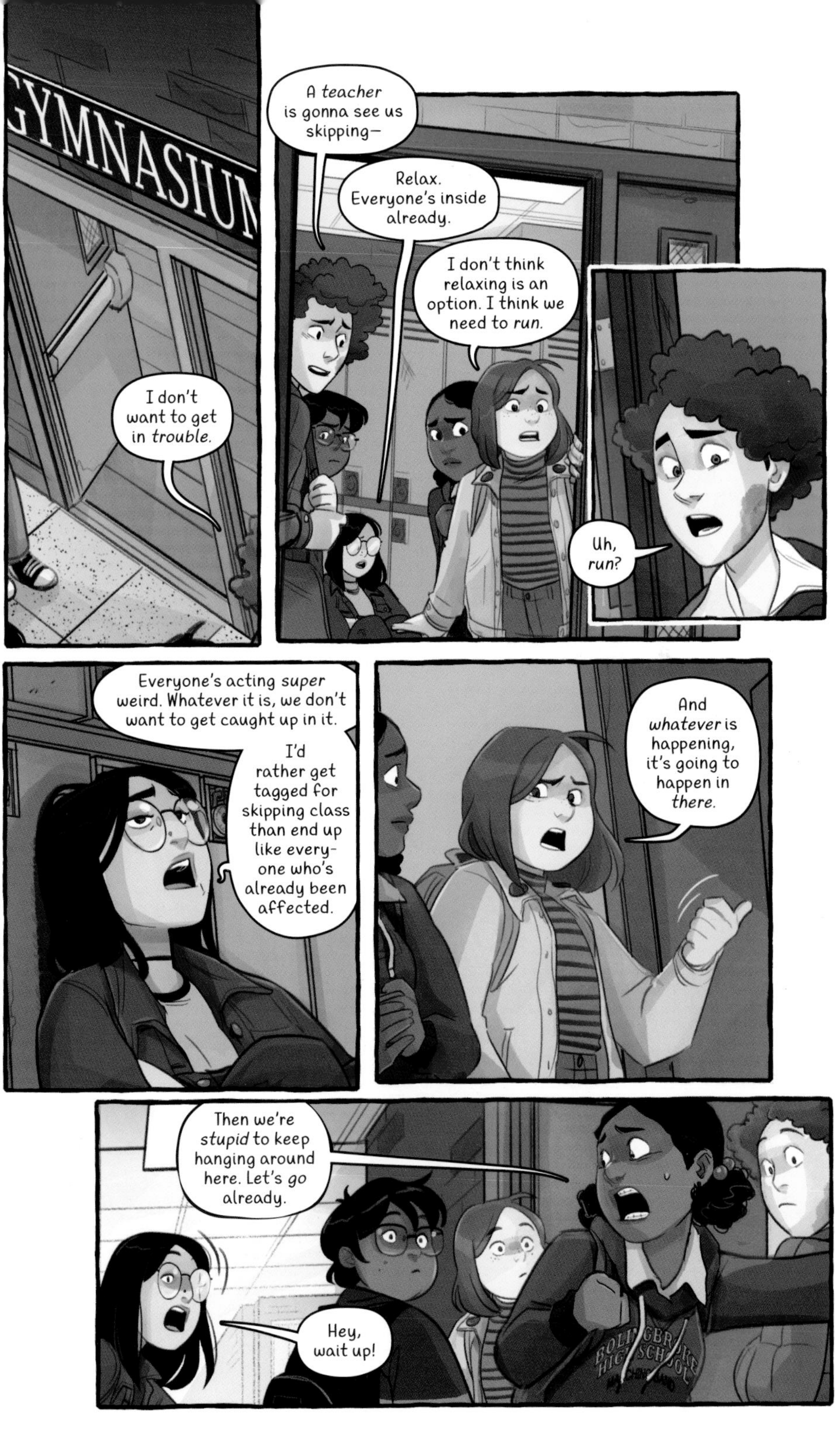
GYMNASIU
I don't want to get in *trouble.*
A *teacher* is gonna see us skipping—
Relax. Everyone's inside already.
I don't think relaxing is an option. I think we need to *run.*
Uh, *run?*
Everyone's acting *super* weird. Whatever it is, we don't want to get caught up in it.
I'd rather get tagged for skipping class than end up like every-one who's already been affected.
And *whatever* is happening, it's going to happen in *there.*
Then we're *stupid* to keep hanging around here. Let's *go* already.
Hey, wait up!

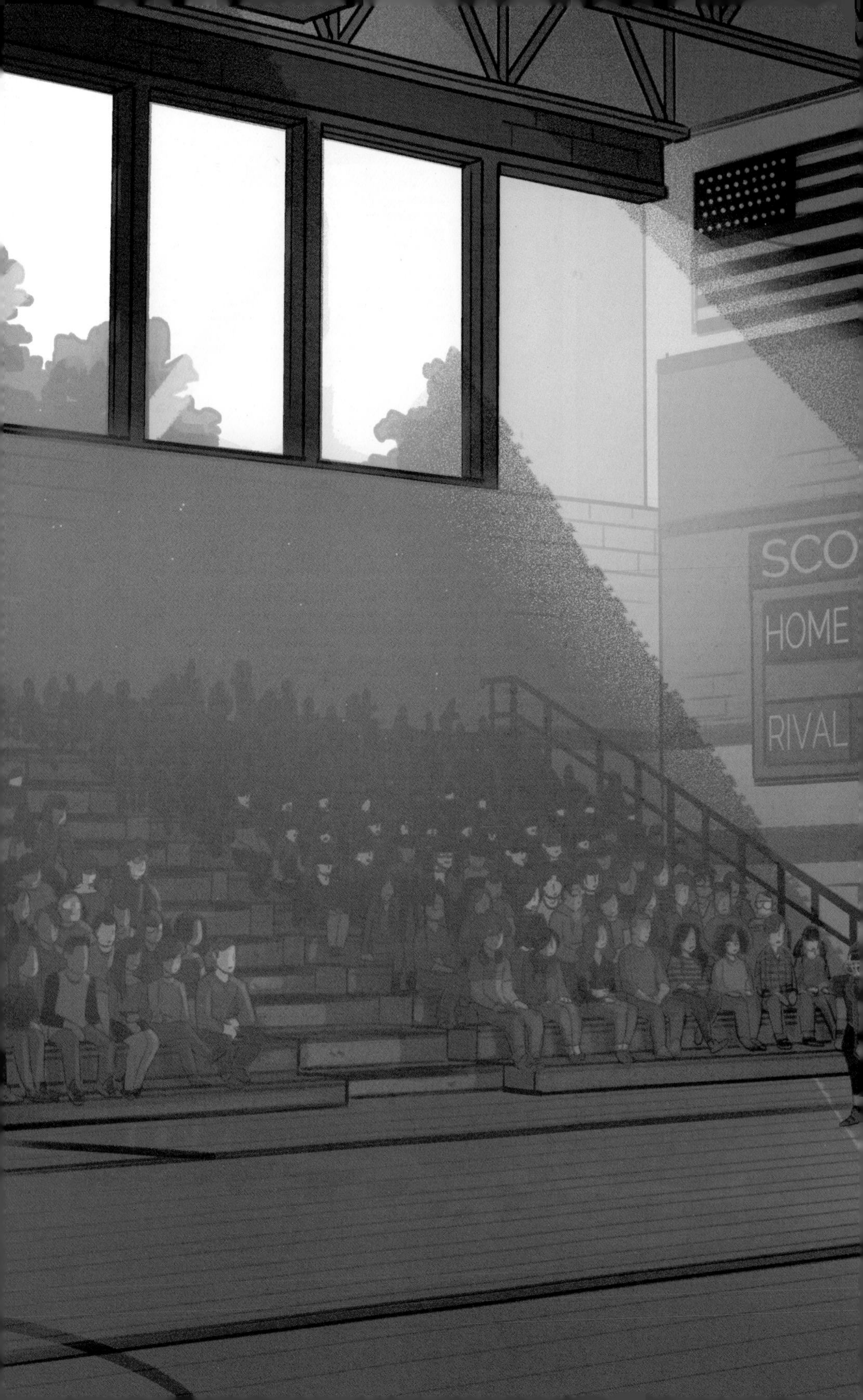
SCO
HOME
RIVAL

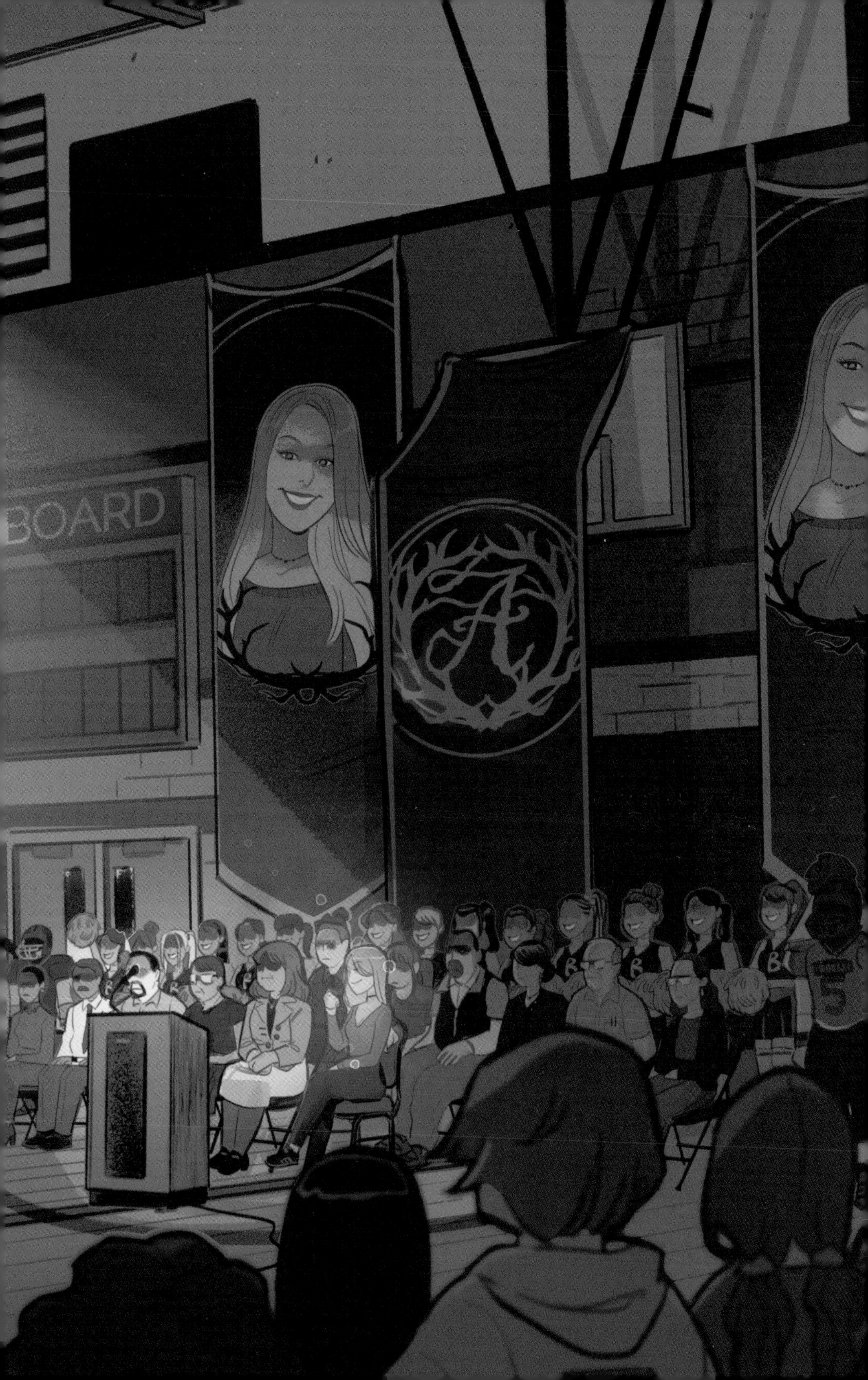
BOARD

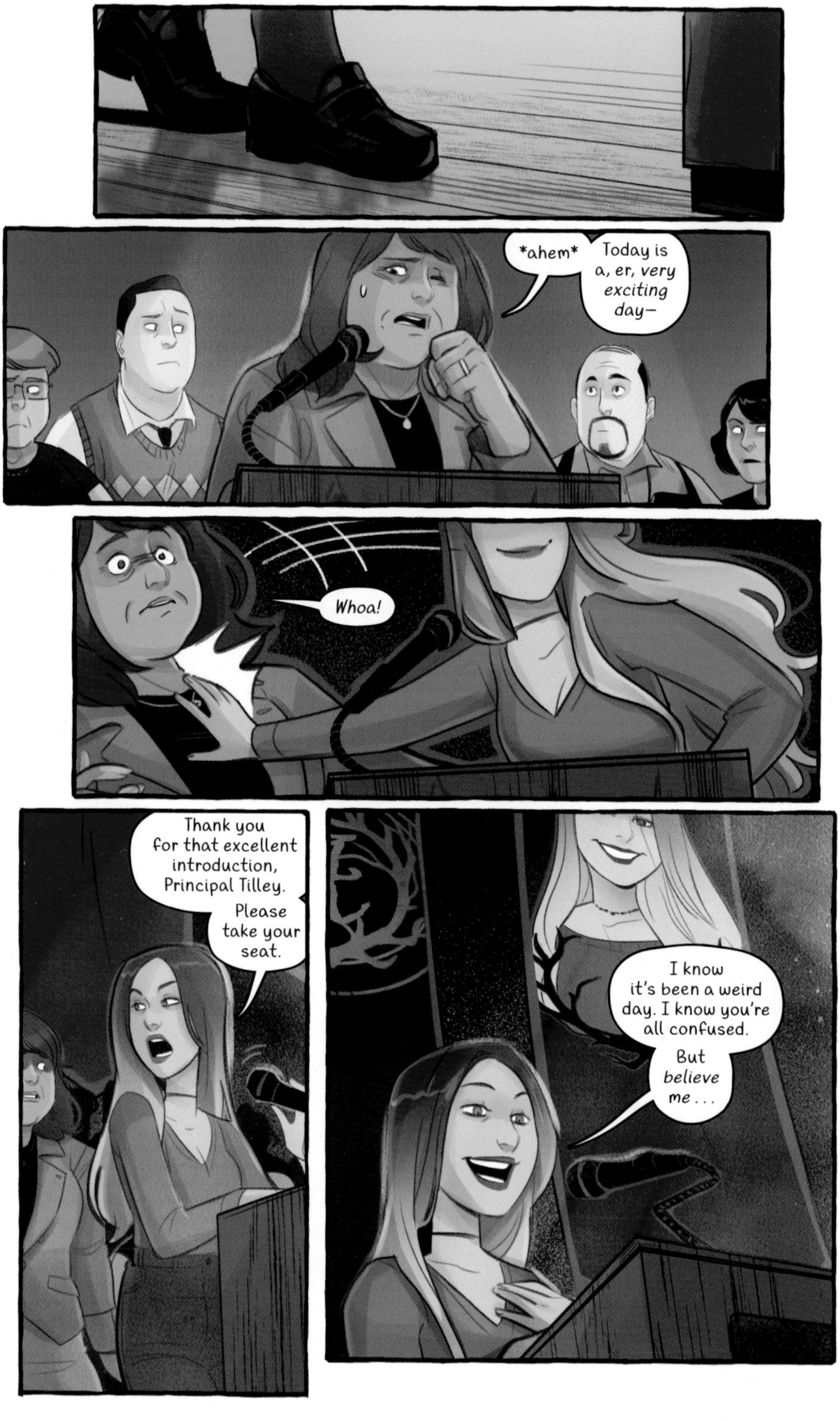
ahem
Today is a, er, very exciting day—
Whoa!
Thank you for that excellent introduction, Principal Tilley.
Please take your seat.
I know it's been a weird day. I know you're all confused.
But believe me . . .

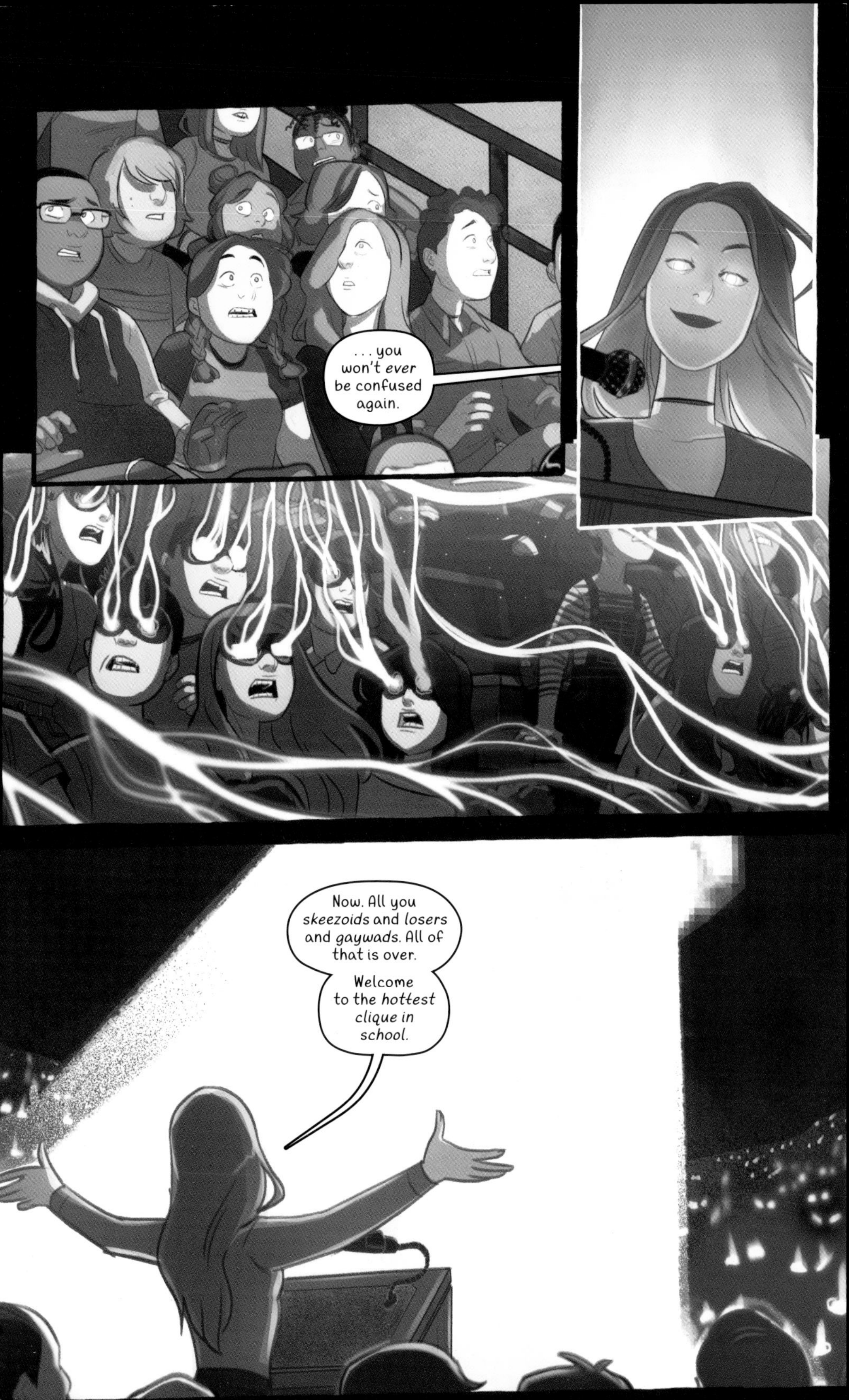
. . . you won't *ever* be confused again.
Now. All you *skeezoids* and *losers* and *gaywads*. All of that is over.
Welcome to the *hottest clique* in school.

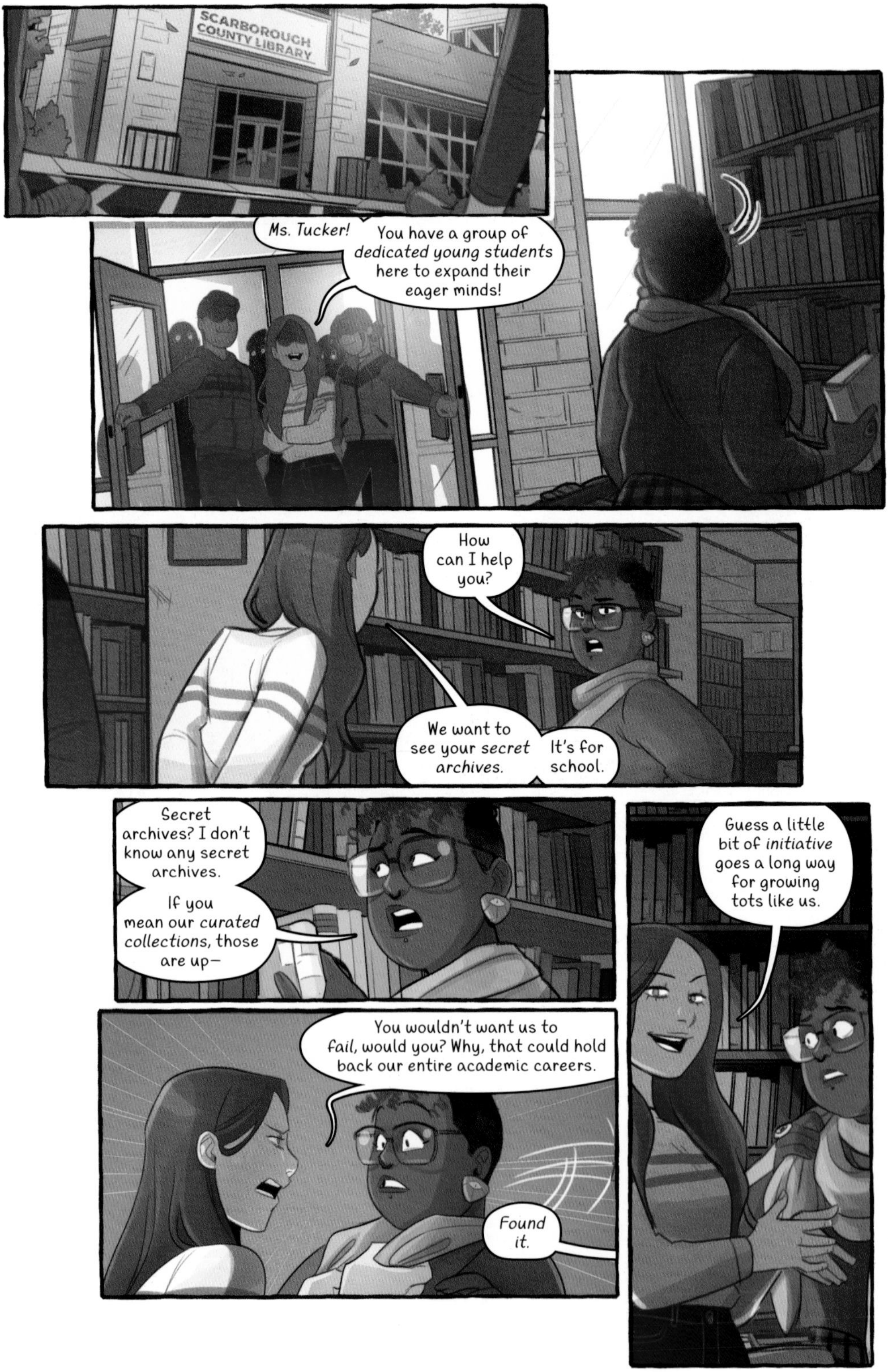
SCARBOROUGH COUNTY LIBRARY
Ms. Tucker!
You have a group of *dedicated young students* here to expand their eager minds!
How can I help you?
We want to see your *secret archives.*
It's for school.
Secret archives? I don't know any secret archives.
If you mean our *curated collections,* those are up—
You wouldn't want us to *fail,* would you? Why, that could hold back our entire academic careers.
Found it.
Guess a little bit of *initiative* goes a long way for growing tots like us.

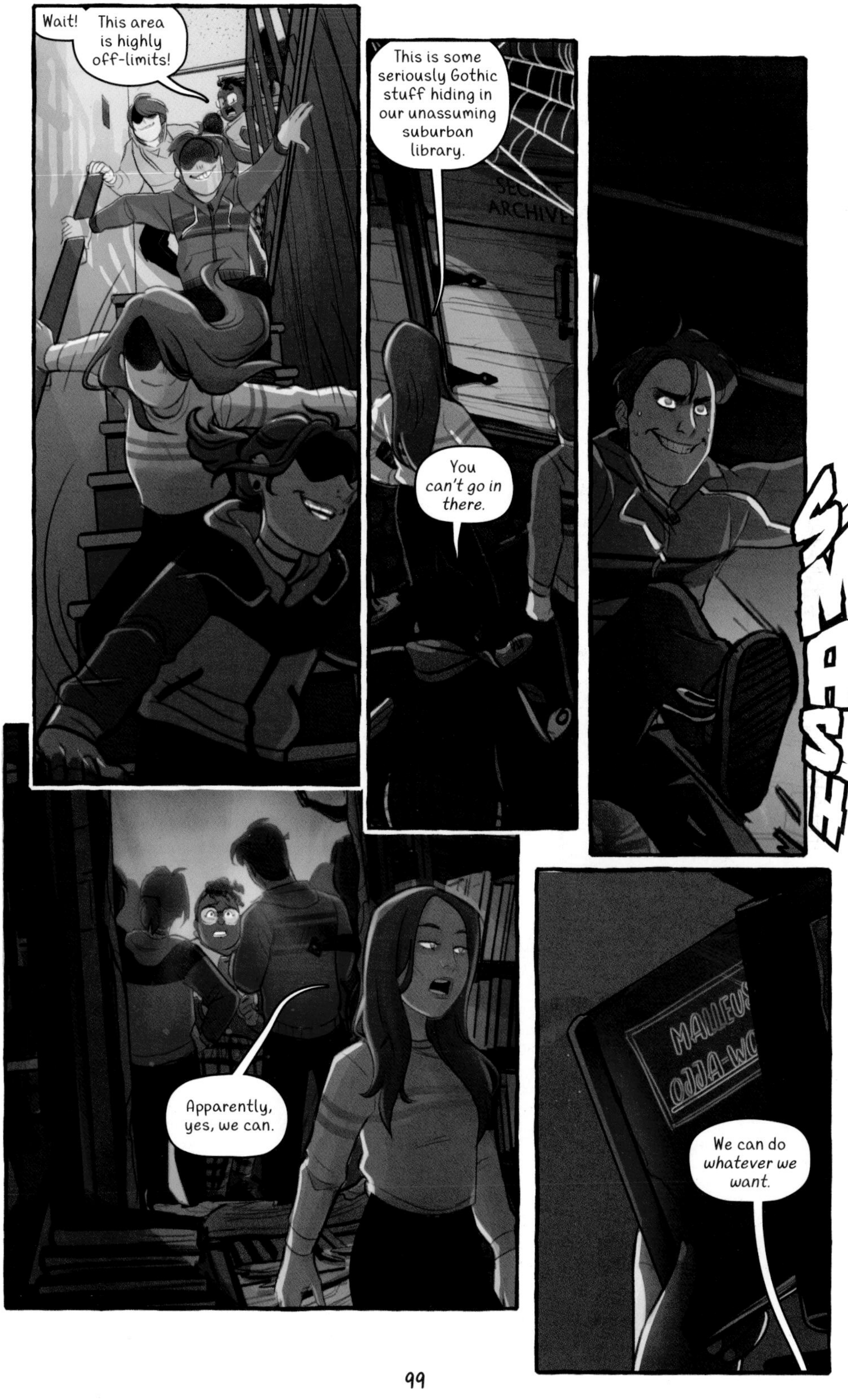
Wait!
This area is highly off-limits!
This is some seriously Gothic stuff hiding in our unassuming suburban library.
SECRET ARCHIVES
You can't go in there.
SMASH
Apparently, yes, we can.
We can do whatever we want.

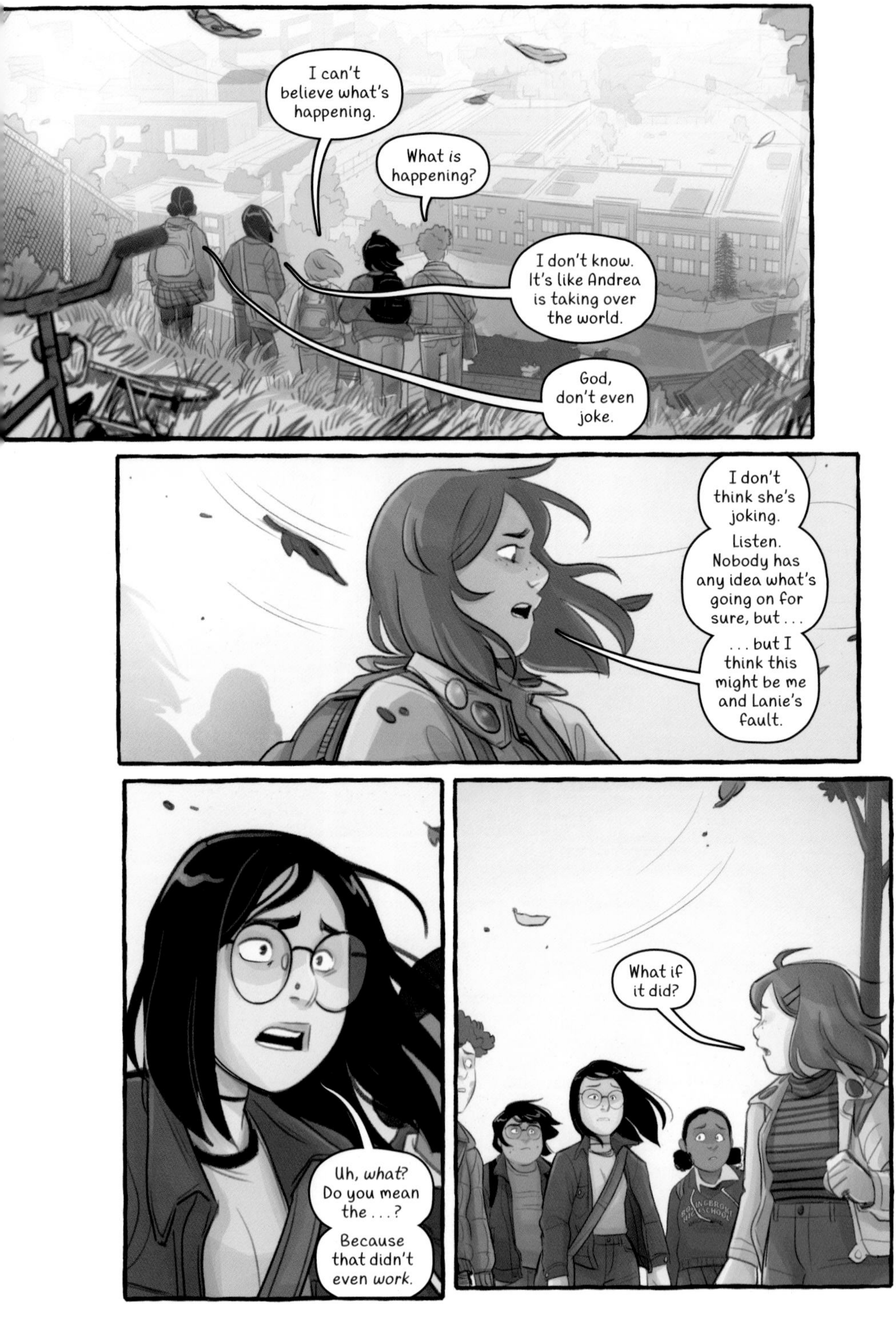
I can't believe what's happening.
What is happening?
I don't know. It's like Andrea is taking over the world.
God, don't even joke.
I don't think she's joking.
Listen. Nobody has any idea what's going on for sure, but . . .
. . . but I think this might be me and Lanie's fault.
Uh, *what?* Do you mean the . . . ?
Because that didn't even *work*.
What if it did?

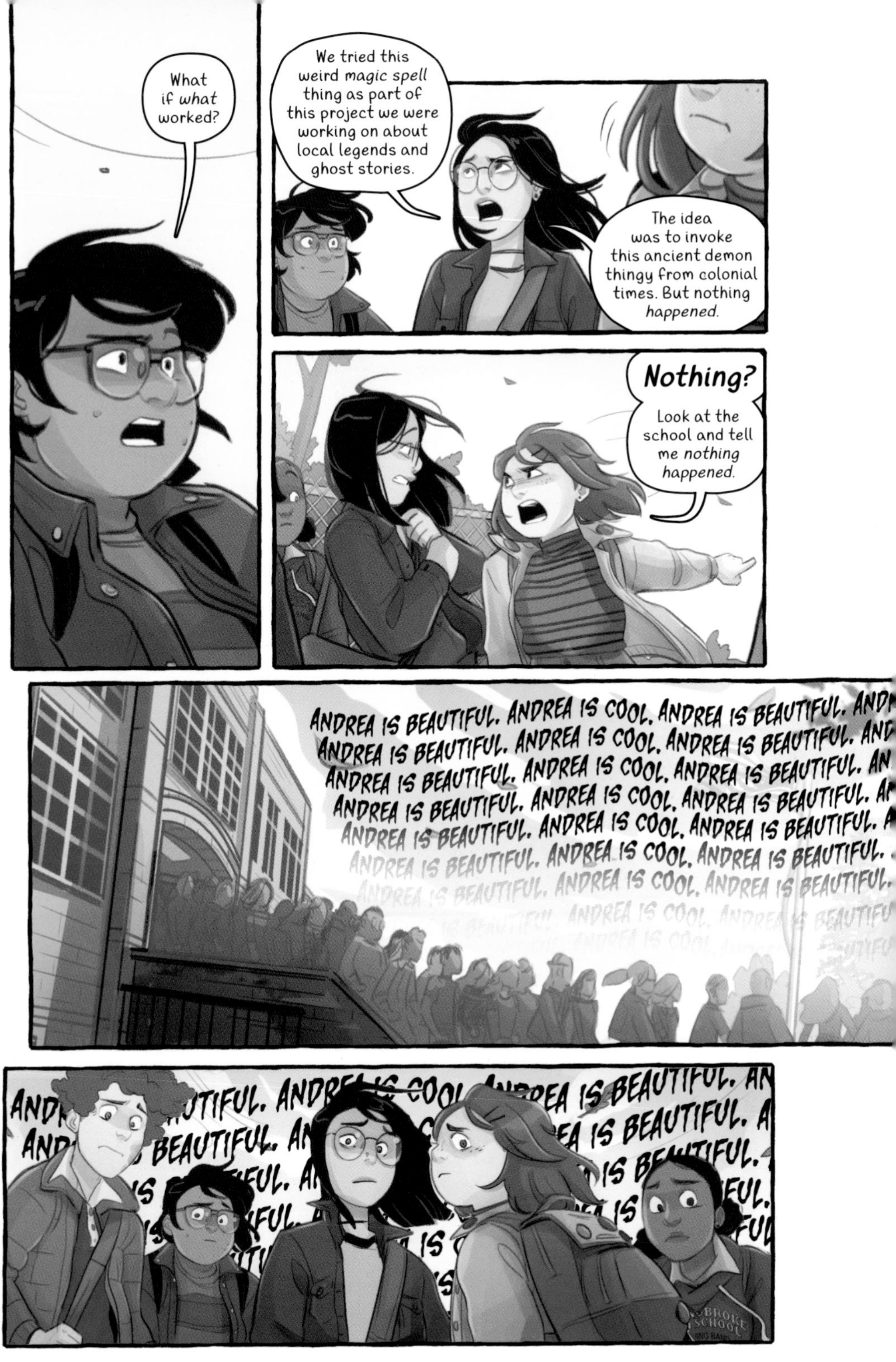
What if *what* worked?
We tried this weird *magic spell* thing as part of this project we were working on about local legends and ghost stories.
The idea was to invoke this ancient demon thingy from colonial times. But nothing *happened.*
Nothing?
Look at the school and tell me *nothing* happened.
ANDREA IS BEAUTIFUL. ANDREA IS COOL. ANDREA IS BEAUTIFUL.
ANDREA IS BEAUTIFUL. ANDREA IS COOL. ANDREA IS BEAUTIFUL.
ANDREA IS BEAUTIFUL. ANDREA IS COOL. ANDREA IS BEAUTIFUL.
ANDREA IS BEAUTIFUL. ANDREA IS COOL. ANDREA IS BEAUTIFUL.
ANDREA IS BEAUTIFUL. ANDREA IS COOL. ANDREA IS BEAUTIFUL.
ANDREA IS BEAUTIFUL. ANDREA IS COOL. ANDREA IS BEAUTIFUL.
ANDREA IS BEAUTIFUL. ANDREA IS COOL. ANDREA IS BEAUTIFUL.
ANDREA IS COOL.

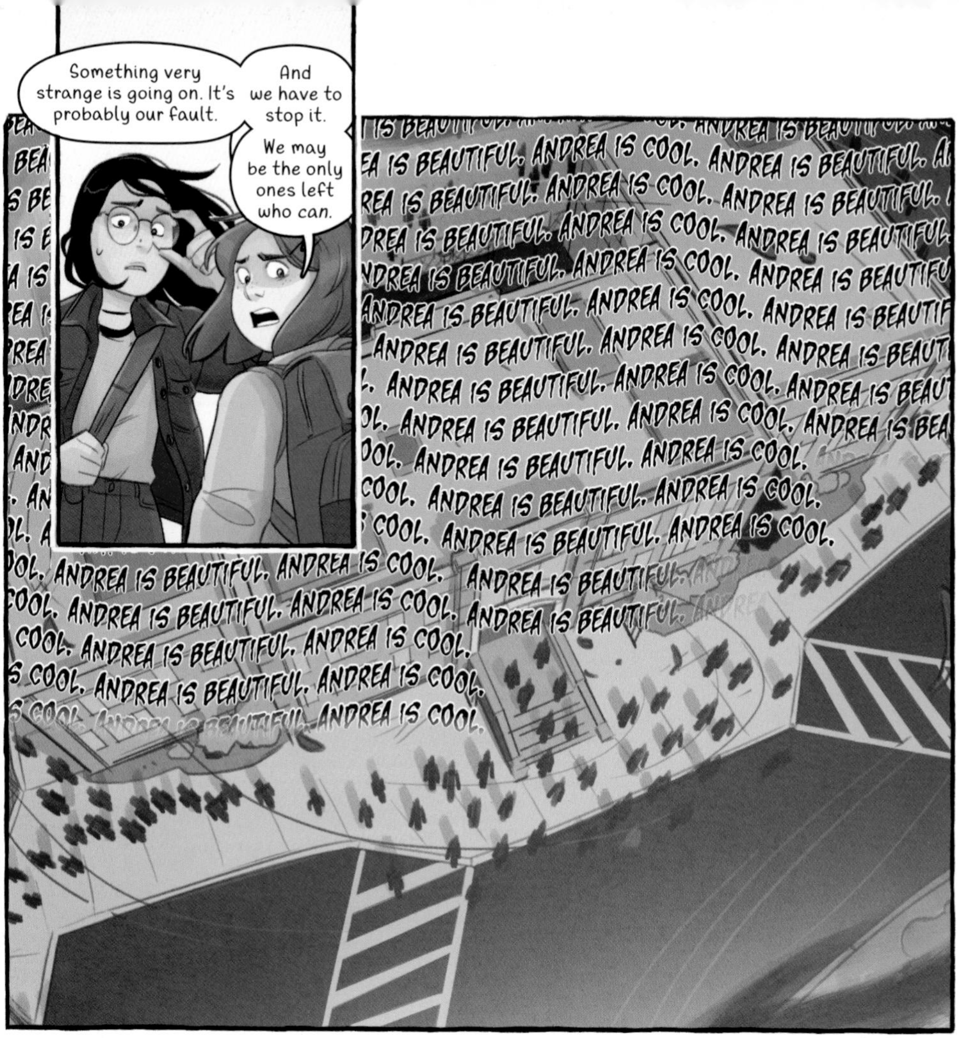
Something very strange is going on. It's probably our fault.
And we have to stop it.
We may be the only ones left who can.
ANDREA IS BEAUTIFUL. ANDREA IS COOL.

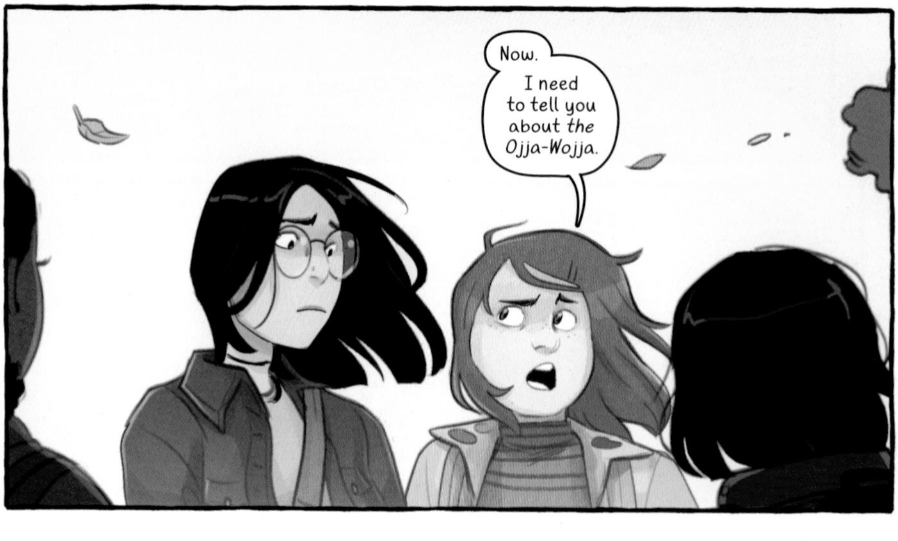
Now. I need to tell you about *the* Ojja-Wojja.

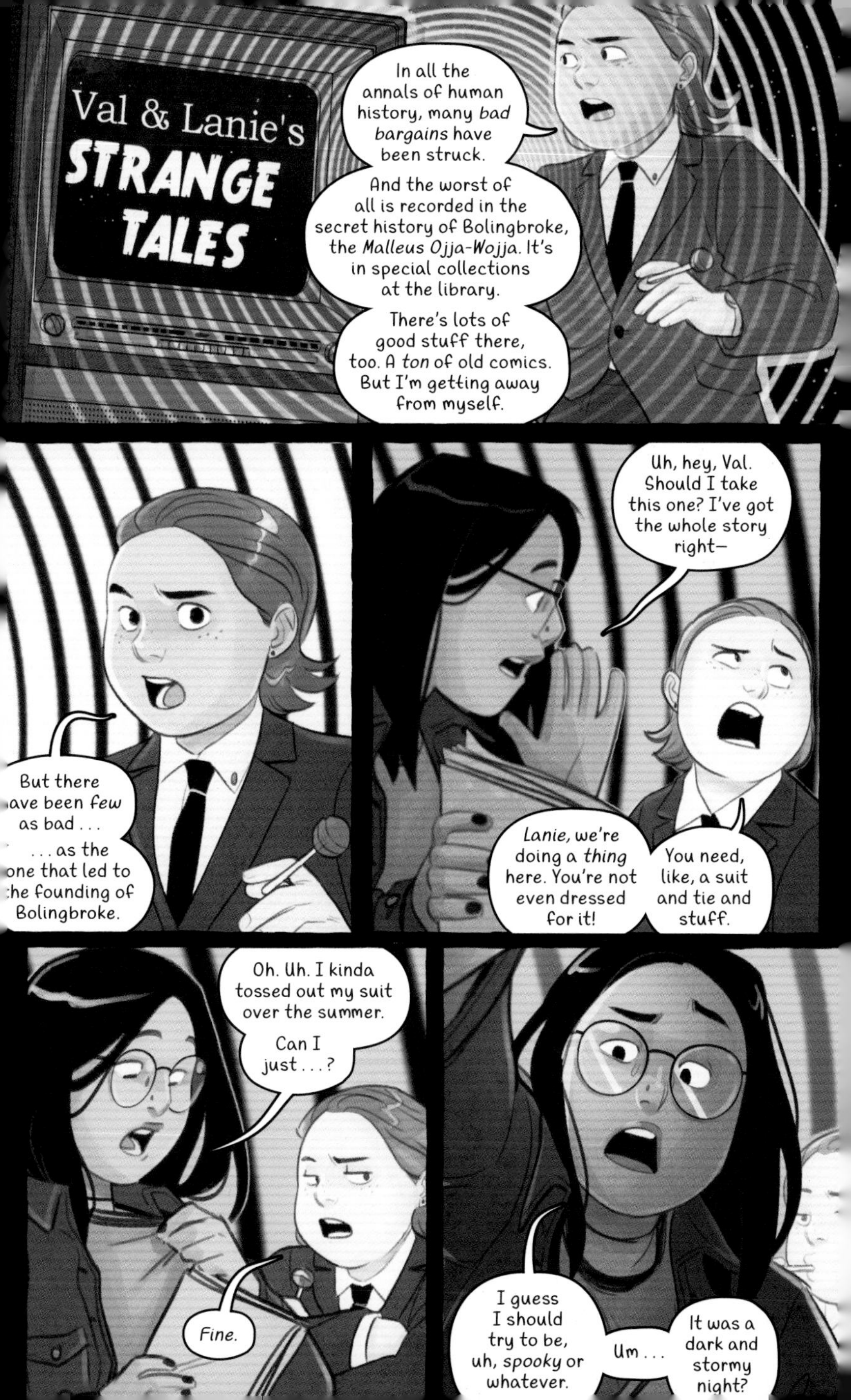
Val & Lanie's
STRANGE TALES
In all the annals of human history, many *bad bargains* have been struck.
And the worst of all is recorded in the secret history of Bolingbroke, the *Malleus Ojja-Wojja*. It's in special collections at the library.
There's lots of good stuff there, too. A *ton* of old comics. But I'm getting away from myself.
But there ave been *few* as bad . . .
. . . as the one that led to he founding of Bolingbroke.
Uh, hey, Val. Should I take this one? I've got the whole story right—
Lanie, we're doing a thing here. You're not even dressed for it!
You need, like, a suit and tie and stuff.
Oh. Uh. I kinda tossed out my suit over the summer.
Can I just . . . ?
Fine.
I guess I should try to be, uh, *spooky* or whatever.
Um . . .
It was a dark and stormy night?

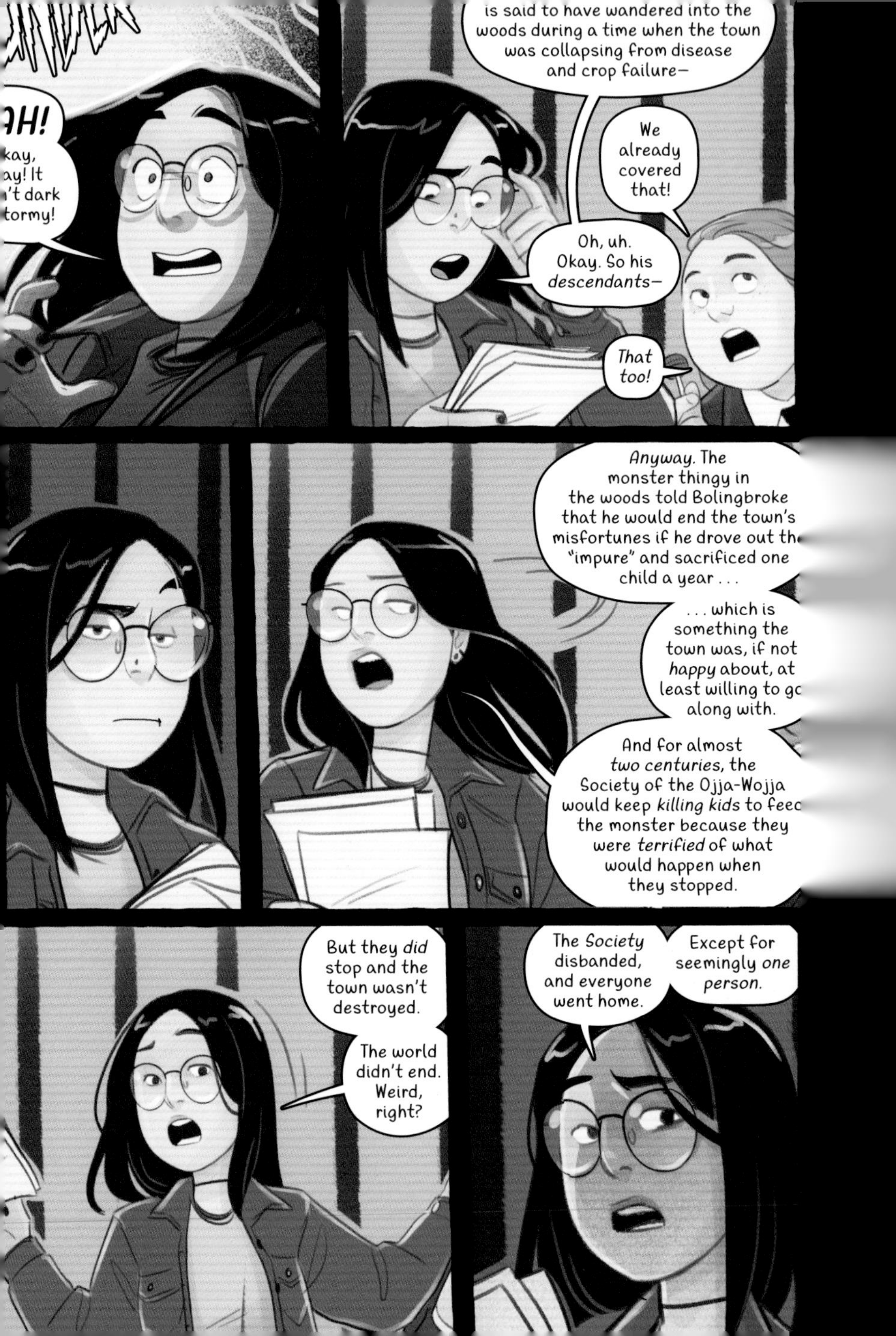

AH!
kay,
ay! It
n't dark
tormy!
is said to have wandered into the woods during a time when the town was collapsing from disease and crop failure—
We already covered that!
Oh, uh. Okay. So his *descendants*—
That too!
Anyway. The monster thingy in the woods told Bolingbroke that he would end the town's misfortunes if he drove out the "impure" and sacrificed one child a year . . .
. . . which is something the town was, if not *happy* about, at least willing to go along with.
And for almost *two centuries*, the Society of the Ojja-Wojja would keep *killing kids* to feed the monster because they were *terrified* of what would happen when they stopped.
But they *did* stop and the town wasn't destroyed.
The world didn't end. Weird, right?
The *Society* disbanded, and everyone went home.
Except for seemingly *one person.*

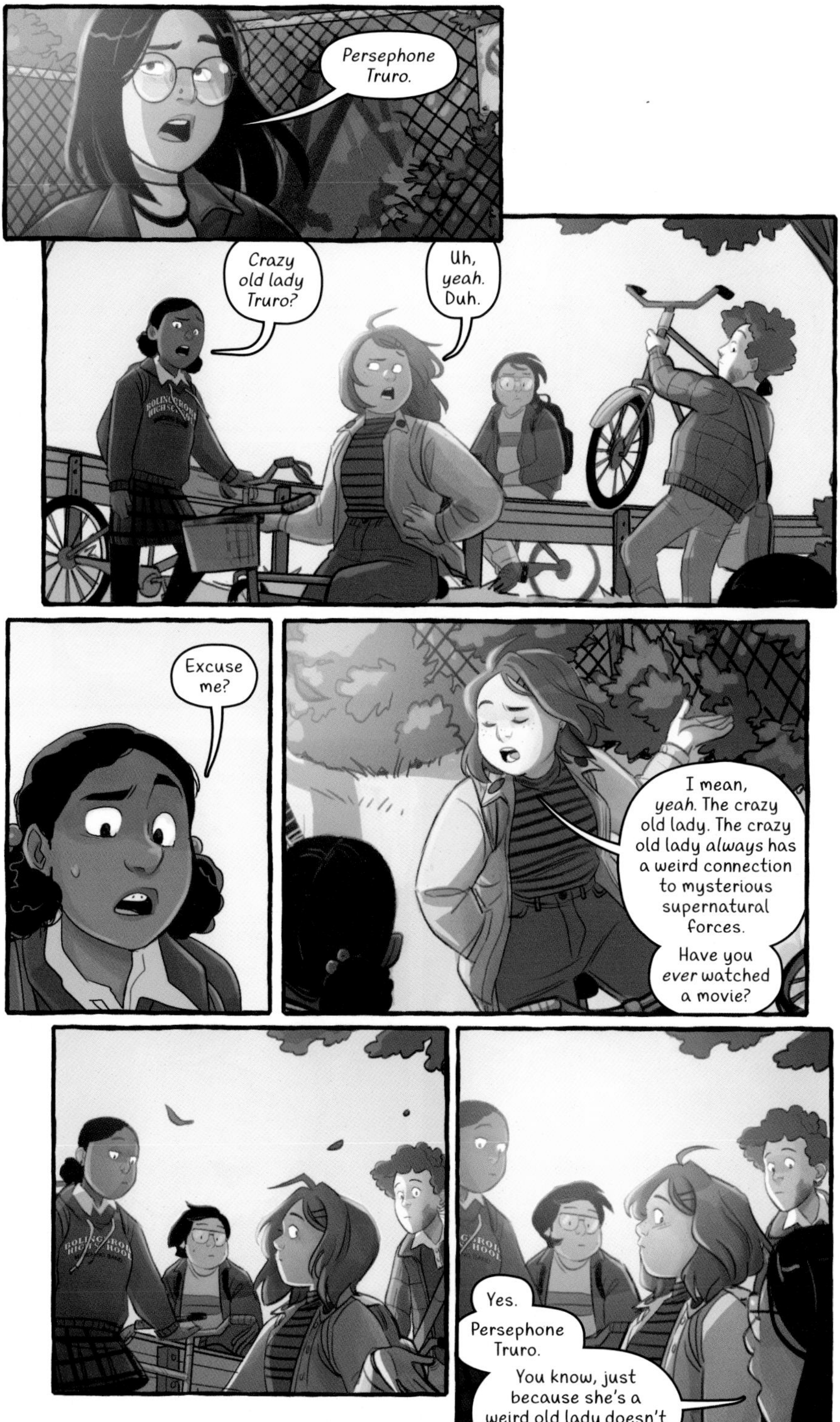
Persephone Truro.
Crazy old lady Truro?
Uh, yeah. Duh.
Excuse me?
I mean, *yeah*. The crazy old lady. The crazy old lady *always* has a weird connection to mysterious supernatural forces.
Have you *ever* watched a movie?
Yes.
Persephone Truro.
You know, just because she's a weird old lady doesn't make her *evil*, Val.

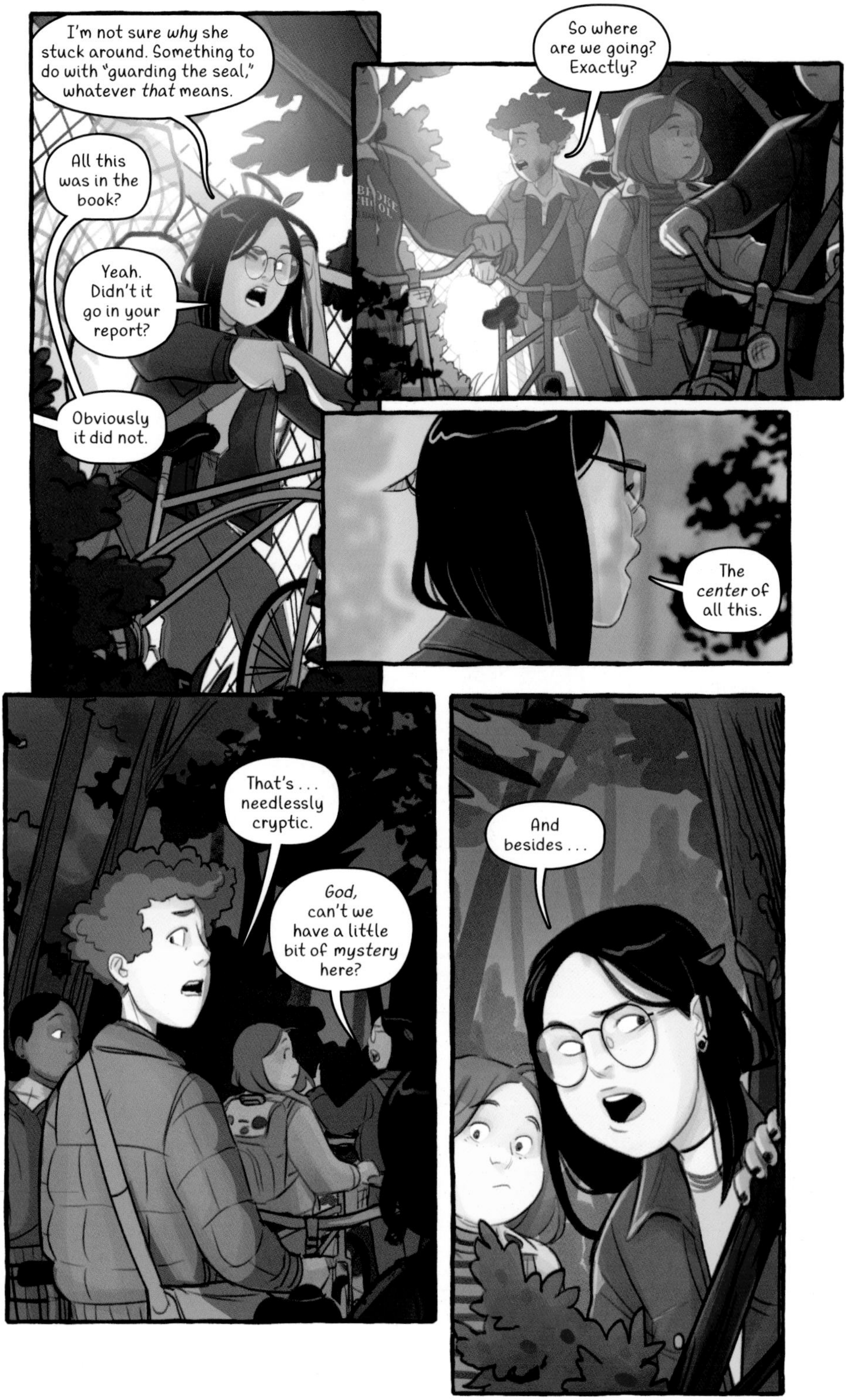
I'm not sure *why* she stuck around. Something to do with "guarding the seal," whatever *that* means.
All this was in the book?
Yeah. Didn't it go in your report?
Obviously it did not.
So where are we going? Exactly?
The *center* of all this.
That's . . . needlessly cryptic.
God, can't we have a little bit of *mystery* here?
And besides . . .

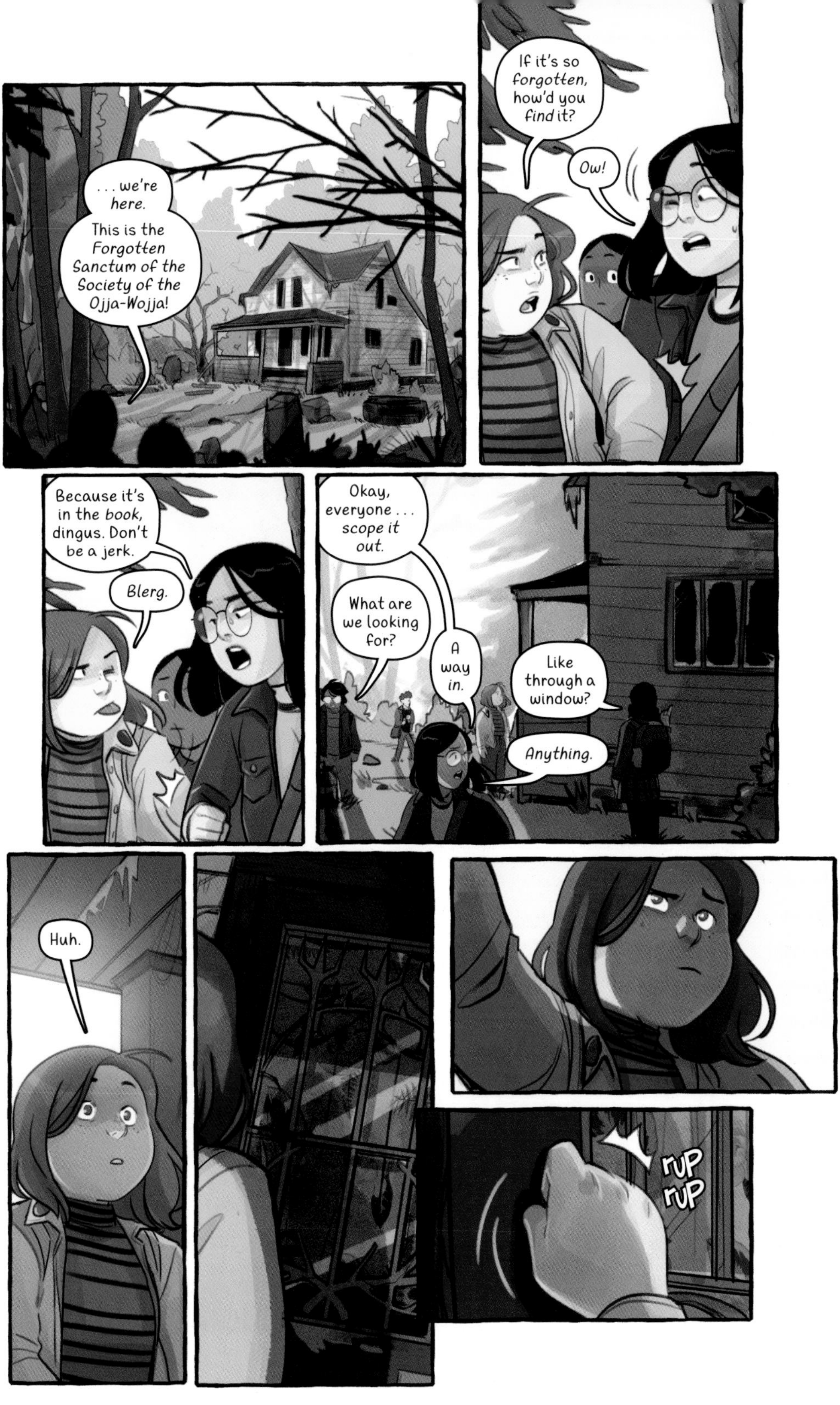

. . . we're here.
This is the Forgotten Sanctum of the Society of the Ojja-Wojja!
If it's so forgotten, how'd you find it?
Ow!
Because it's in the book, dingus. Don't be a jerk.
Blerg.
Okay, everyone . . . scope it out.
What are we looking for?
A way in.
Like through a window?
Anything.
Huh.
rup rup

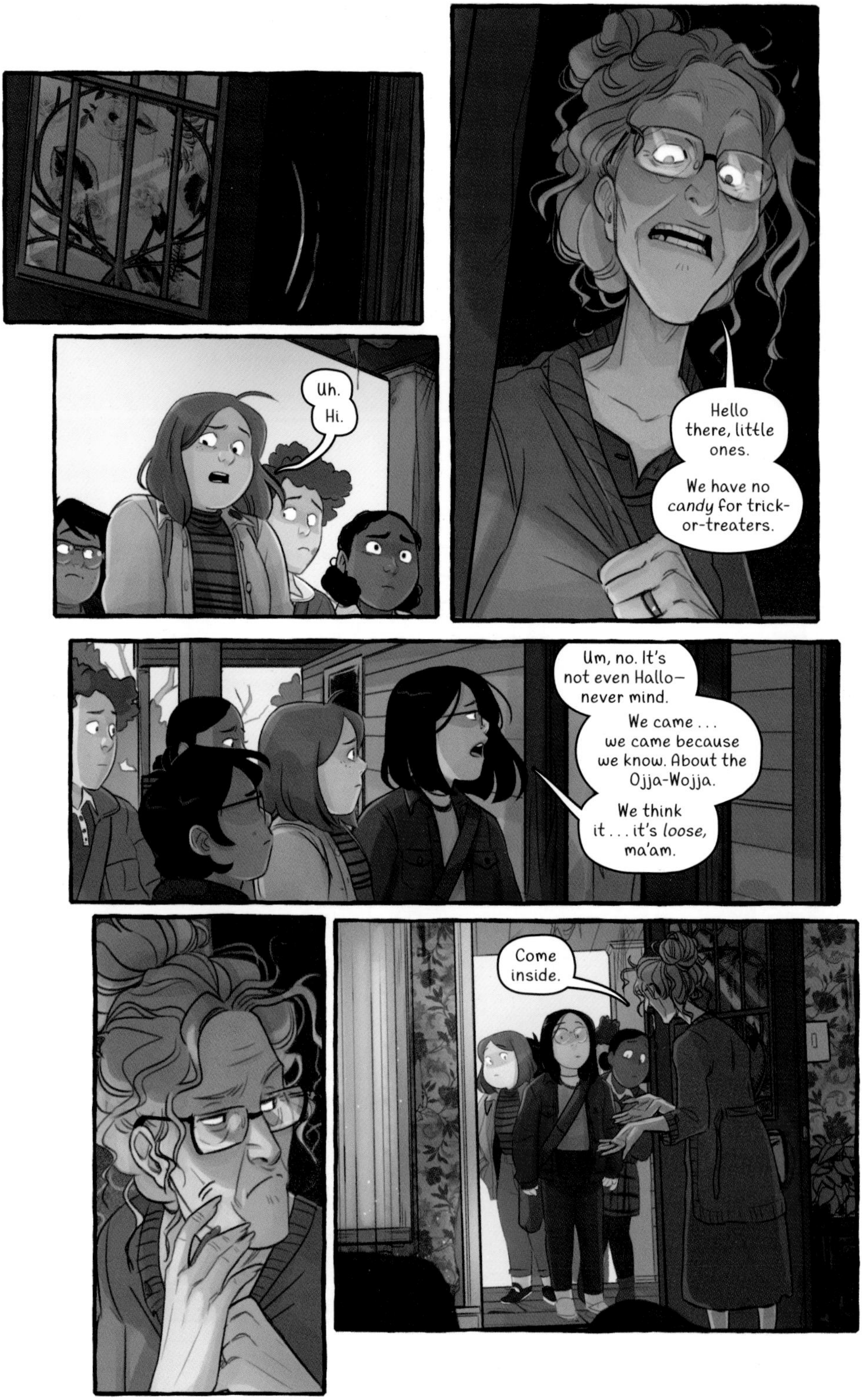
Hello there, little ones.
We have no *candy* for trick-or-treaters.
Uh. Hi.
Um, no. It's not even Hallo— never mind.
We came . . . we came because we know. About the Ojja-Wojja.
We think it . . . it's *loose,* ma'am.
Come inside.

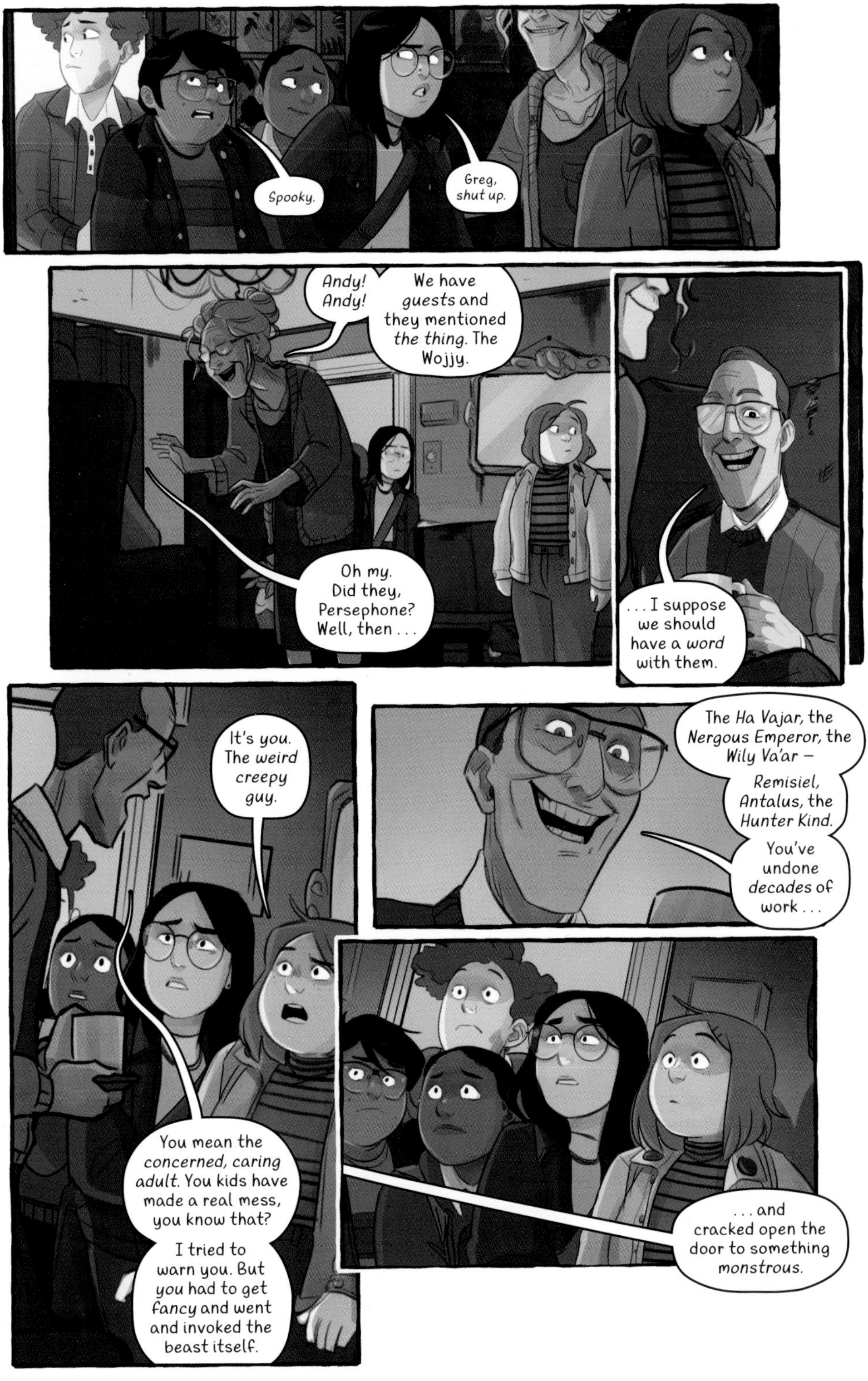
Spooky.
Greg, shut up.
Andy! Andy!
We have guests and they mentioned the thing. The Wojjy.
Oh my. Did they, Persephone? Well, then . . .
. . . I suppose we should have a word with them.
It's you. The weird creepy guy.
You mean the concerned, caring adult. You kids have made a real mess, you know that?
I tried to warn you. But you had to get fancy and went and invoked the beast itself.
The Ha Vajar, the Nergous Emperor, the Wily Va'ar —
Remisiel, Antalus, the Hunter Kind.
You've undone decades of work . . .
. . . and cracked open the door to something monstrous.

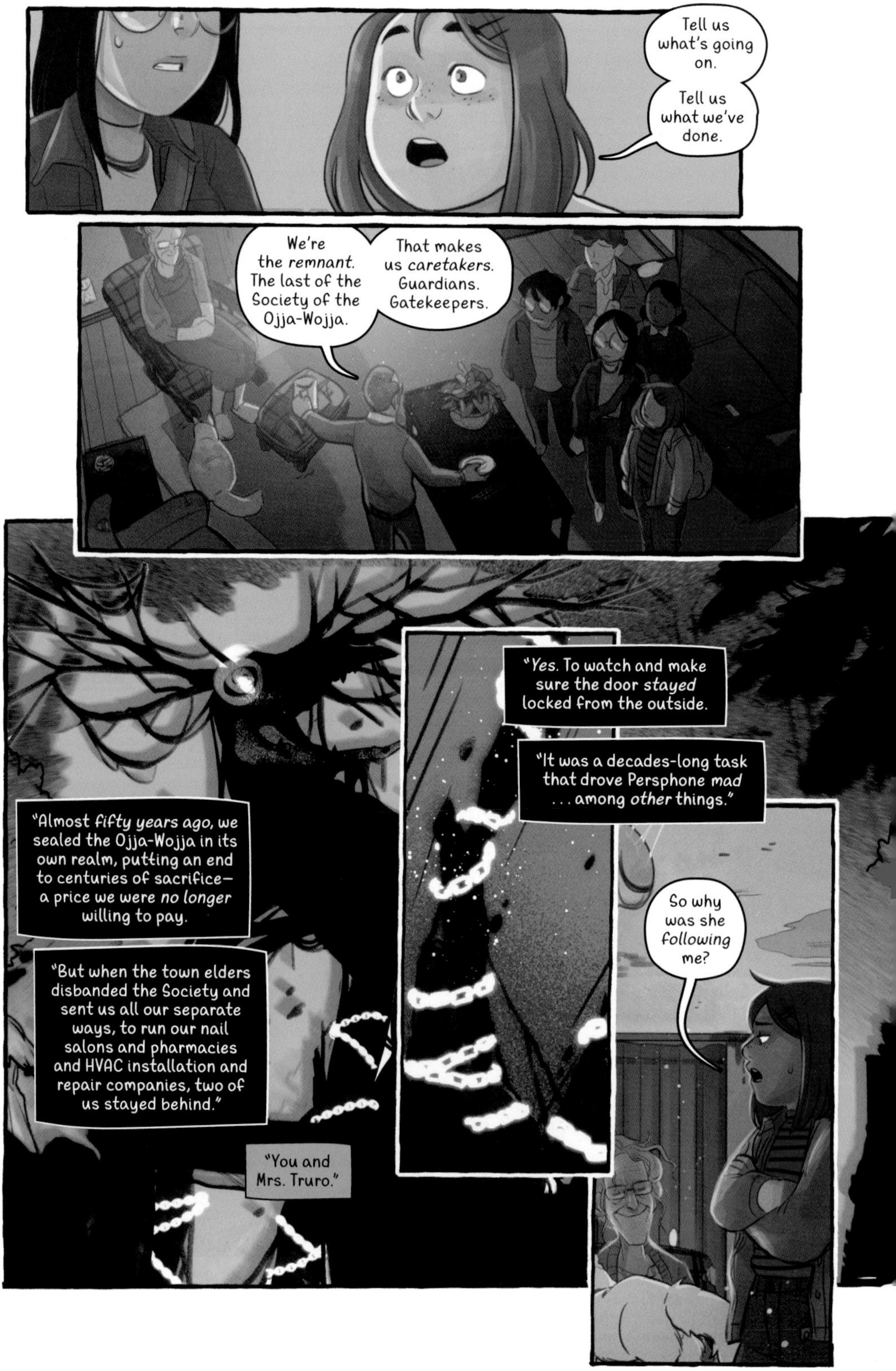
Tell us what's going on.
Tell us what we've done.
We're the *remnant.* The last of the Society of the Ojja-Wojja.
That makes us *caretakers.* Guardians. Gatekeepers.
"Almost *fifty years ago,* we sealed the Ojja-Wojja in its own realm, putting an end to centuries of sacrifice—a price we were *no longer* willing to pay.
"But when the town elders disbanded the Society and sent us all our separate ways, to run our nail salons and pharmacies and HVAC installation and repair companies, two of us stayed behind."
"You and Mrs. Truro."
"*Yes.* To watch and make sure the door *stayed* locked from the outside.
"It was a decades-long task that drove Persphone *mad* . . . among *other* things."
So why was she *following* me?

I wasn't. I was waiting for the Rider.

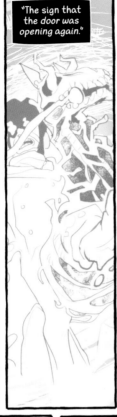

"The sign that the *door was opening again.*"

I *knew* we weren't seeing things.

So the *only* reason the Rider appeared was because the... Ojja-Wojja was *already* opening the door to our plane of existence?

That's right.

Soooo the Rider is a *pan-dimensional being* from another universe who serves as the herald of an alien monster bent on conquering all of space and time?

No. The Rider is a ghost. But he's only visible when the, er, "veil between worlds" is weak. I usually just call it "the gap."

I hope they have a *better selection* than the store. Get it?

The... store? Like... the Gap?

Funny joke, son. But the gap is serious business.

It's either narrow or it's wide. Wide enough, and things start busting through. And *you guys* had to go ahead and wake the old thing up *right* when the gap was at its widest.

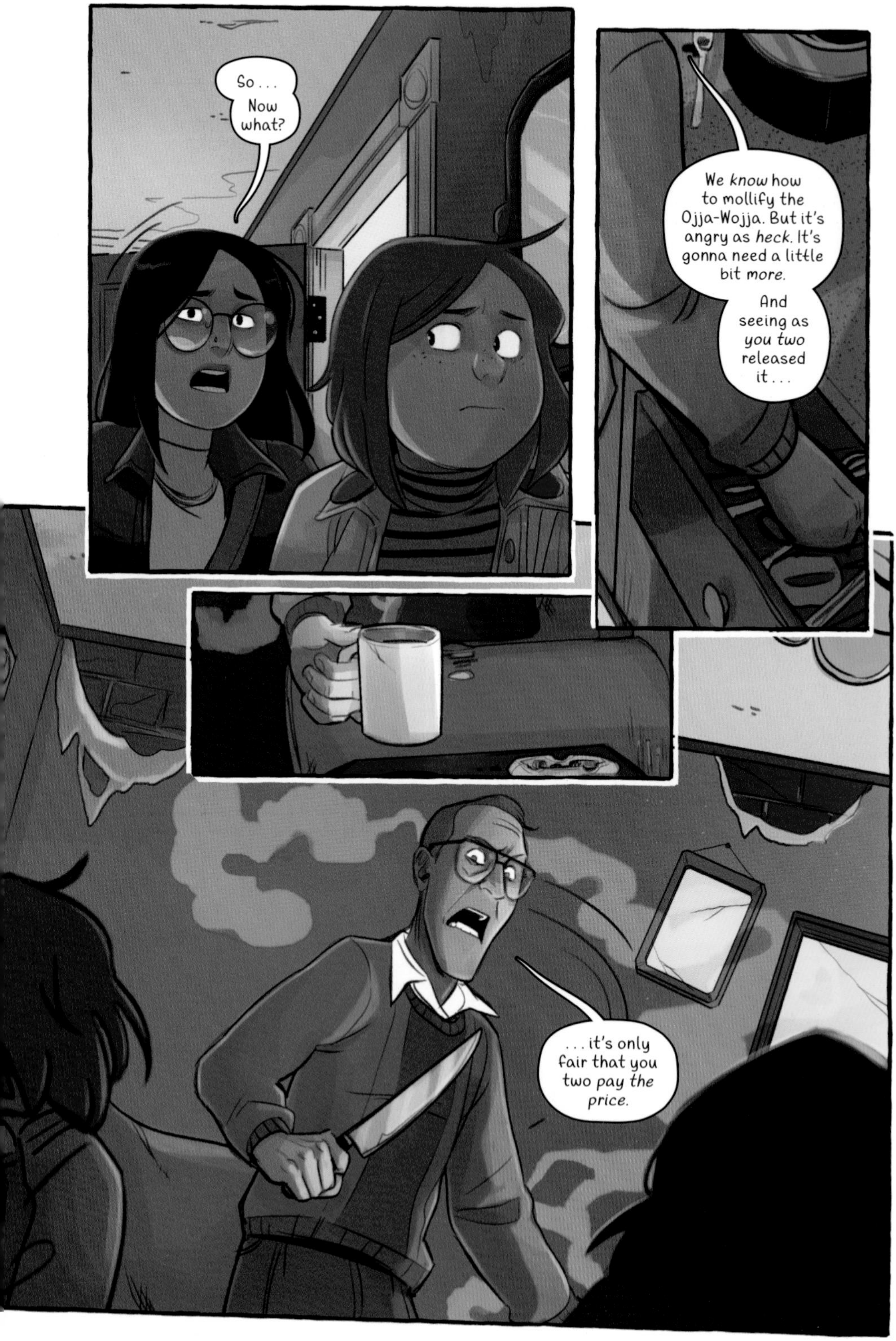
So . . . Now what?
We *know* how to mollify the Ojja-Wojja. But it's angry as *heck*. It's gonna need a little bit *more*.
And seeing as *you two* released it . . .
. . . it's only fair that you two *pay the price*.

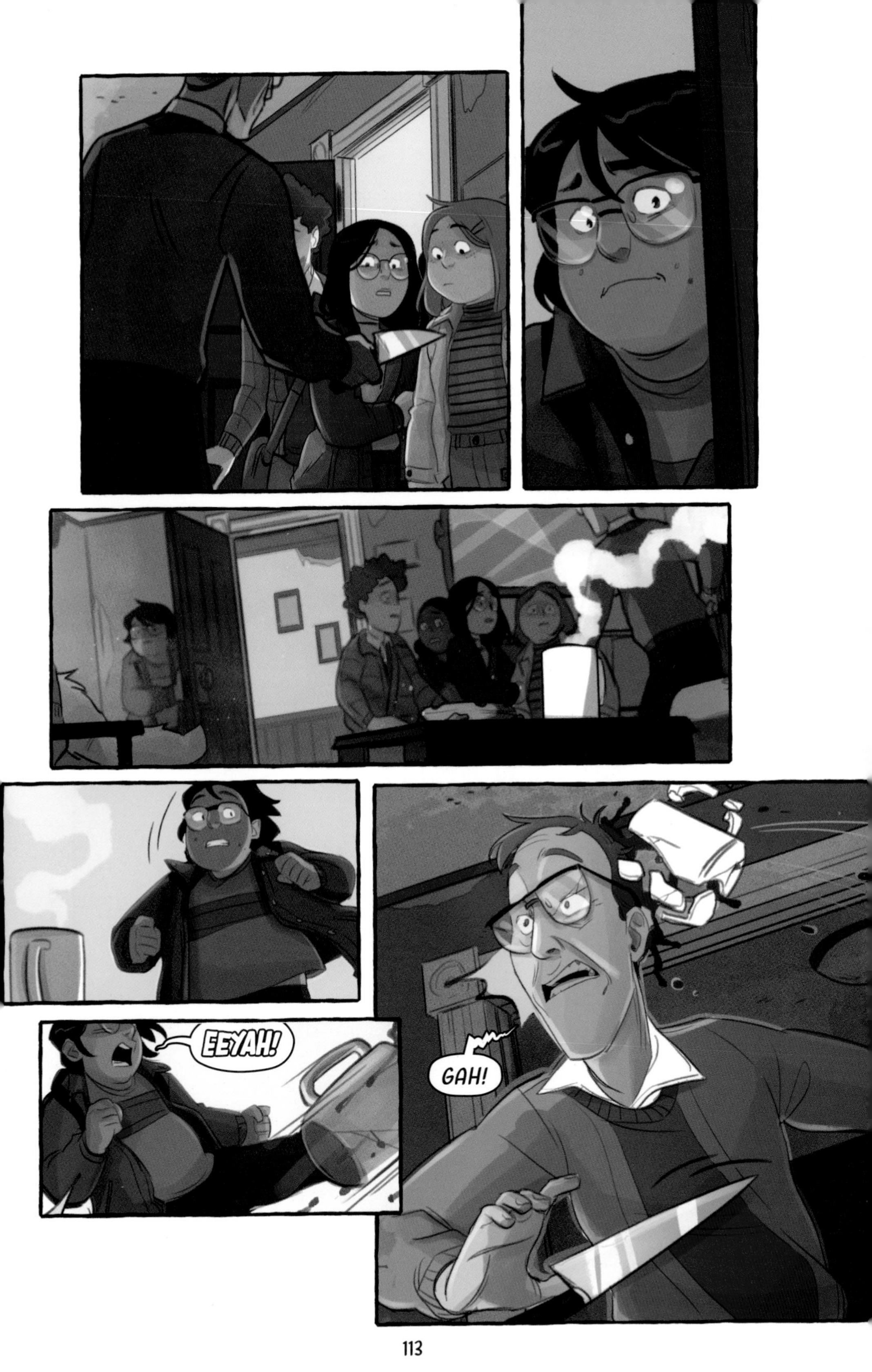
EEYAH!
GAH!

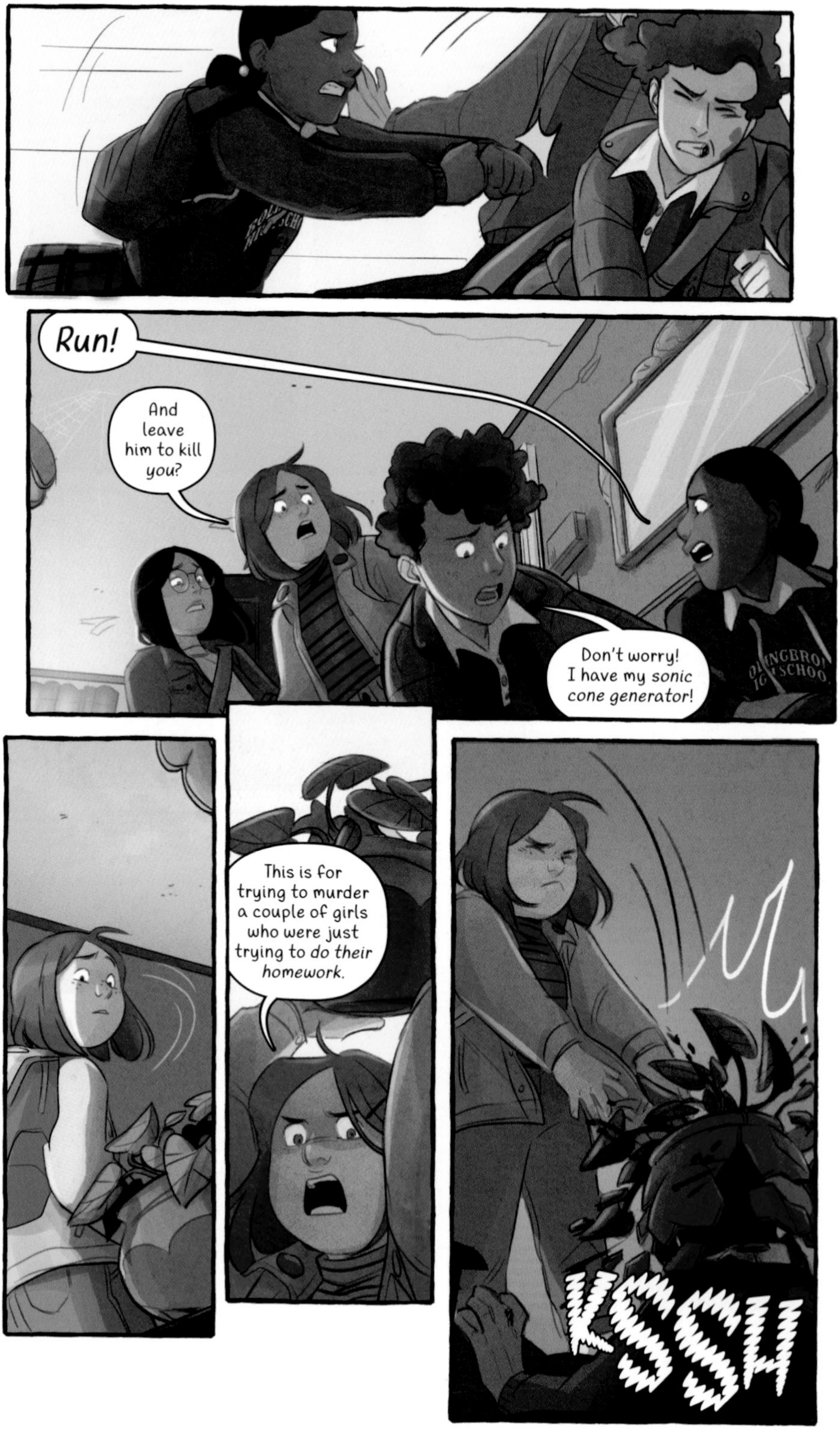

Run!
And leave him to kill you?
Don't worry! I have my sonic cone generator!
This is for trying to murder a couple of girls who were just trying to do their homework.
KSSH

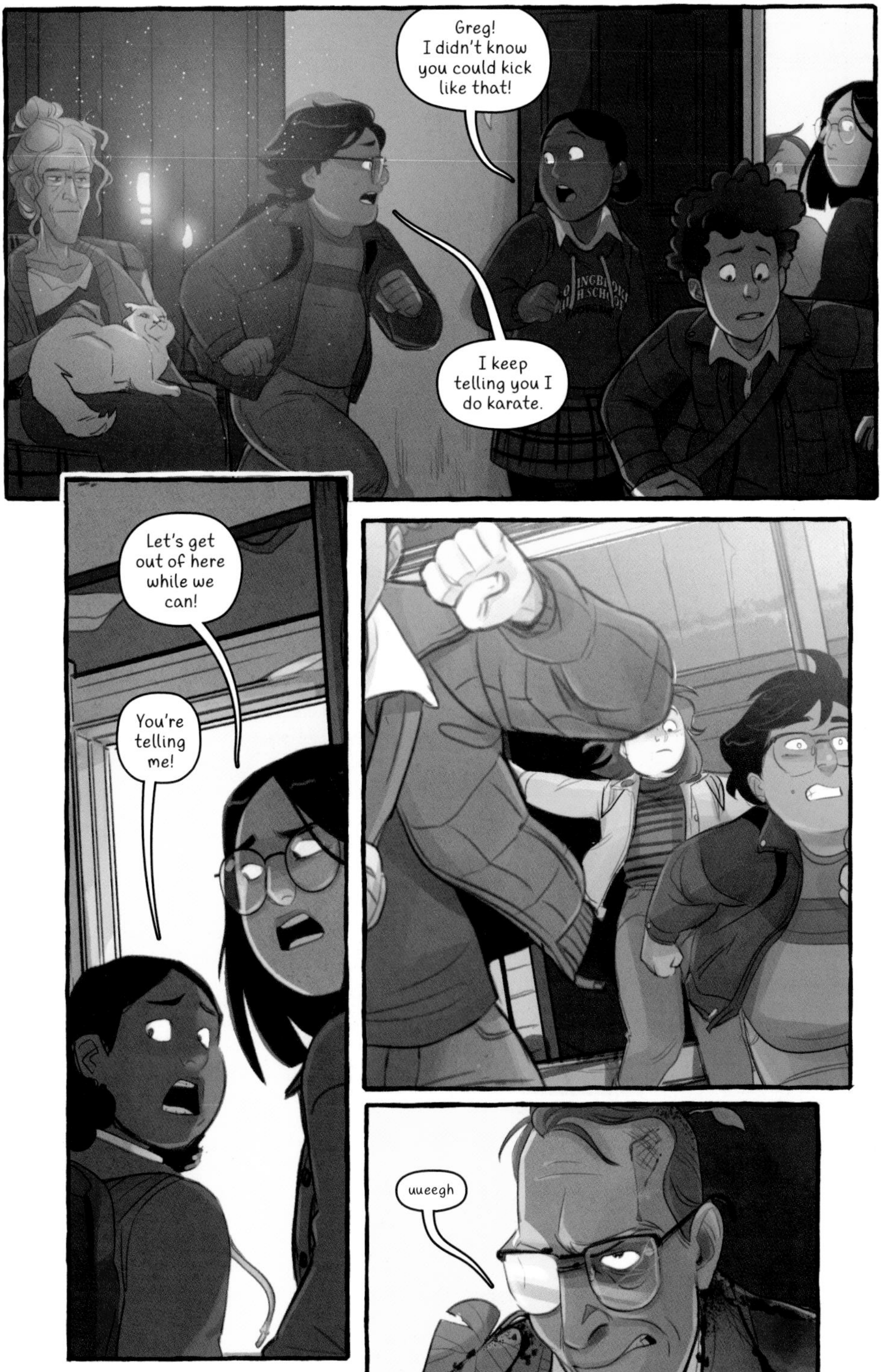
Greg! I didn't know you could kick like that!
I keep telling you I do karate.
Let's get out of here while we can!
You're telling me!
uueegh

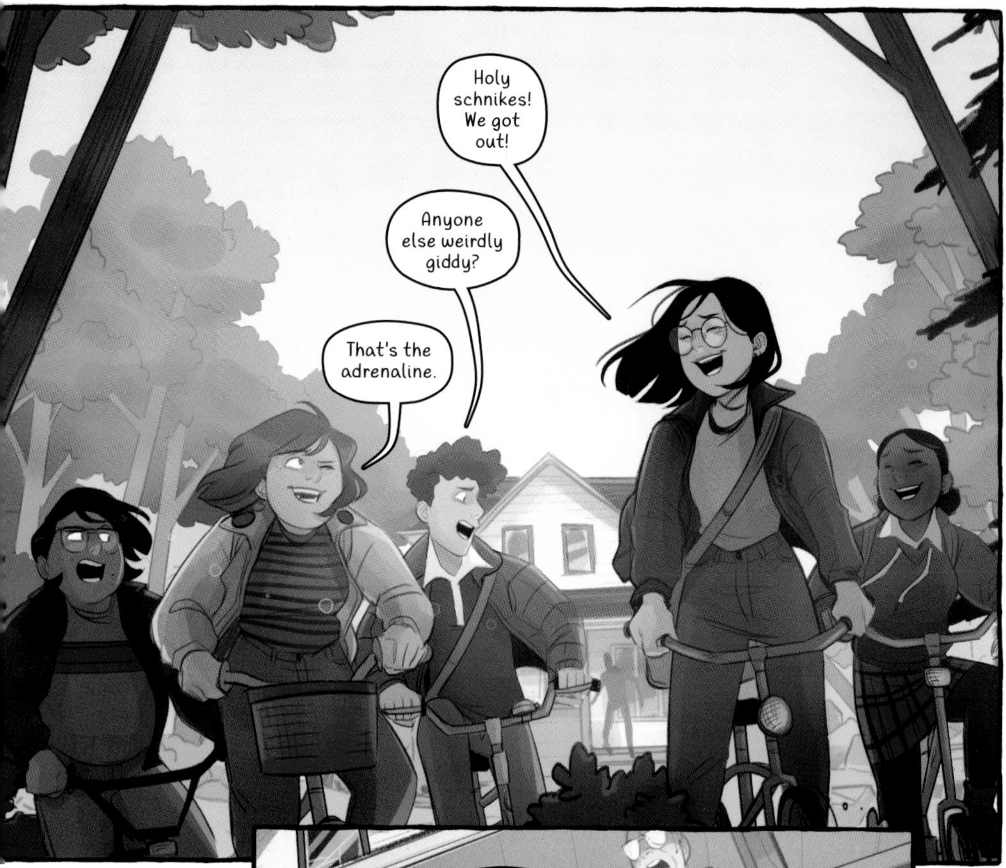
Holy schnikes! We got out!
Anyone else weirdly giddy?
That's the adrenaline.

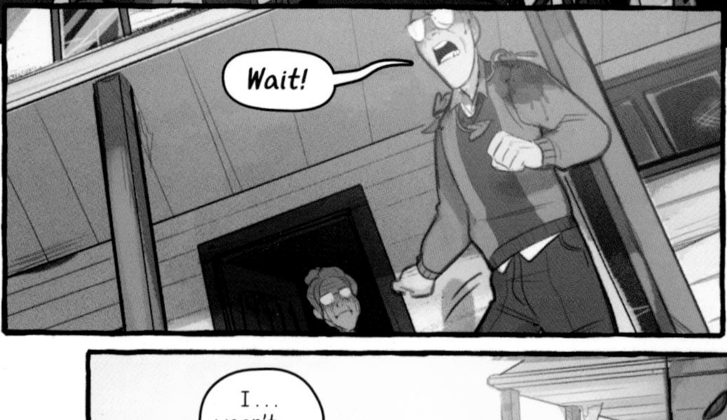
Wait!

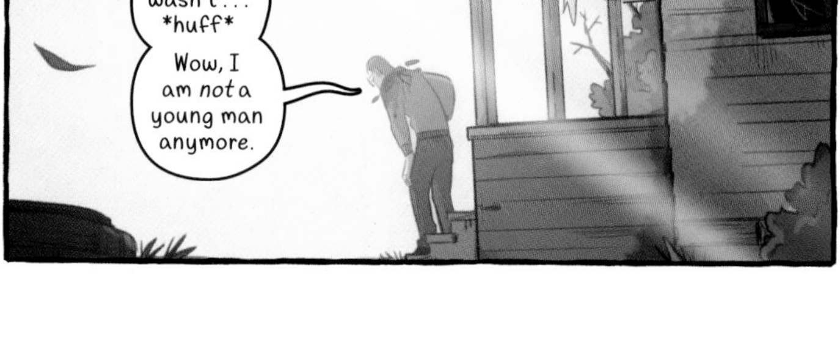
I... wasn't... *huff*
Wow, I am *not* a young man anymore.

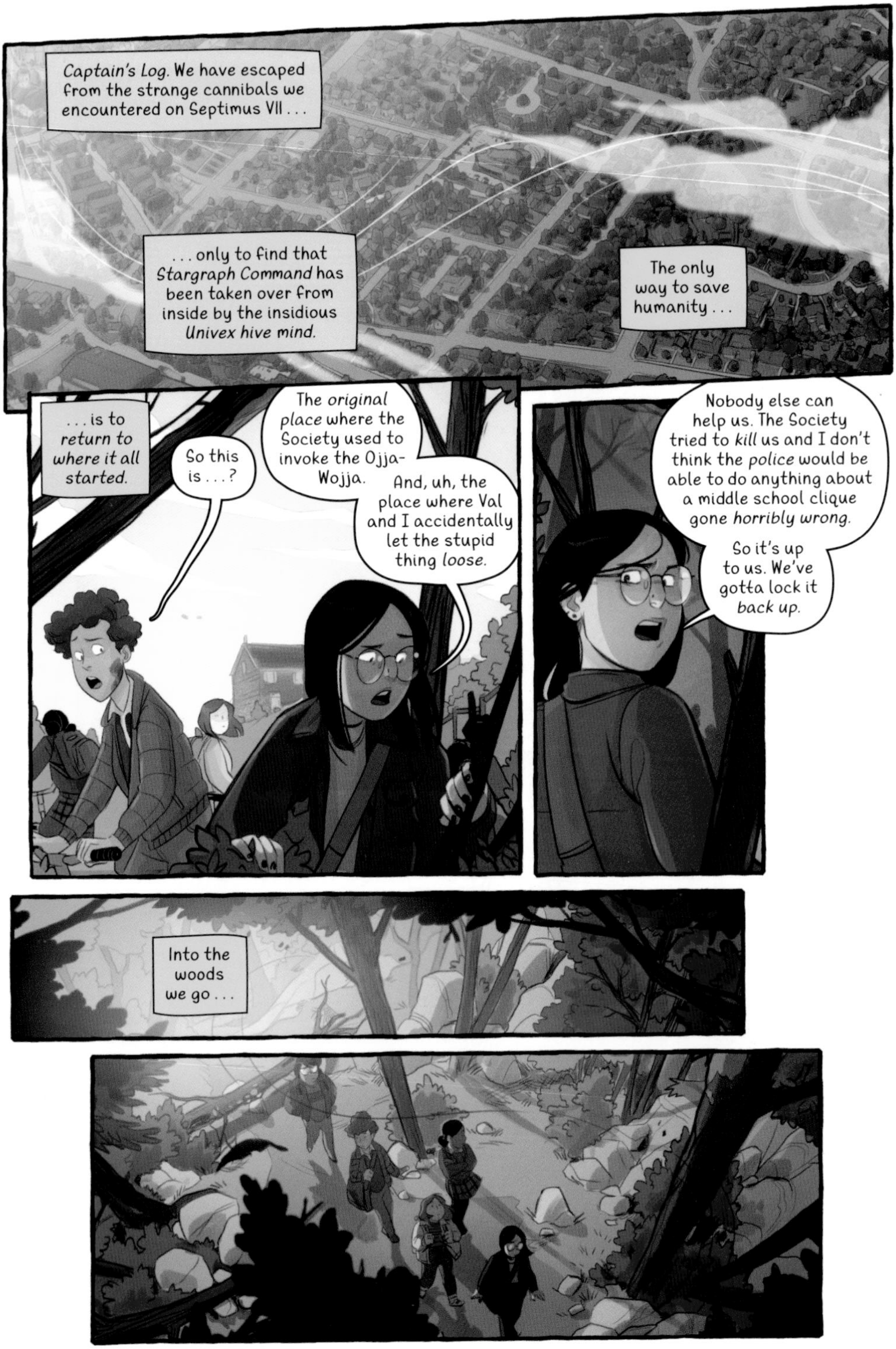

Captain's Log. We have escaped from the strange cannibals we encountered on Septimus VII . . .
. . . only to find that *Stargraph Command* has been taken over from inside by the insidious *Univex hive mind.*
The only way to save humanity . . .
. . . is to *return to where it all started.*
So this is . . . ?
The *original place* where the Society used to invoke the Ojja-Wojja.
And, uh, the place where Val and I accidentally let the stupid thing *loose.*
Nobody else can help us. The Society tried to *kill* us and I don't think the *police* would be able to do anything about a middle school clique gone *horribly wrong.*
So it's up to us. We've gotta lock it *back up.*
Into the woods we go . . .

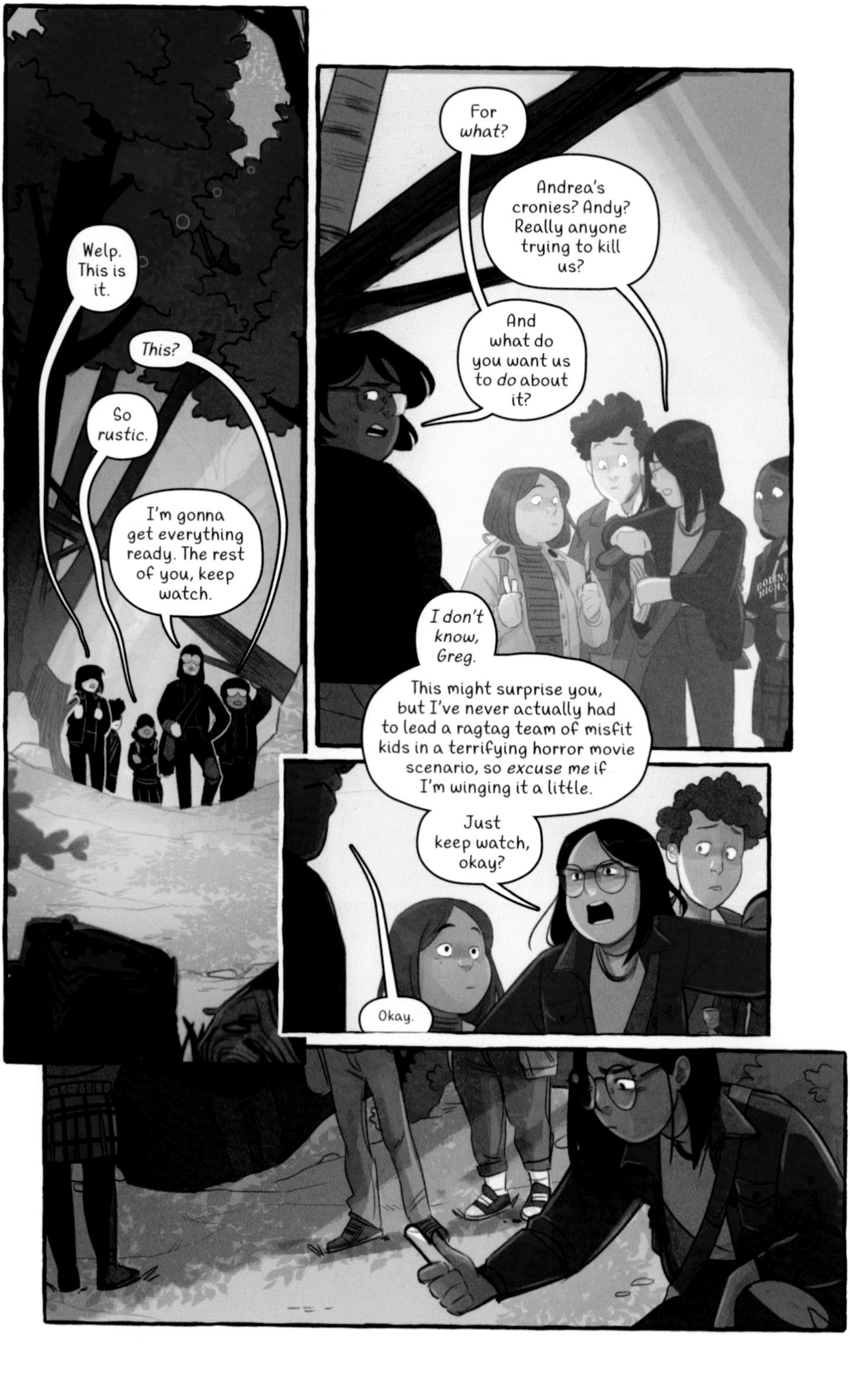
Welp. This is it.
This?
So rustic.
I'm gonna get everything ready. The rest of you, keep watch.
For what?
Andrea's cronies? Andy? Really anyone trying to kill us?
And what do you want us to do about it?
I don't know, Greg.
This might surprise you, but I've never actually had to lead a ragtag team of misfit kids in a terrifying horror movie scenario, so excuse me if I'm winging it a little.
Just keep watch, okay?
Okay.

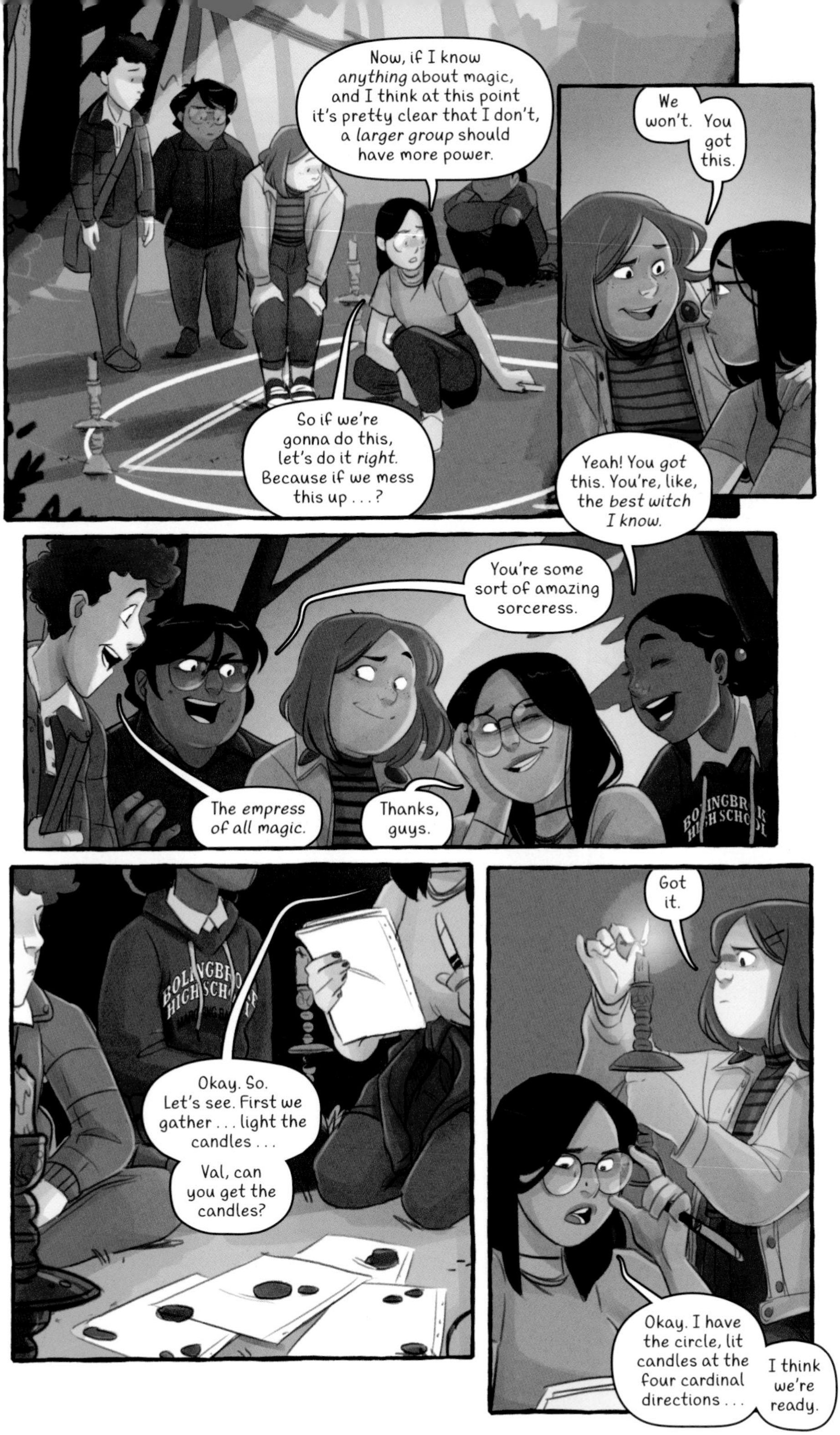
Now, if I know *anything* about magic, and I think at this point it's pretty clear that I don't, a *larger group* should have more power.
So if we're gonna do this, let's do it *right*. Because if we mess this up . . . ?
We won't. You got this.
Yeah! You *got* this. You're, like, the *best witch I know*.
You're some sort of amazing sorceress.
The *empress of all magic*.
Thanks, guys.
Okay. So. Let's see. First we gather . . . light the candles . . .
Val, can you get the candles?
Got it.
Okay. I have the circle, lit candles at the four cardinal directions . . .
I think we're ready.

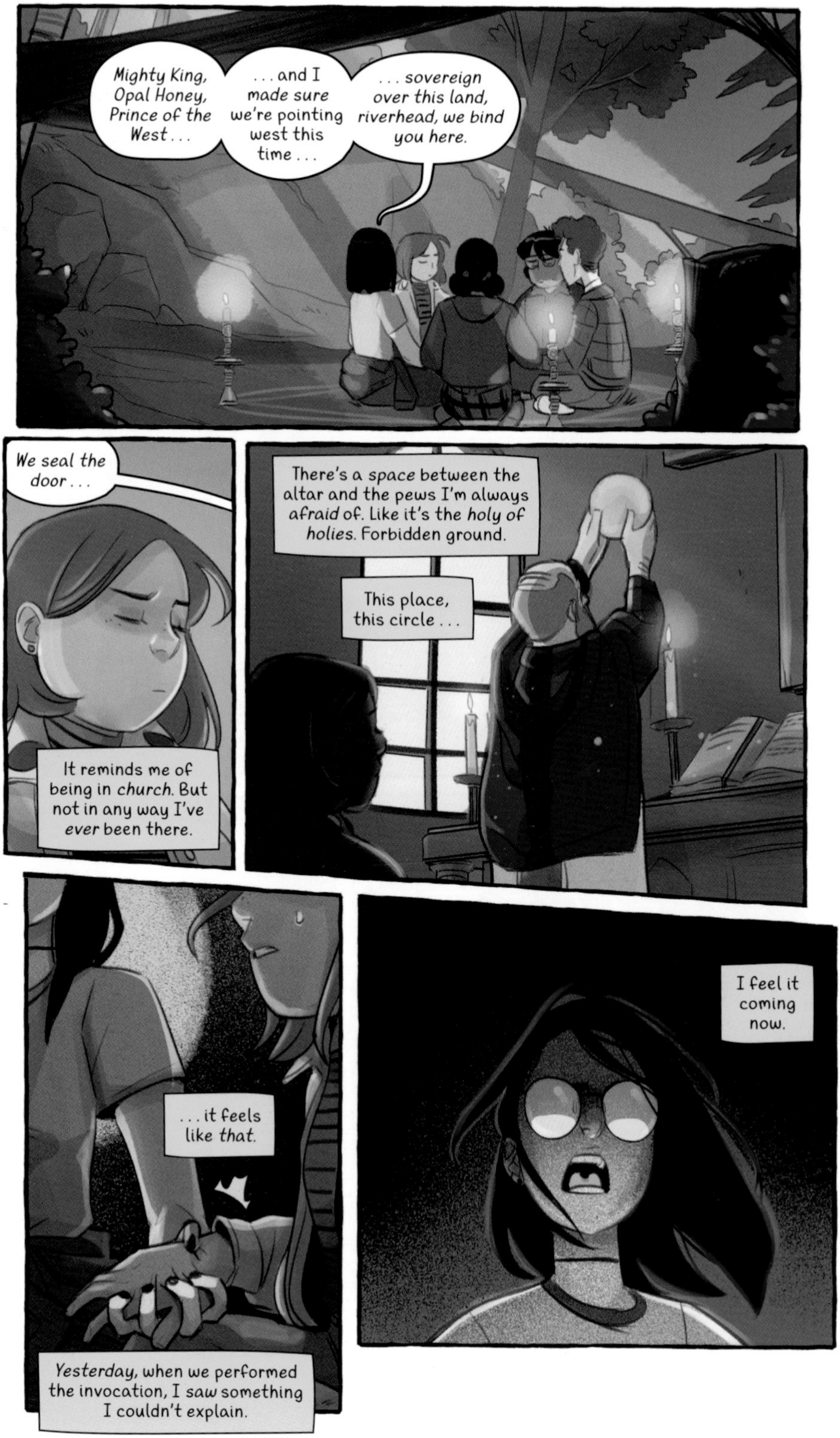
Mighty King, Opal Honey, Prince of the West . . .
. . . and I made sure we're pointing west this time . . .
. . . sovereign over this land, riverhead, we bind you here.
We seal the door . . .
It reminds me of being in *church*. But not in any way I've *ever* been there.
There's a *space* between the altar and the pews I'm always *afraid* of. Like it's the *holy of holies*. Forbidden ground.
This place, this circle . . .
. . . it feels like *that*.
Yesterday, when we performed the invocation, I saw something I couldn't explain.
I feel it coming now.

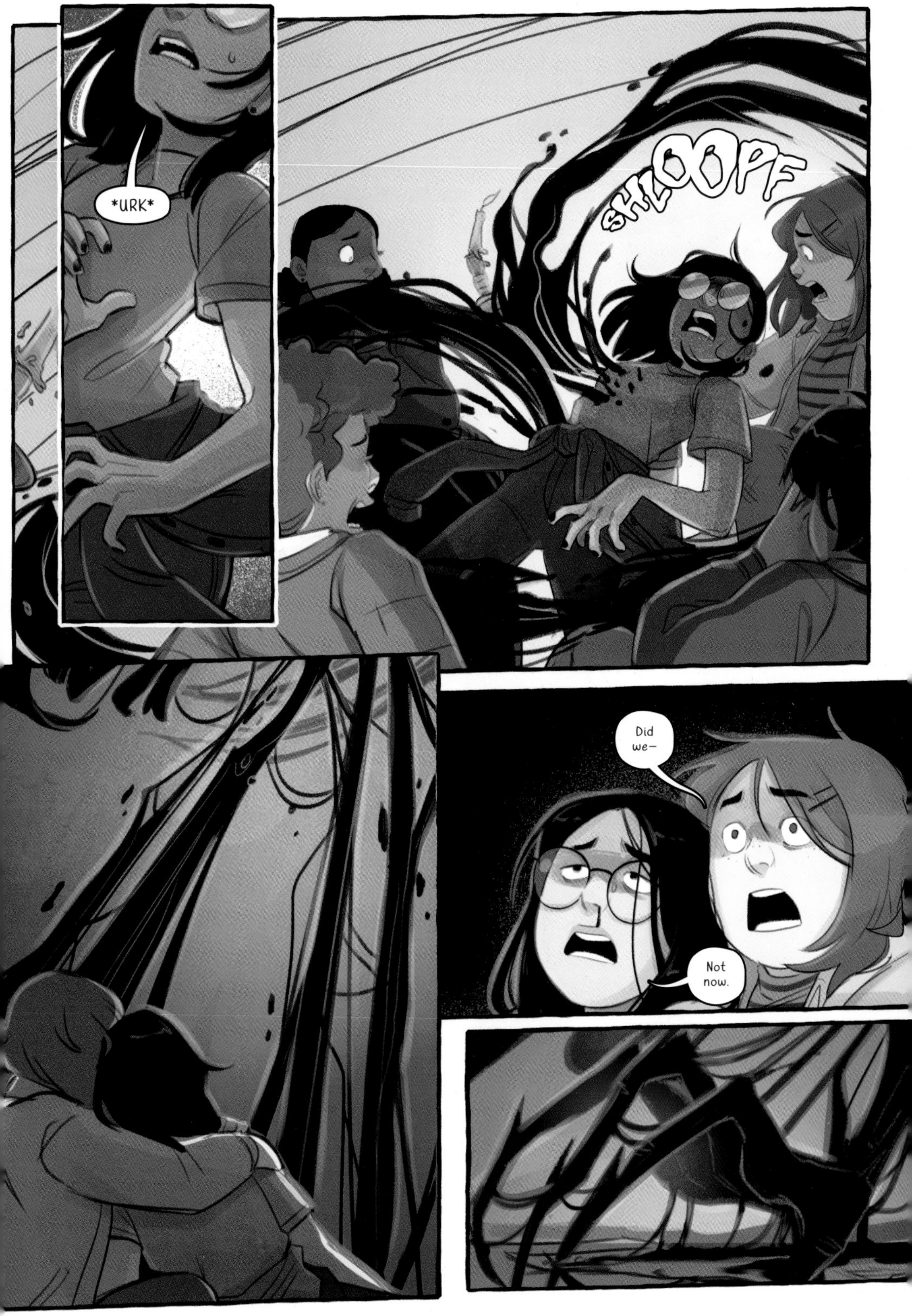
URK
SHLOOPF
Did we—
Not now.

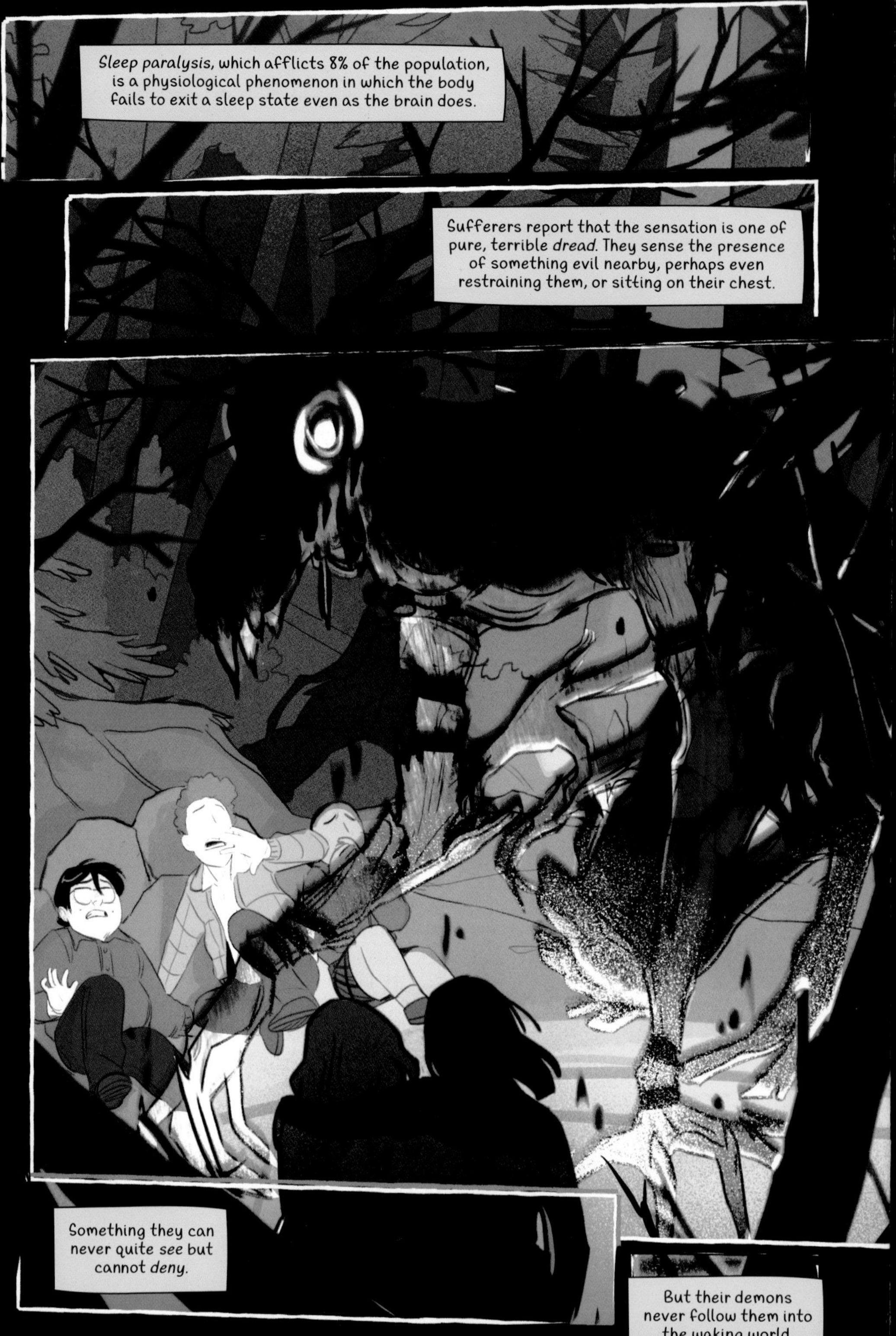
Sleep paralysis, which afflicts 8% of the population, is a physiological phenomenon in which the body fails to exit a sleep state even as the brain does.
Sufferers report that the sensation is one of pure, terrible *dread*. They sense the presence of something evil nearby, perhaps even restraining them, or sitting on their chest.
Something they can never quite *see* but cannot *deny*.
But their demons never follow them into the waking world.

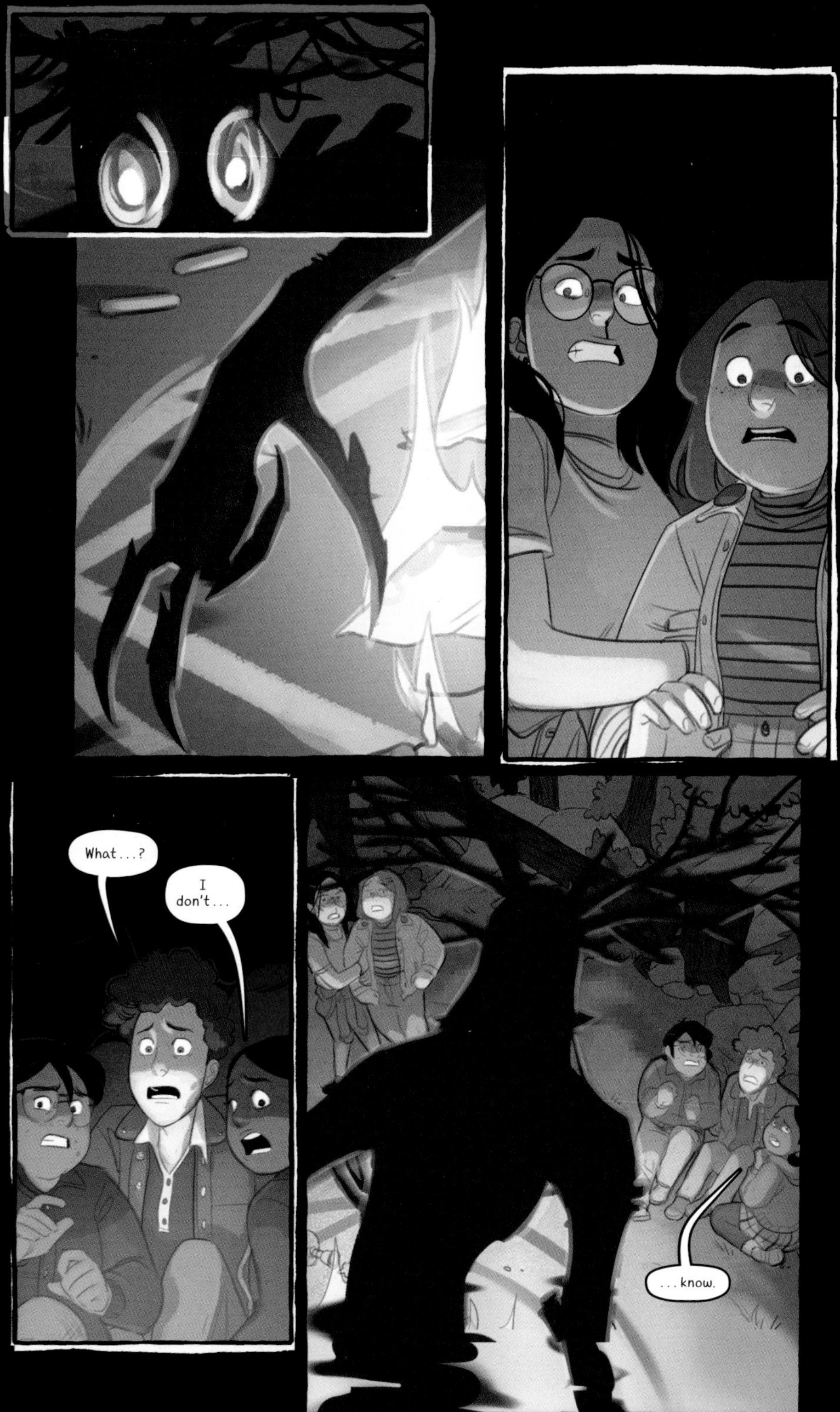
What...?
I don't...
...know.

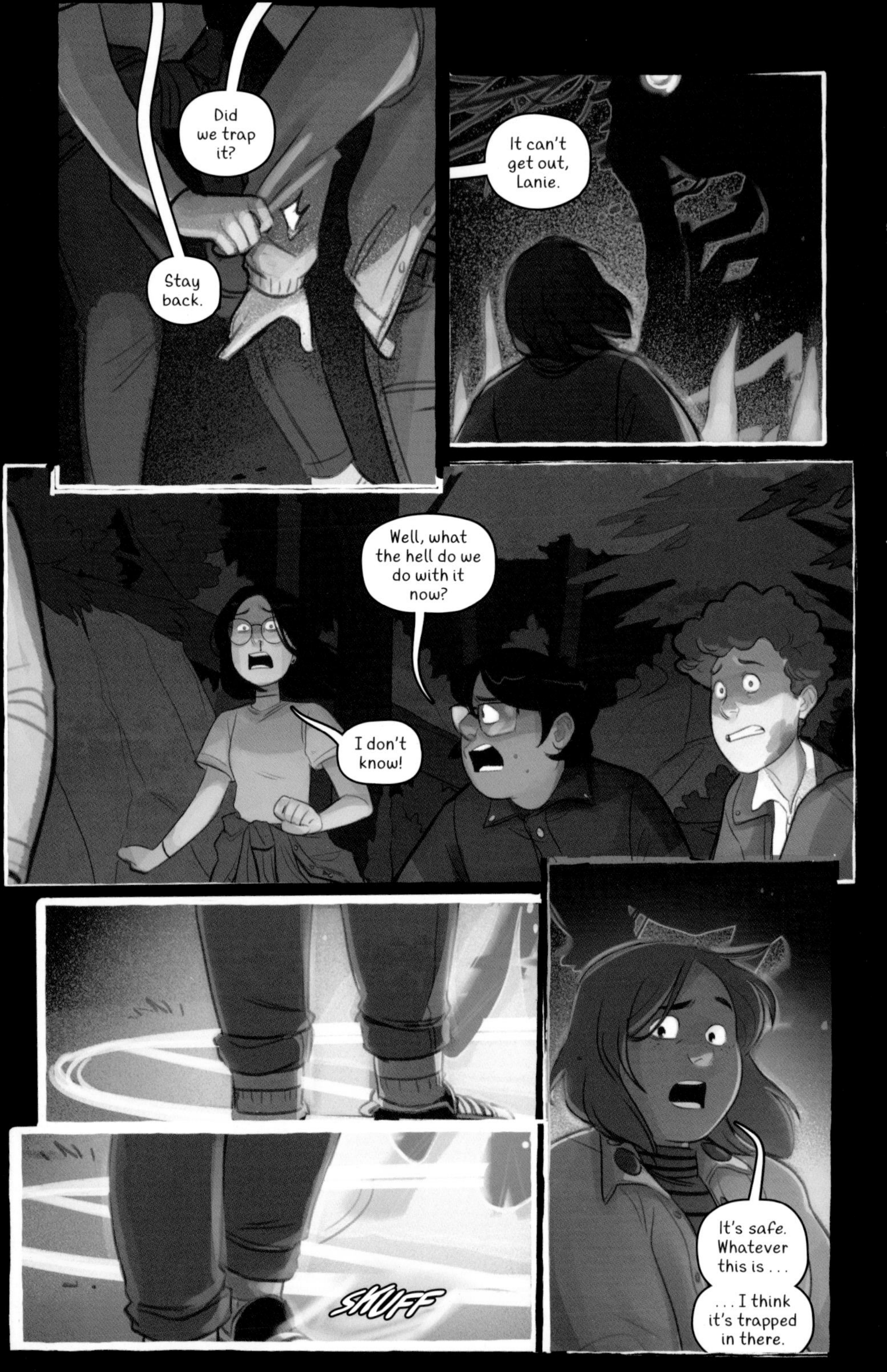
Did we trap it?
Stay back.
It can't get out, Lanie.
Well, what the hell do we do with it now?
I don't know!
SKUFF
It's safe. Whatever this is . . .
. . . I think it's trapped in there.

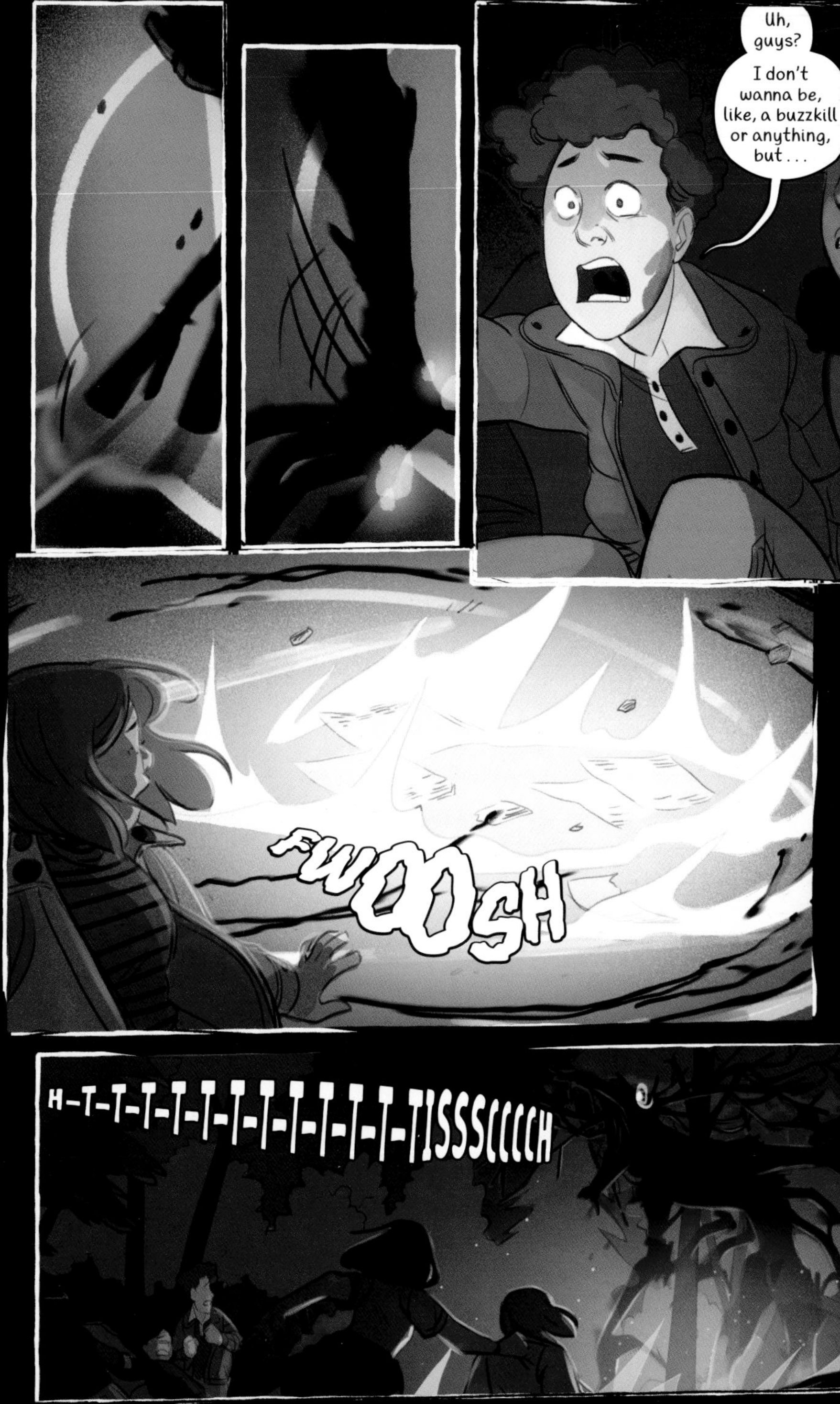
Uh, guys?
I don't wanna be, like, a buzzkill or anything, but . . .
FWOOSH
H-T-T-T-T-T-T-T-T-T-T-T-T-TISSSCCCCH

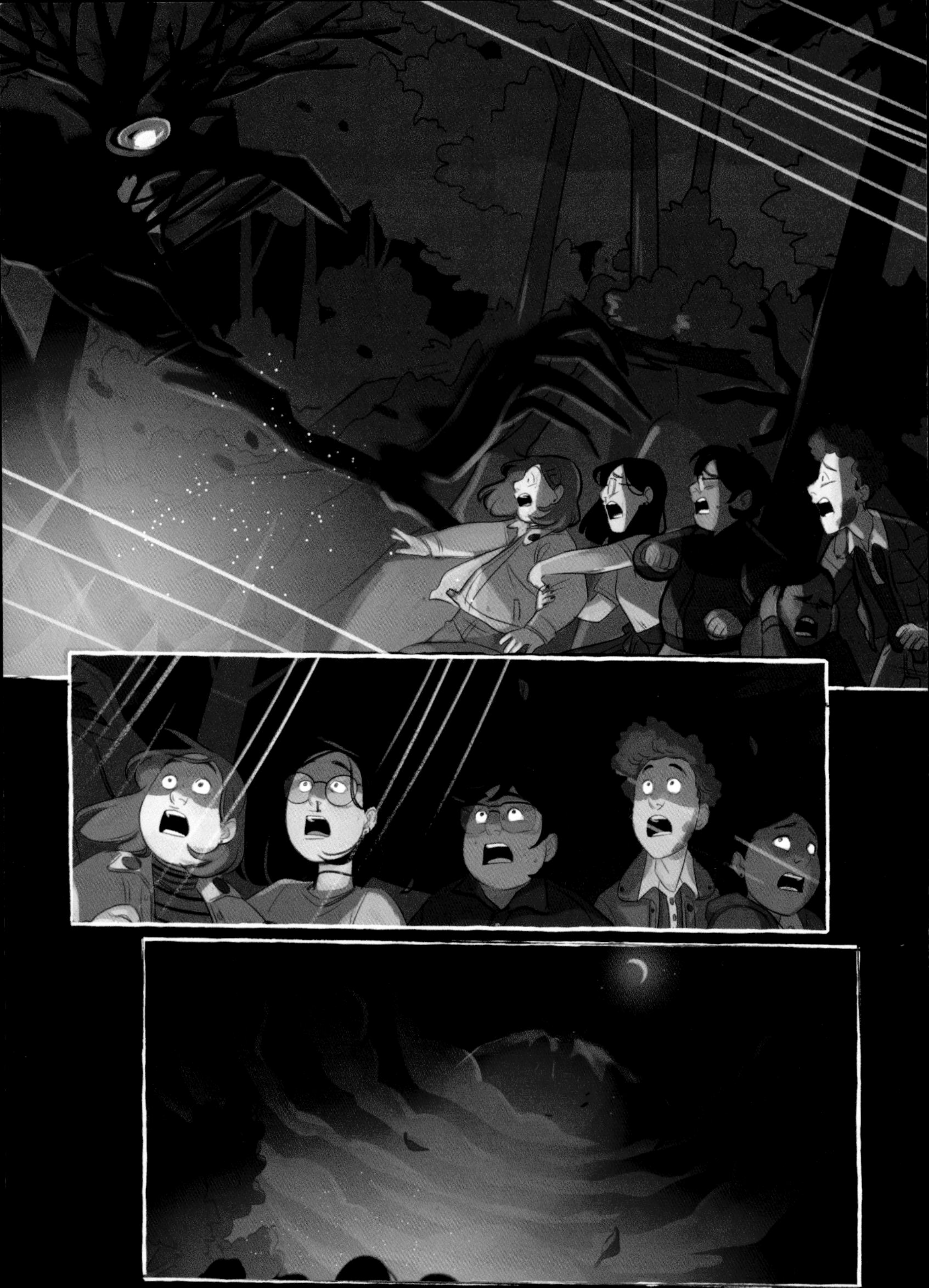

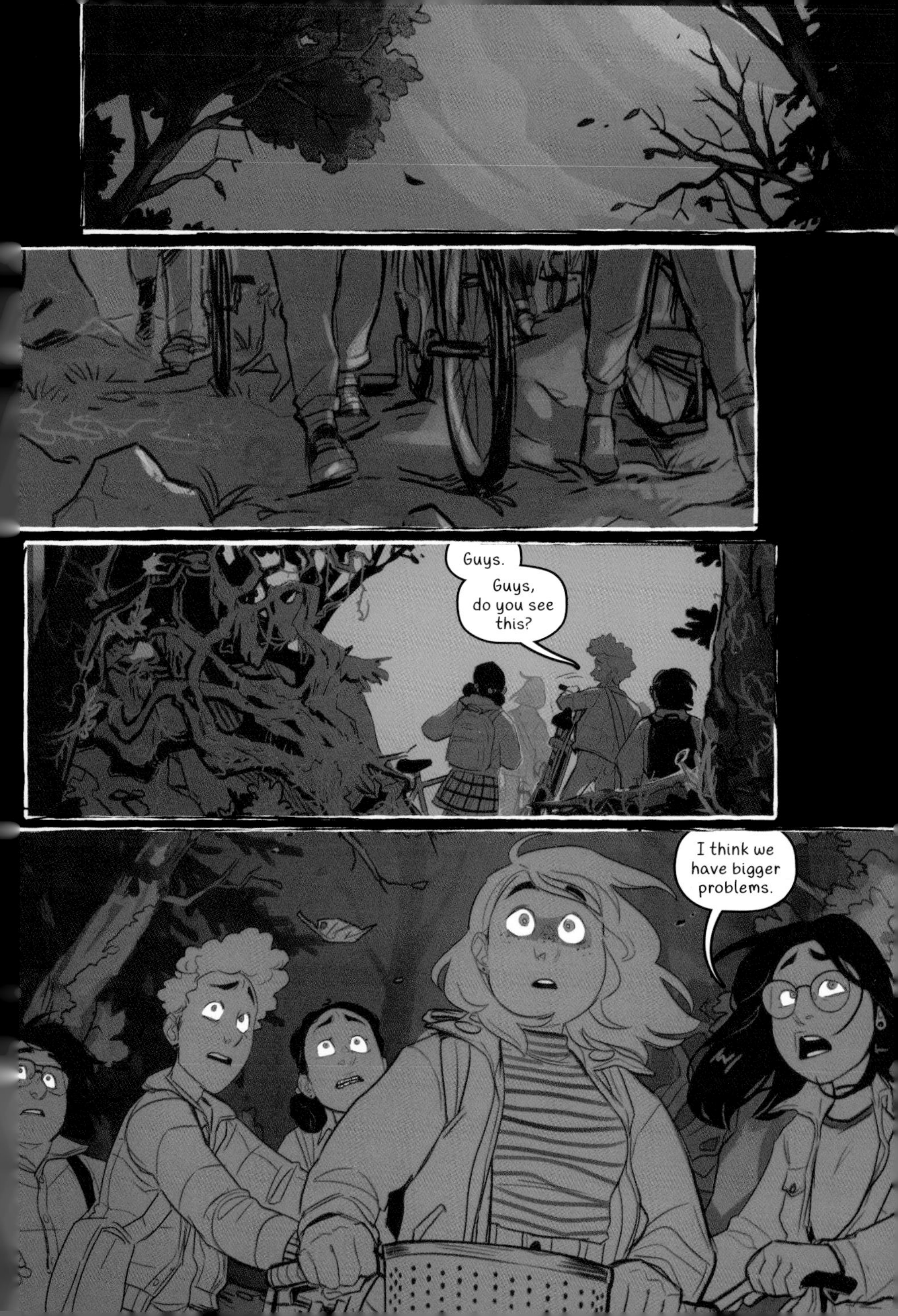

Guys.
Guys, do you see this?
I think we have bigger problems.

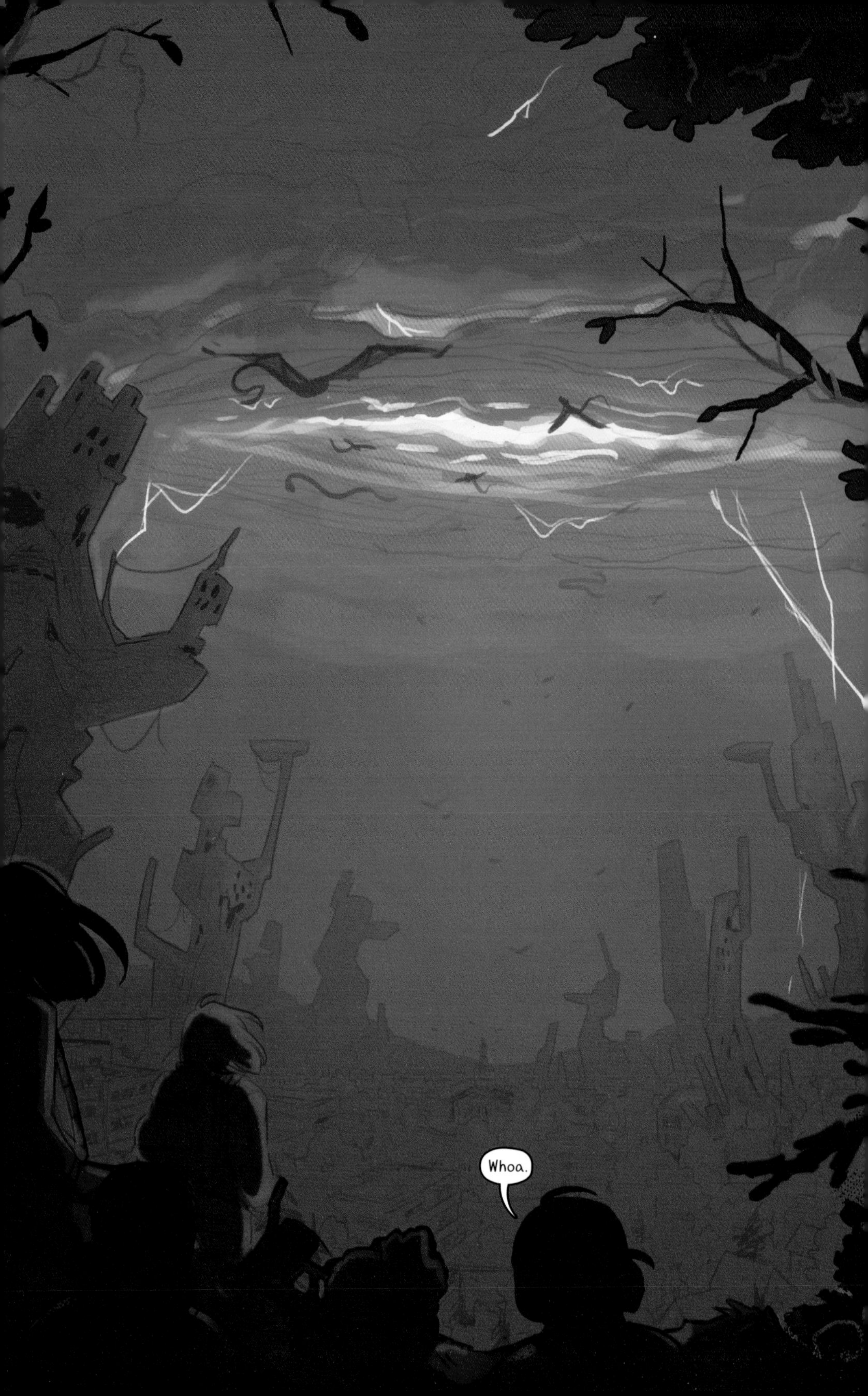
Whoa.

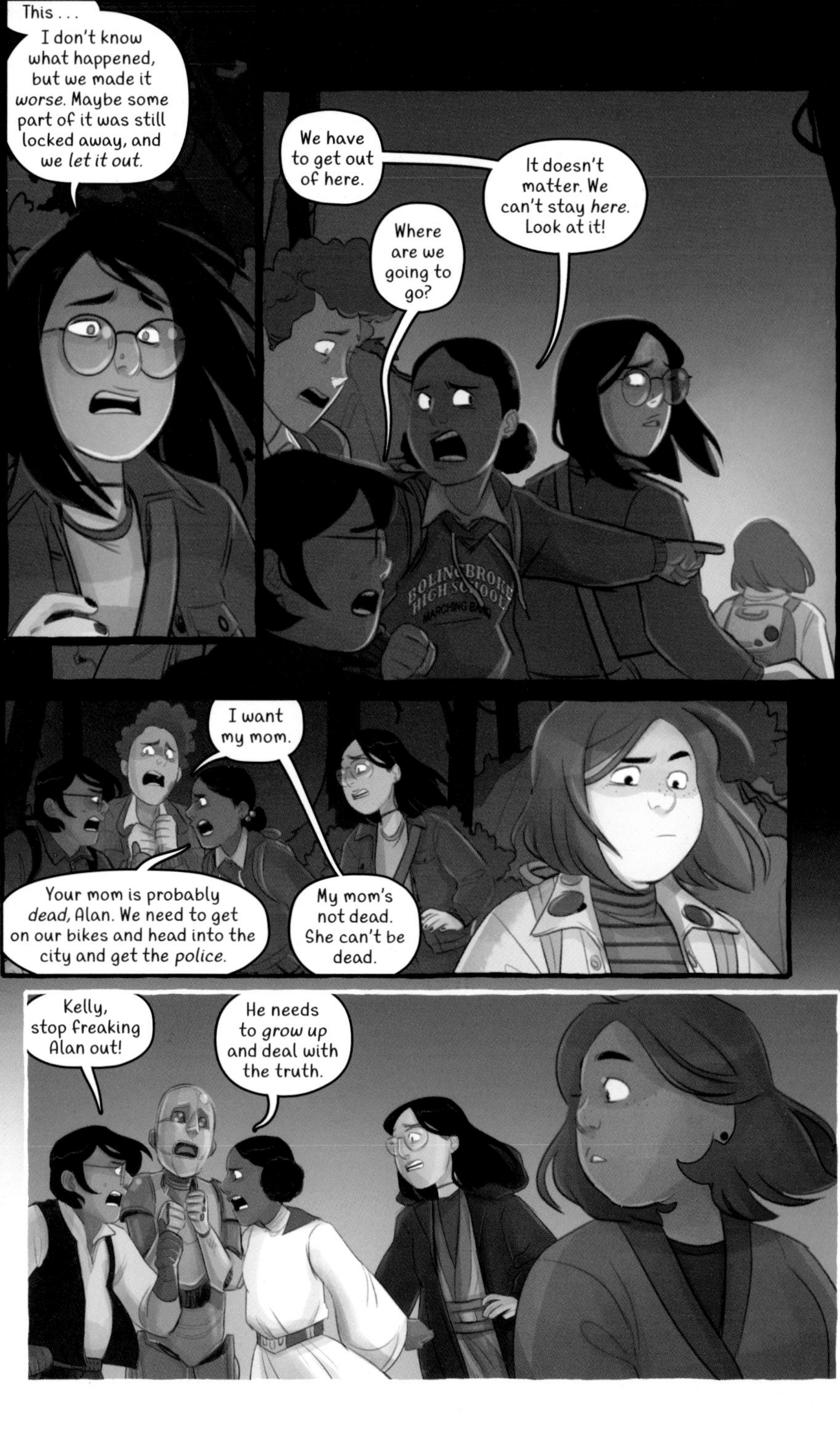
This . . .
I don't know what happened, but we made it *worse*. Maybe some part of it was still locked away, and we *let it out*.
We have to get out of here.
Where are we going to go?
It doesn't matter. We can't stay *here*. Look at it!
BOLINGBROKE HIGH SCHOOL MARCHING BAND
I want my mom.
Your mom is probably *dead*, Alan. We need to get on our bikes and head into the city and get the *police*.
My mom's not dead. She can't be dead.
Kelly, stop freaking Alan out!
He needs to *grow up* and deal with the truth.

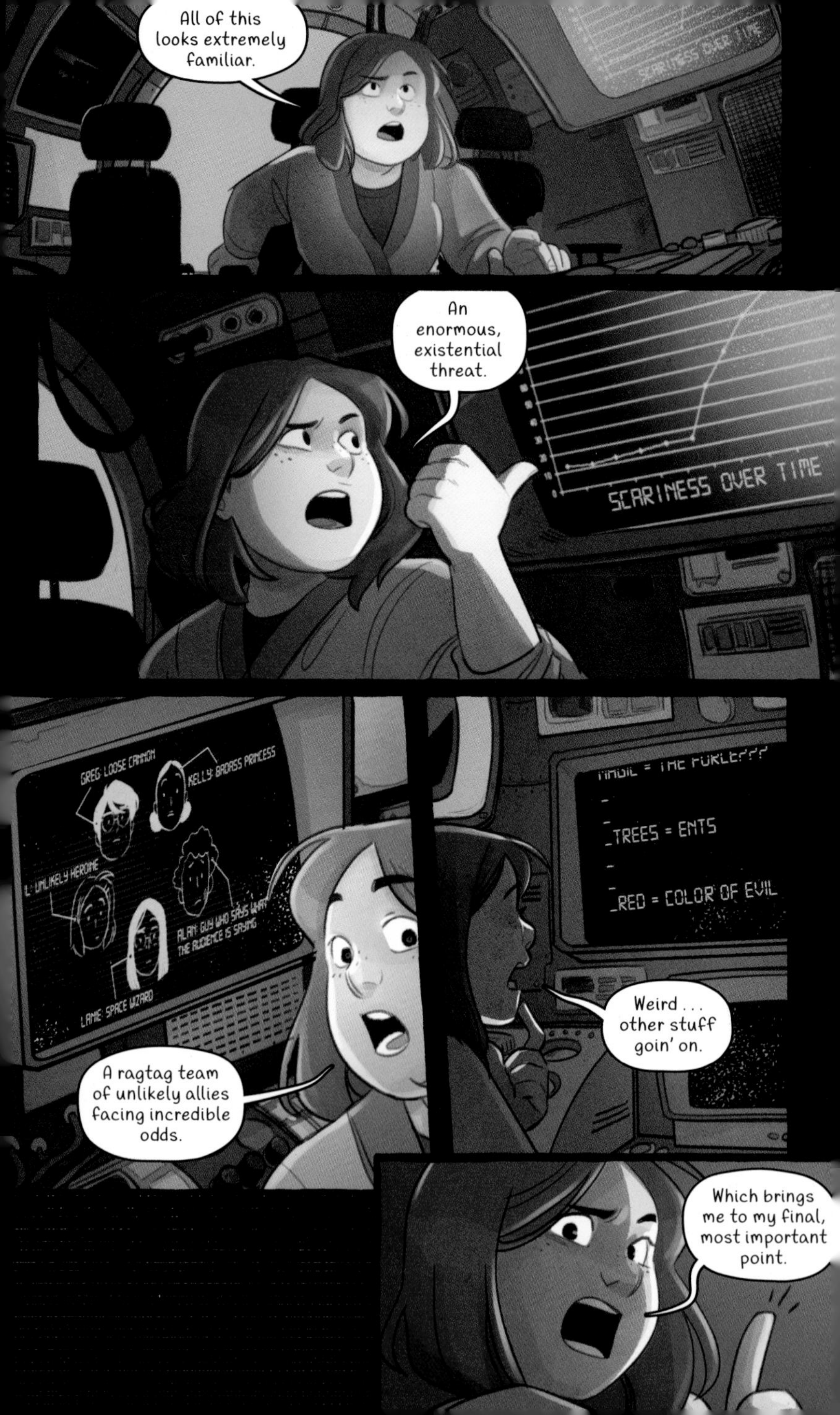
All of this looks extremely familiar.
SCARINESS OVER TIME
An enormous, existential threat.
SCARINESS OVER TIME
GREG: LOOSE CANNON
KELLY: BADASS PRINCESS
L: UNLIKELY HEROINE
ALAN: GUY WHO SAYS WHAT THE AUDIENCE IS SAYING
LANIE: SPACE WIZARD
A ragtag team of unlikely allies facing incredible odds.
TREES = ENTS
RED = COLOR OF EVIL
Weird . . . other stuff goin' on.
Which brings me to my final, most important point.

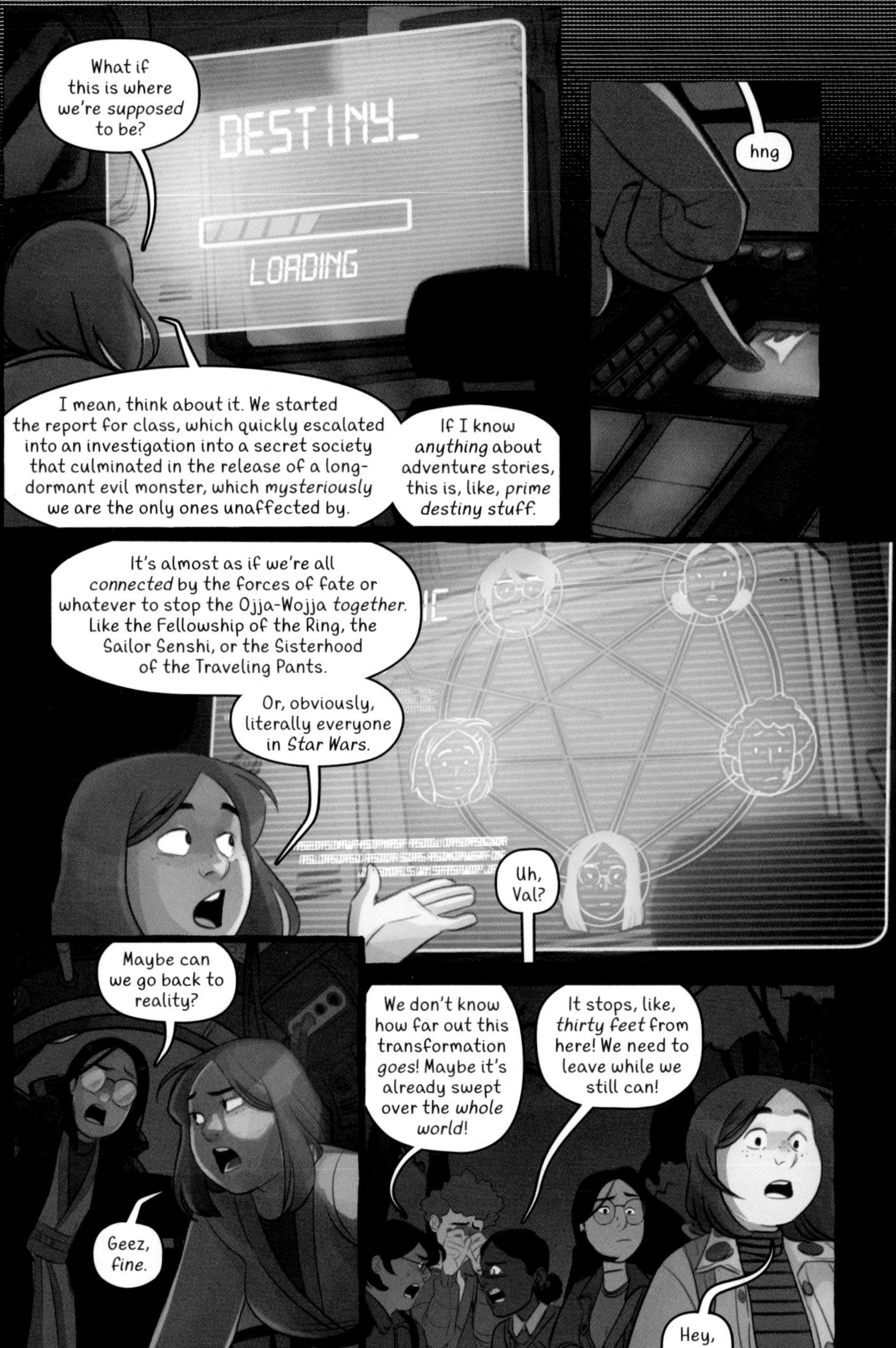
What if this is where we're *supposed* to be?
DESTINY_
LOADING
hng
I mean, think about it. We started the report for class, which quickly escalated into an investigation into a secret society that culminated in the release of a long-dormant evil monster, which *mysteriously* we are the only ones unaffected by.
If I know *anything* about adventure stories, this is, like, *prime destiny stuff.*
It's almost as if we're all *connected* by the forces of fate or whatever to stop the Ojja-Wojja *together.* Like the Fellowship of the Ring, the Sailor Senshi, or the Sisterhood of the Traveling Pants.
Or, obviously, literally everyone in *Star Wars.*
Uh, Val?
Maybe can we go back to reality?
Geez, *fine.*
We don't know how far out this transformation *goes!* Maybe it's already swept over the *whole world!*
It stops, like, *thirty feet* from here! We need to leave while we still can!
Hey, guys.

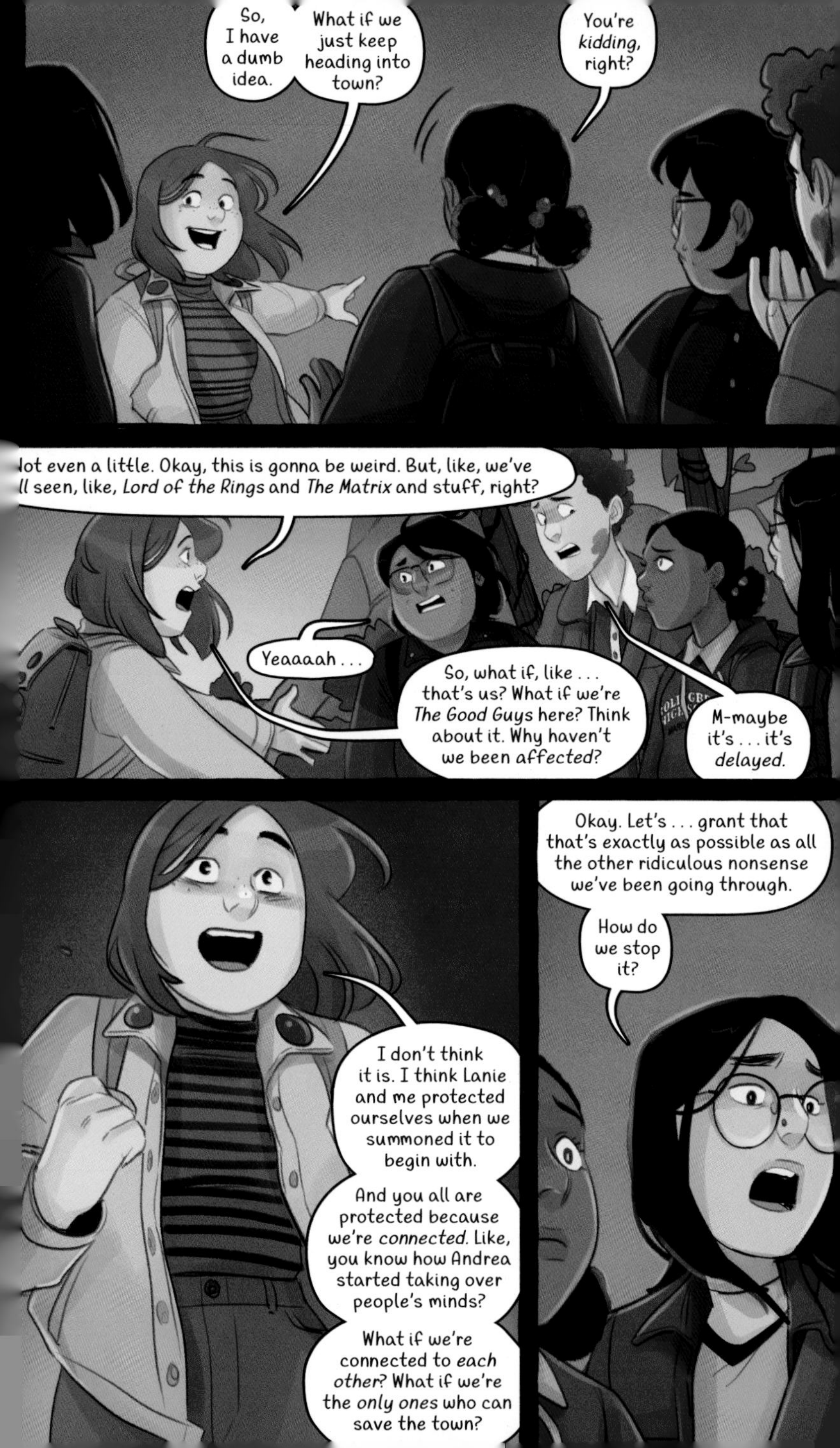
So, I have a dumb idea.
What if we just keep heading into town?
You're kidding, right?
Not even a little. Okay, this is gonna be weird. But, like, we've all seen, like, Lord of the Rings and The Matrix and stuff, right?
Yeaaaah . . .
So, what if, like . . . that's us? What if we're The Good Guys here? Think about it. Why haven't we been affected?
M-maybe it's . . . it's delayed.
I don't think it is. I think Lanie and me protected ourselves when we summoned it to begin with.
And you all are protected because we're connected. Like, you know how Andrea started taking over people's minds?
What if we're connected to each other? What if we're the only ones who can save the town?
Okay. Let's . . . grant that that's exactly as possible as all the other ridiculous nonsense we've been going through.
How do we stop it?

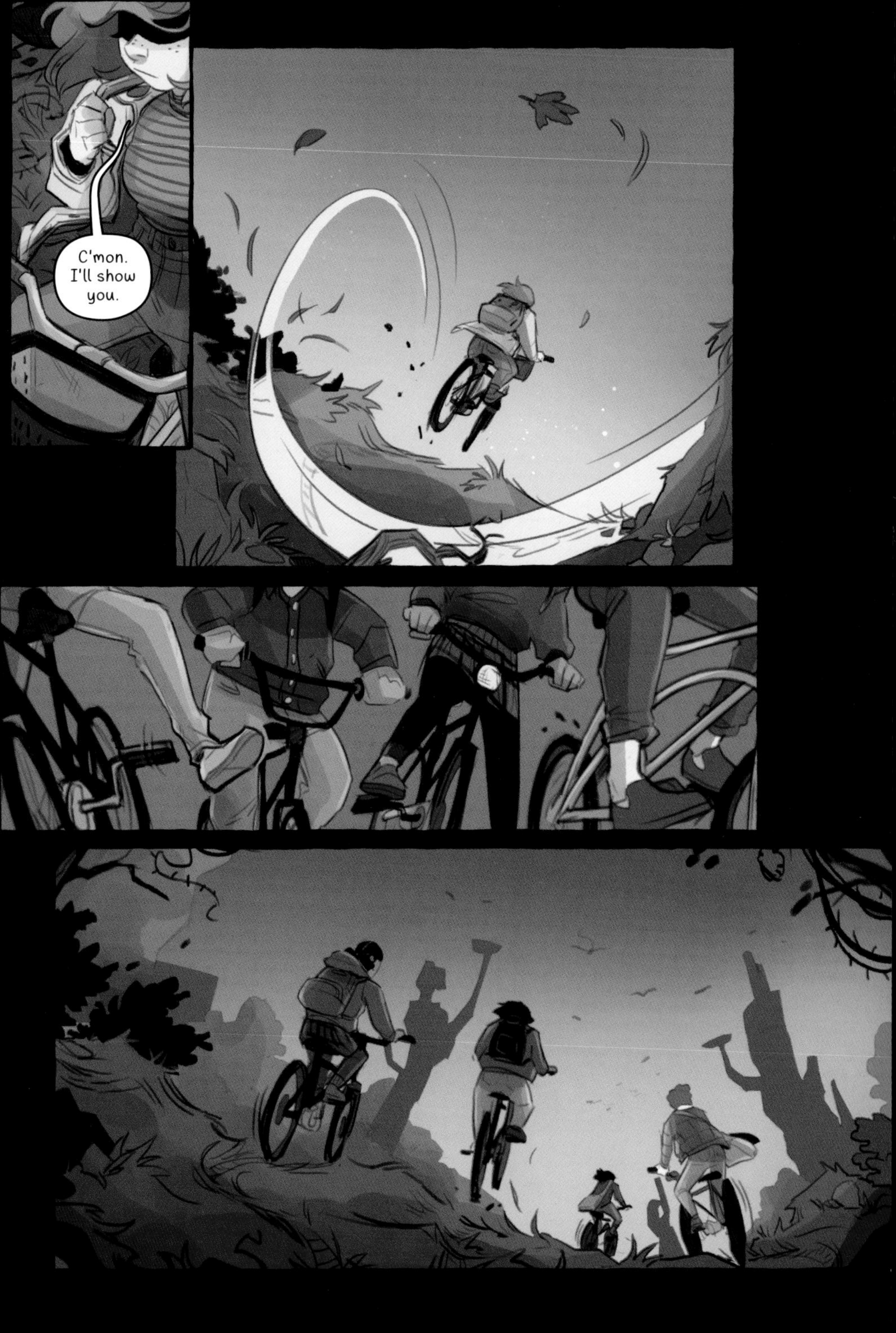
C'mon. I'll show you.

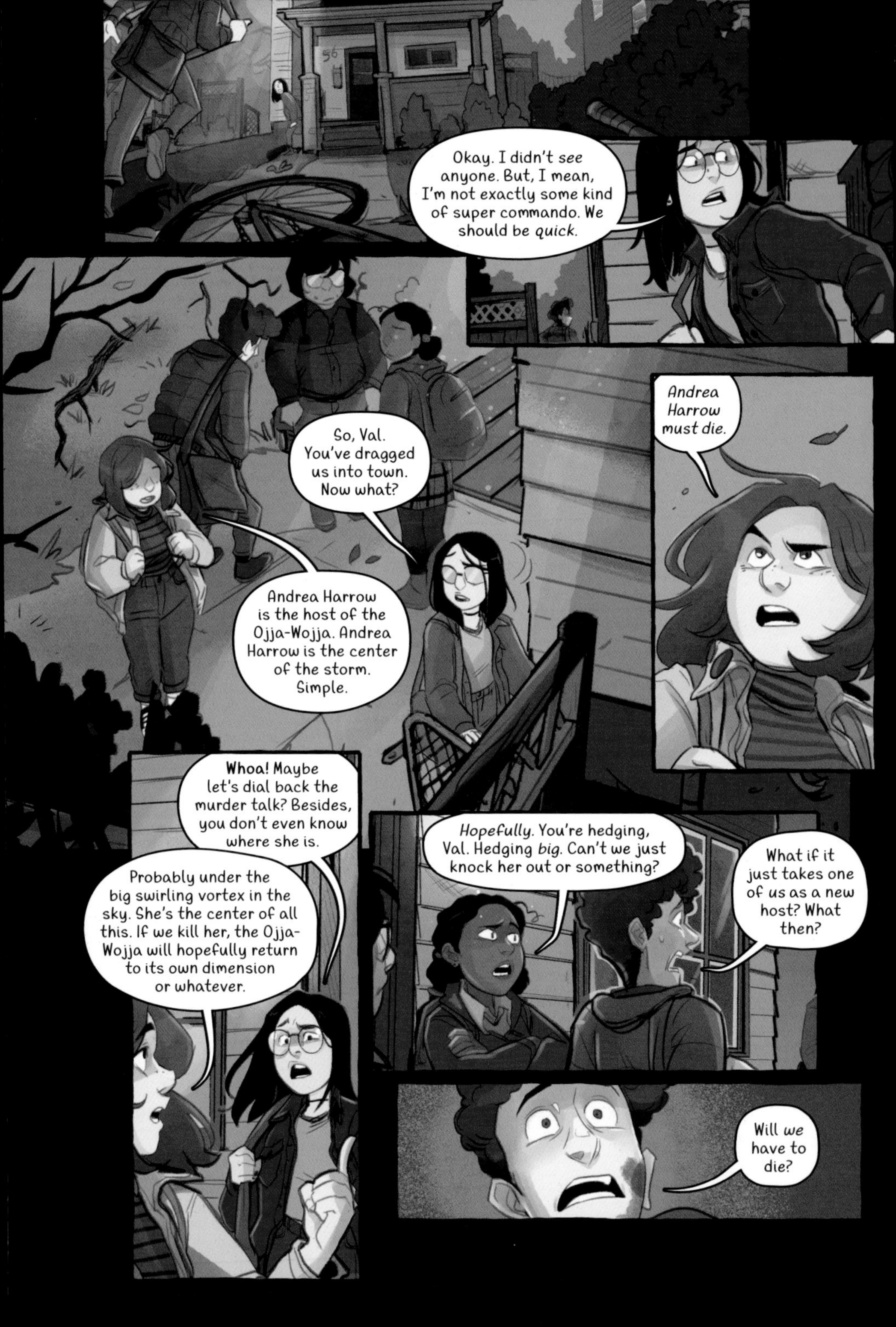
Okay. I didn't *see* anyone. But, I mean, I'm not exactly some kind of super commando. We should be *quick*.
So, Val. You've dragged us into town. Now what?
Andrea Harrow is the host of the Ojja-Wojja. Andrea Harrow is the center of the storm. Simple.
Andrea Harrow must die.
Whoa! Maybe let's dial back the murder talk? Besides, you don't even know where she is.
Probably under the big swirling vortex in the sky. She's the center of all this. If we kill her, the Ojja-Wojja will hopefully return to its own dimension or whatever.
Hopefully. You're hedging, Val. Hedging *big*. Can't we just knock her out or something?
What if it just takes one of us as a new host? What then?
Will *we* have to die?

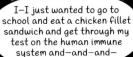
I—I just wanted to go to school and eat a chicken fillet sandwich and get through my test on the human immune system and—and—and—

I'm thirteen years old! I'm a *kid* and—and—and kids are supposed to just, like, play Xbox and eat candy and not *fight monster ghosts!*

And now I'm wondering if we're going to have to *literally murder* each other!

This isn't okay! None of this is okay!

I just want to go *home!* I . . .

—and now I'm wondering if I'm about to die and if my mom is already dead and I just want to go *home.*

I woke up this morning and I had my Corn Pops and then we decided that we're going to kill Andrea Harrow!

Shh. It's okay. It's okay to be afraid. Nobody wanted this.

It *is* scary. It *is* dangerous. And we *are* kids. But your mom? She's counting on us right now. On *you.*

Your mom would want you to be brave.

My mom would want to make sure I had my inhaler.

Good. And do you?

It's in my backpack.

Then you're doing your mom proud. We got this.

There!

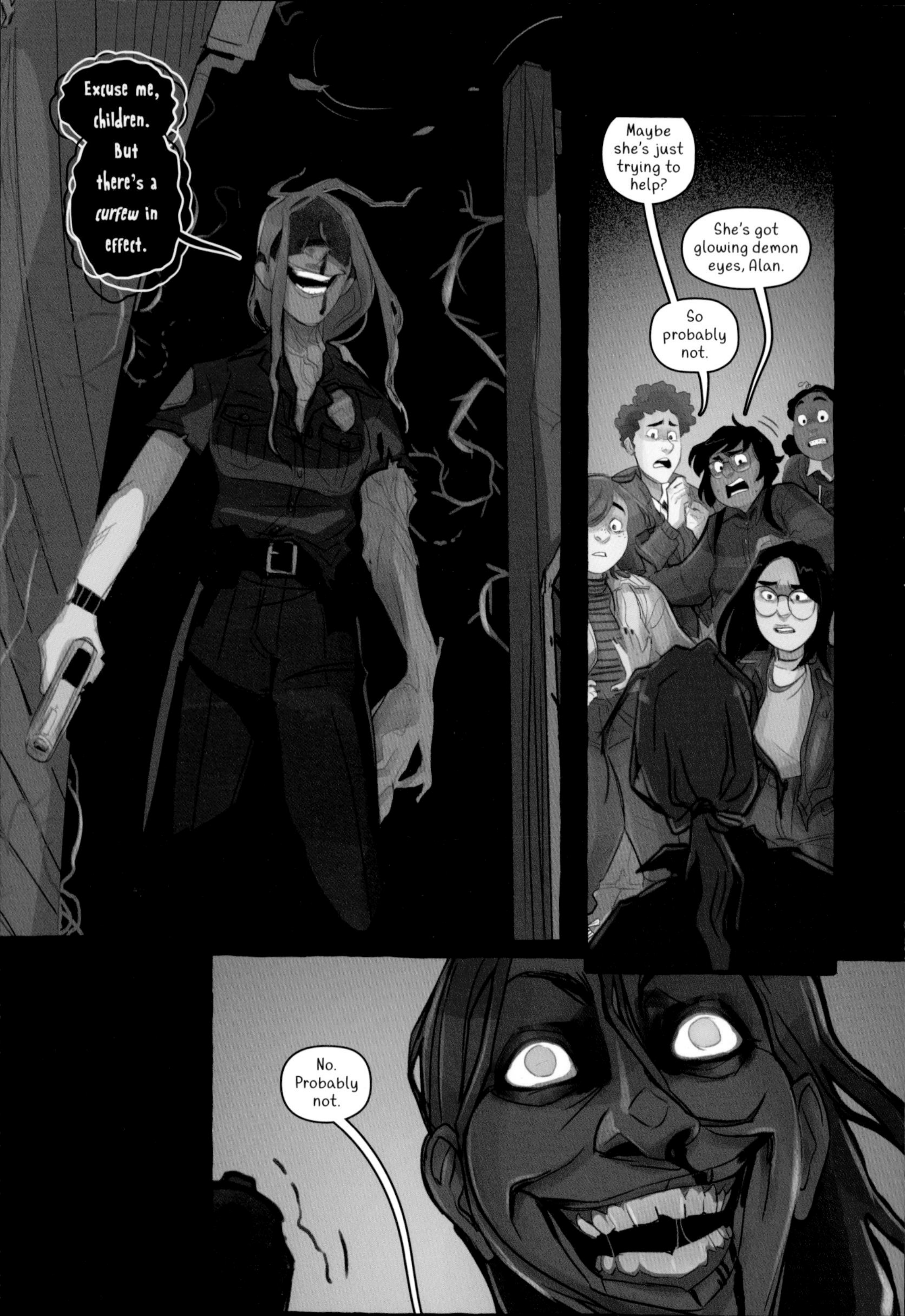
Excuse me, children. But there's a curfew in effect.
Maybe she's just trying to help?
She's got glowing demon eyes, Alan.
So probably not.
No. Probably not.

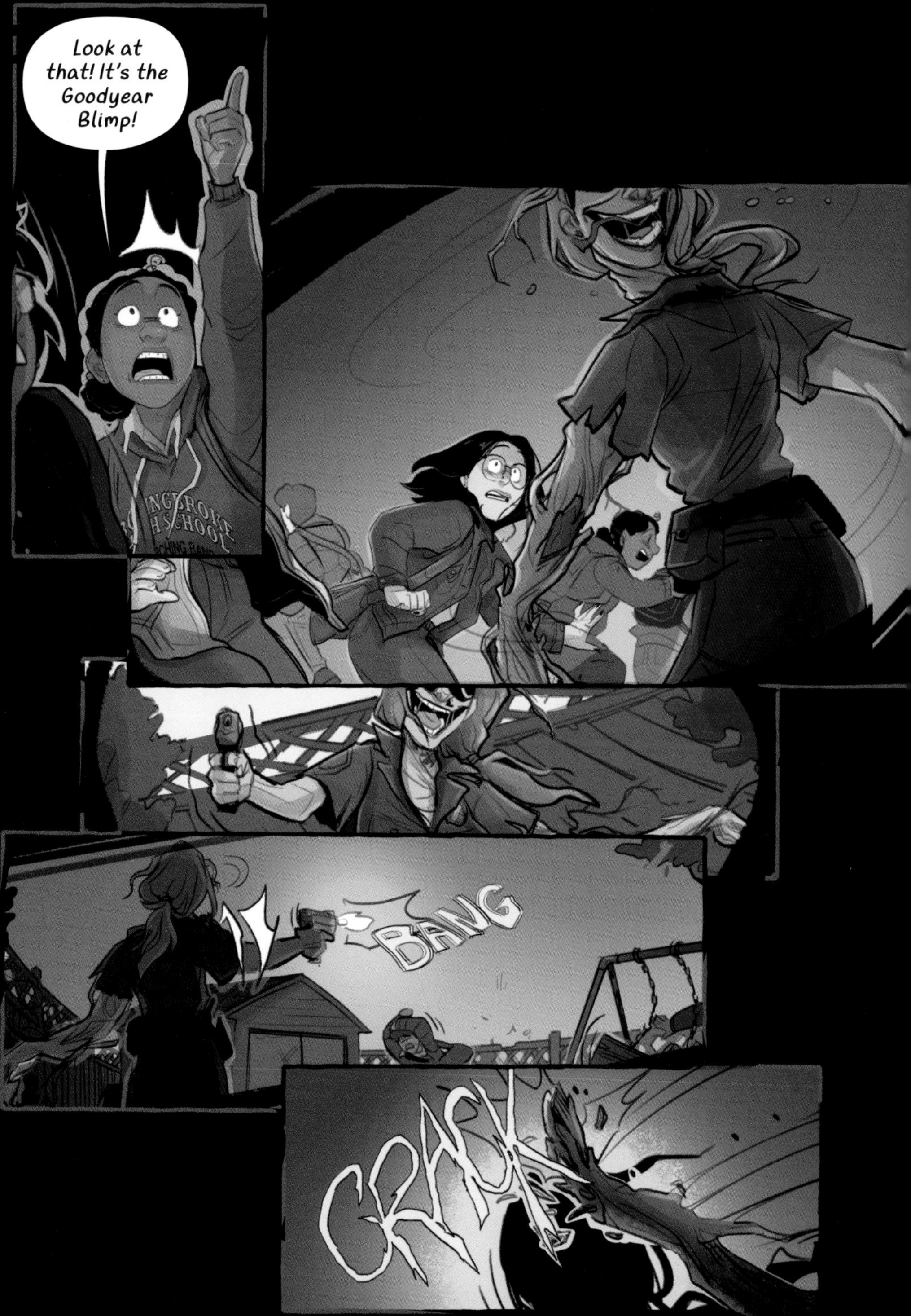
Look at that! It's the Goodyear Blimp!
BANG
CRACK

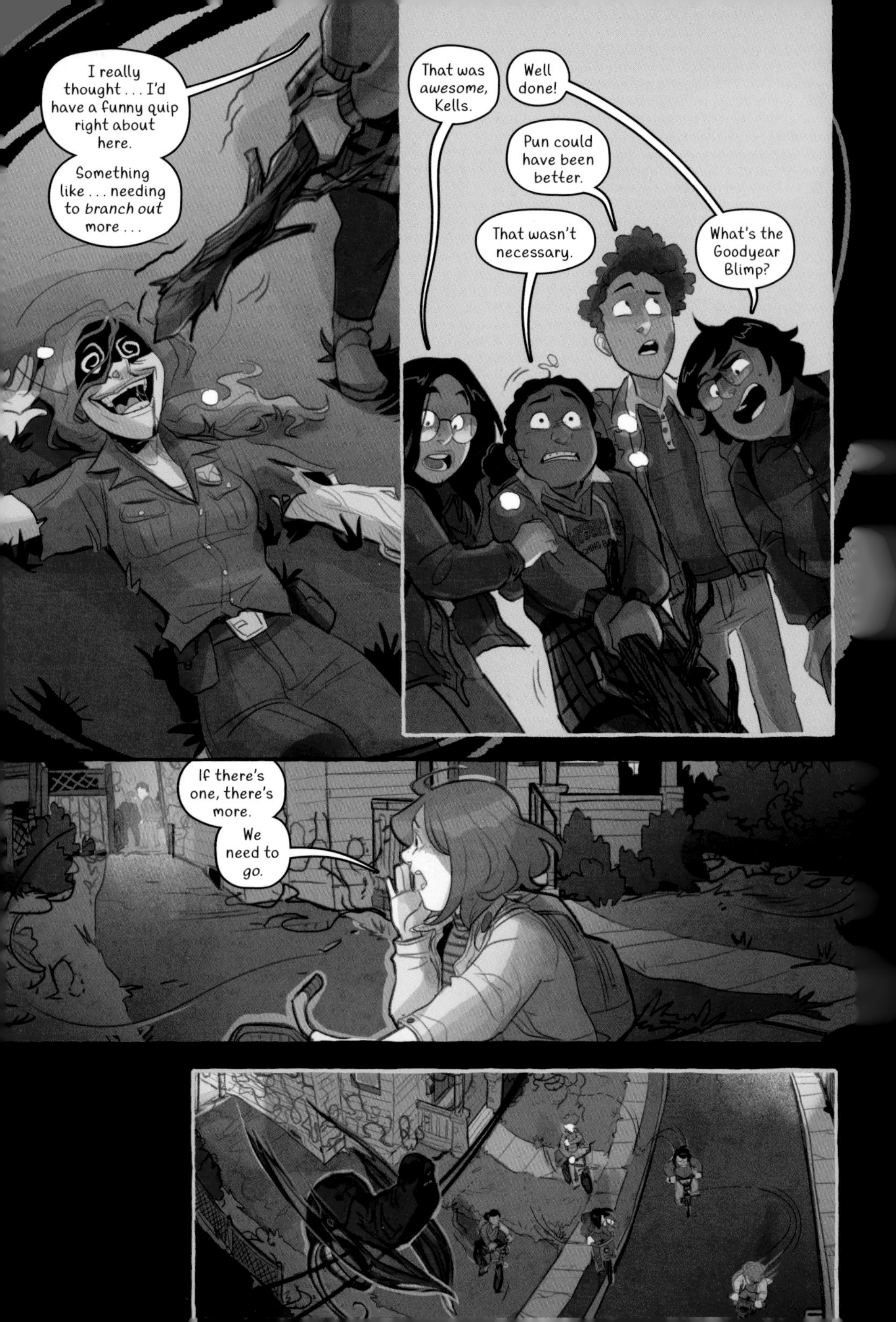

I really thought . . . I'd have a funny quip right about here.
Something like . . . needing to *branch out* more . . .
That was *awesome*, Kells.
Well done!
Pun could have been better.
That wasn't necessary.
What's the Goodyear Blimp?
If there's one, there's more.
We need to *go*.

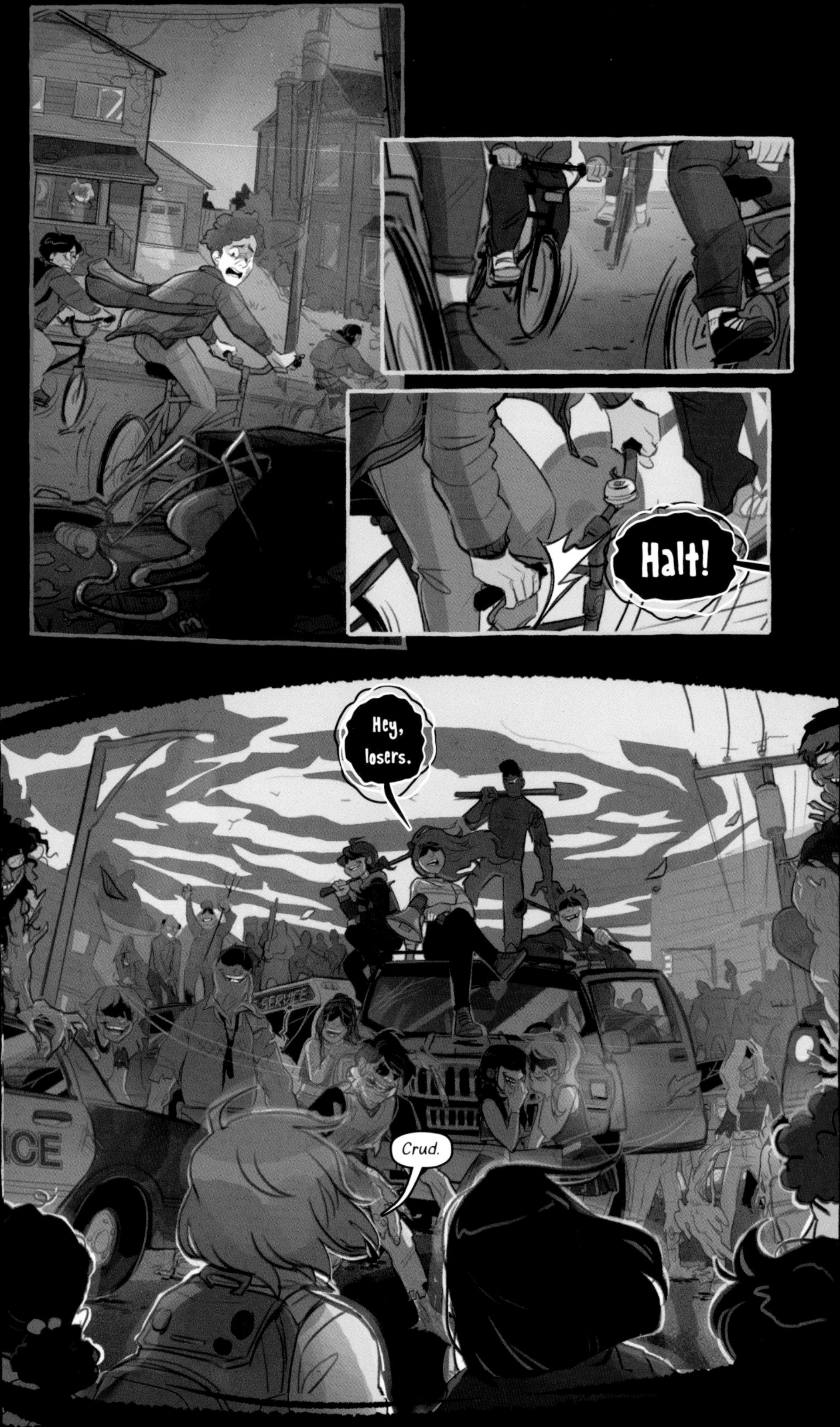
Halt!
Hey, losers.
Crud.

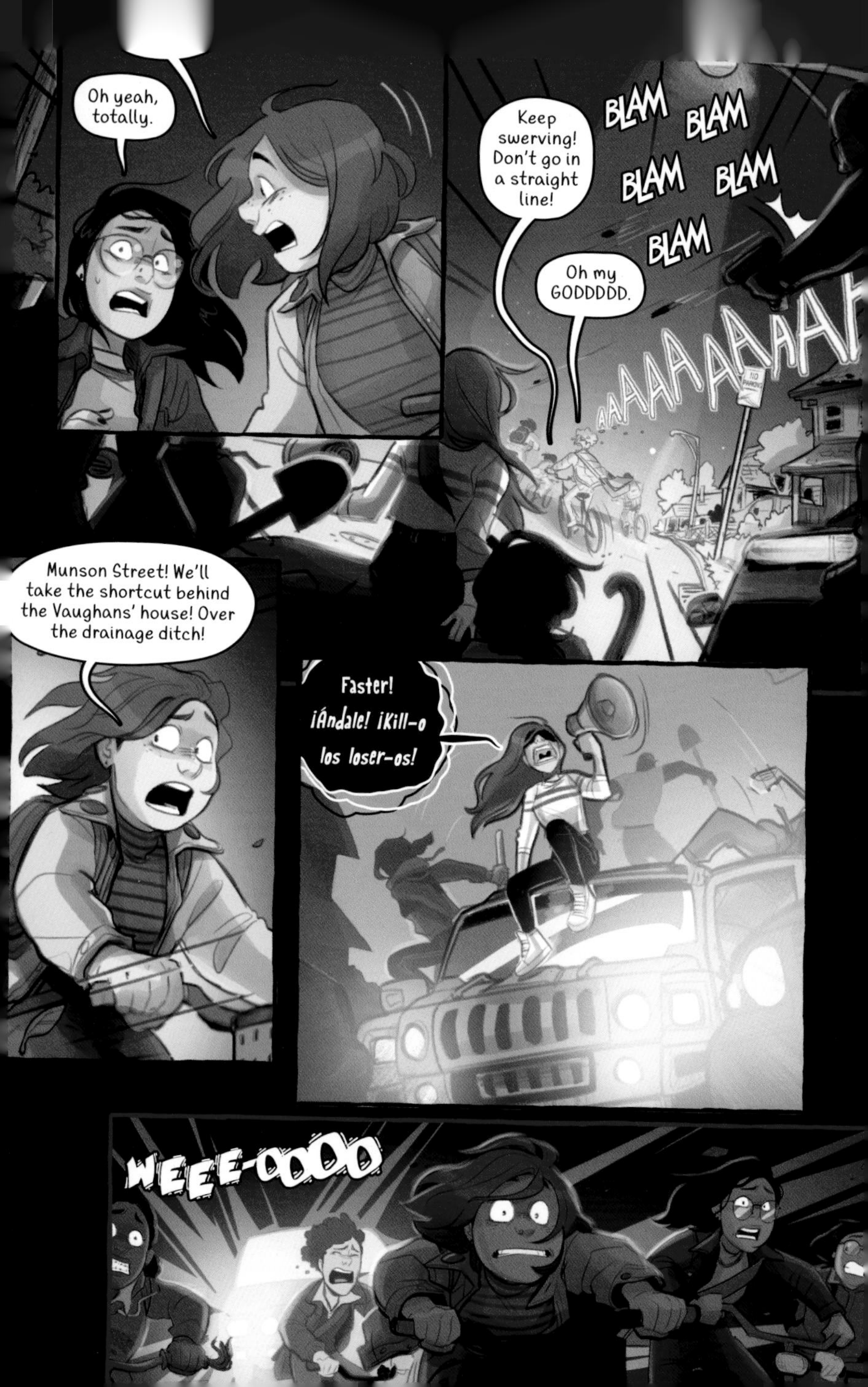
Oh yeah, totally.
Keep swerving! Don't go in a straight line!
BLAM BLAM BLAM BLAM BLAM
Oh my GODDDDD.
AAAAAAAAAAAH
NO PARKING
Munson Street! We'll take the shortcut behind the Vaughans' house! Over the drainage ditch!
Faster! ¡Ándale! ¡Kill-o los loser-os!
WEEE-OOOO

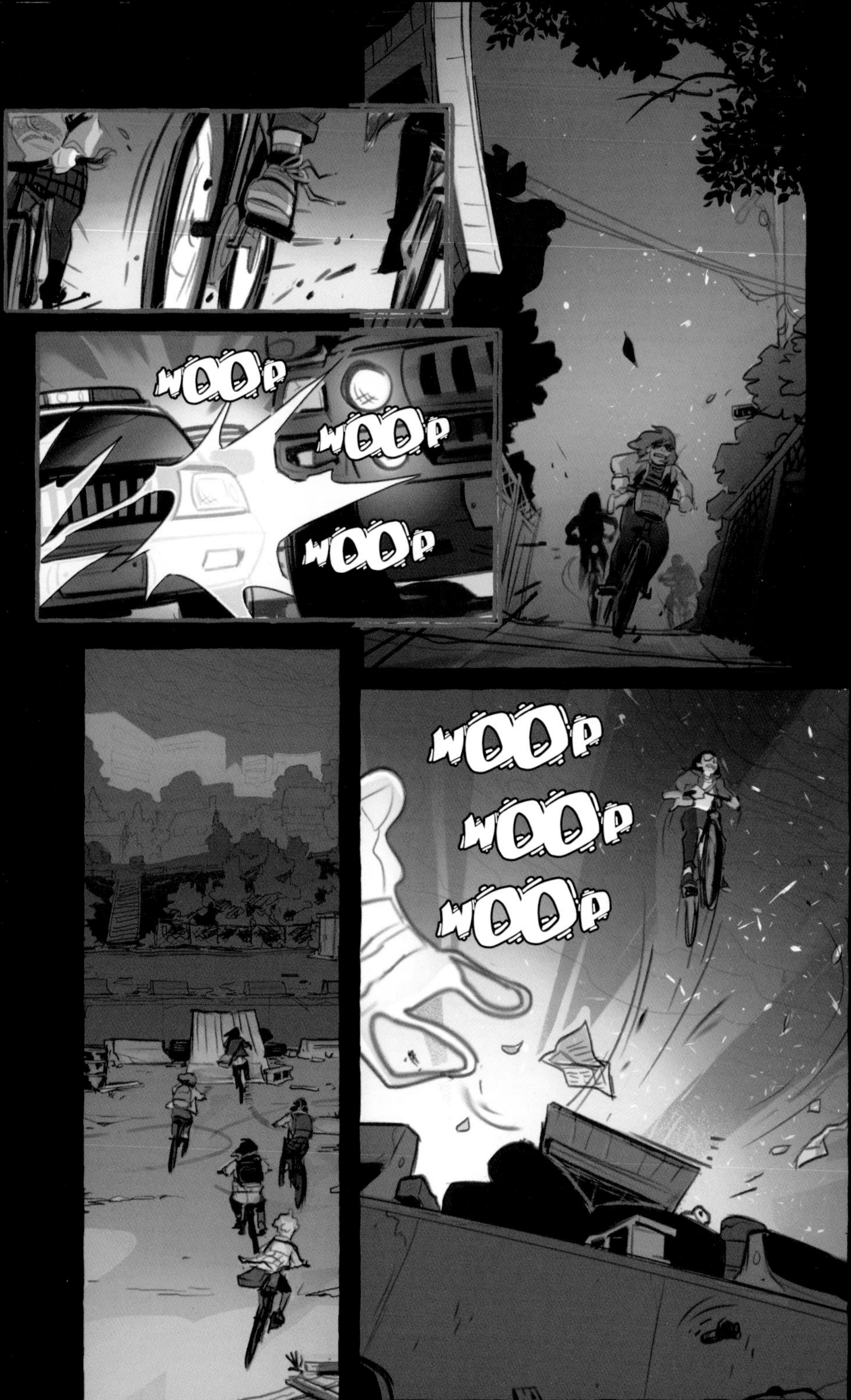
WOOP
WOOP
WOOP
WOOP
WOOP
WOOP

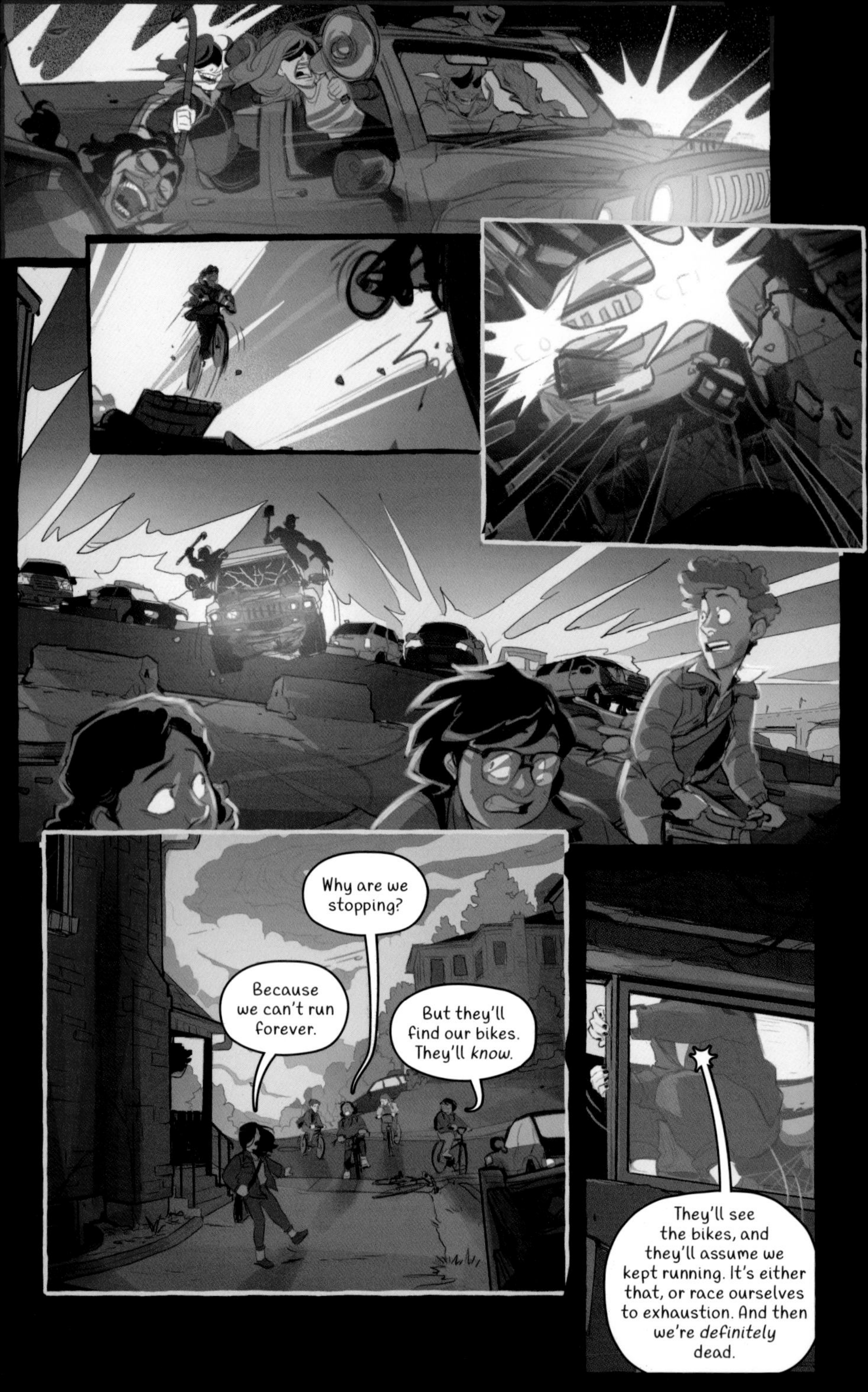
Why are we stopping?
Because we can't run forever.
But they'll find our bikes. They'll *know.*
They'll see the bikes, and they'll assume we kept running. It's either that, or race ourselves to exhaustion. And then we're *definitely* dead.

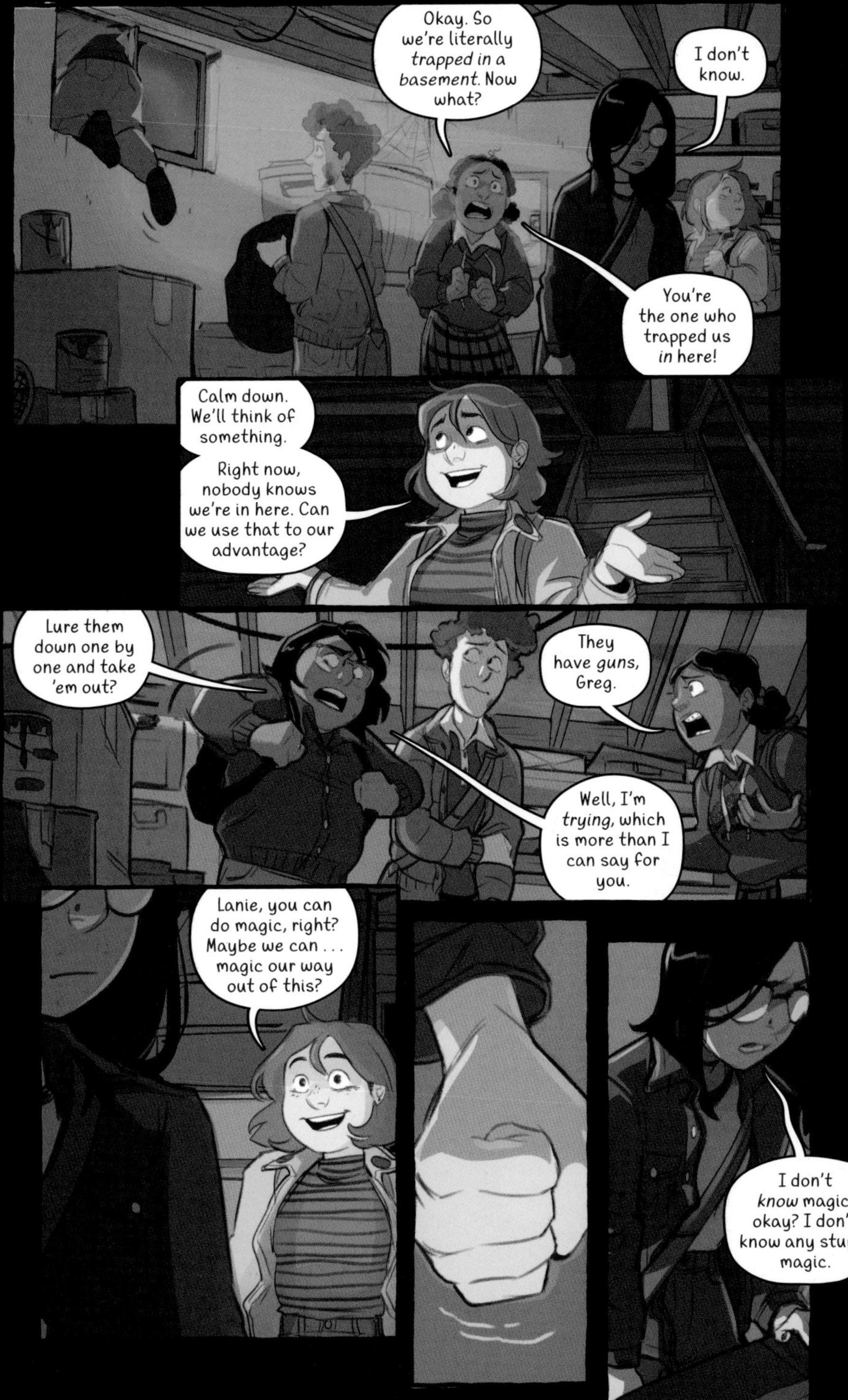
Okay. So we're literally *trapped in a basement*. Now what?
I don't know.
You're the one who trapped us *in* here!
Calm down. We'll think of something.
Right now, nobody knows we're in here. Can we use that to our advantage?
Lure them down one by one and take 'em out?
They have *guns*, Greg.
Well, I'm *trying*, which is more than I can say for you.
Lanie, you can do magic, right? Maybe we can . . . magic our way out of this?
I don't *know* magic, okay? I don't know any stupid magic.

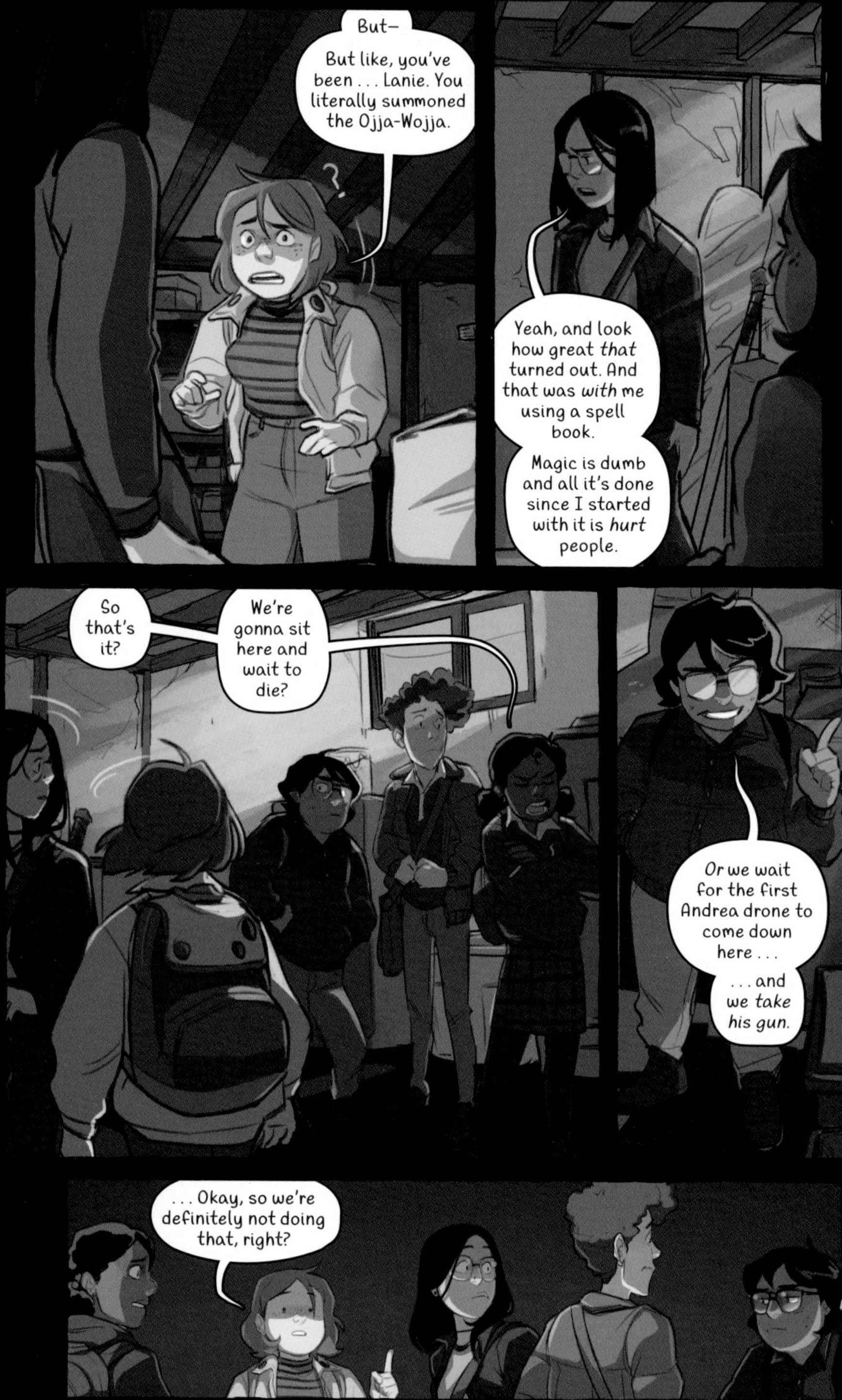

But–
But like, you've been . . . Lanie. You literally summoned the Ojja-Wojja.
?
Yeah, and look how great *that* turned out. And that was *with* me using a spell book.
Magic is dumb and all it's done since I started with it is *hurt* people.
So that's it?
We're gonna sit here and wait to die?
Or we wait for the first Andrea drone to come down here . . .
. . . and we take his gun.
. . . Okay, so we're definitely not doing that, right?

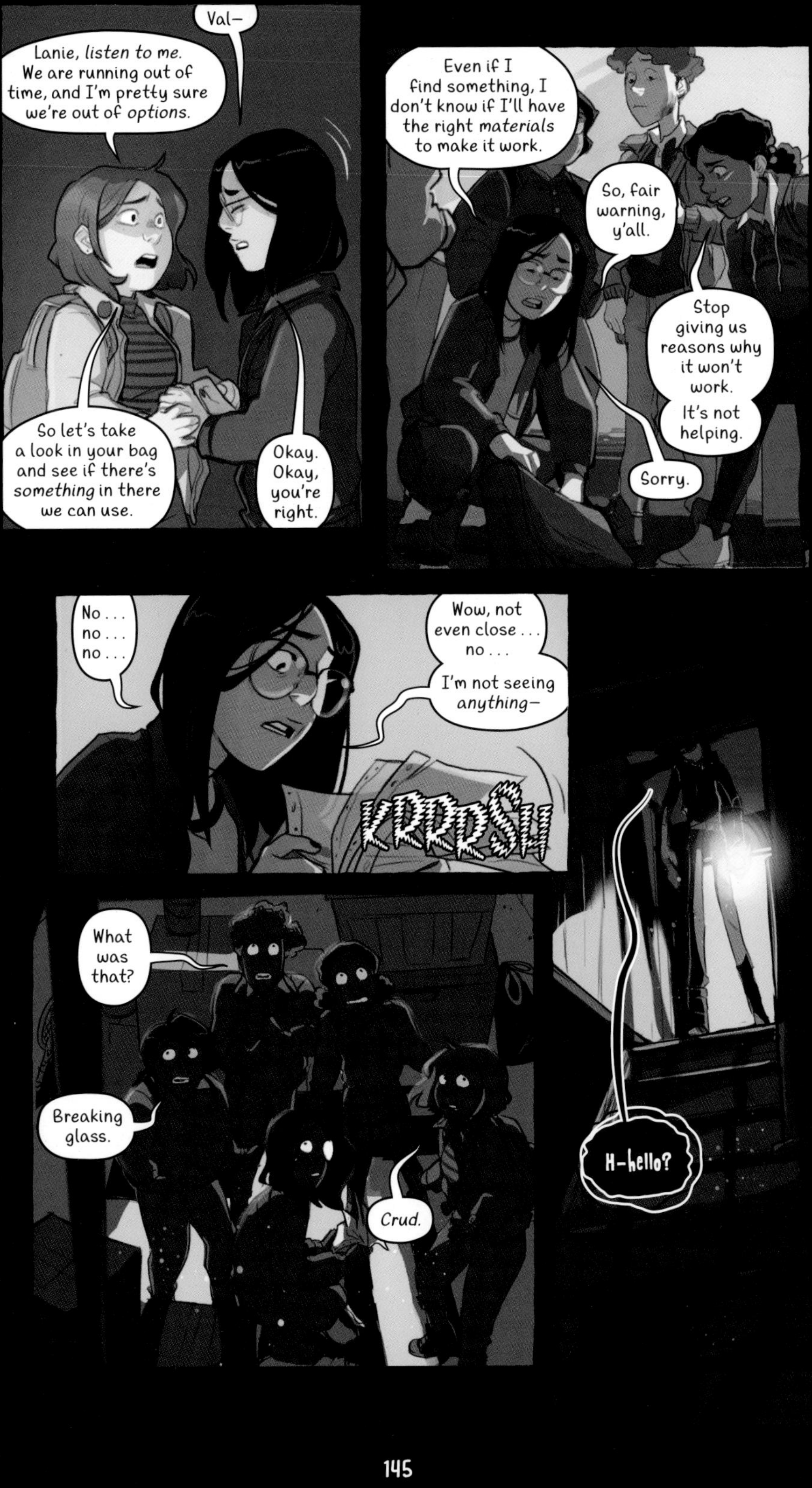
Lanie, *listen to me.* We are running out of time, and I'm pretty sure we're out of *options.*
Val—
So let's take a look in your bag and see if there's *something* in there we can use.
Okay. Okay, you're right.
Even if I find something, I don't know if I'll have the right *materials* to make it work.
So, fair warning, y'all.
Stop giving us reasons why it won't work.
It's not helping.
Sorry.
No . . . no . . . no . . .
Wow, not even close . . . no . . .
I'm not seeing *anything*—
KRRRSH
What was that?
Breaking glass.
Crud.
H-hello?

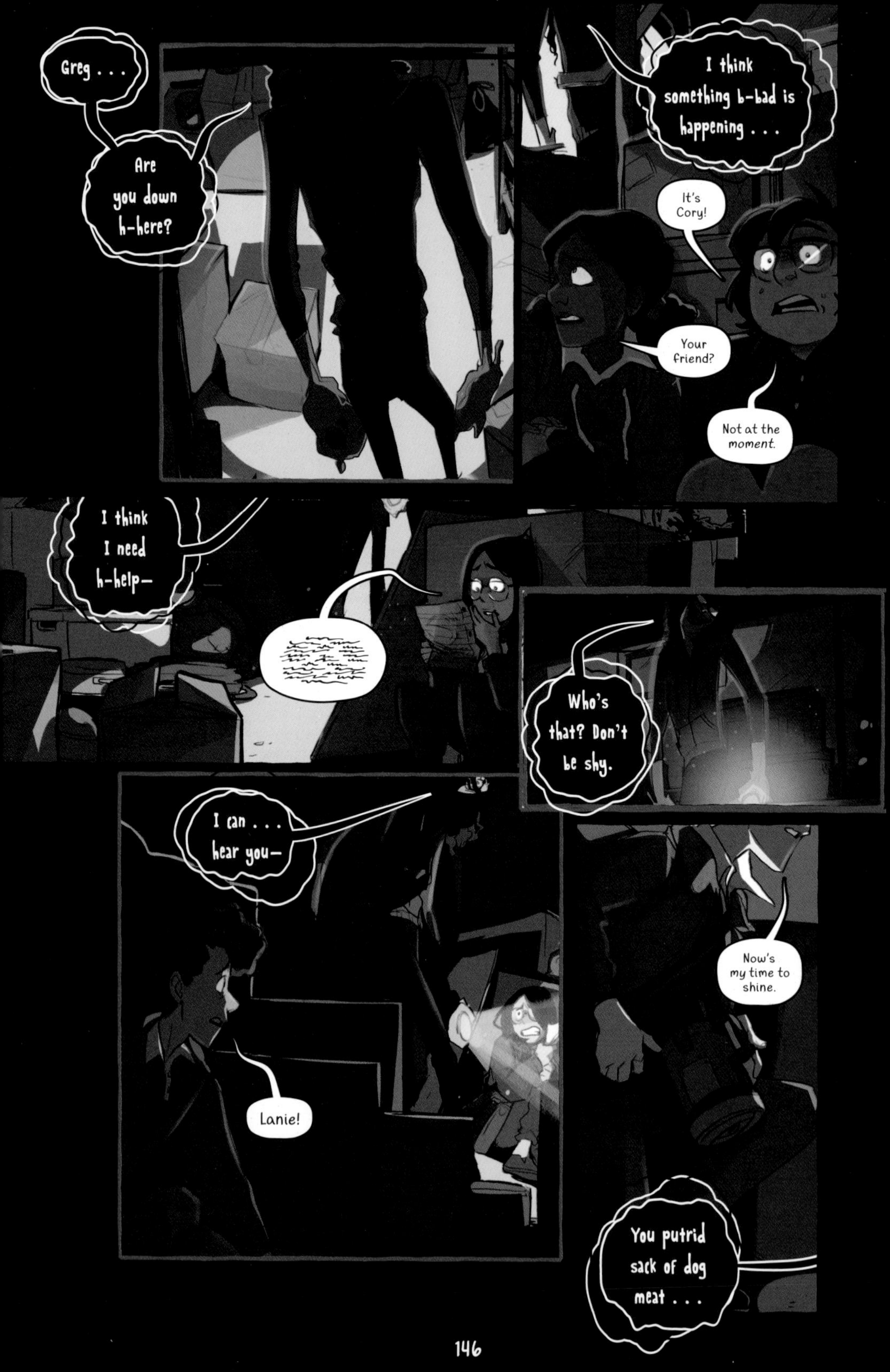
Greg . . .
Are you down h-here?
I think something b-bad is happening . . .
It's Cory!
Your friend?
Not at the moment.
I think I need h-help—
Who's that? Don't be shy.
I can . . . hear you—
Lanie!
Now's my time to shine.
You putrid sack of dog meat . . .

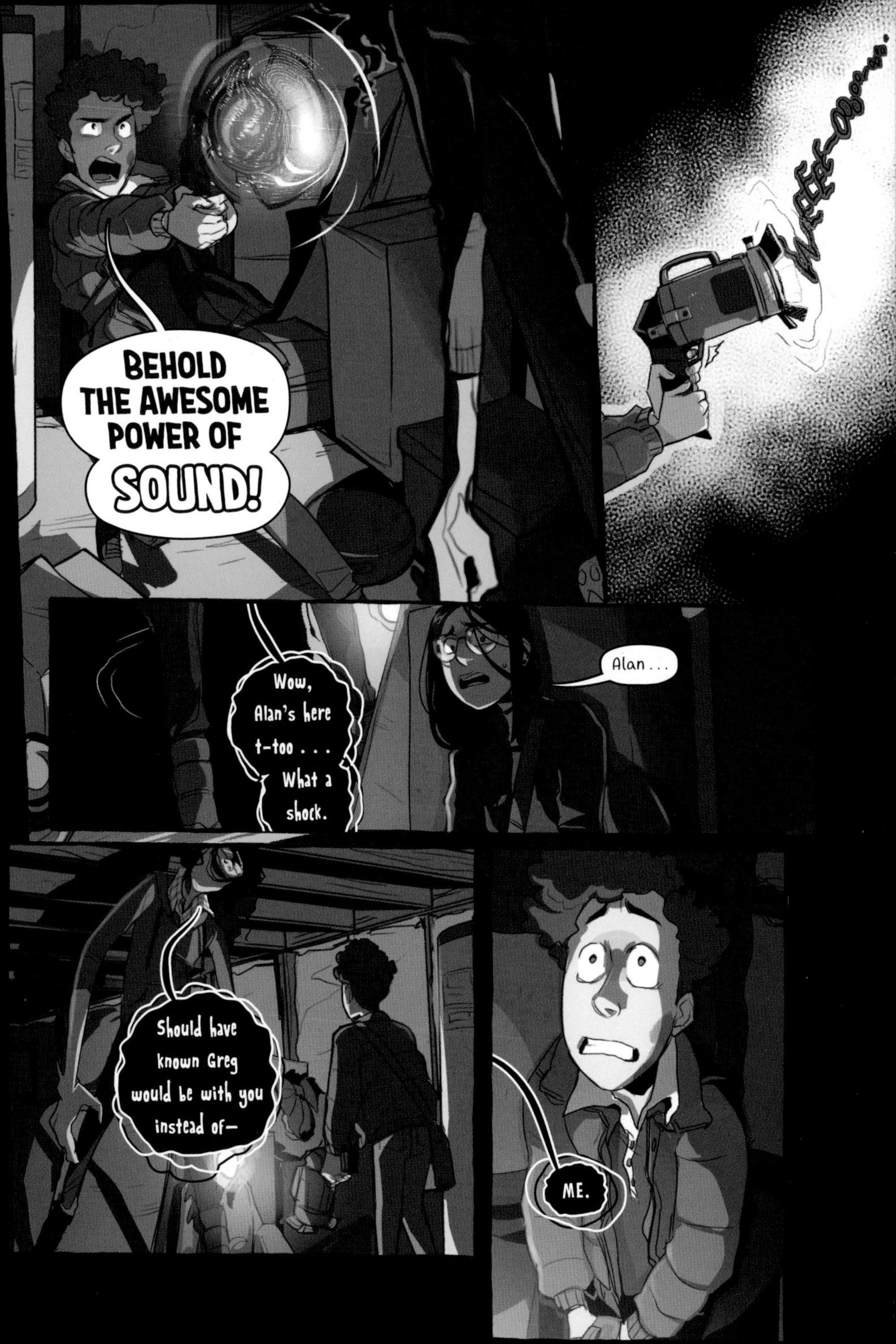

BEHOLD THE AWESOME POWER OF SOUND!
WHEEEE-OOooo...
Wow, Alan's here t-too . . . What a shock.
Alan . . .
Should have known Greg would be with you instead of—
ME.

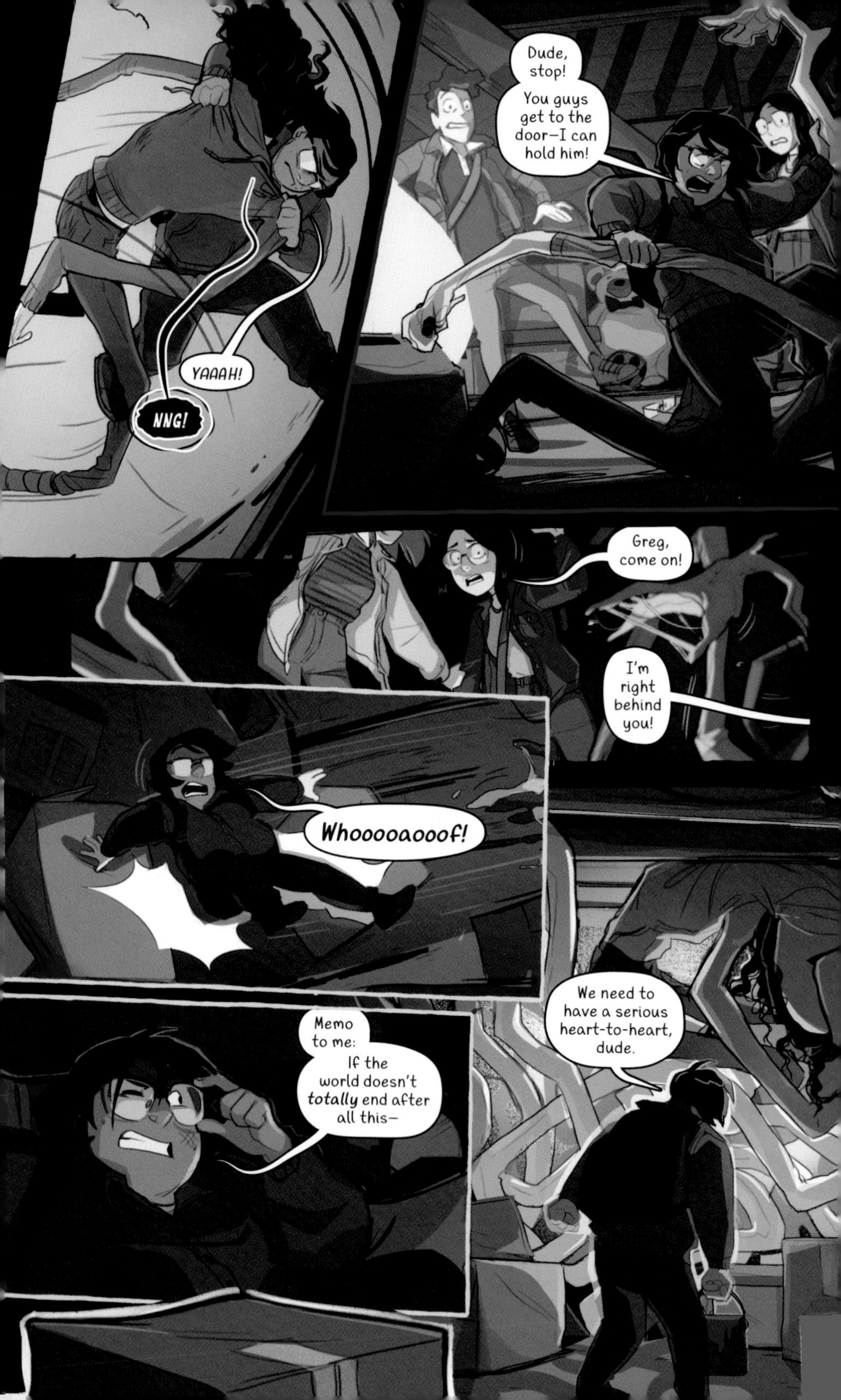
YAAAH!
NNG!
Dude, stop!
You guys get to the door—I can hold him!
Greg, come on!
I'm right behind you!
Whooooaooof!
Memo to me:
If the world doesn't *totally* end after all this—
We need to have a serious heart-to-heart, dude.

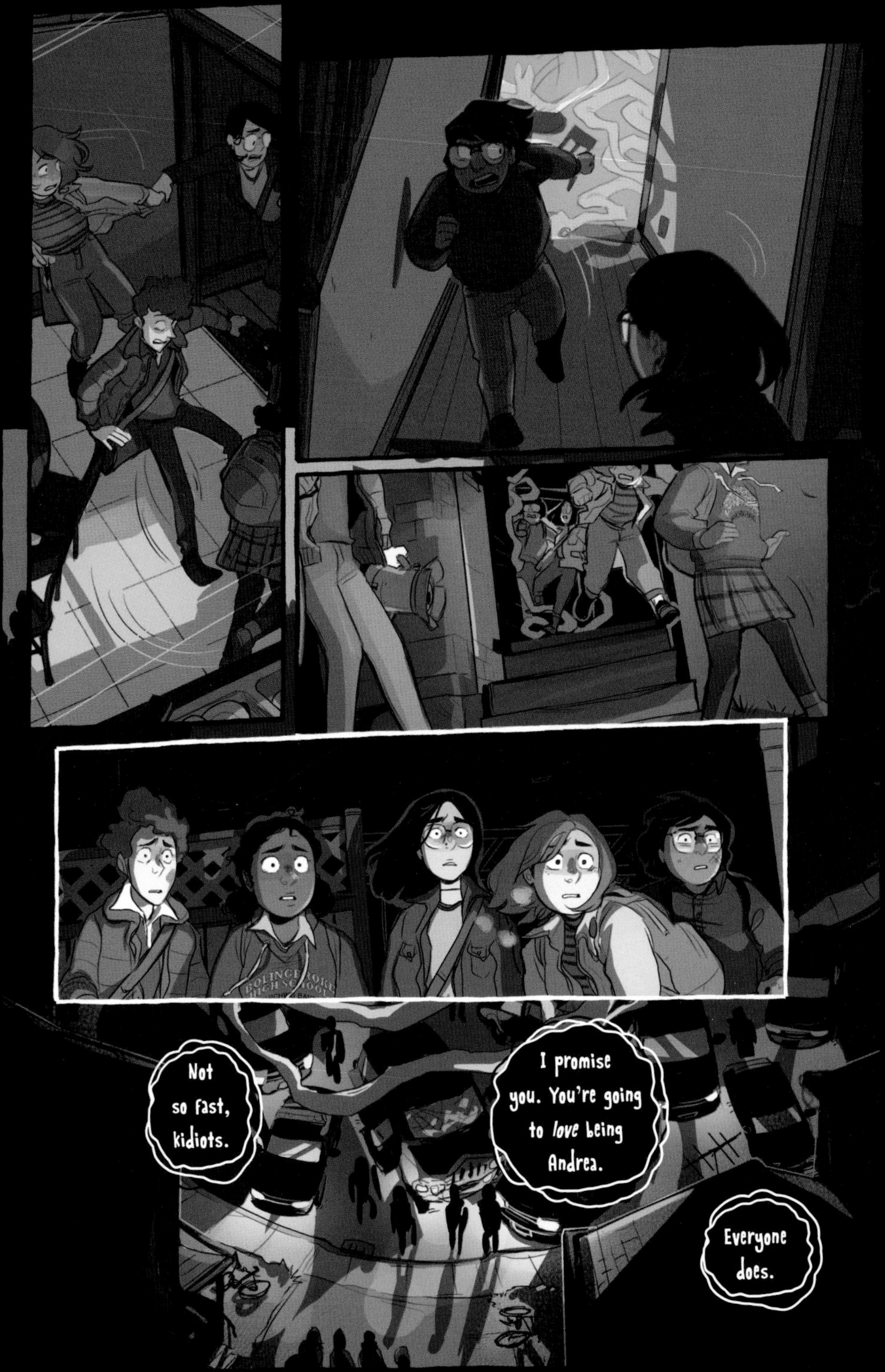
Not so fast, kidiots.
I promise you. You're going to *love* being Andrea.
Everyone does.

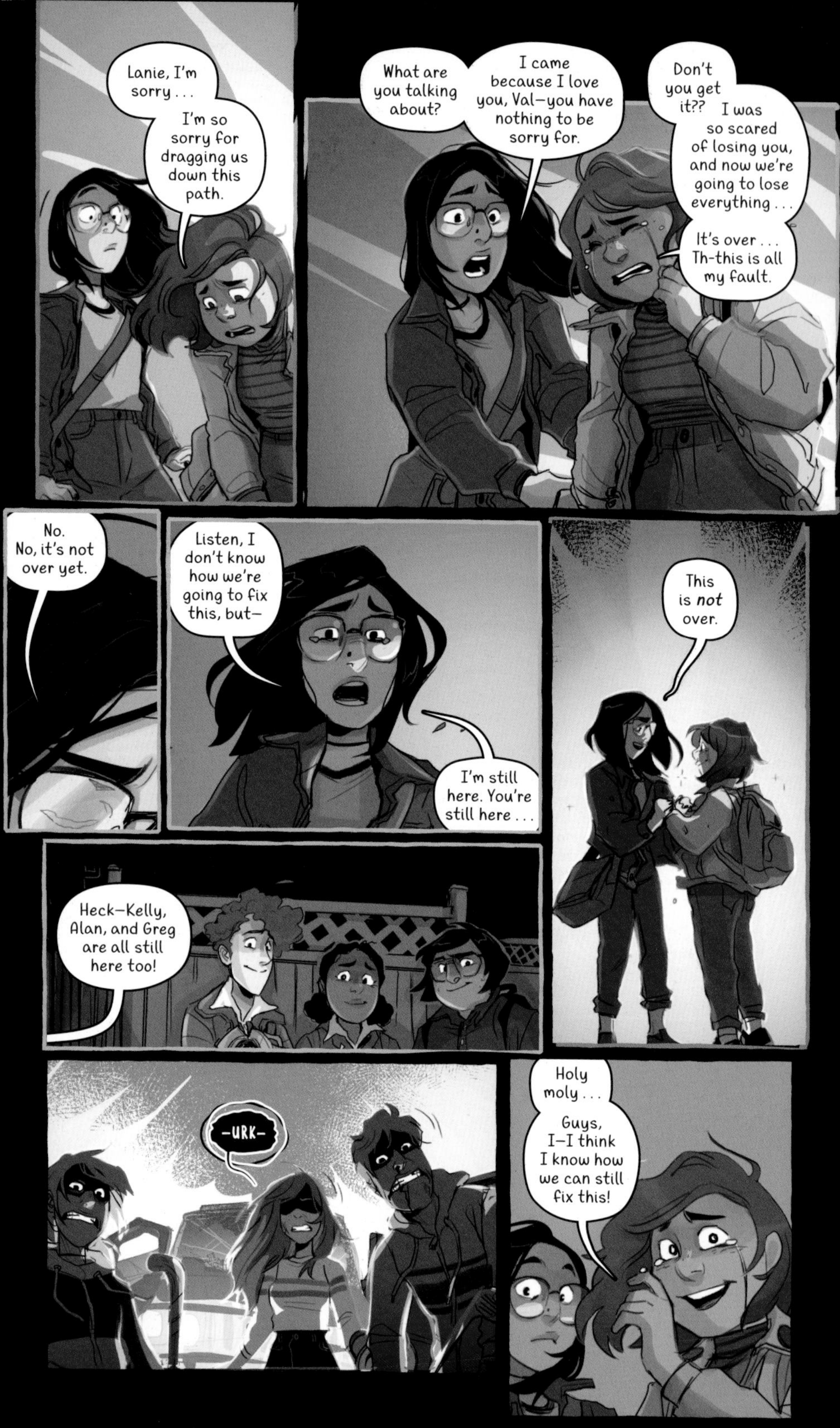
Lanie, I'm sorry . . .
I'm so sorry for dragging us down this path.
What are you talking about?
I came because I love you, Val—you have nothing to be sorry for.
Don't you get it?? I was so scared of losing you, and now we're going to lose everything . . .
It's over . . . Th-this is all my fault.
No. No, it's not over yet.
Listen, I don't know how we're going to fix this, but—
I'm still here. You're still here . . .
This is *not* over.
Heck—Kelly, Alan, and Greg are all still here too!
—URK—
Holy moly . . .
Guys, I—I think I know how we can still fix this!

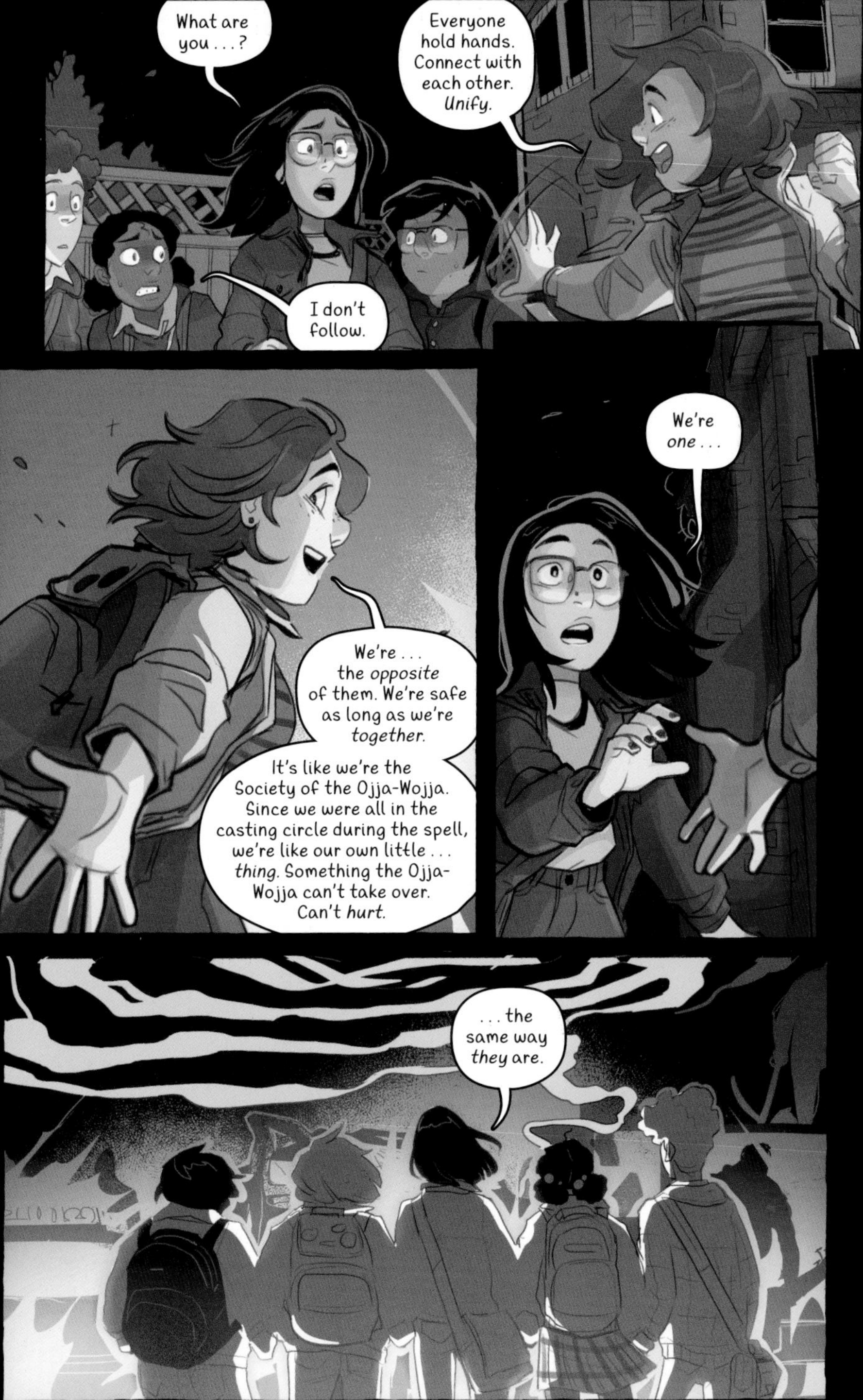
What are you . . . ?
Everyone hold hands. Connect with each other. *Unify.*
I don't follow.
We're . . . the *opposite* of them. We're safe as long as we're *together.*
It's like we're the Society of the Ojja-Wojja. Since we were all in the casting circle during the spell, we're like our own little . . . *thing.* Something the Ojja-Wojja can't take over. Can't *hurt.*
We're one . . .
. . . the same way *they* are.

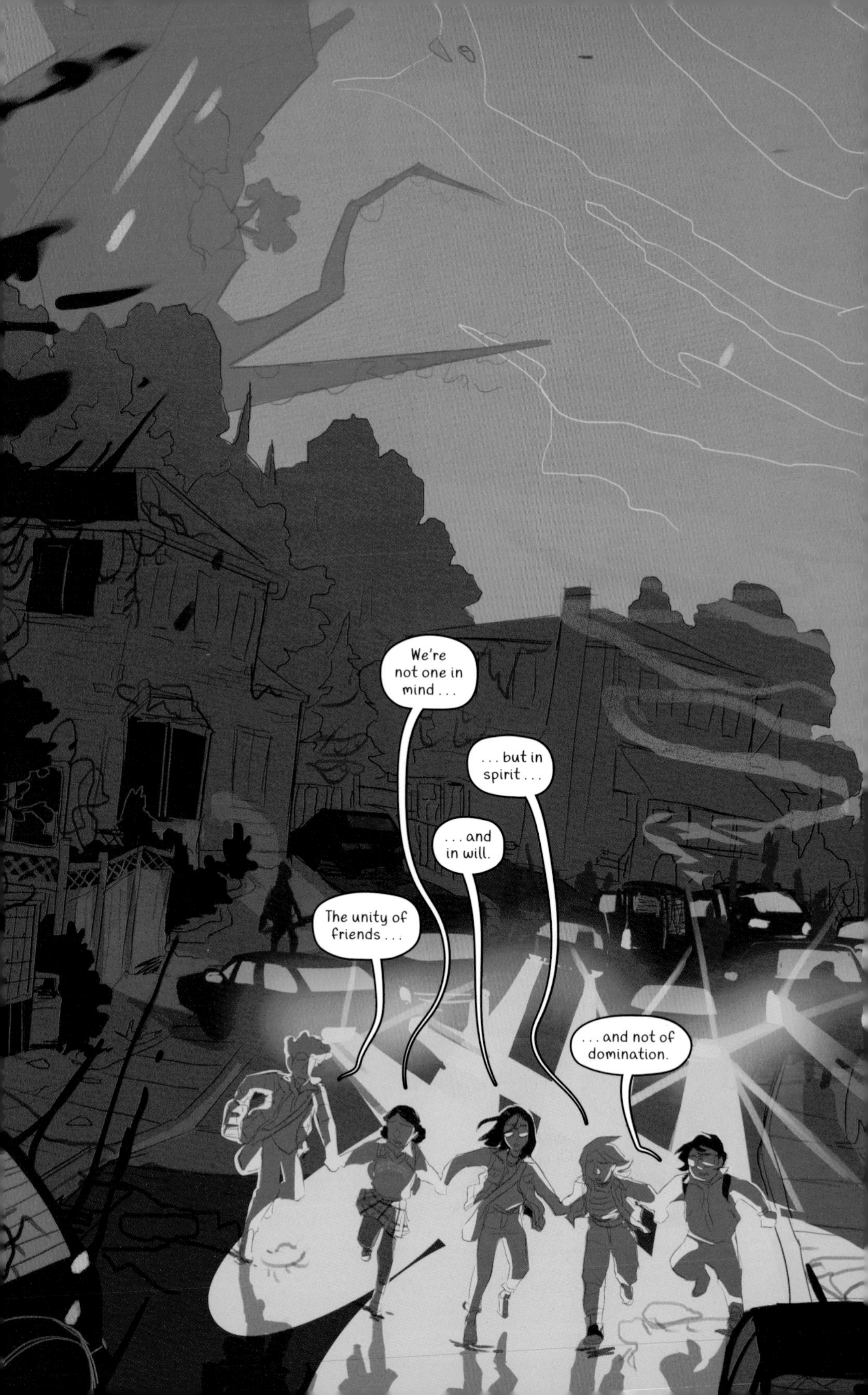
We're not one in mind . . .
. . . but in spirit . . .
. . . and in will.
The unity of friends . . .
. . . and not of domination.

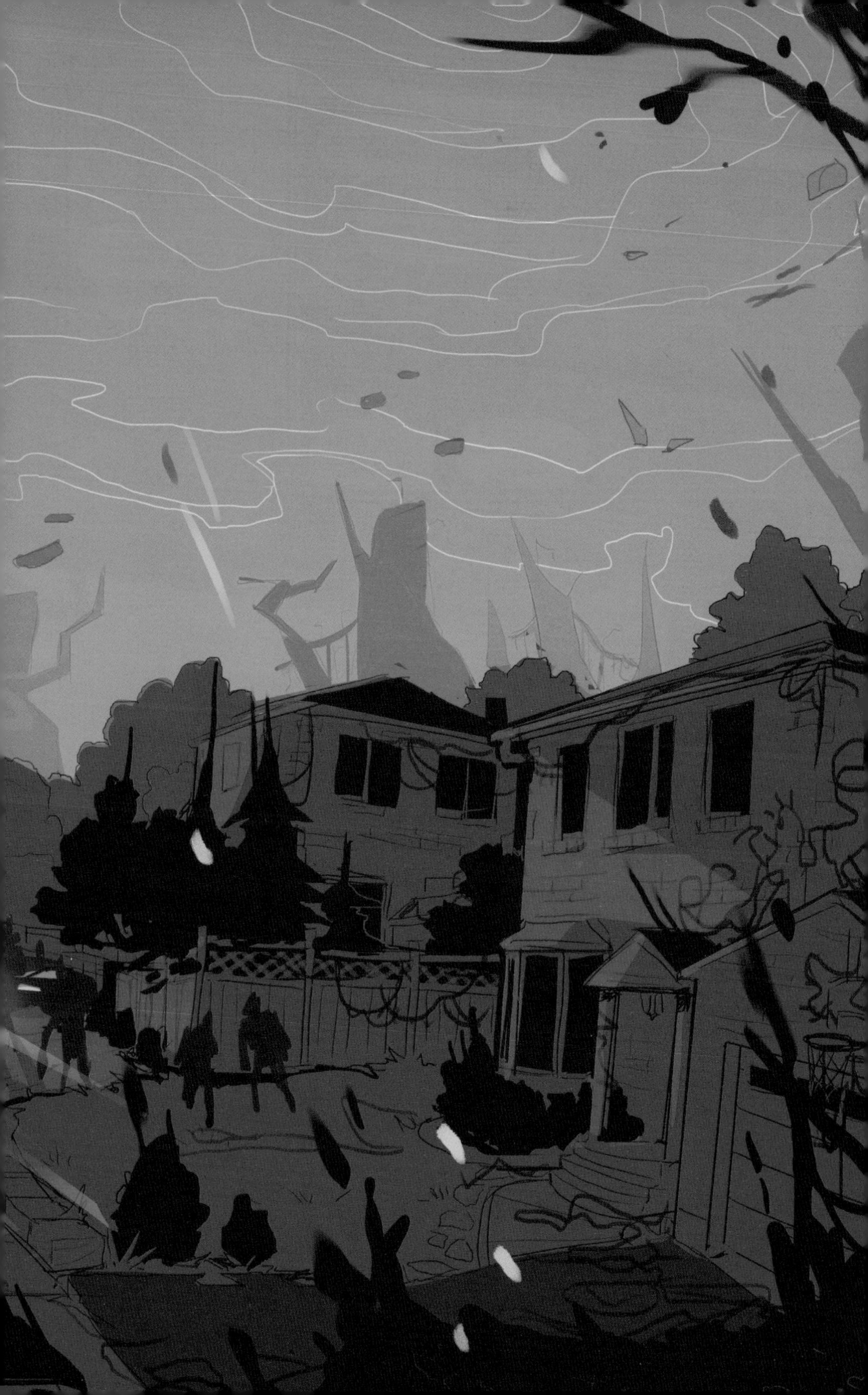

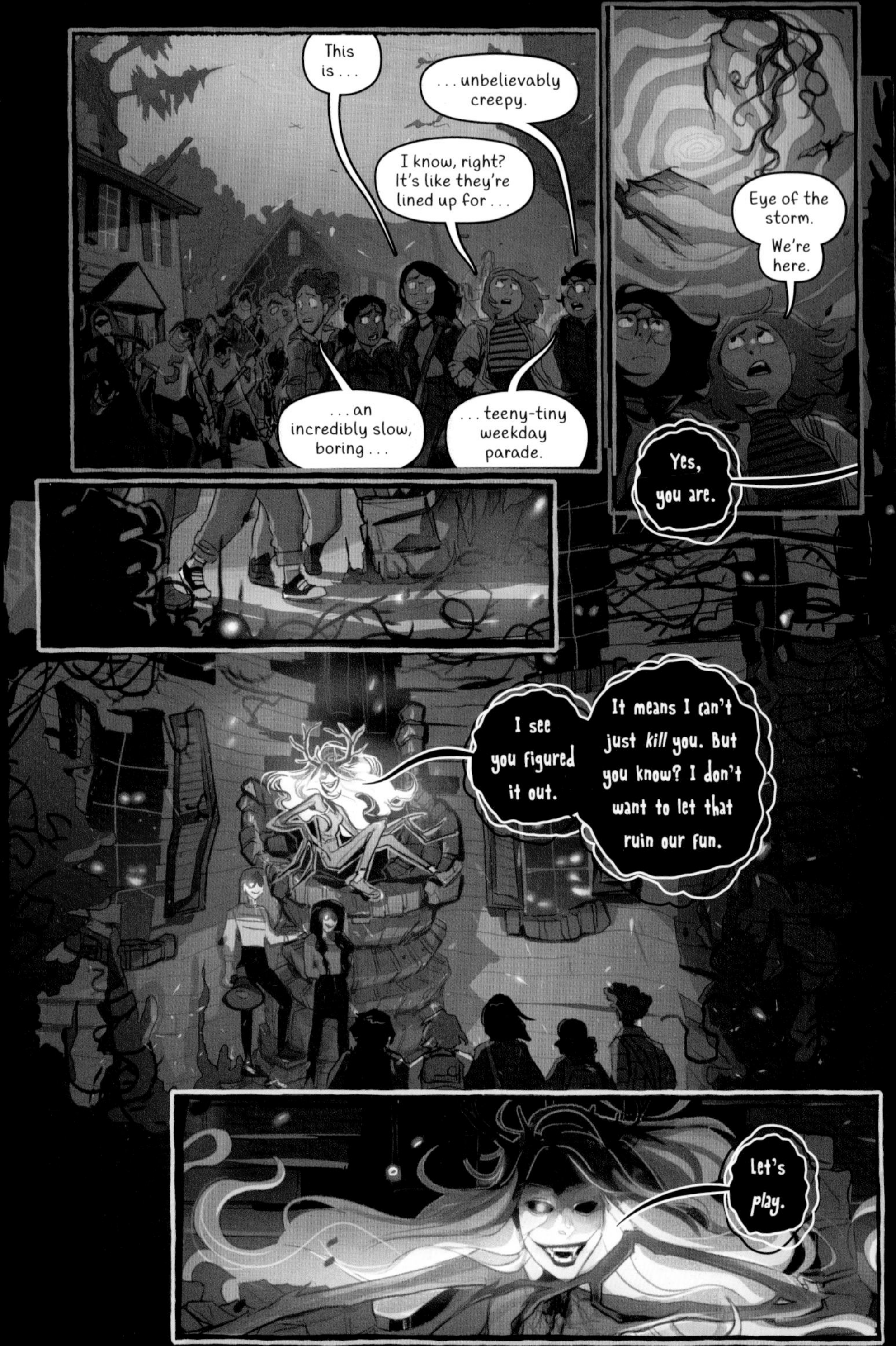
This is . . .
. . . unbelievably creepy.
I know, right? It's like they're lined up for . . .
. . . an incredibly slow, boring . . .
. . . teeny-tiny weekday parade.
Eye of the storm.
We're here.
Yes, you are.
I see you figured it out.
It means I can't just *kill* you. But you know? I don't want to let that ruin our fun.
Let's *play*.

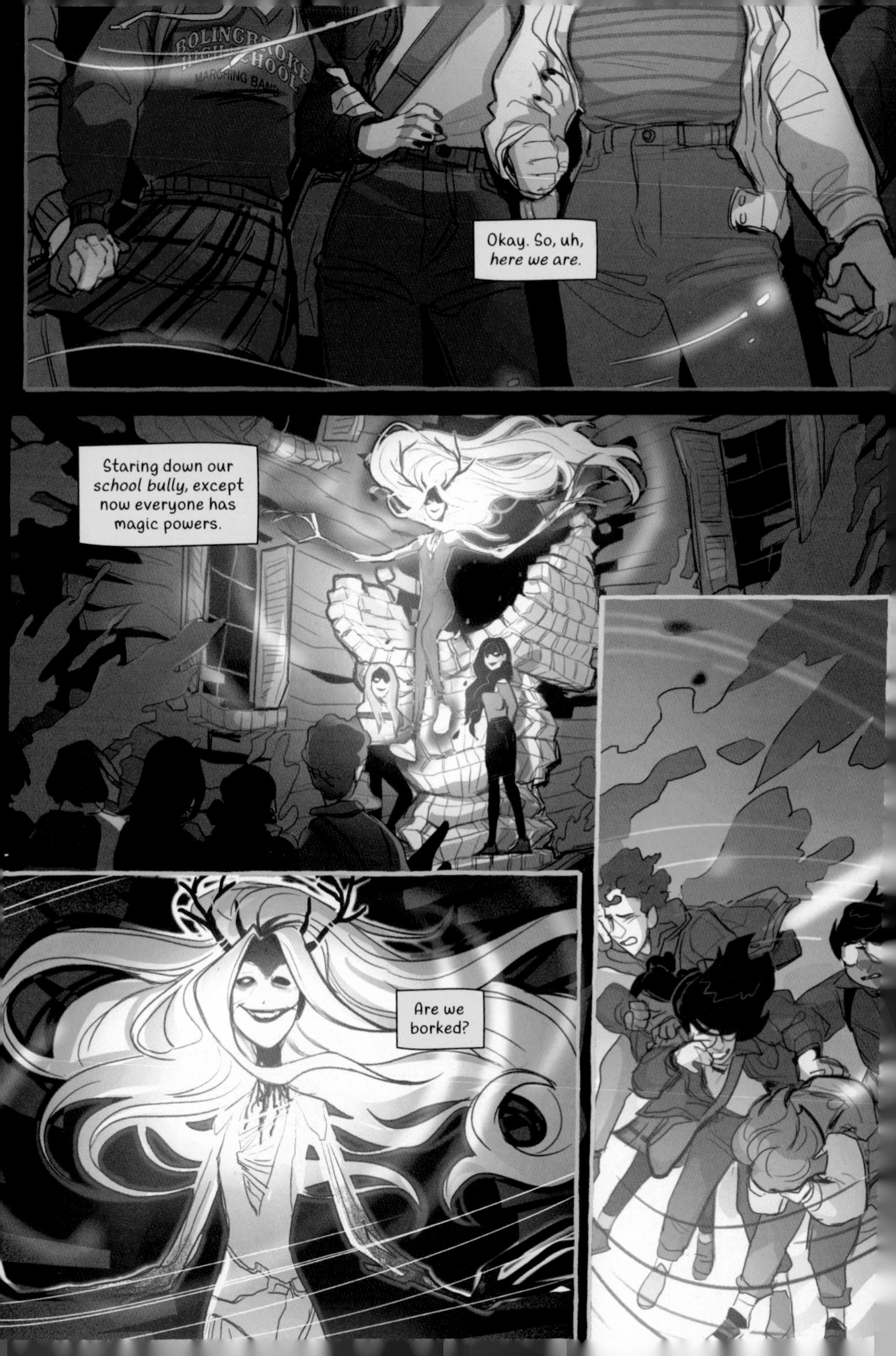
BOLINGBROKE HIGH SCHOOL MARCHING BAND
Okay. So, uh, here we are.
Staring down our *school bully*, except now everyone has magic powers.
Are we borked?

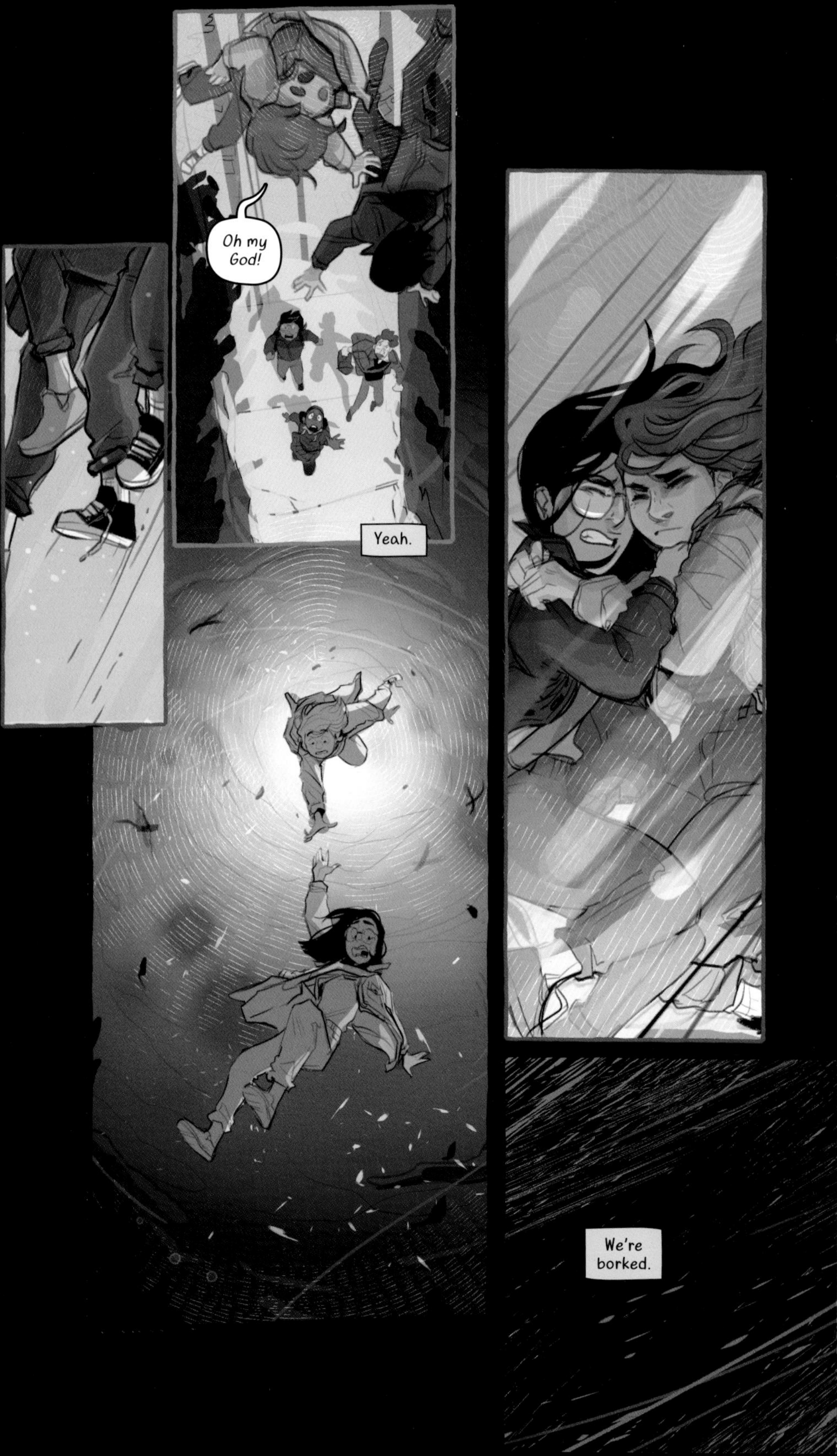
Oh my God!
Yeah.
We're borked.

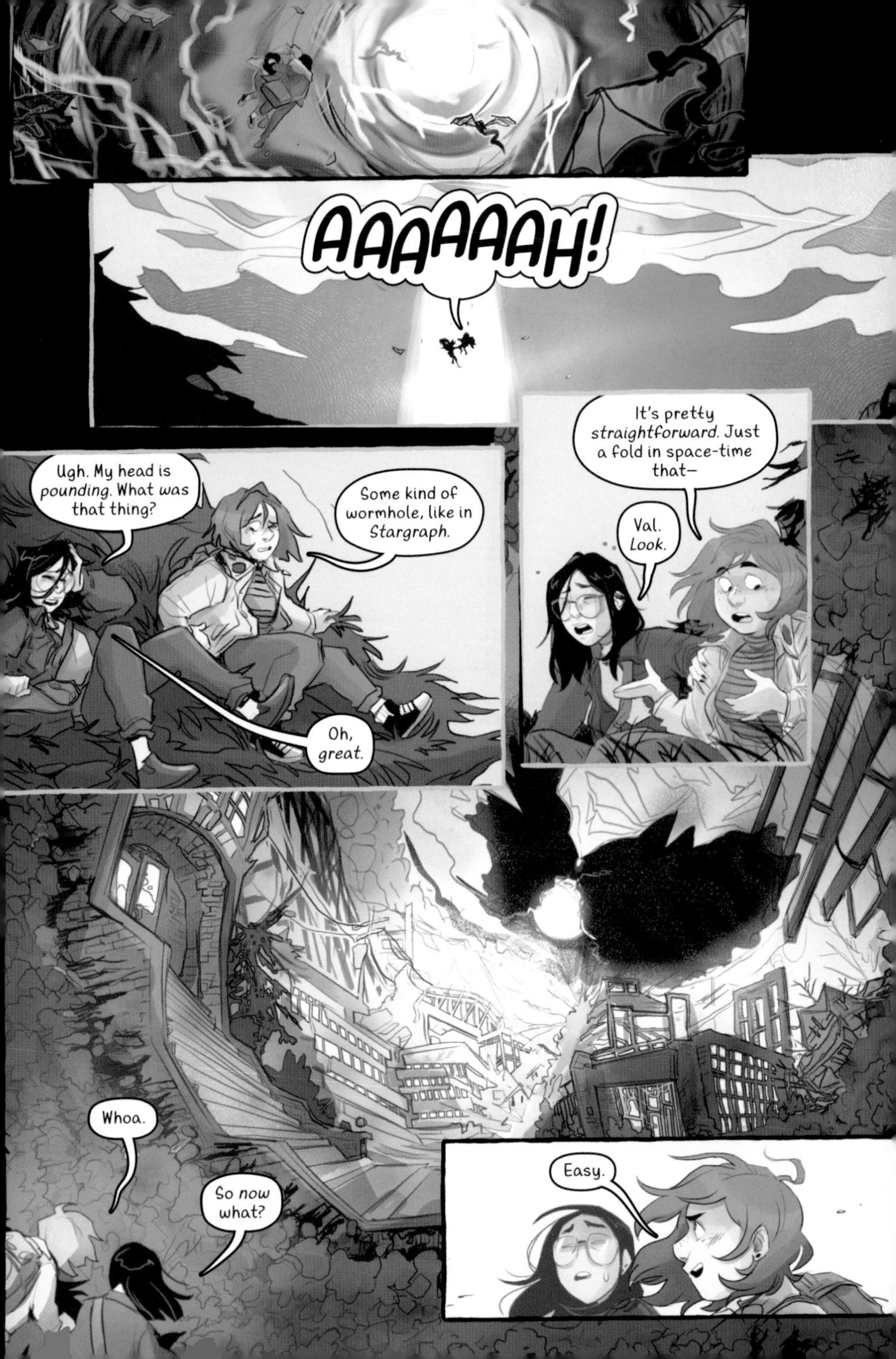
AAAAAAH!
Ugh. My head is pounding. What was that thing?
Some kind of wormhole, like in Stargraph.
Oh, great.
It's pretty straightforward. Just a fold in space-time that–
Val. Look.
Whoa.
So now what?
Easy.

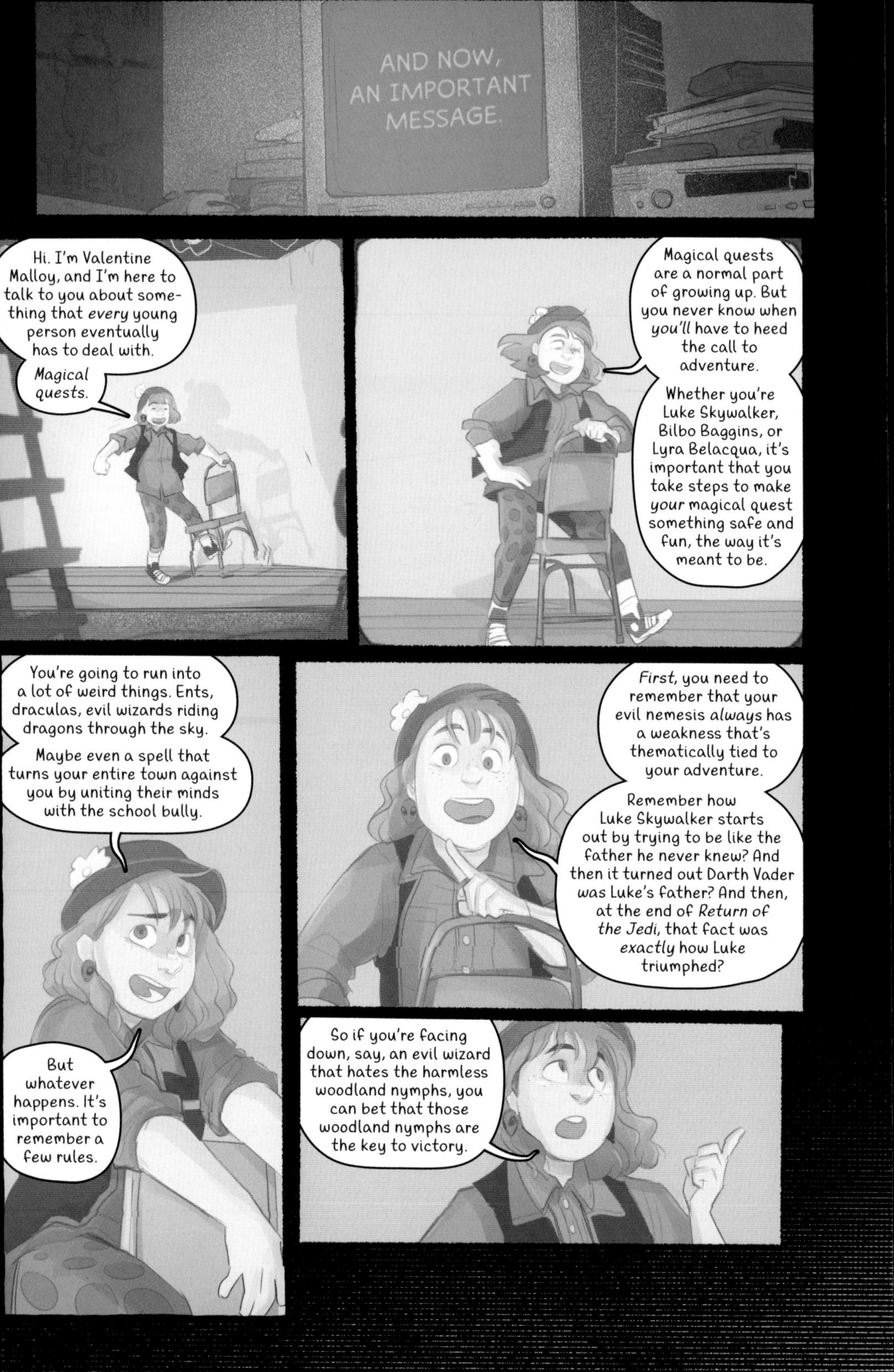
AND NOW, AN IMPORTANT MESSAGE.
Hi. I'm Valentine Malloy, and I'm here to talk to you about something that *every* young person eventually has to deal with.
Magical quests.
Magical quests are a normal part of growing up. But you never know when *you'll* have to heed the call to adventure.
Whether you're Luke Skywalker, Bilbo Baggins, or Lyra Belacqua, it's important that you take steps to make *your* magical quest something safe and fun, the way it's meant to be.
You're going to run into a lot of weird things. Ents, draculas, evil wizards riding dragons through the sky.
Maybe even a spell that turns your entire town against you by uniting their minds with the school bully.
But whatever happens. It's important to remember a few rules.
First, you need to remember that your evil nemesis *always* has a weakness that's thematically tied to your adventure.
Remember how Luke Skywalker starts out by trying to be like the father he never knew? And then it turned out Darth Vader *was* Luke's father? And then, at the end of *Return of the Jedi*, that fact was *exactly* how Luke triumphed?
So if you're facing down, say, an evil wizard that hates the harmless woodland nymphs, you can bet that those woodland nymphs are the key to victory.

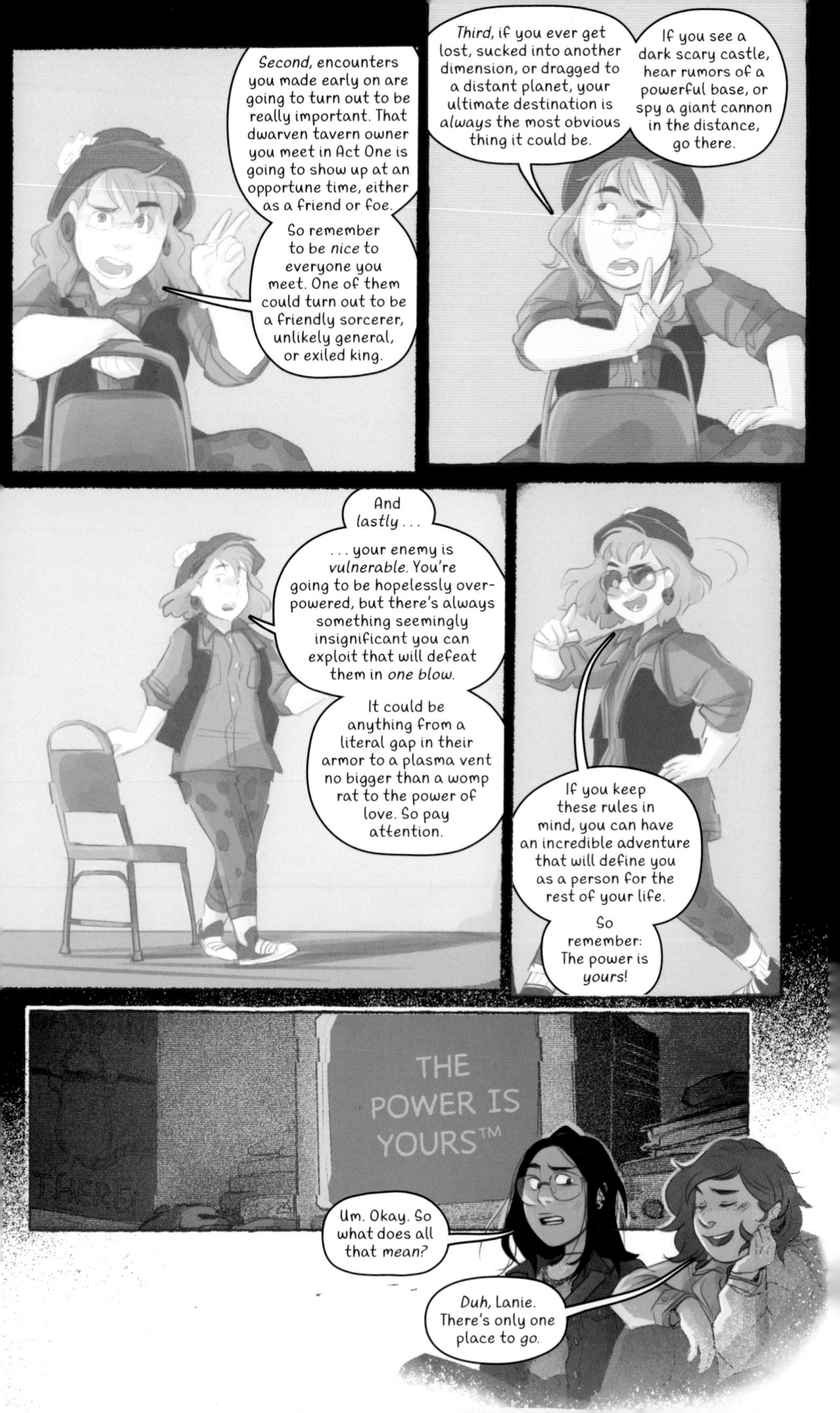

Second, encounters you made early on are going to turn out to be really important. That dwarven tavern owner you meet in Act One is going to show up at an opportune time, either as a friend or foe.

So remember to be *nice* to everyone you meet. One of them could turn out to be a friendly sorcerer, unlikely general, or exiled king.

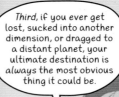

Third, if you ever get lost, sucked into another dimension, or dragged to a distant planet, your ultimate destination is *always* the most obvious thing it could be.

If you see a dark scary castle, hear rumors of a powerful base, or spy a giant cannon in the distance, go there.

And lastly . . .

. . . your enemy is *vulnerable*. You're going to be hopelessly overpowered, but there's always something seemingly insignificant you can exploit that will defeat them in *one blow*.

It could be anything from a literal gap in their armor to a plasma vent no bigger than a womp rat to the power of love. So pay attention.

If you keep these rules in mind, you can have an incredible adventure that will define you as a person for the rest of your life.

So remember: The power is yours!

THE POWER IS YOURS™

Um. Okay. So what does all that *mean*?

Duh, Lanie. There's only one place to go.

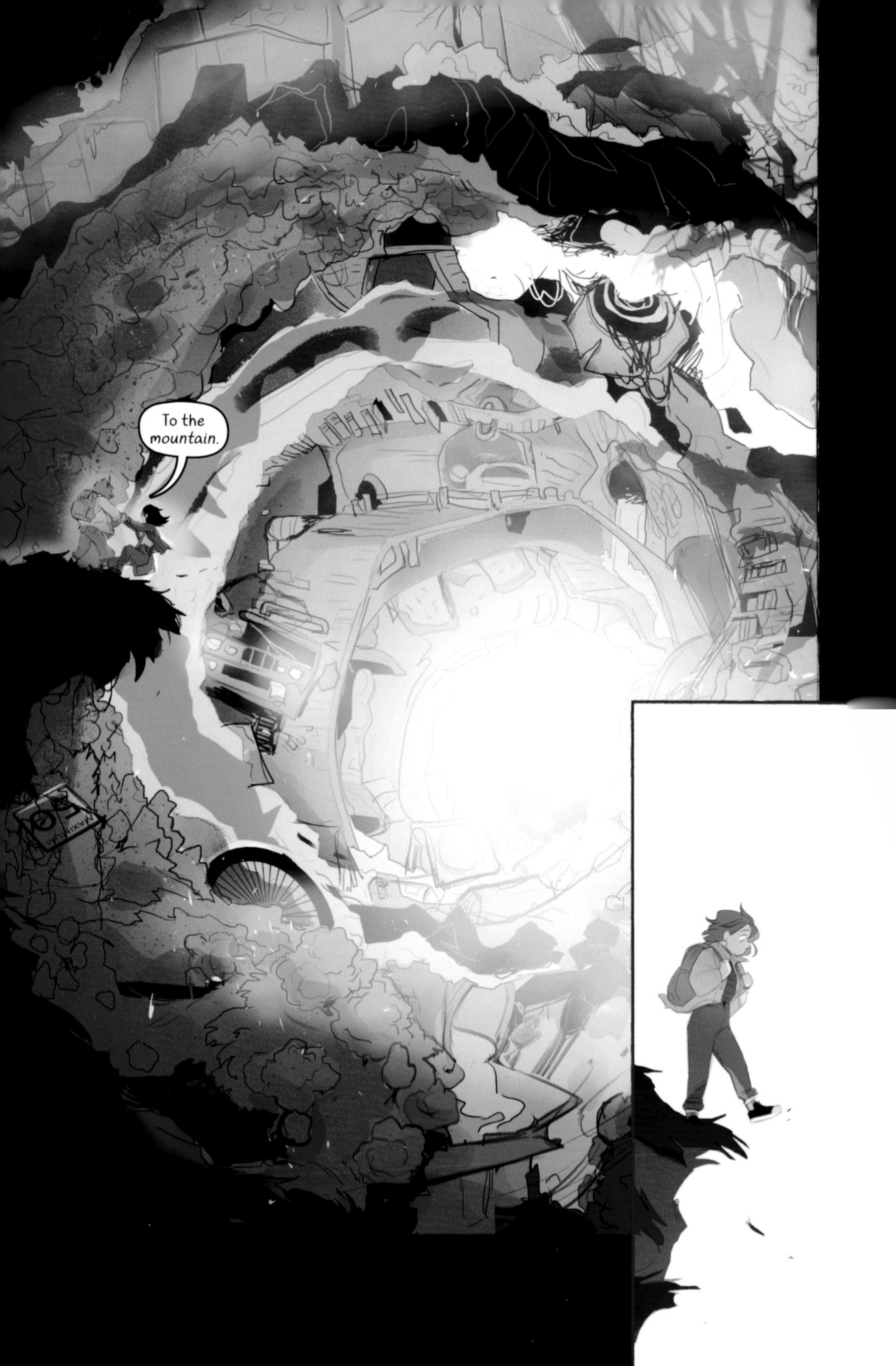
To the mountain.

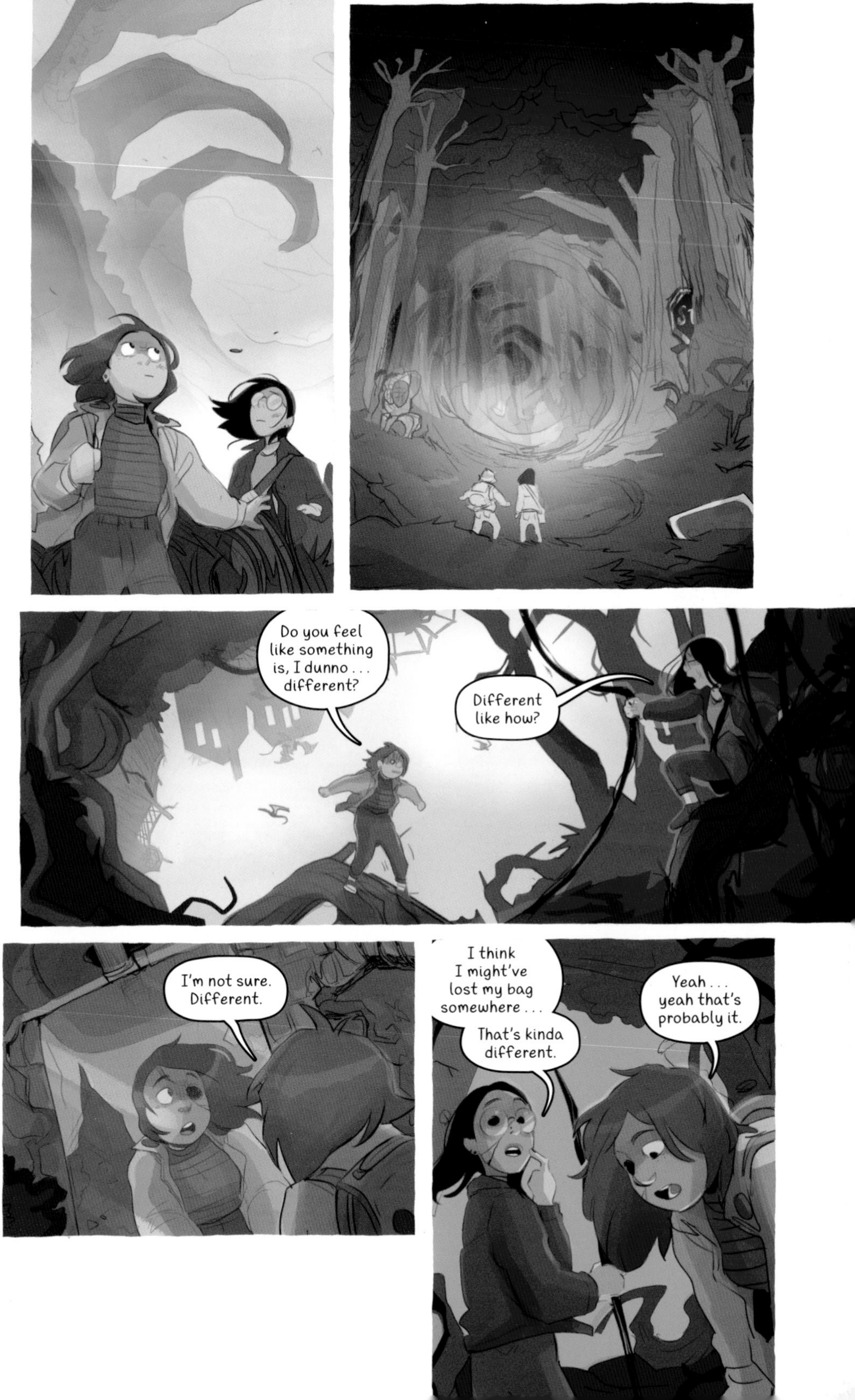
Do you feel like something is, I dunno . . . different?
Different like how?
I'm not sure. Different.
I think I might've lost my bag somewhere . . .
That's kinda different.
Yeah . . . yeah that's probably it.

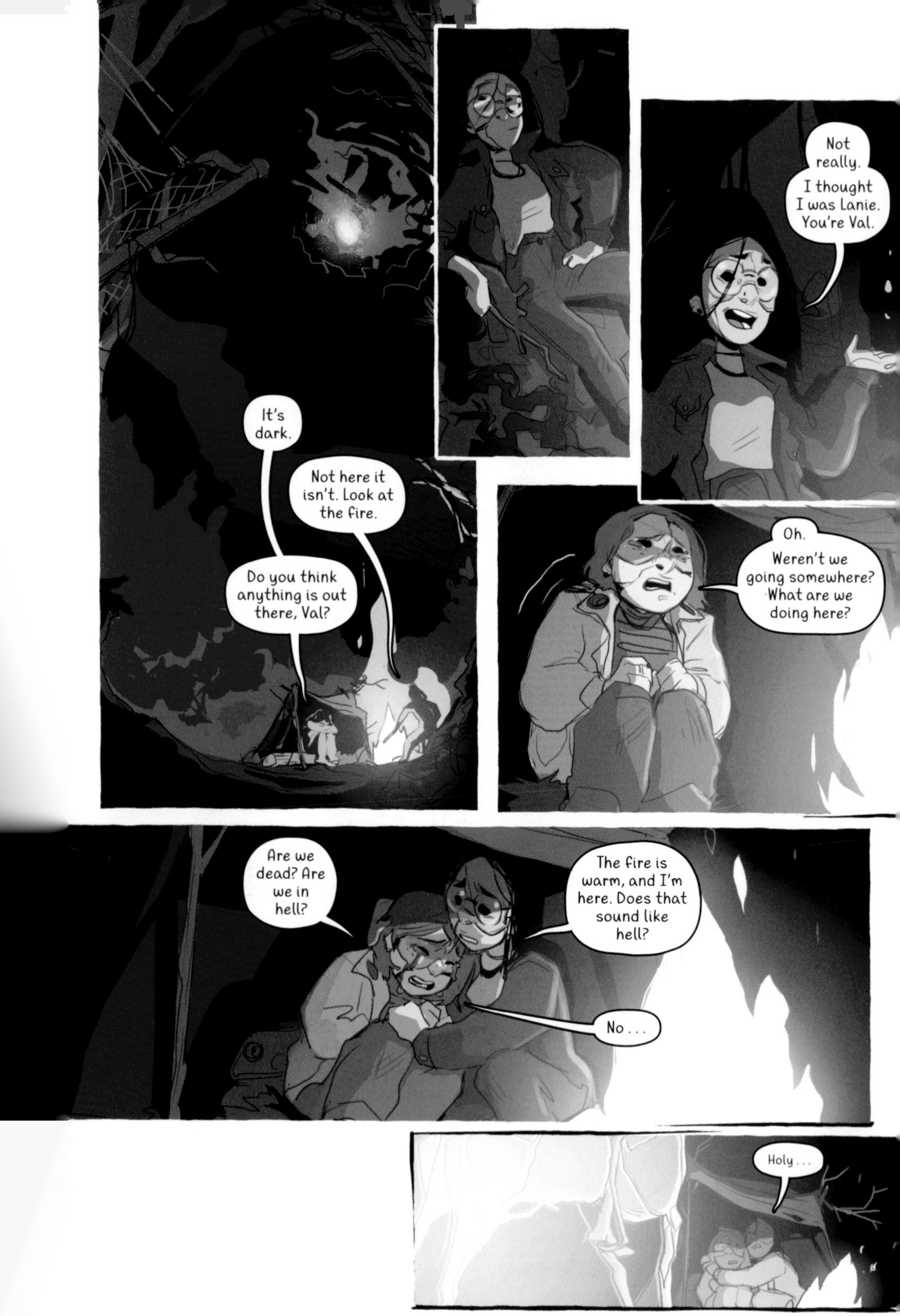

It's dark.
Not here it isn't. Look at the fire.
Do you think anything is out there, Val?
Not really. I thought I was Lanie. You're Val.
Oh. Weren't we going somewhere? What are we doing here?
Are we dead? Are we in hell?
The fire is warm, and I'm here. Does that sound like hell?
No . . .
Holy . . .

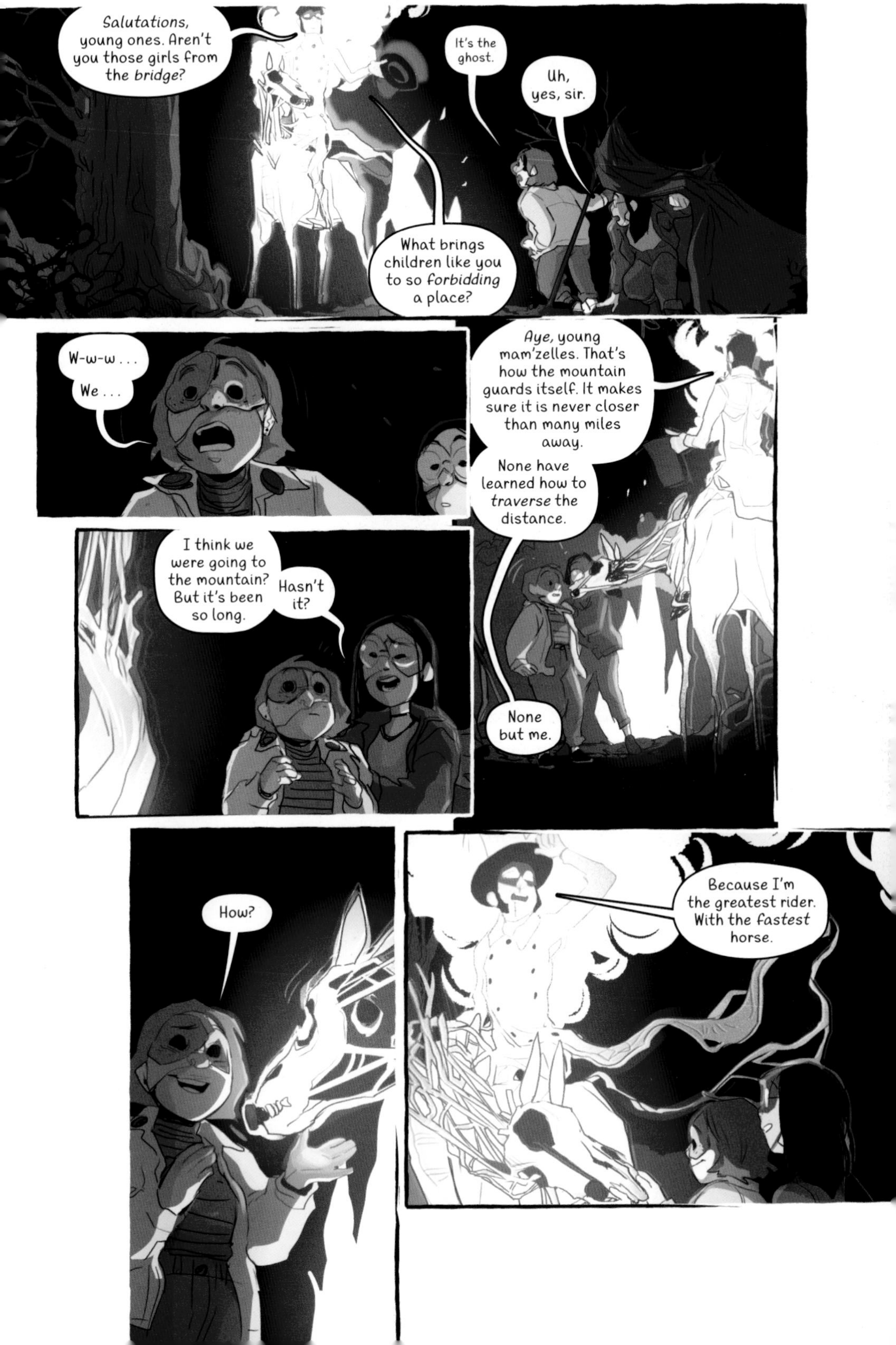
Salutations, young ones. Aren't you those girls from the *bridge*?
It's the ghost.
Uh, yes, sir.
What brings children like you to so *forbidding* a place?
W-w-w . . .
We . . .
I think we were going to the mountain? But it's been so long.
Hasn't it?
Aye, young mam'zelles. That's how the mountain guards itself. It makes sure it is never closer than many miles away.
None have learned how to *traverse* the distance.
None but me.
How?
Because I'm the greatest rider. With the *fastest* horse.

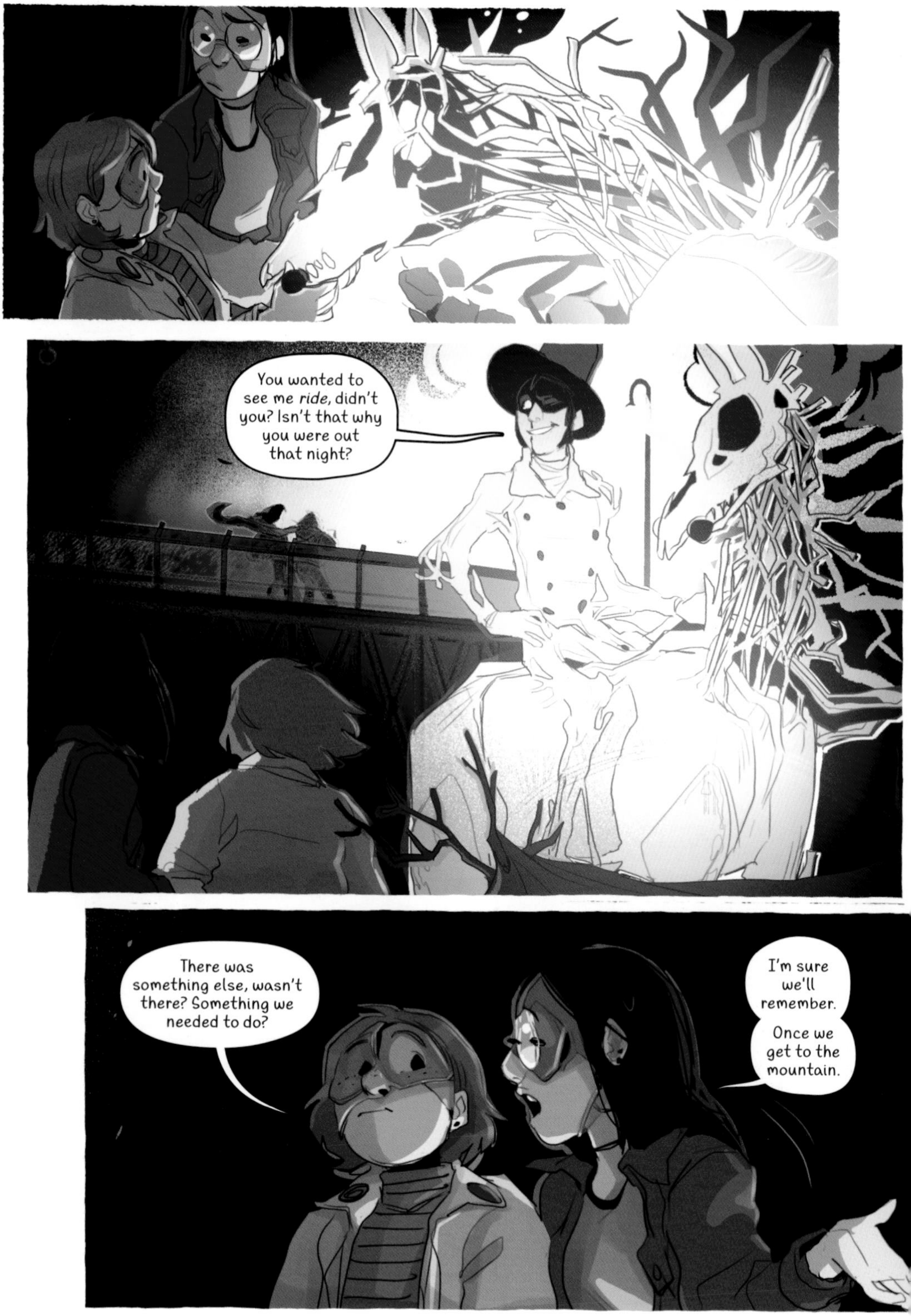
You wanted to see me *ride*, didn't you? Isn't that why you were out that night?
There was something else, wasn't there? Something we needed to do?
I'm sure we'll remember.
Once we get to the mountain.

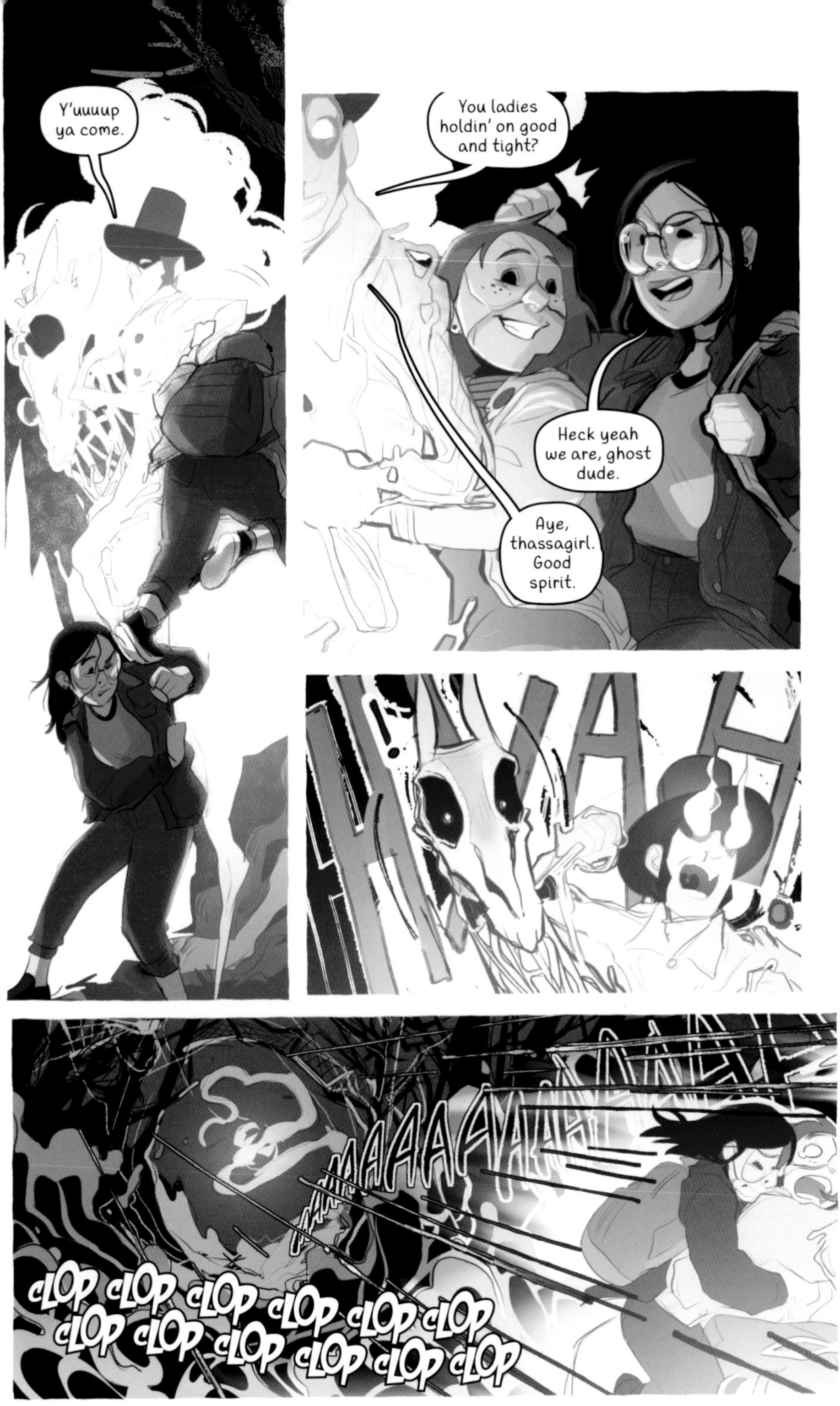
Y'uuuup ya come.
You ladies holdin' on good and tight?
Heck yeah we are, ghost dude.
Aye, thassagirl. Good spirit.
CLOP CLOP CLOP CLOP CLOP CLOP
CLOP CLOP CLOP CLOP CLOP CLOP

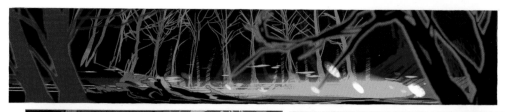

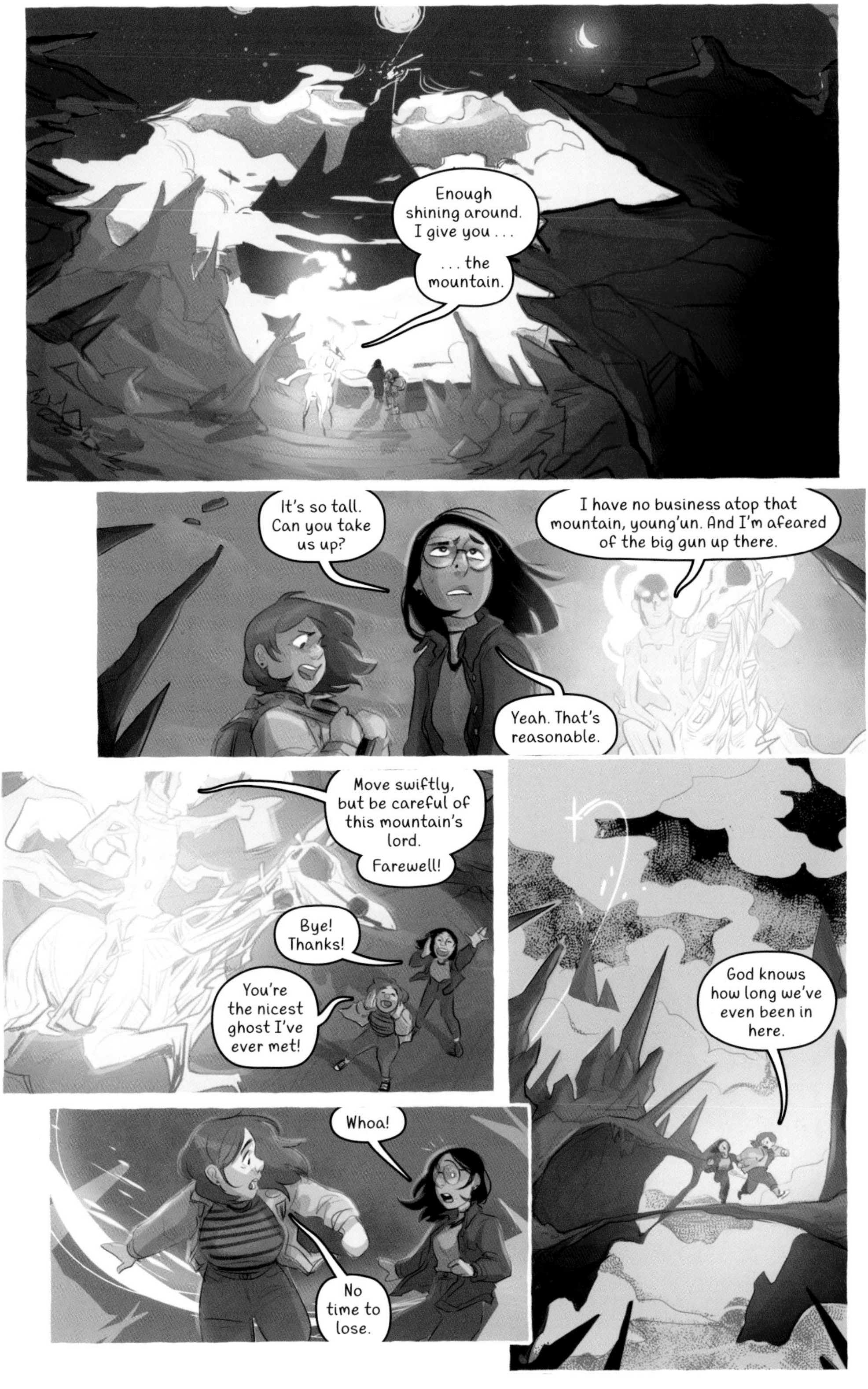
Enough shining around. I give you . . .
. . . the mountain.
It's so tall. Can you take us up?
I have no business atop that mountain, young'un. And I'm afeared of the big gun up there.
Yeah. That's reasonable.
Move swiftly, but be careful of this mountain's lord.
Farewell!
Bye! Thanks!
You're the nicest ghost I've ever met!
Whoa!
No time to lose.
God knows how long we've even been in here.

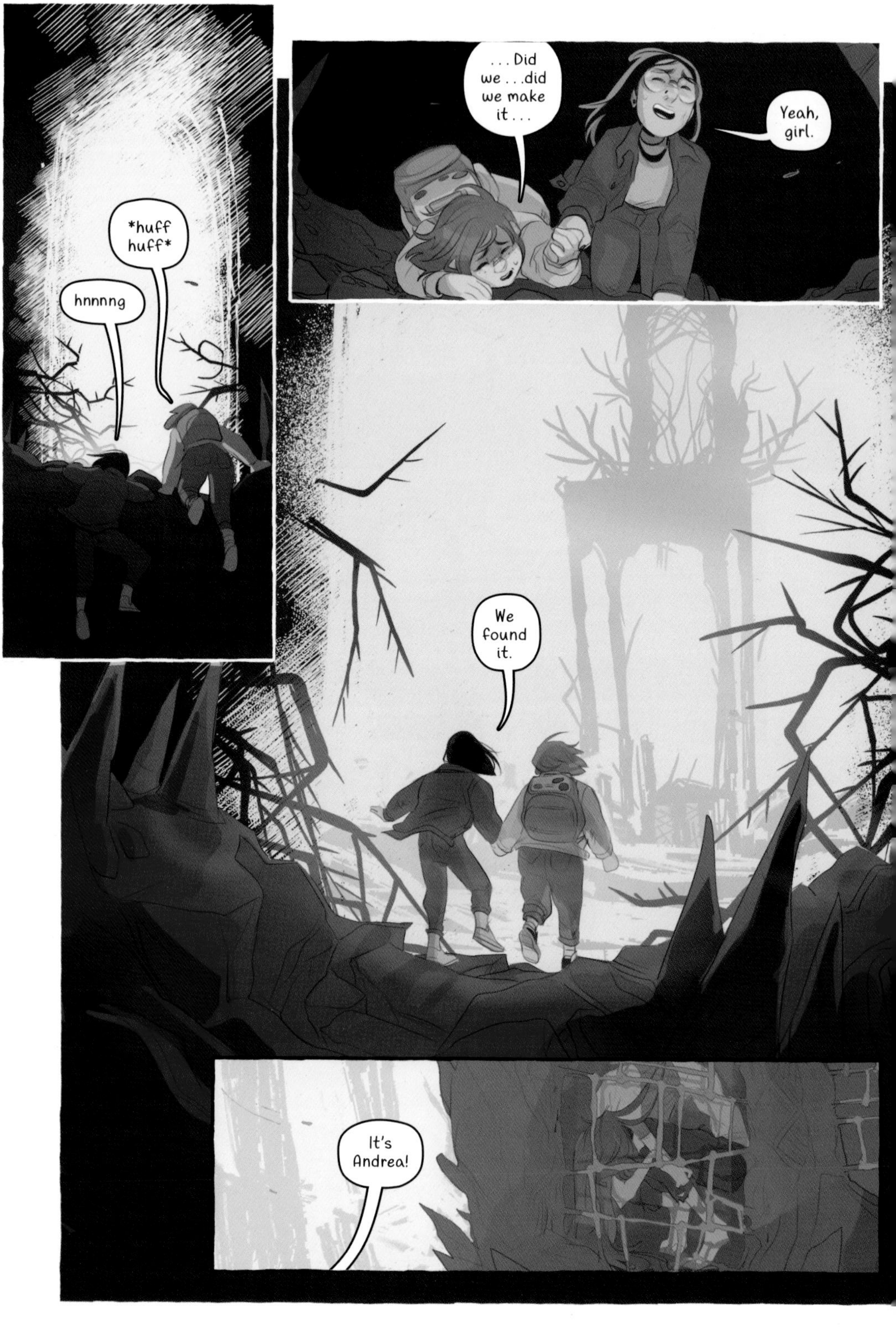
huff huff
hnnnng
. . . Did we . . . did we make it . . .
Yeah, girl.
We found it.
It's Andrea!

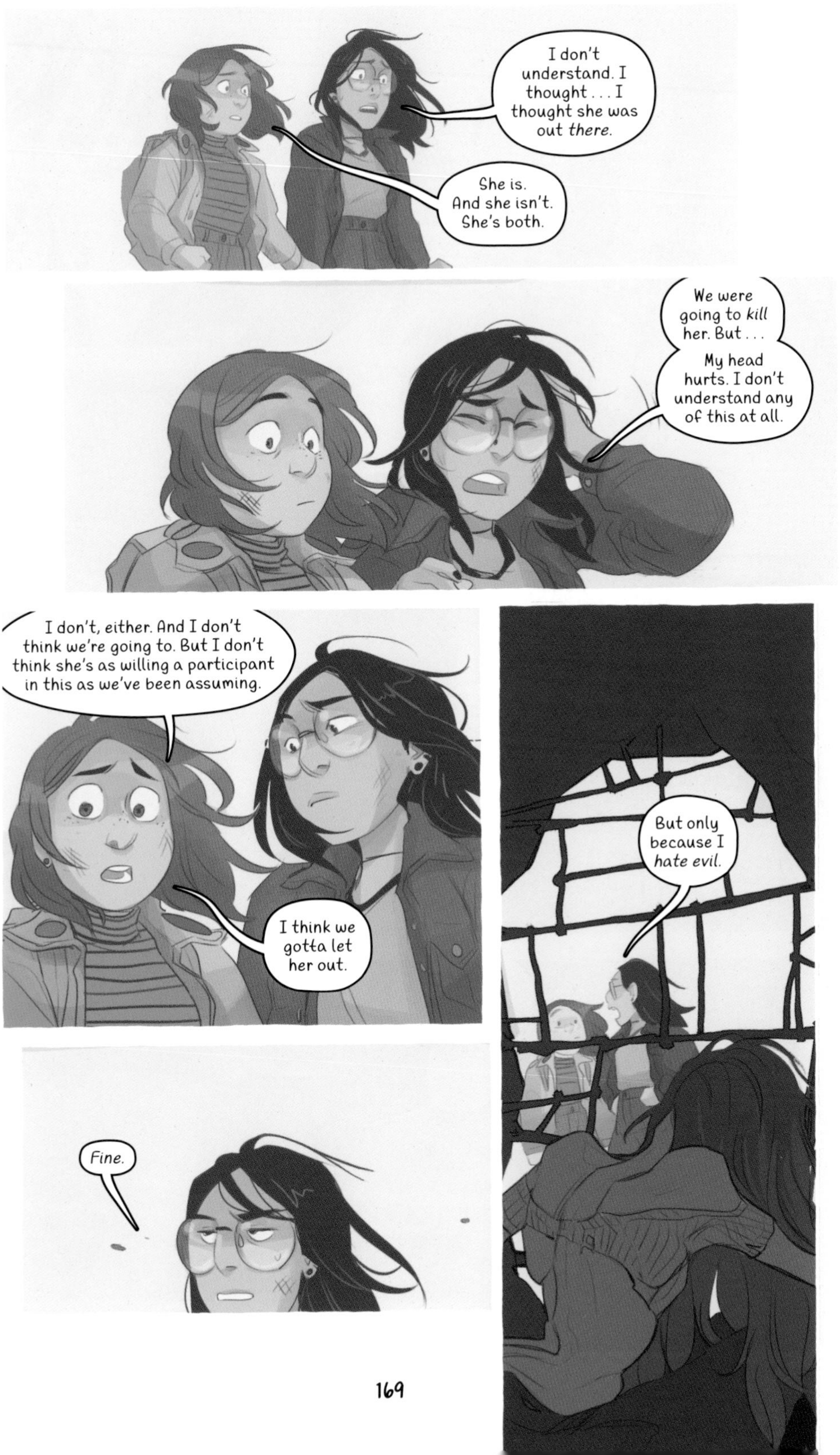
I don't understand. I thought . . . I thought she was out *there*.
She is. And she isn't. She's both.
We were going to *kill* her. But . . .
My head hurts. I don't understand any of this at all.
I don't, either. And I don't think we're going to. But I don't think she's as willing a participant in this as we've been assuming.
I think we gotta let her out.
But only because I *hate evil*.
Fine.

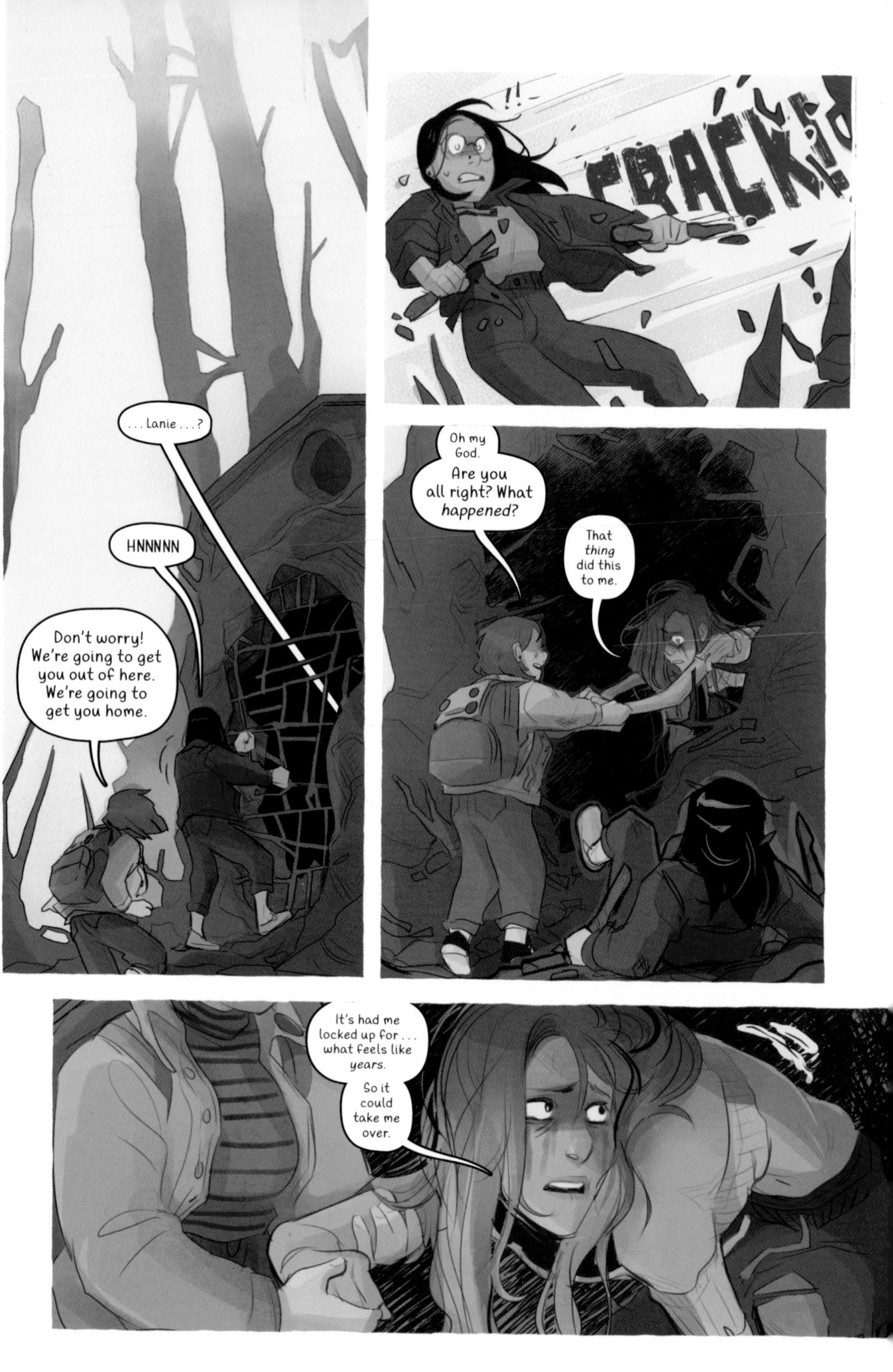
!!
CRACK!
. . . Lanie . . . ?
HNNNNN
Don't worry! We're going to get you out of here. We're going to get you home.
Oh my God.
Are you all right? What happened?
That thing did this to me.
It's had me locked up for . . . what feels like years.
So it could take me over.

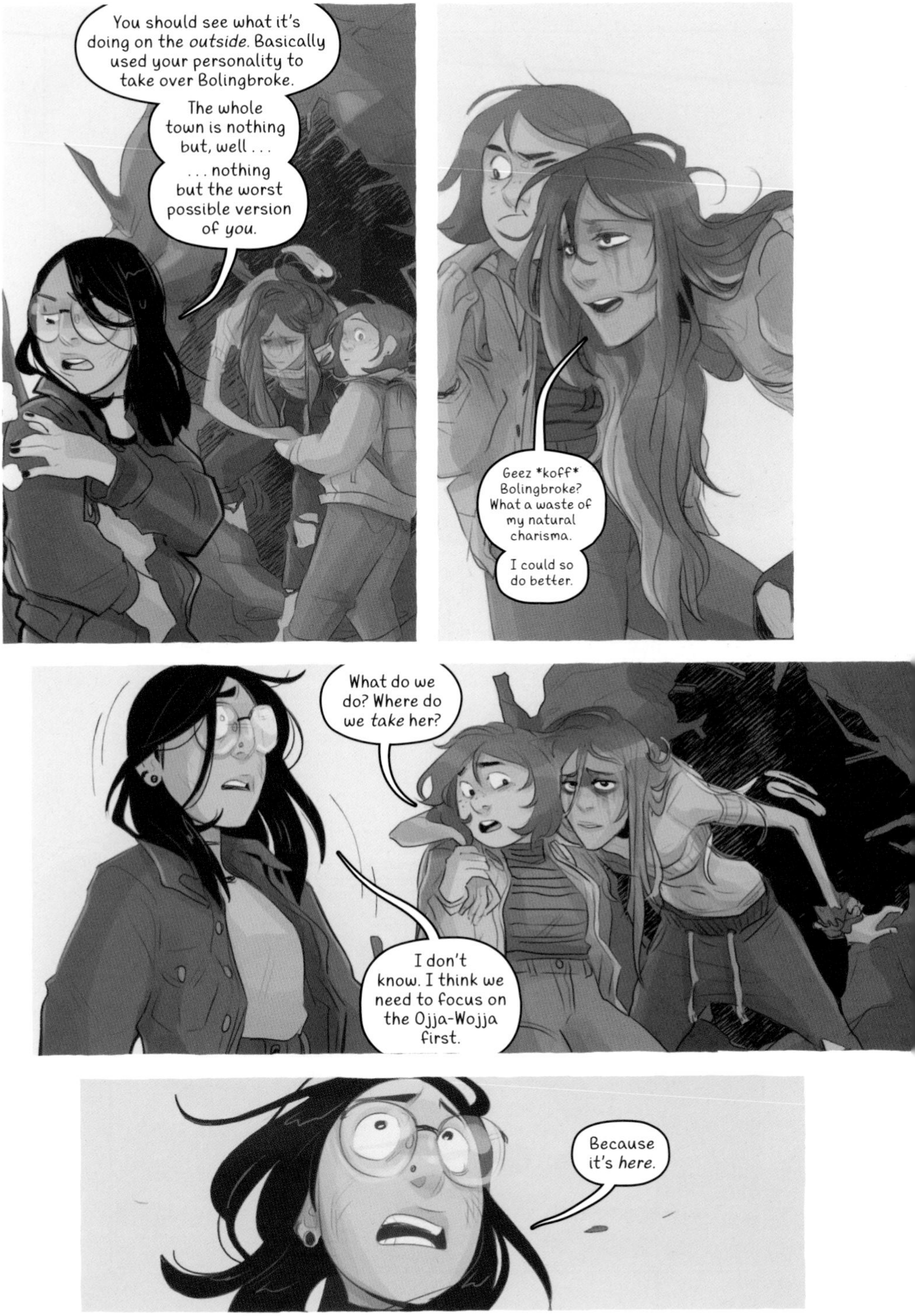
You should see what it's doing on the *outside*. Basically used your personality to take over Bolingbroke.
The whole town is nothing but, well . . .
. . . nothing but the worst possible version of *you*.
Geez *koff* Bolingbroke? What a waste of my natural charisma.
I could so do better.
What do we do? Where do we *take* her?
I don't know. I think we need to focus on the Ojja-Wojja first.
Because it's *here*.

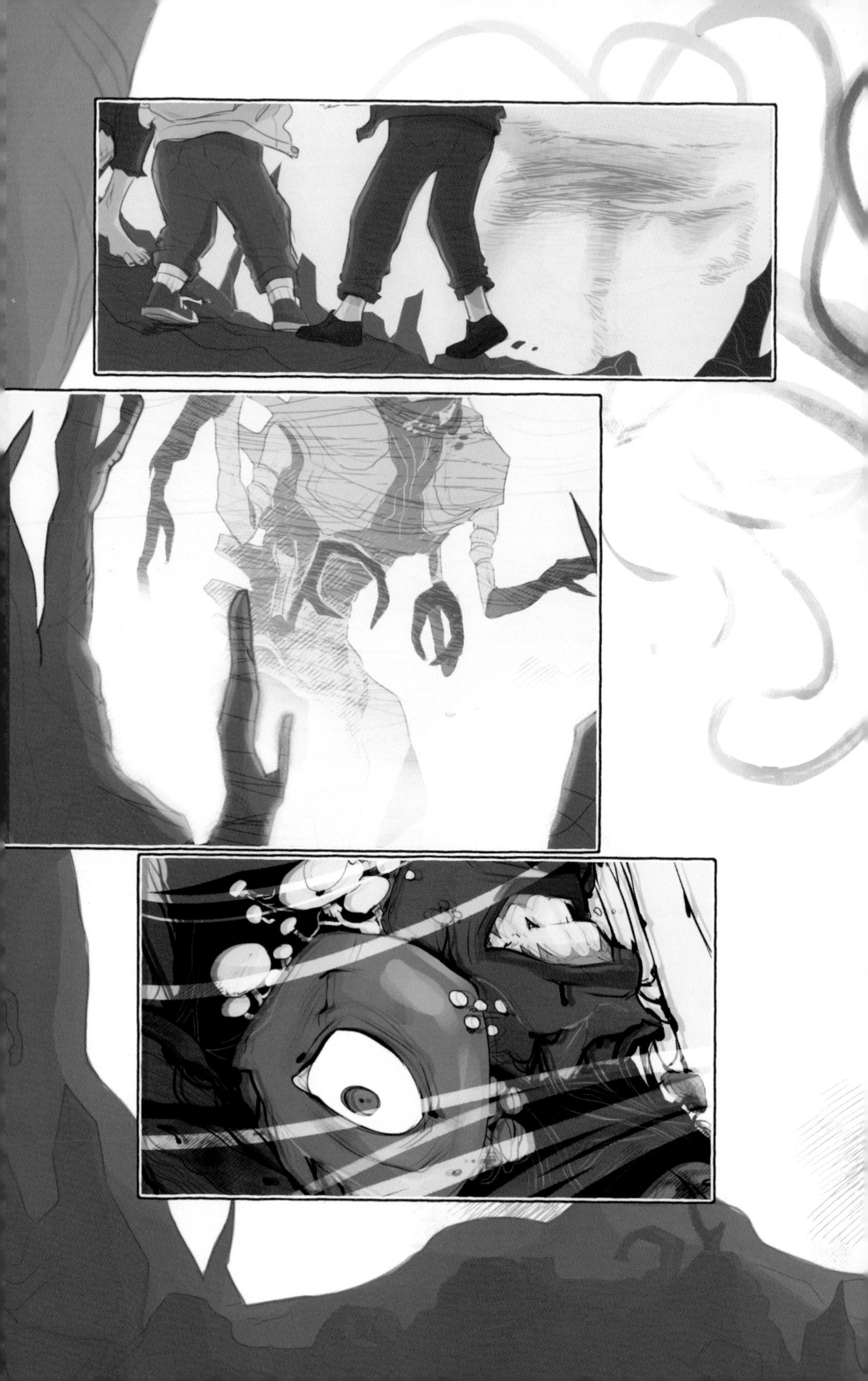

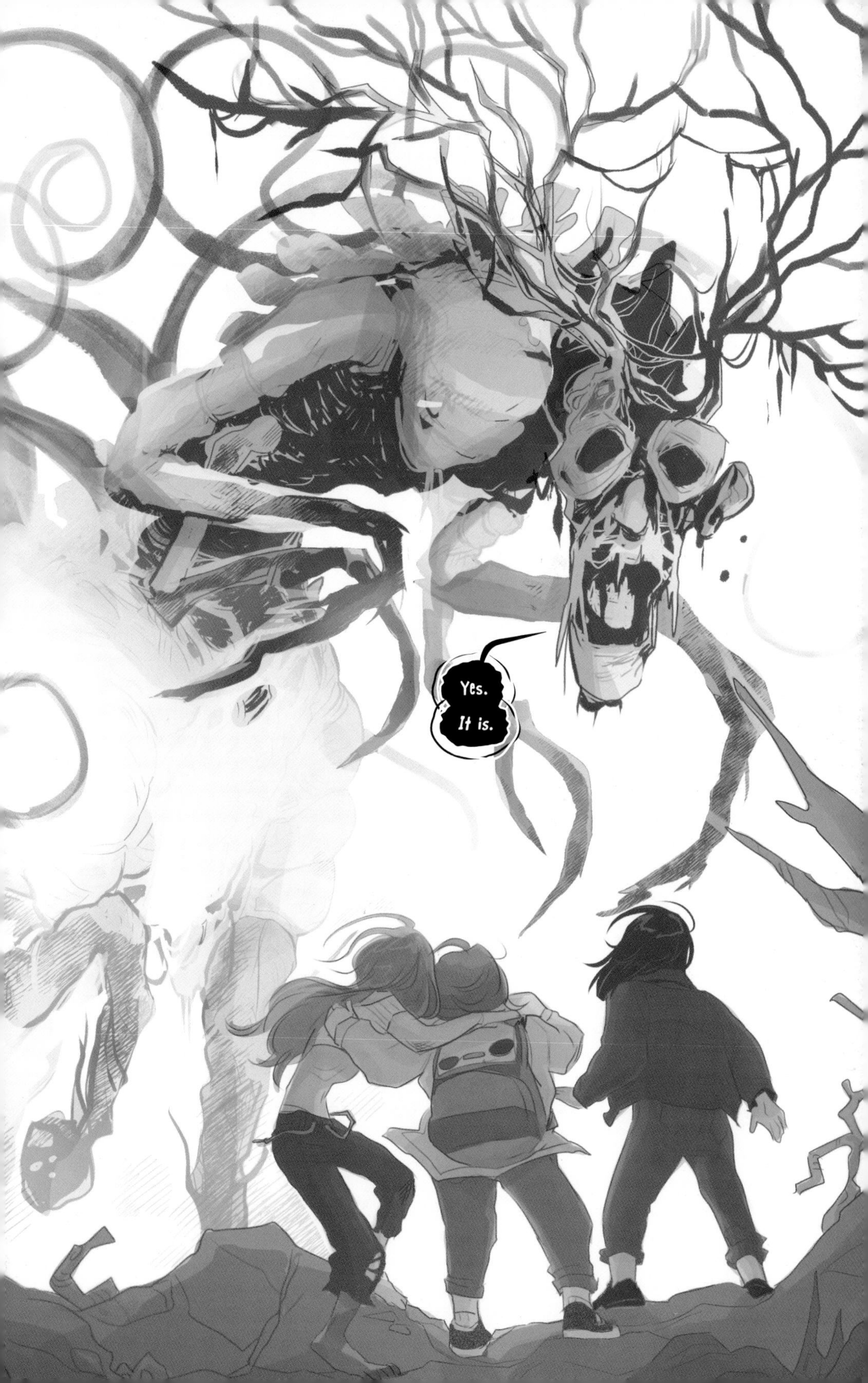
Yes.
It is.

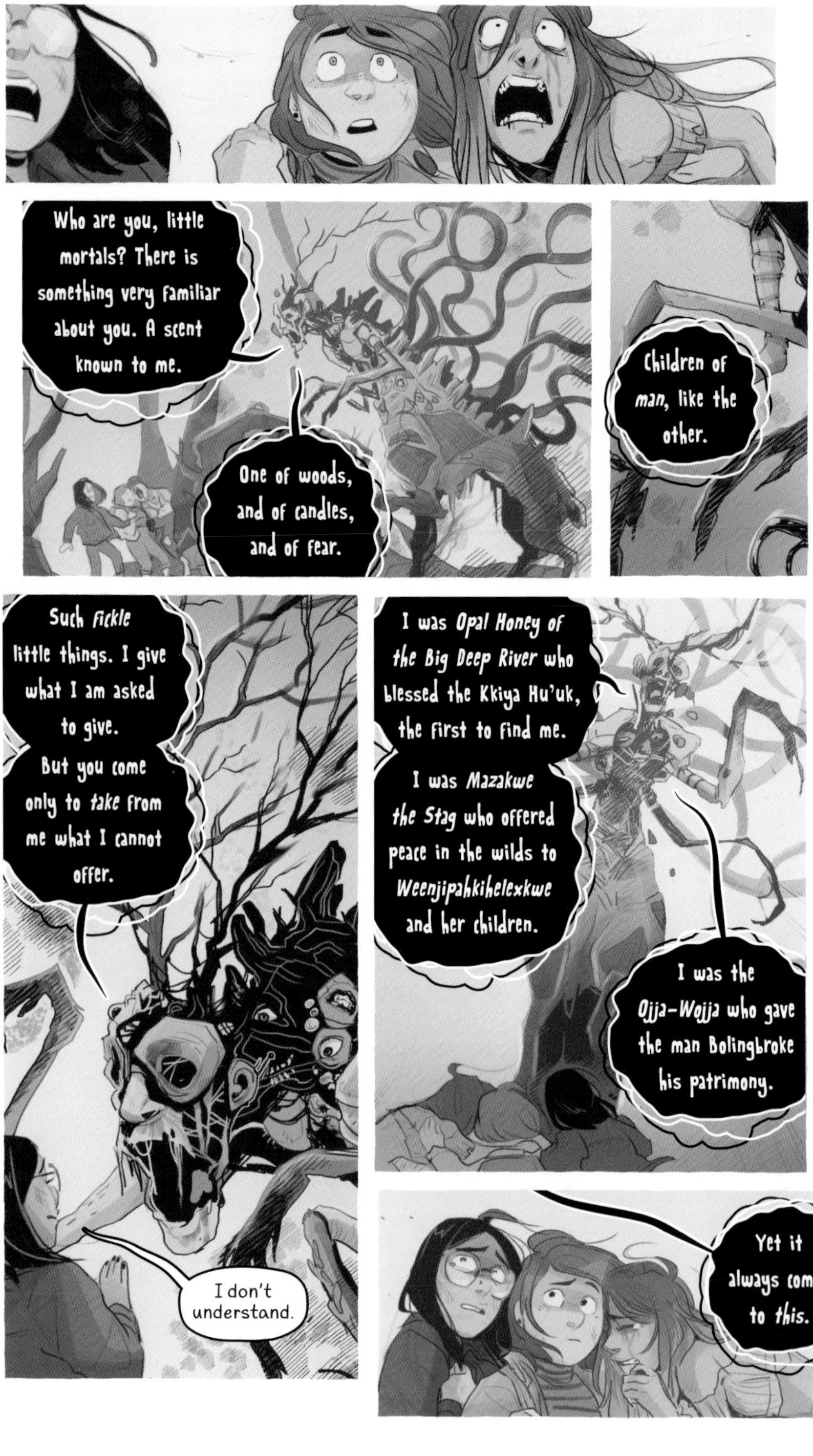

Who are you, little mortals? There is something very familiar about you. A scent known to me.
One of woods, and of candles, and of fear.
Children of *man*, like the other.
Such *fickle* little things. I give what I am asked to give.
But you come only to *take* from me what I cannot offer.
I don't understand.
I was *Opal Honey of the Big Deep River* who blessed the Kkiya Hu'uk, the first to find me.
I was *Mazakwe the Stag* who offered peace in the wilds to *Weenjipahkihelexkwe* and her children.
I was the *Ojja-Wojja* who gave the man Bolingbroke his patrimony.
Yet it always comes to *this*.

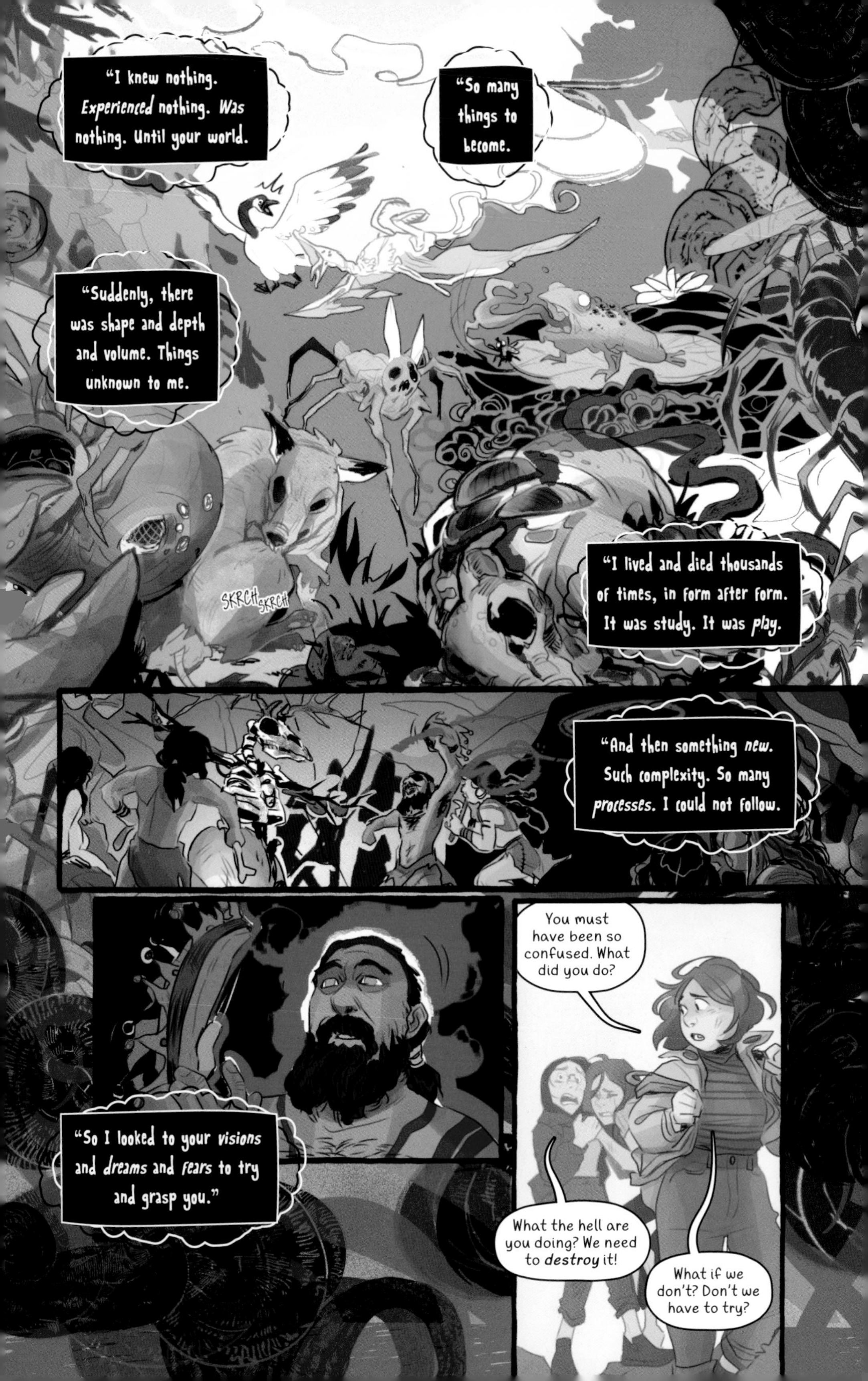
"I knew nothing. Experienced nothing. Was nothing. Until your world.
"So many things to become.
"Suddenly, there was shape and depth and volume. Things unknown to me.
SKRCH SKRCH
"I lived and died thousands of times, in form after form. It was study. It was play.
"And then something new. Such complexity. So many processes. I could not follow.
"So I looked to your visions and dreams and fears to try and grasp you."
You must have been so confused. What did you do?
What the hell are you doing? We need to destroy it!
What if we don't? Don't we have to try?

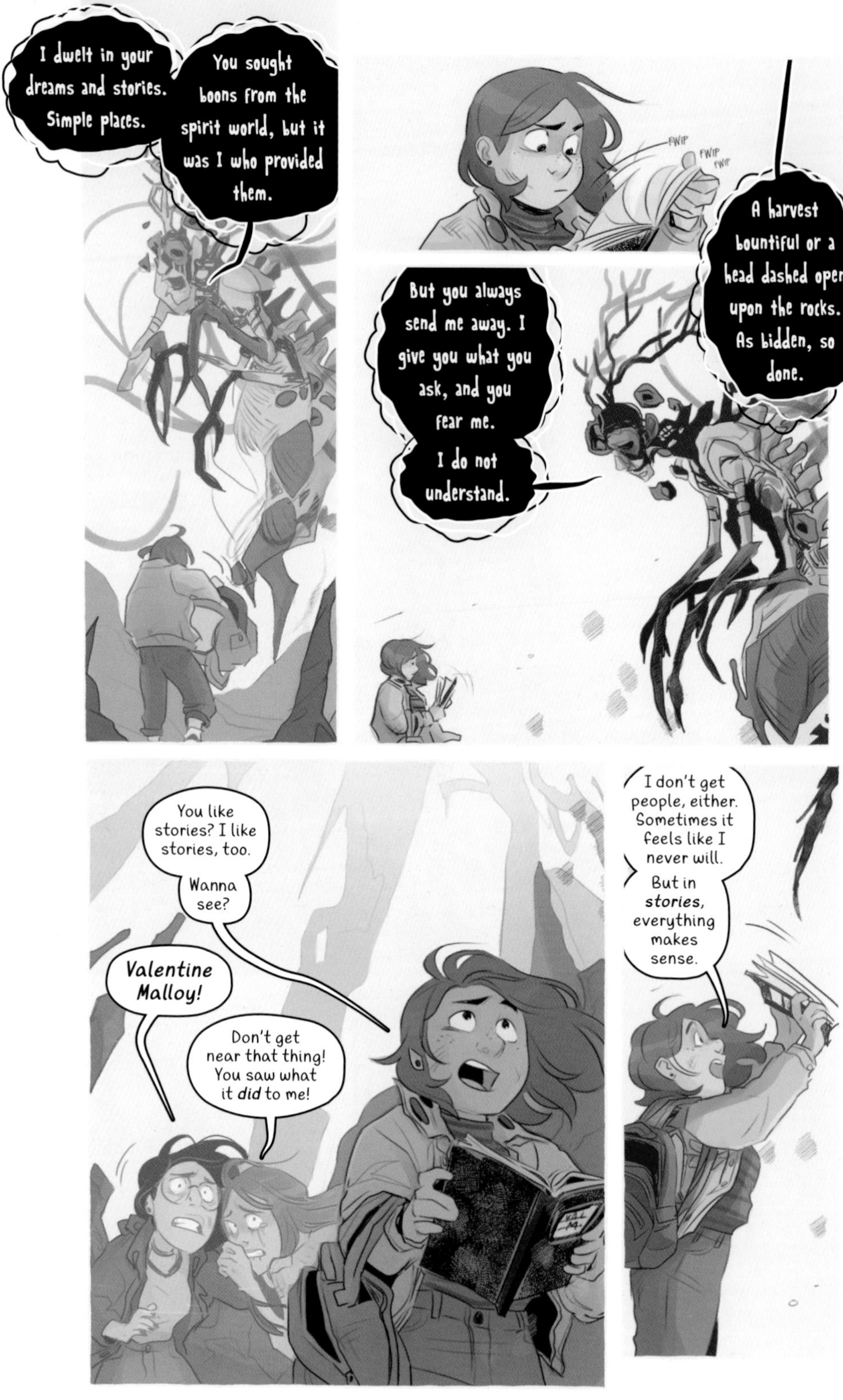
I dwelt in your dreams and stories. Simple places.
You sought boons from the spirit world, but it was I who provided them.
FWIP FWIP FWIP
A harvest bountiful or a head dashed open upon the rocks. As bidden, so done.
But you always send me away. I give you what you ask, and you fear me.
I do not understand.
You like stories? I like stories, too.
Wanna see?
Valentine Malloy!
Don't get near that thing! You saw what it *did* to me!
I don't get people, either. Sometimes it feels like I never will.
But in *stories*, everything makes sense.

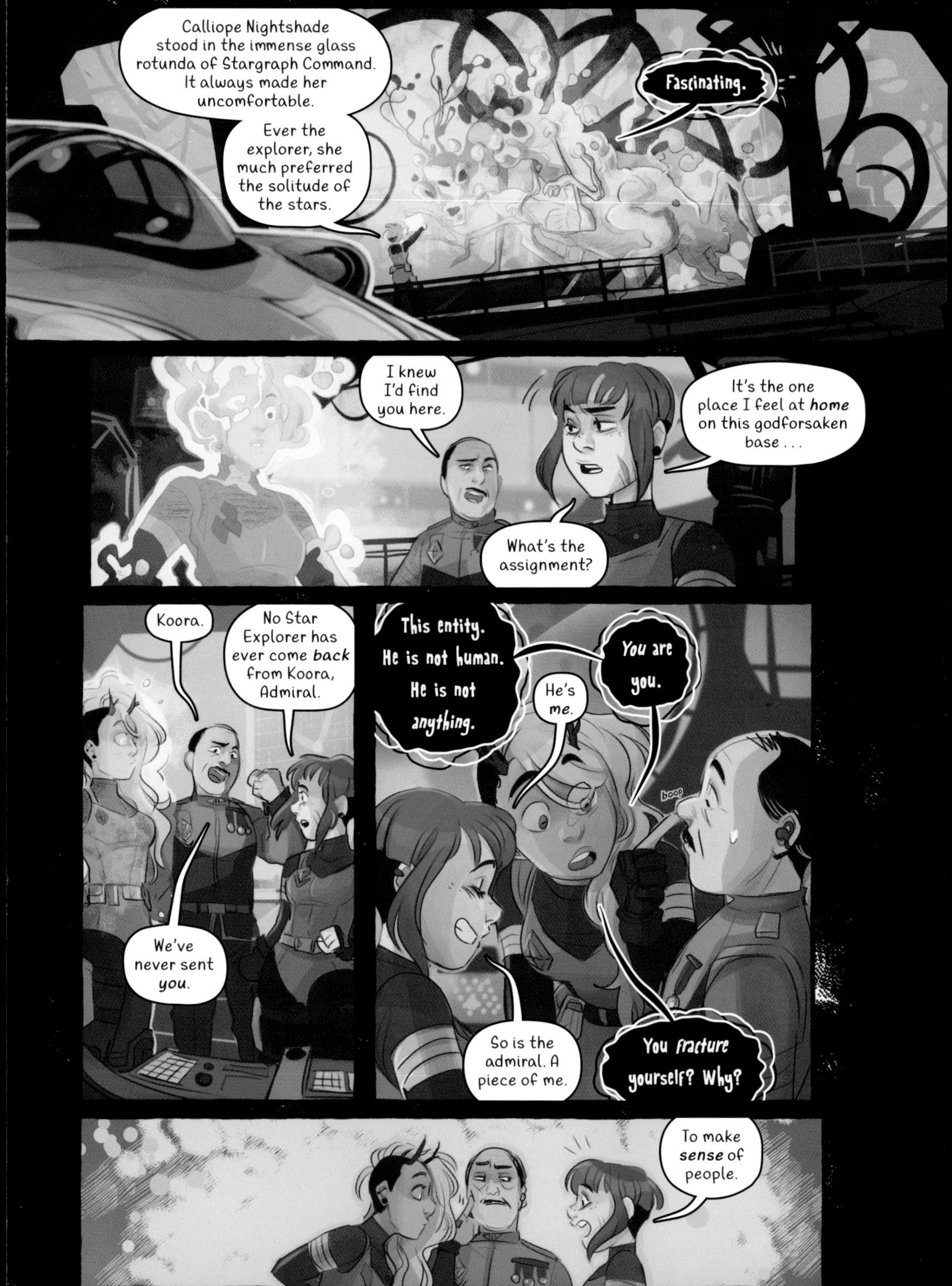
Calliope Nightshade stood in the immense glass rotunda of Stargraph Command. It always made her uncomfortable.
Ever the explorer, she much preferred the solitude of the stars.
Fascinating.
I knew I'd find you here.
It's the one place I feel at *home* on this godforsaken base . . .
What's the assignment?
Koora.
No Star Explorer has ever come *back* from Koora, Admiral.
We've never sent *you*.
This entity. He is not human. He is not anything.
He's *me*.
You are you.
boop
So is the admiral. A piece of me.
You *fracture* yourself? Why?
To make *sense* of people.

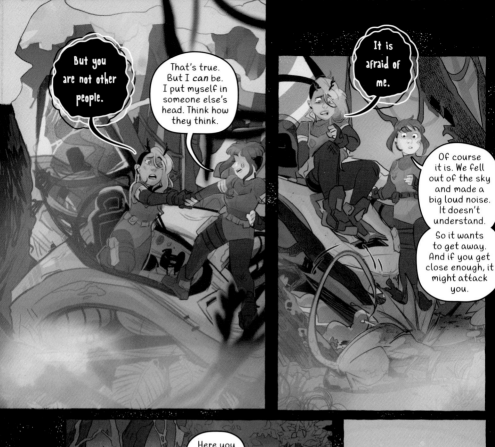

But you are not other people.

That's true. But I *can* be. I put myself in someone else's head. Think how they think.

It is afraid of me.

Of course it is. We fell out of the sky and made a big loud noise. It doesn't understand.

So it wants to get away. And if you get close enough, it might attack you.

Here you go, little guy.

kwa

You are the monkey and yourself.

I'm whatever I want to be.

Is there more?

There is always more.

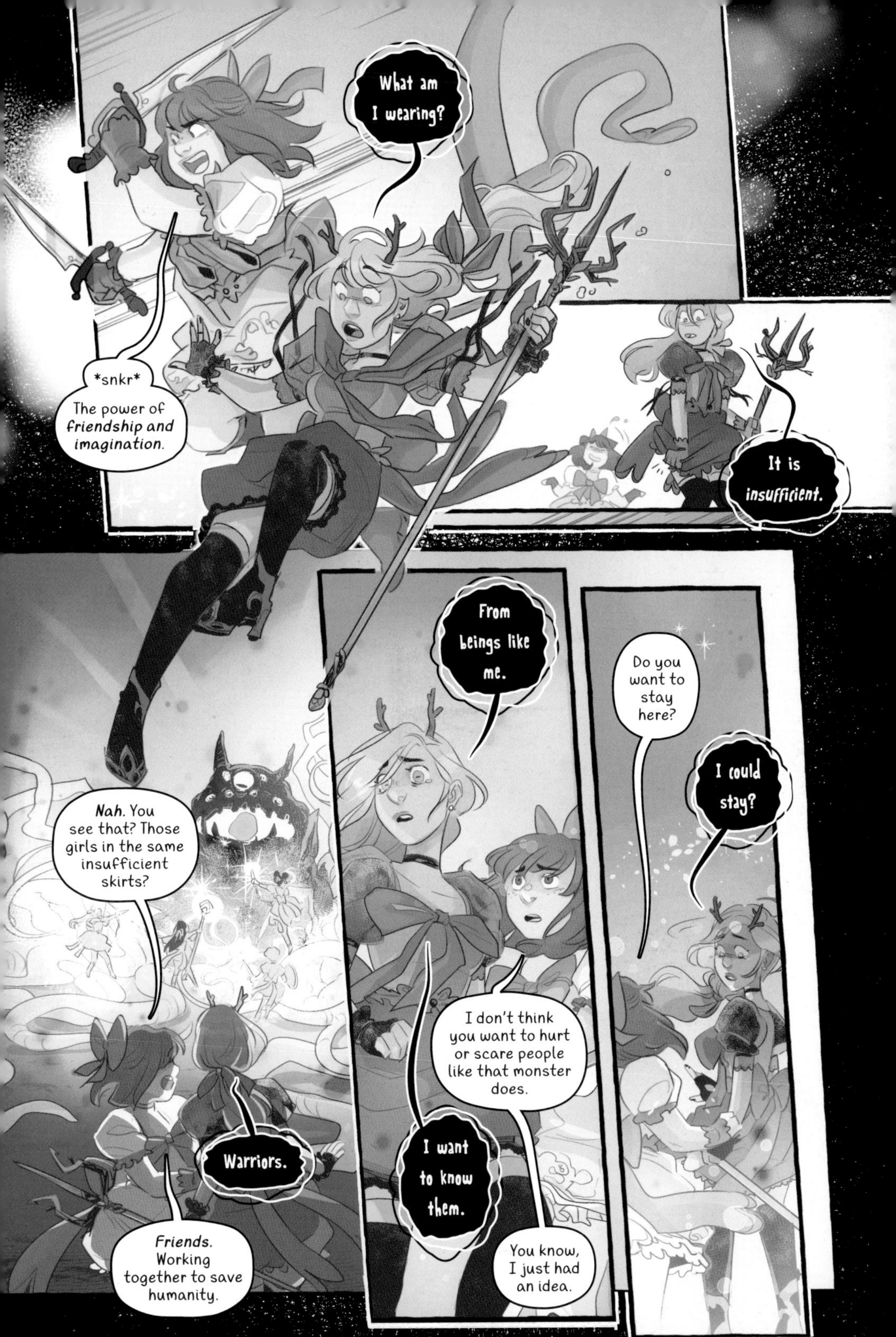
What am I wearing?
snkr
The power of friendship and imagination.
It is insufficient.
Nah. You see that? Those girls in the same insufficient skirts?
Warriors.
Friends. Working together to save humanity.
From beings like me.
I don't think you want to hurt or scare people like that monster does.
I want to know them.
You know, I just had an idea.
Do you want to stay here?
I could stay?

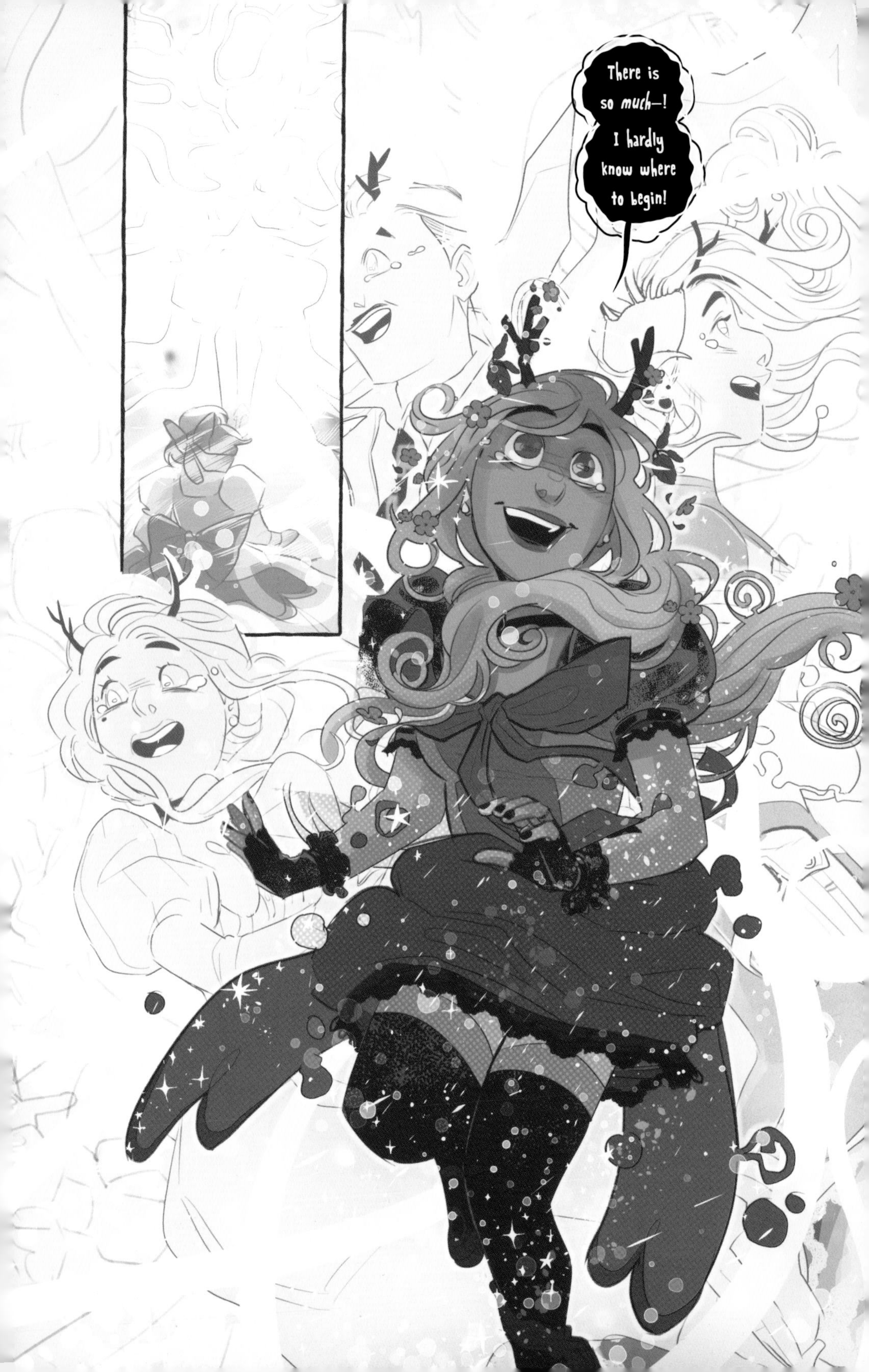
There is so *much*—! I hardly know where to begin!

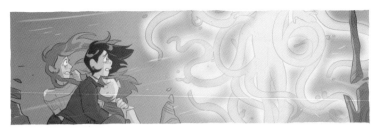

Stay back.

I said *stay back!*

What the—

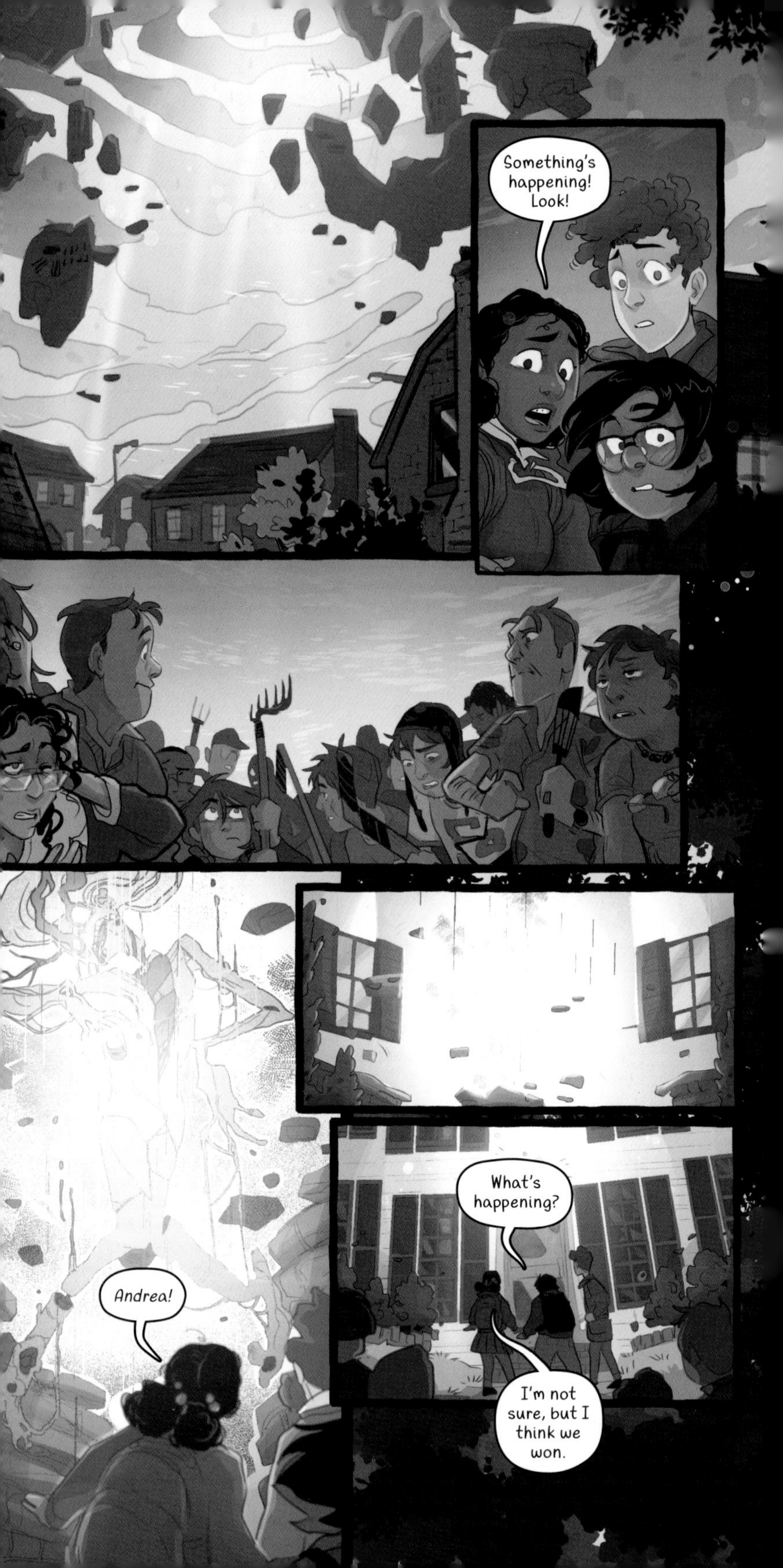
Something's happening! Look!
Andrea!
What's happening?
I'm not sure, but I think we won.

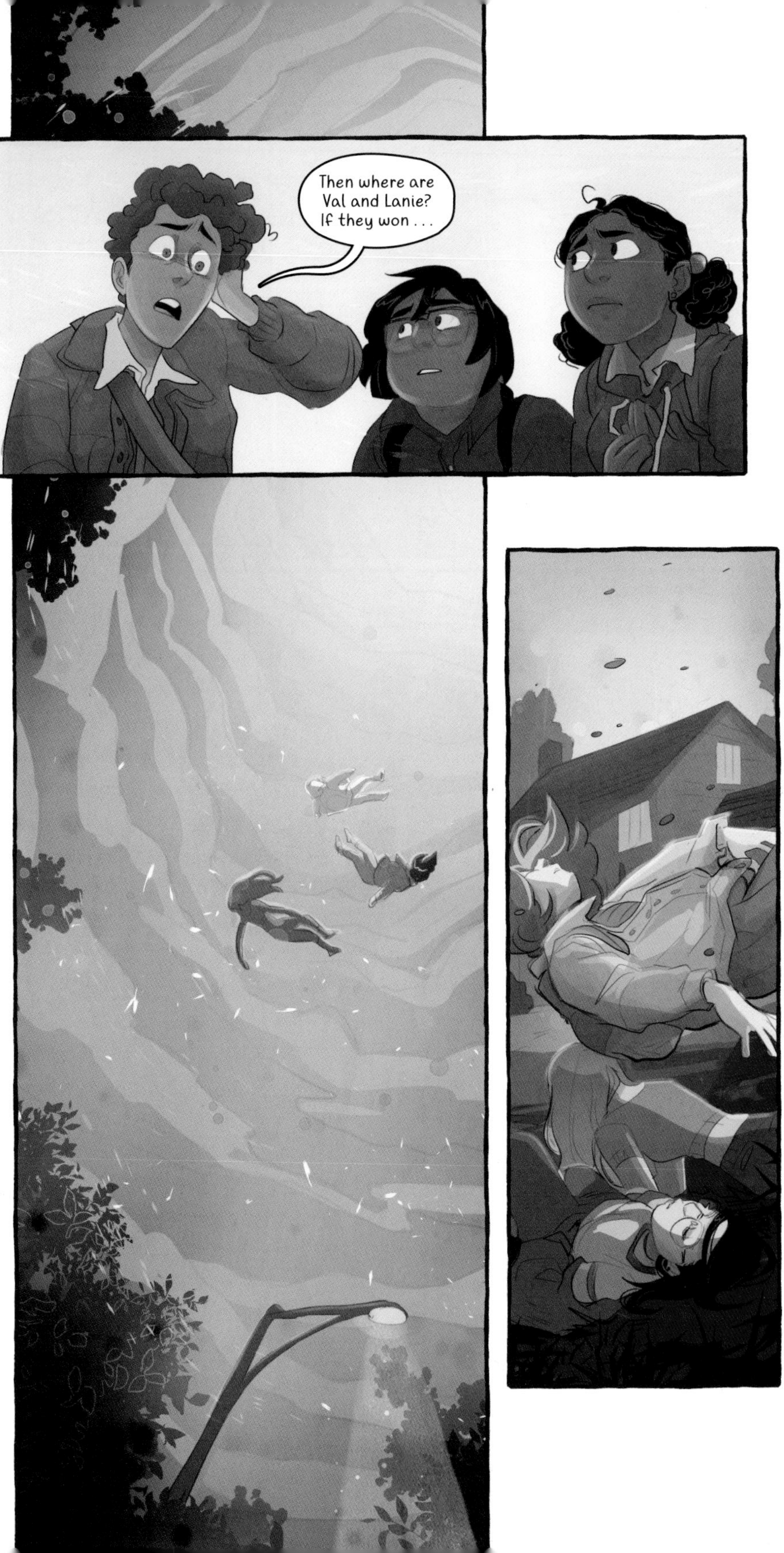
Then where are Val and Lanie? If they won . . .

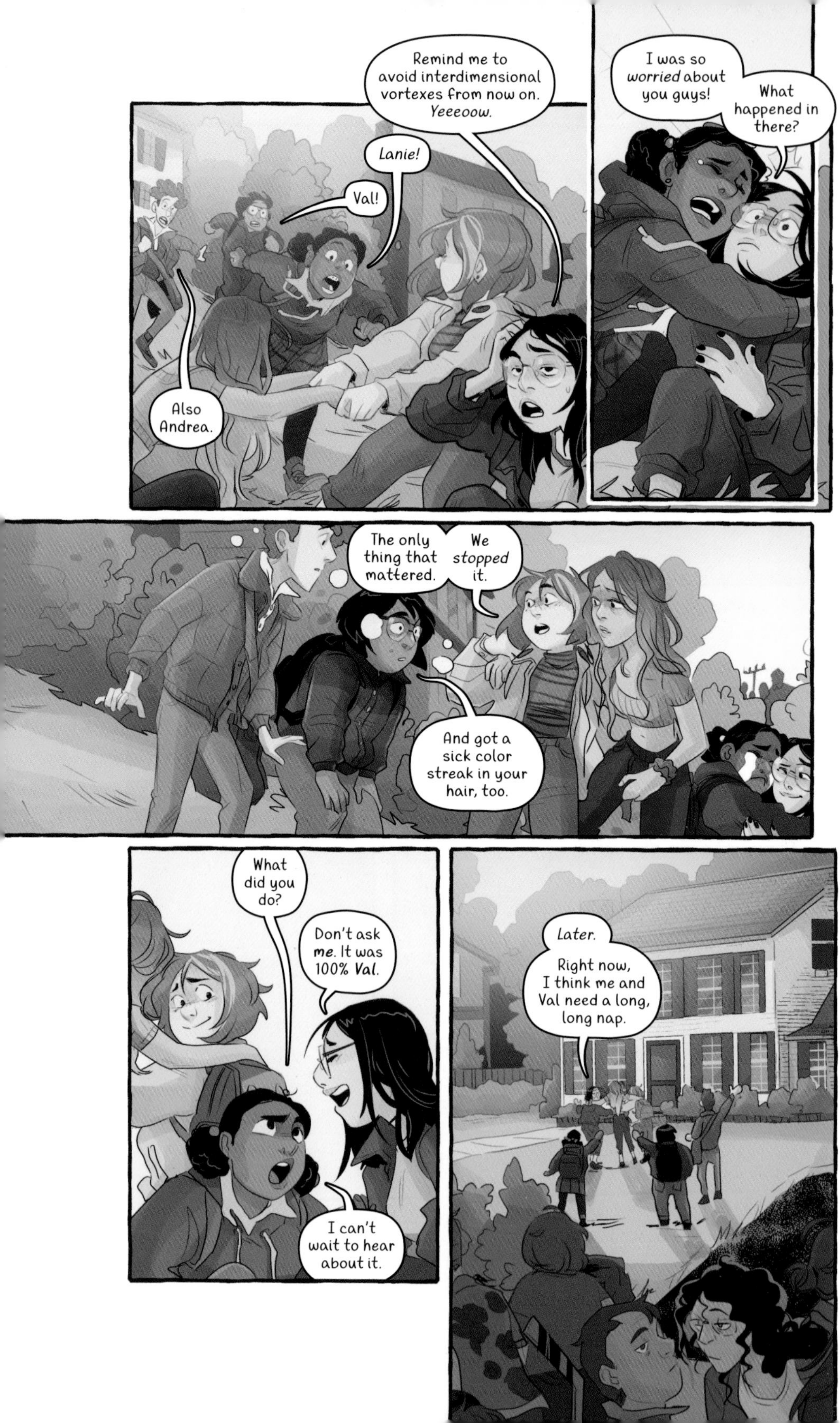

Remind me to avoid interdimensional vortexes from now on. *Yeeeoow.*
Lanie!
Val!
Also Andrea.
I was so *worried* about you guys!
What happened in there?
We *stopped* it.
The only thing that mattered.
And got a sick color streak in your hair, too.
What did you do?
Don't ask **me**. It was 100% **Val**.
I can't wait to hear about it.
Later.
Right now, I think me and Val need a long, long nap.

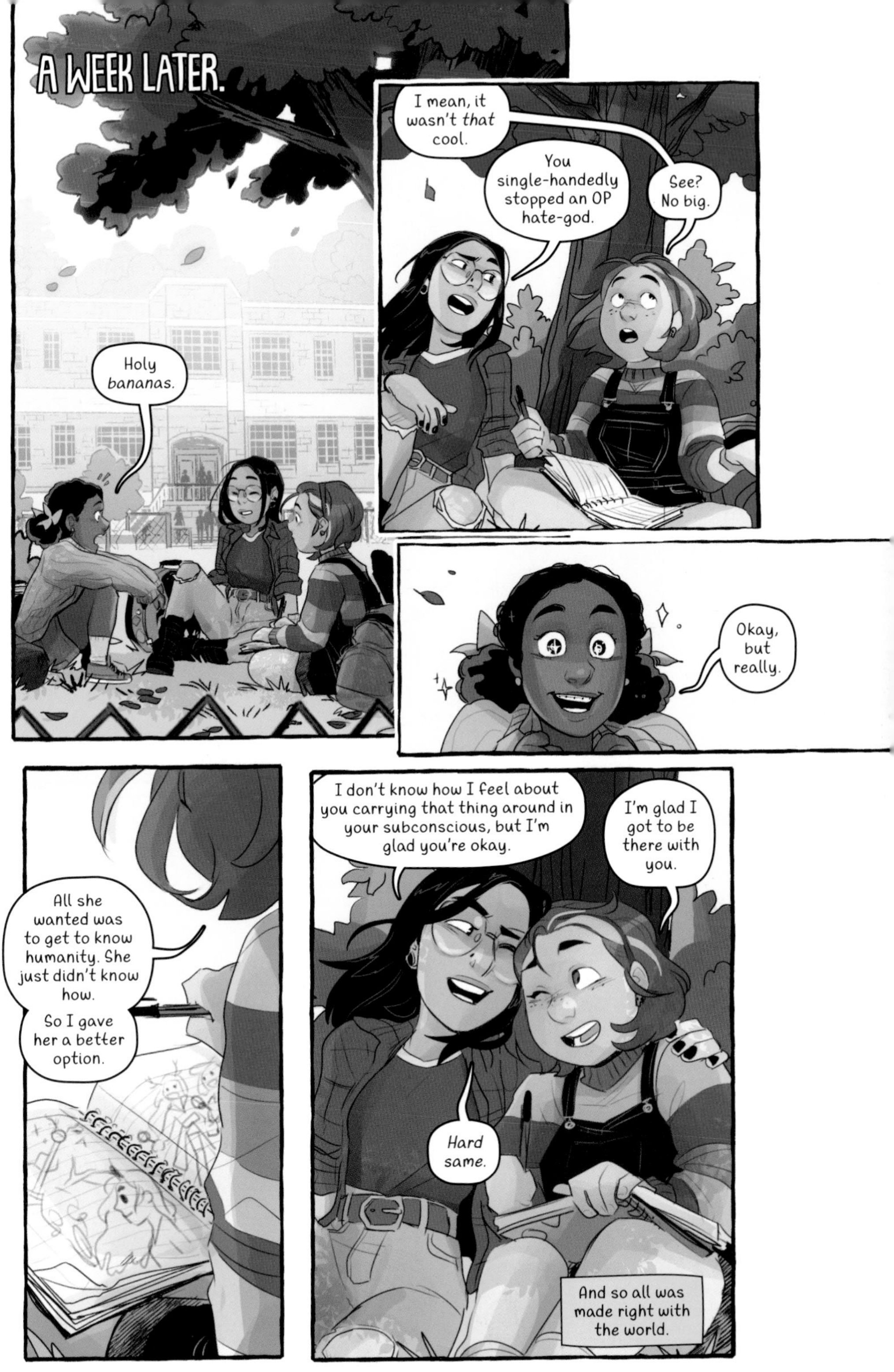
A WEEK LATER.
Holy *bananas*.
I mean, it wasn't *that* cool.
You single-handedly stopped an OP hate-god.
See? No big.
Okay, but really.
All she wanted was to get to know humanity. She just didn't know how.
So I gave her a better option.
I don't know how I feel about you carrying that thing around in your subconscious, but I'm glad you're okay.
I'm glad I got to be there with you.
Hard same.
And so all was made right with the world.

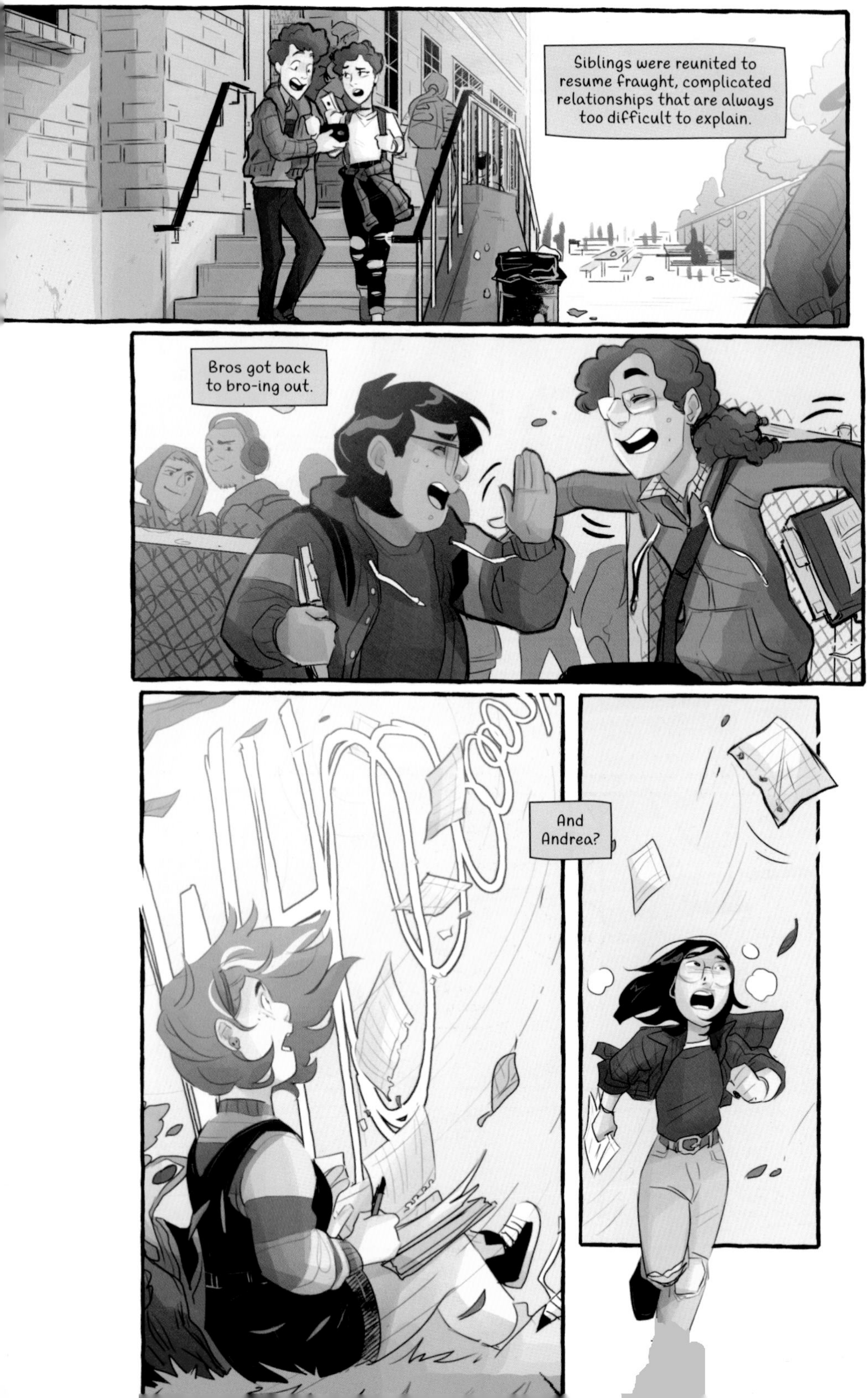
Siblings were reunited to resume fraught, complicated relationships that are always too difficult to explain.
Bros got back to bro-ing out.
And Andrea?

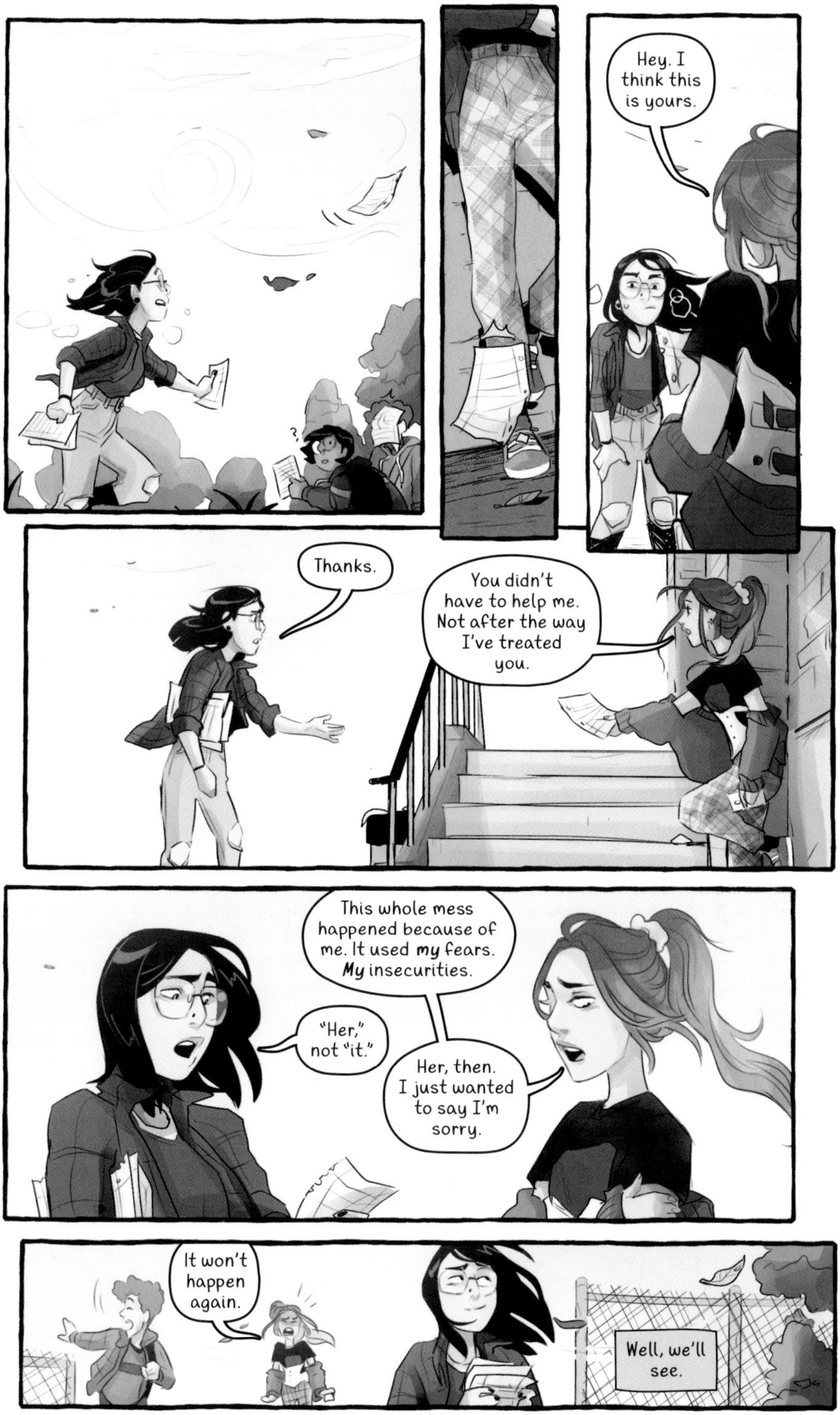
Hey. I think this is yours.
Thanks.
You didn't have to help me. Not after the way I've treated you.
This whole mess happened because of me. It used **my** fears. **My** insecurities.
"Her," not "it."
Her, then. I just wanted to say I'm sorry.
It won't happen again.
Well, we'll see.

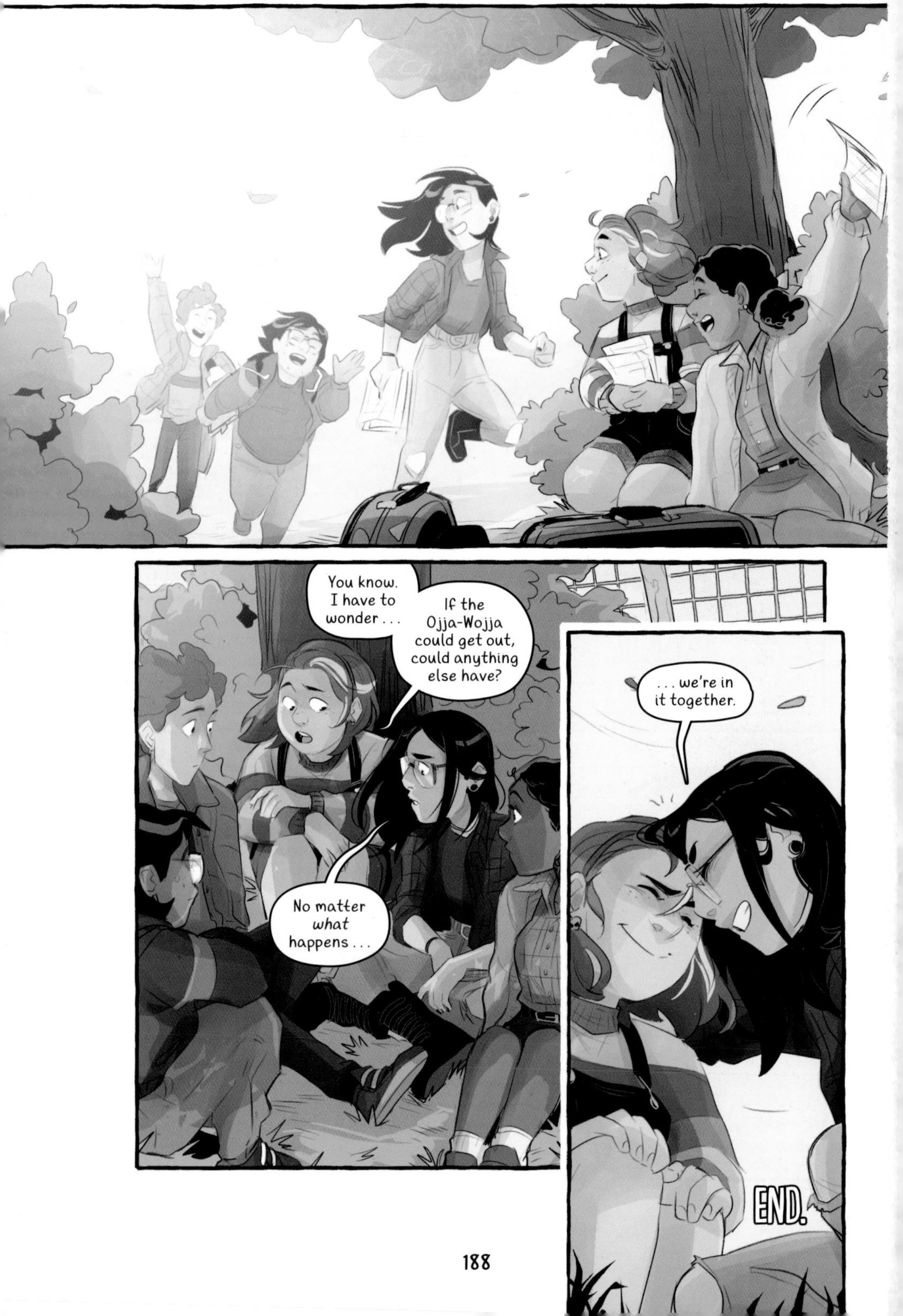
You know. I have to wonder . . .
If the Ojja-Wojja could get out, could anything else have?
No matter *what* happens . . .
. . . we're in it together.
END.